# HEDONISM

---

## AN EROTIC ANTHOLOGY

## VICTORIA RUSH

# COPYRIGHT

*For the uninhibited...*

# VOLUME ONE

## SWEDISH SAUNA

**1**

———

I knew this trip was going to be different as soon as I stepped onto the plane. The flight attendants aboard my SAS flight to Stockholm were drop-dead gorgeous. Not just typical cute-stewardesses pretty, like top supermodel stunning. Every one of them was tall, slim, and *built*. With high cheekbones, full pouty lips, and steel-blue eyes, I felt like was like I was being transported to another *planet*, not another country. One where everybody had natural blonde hair, sexy figures, and movie-star looks.

As I streamed down the aisle with the other passengers, I couldn't stop staring at the crew as they greeted the travelers with perfect smiles and lilting European accents. Instantly smitten, I felt my skin beginning to moisten while I gawked at them like a star-struck colt. When a hunky male attendant in a tight blue uniform offered to help me lift my overstuffed carry-on bag into the overhead storage compartment, I stuttered like an infatuated schoolgirl.

"Can I help you with that madam?" he offered.

"Um, yes," I said, flushing unconsciously. "I guess I overpacked for such a short trip."

As he effortlessly lifted my bag into the bin, I watched his pec muscles bulging under his neatly pressed shirt, with my face mere inches away from his chest.

"How long will you be staying in Sweden?" he asked, flashing me a full set of pearly whites.

With his handsome face and tall muscular build, he looked like a dead-ringer for the Scandinavian actor Alexander Skarsgard.

"Just a couple of weeks," I muttered.

"You can't be too careful at this time of the year," he said. "Wintertime in Sweden can be quite chilly and the nights are very long. It's best to bundle up."

"Thank you," I said, smiling at him warmly.

"Enjoy your stay," he nodded before moving down the aisle to assist another passenger.

When I plopped down into my seat, I suddenly became conscious of how wet my panties had become in the short time I'd been on the plane. A slightly older woman sitting across the aisle from me glanced at the beads of perspiration on my forehead and smiled.

"He had the same effect on me," she grinned. "Do you think *everyone* in Sweden is this beautiful?"

"I don't know," I said, shaking my head. "But if so, this should be one hell of an interesting trip."

I pulled out my phone and pretended to text someone on the screen. I knew it was going to be a long flight overseas, and I didn't want another Chatty-Cathy burning up my ear the entire way. I didn't want to lose another moment soaking up the dazzling flight attendants as they walked up and down the aisle.

When the doors finally closed and the jet began to pull away from the gate, I was happy to have an unobstructed view of the pretty stewardesses from my perch at the back of the forward cabin. As the lead flight attendant provided instructions over the intercom system, her pretty assistant took up position at the front of the aisle and smiled at me. Normally, I ignored these boring safety demonstrations, burying my head in a newspaper or playing games on my phone. But on this flight, virtually every passenger in the first-class compartment sat upright in rapt attention, with all eyes on the model at the front of the room.

While the attendant demonstrated how to properly use the seatbelts and oxygen masks, I squeezed my legs together to quell my throbbing pussy. Beyond her perfect bone structure and pretty updo under her tight bellman's cap, her skin was absolutely flawless. Her creamy alabaster tone radiated a natural blush over her Nordic cheekbones, her ramrod-straight posture reinforcing the impression of watching a model on the catwalk. When she raised her arms to point out the location of the emergency exits, her full breasts pressed against the front of her blouse, showing off her Amazon-perfect physique.

*Jesus*, I thought, listening to myself audibly panting as I watched her go through the motions. *No wonder men joke about the Swedish Bikini Team as their ultimate fantasy. These people really are as gorgeous as the legend says.*

As I sat in my chair getting more and more turned on watching the sexy flight attendant, I felt like I had a front-row seat at a Paris fashion show. I had the blind fortune of checking out some of the most beautiful people on Earth from in my own personal viewing room. Even my first-class leather chair made it seem like I was sitting in my home studio watching an Ingmar Bergman movie. I was glad the window seat next to me hadn't been filled, as I squirmed between the armrests trying to give my aching clit some much-needed stimulation.

But as I began to fantasize about taking the sexy flight attendant into one of the lavatories for a mile-high fling, the demonstration abruptly ended and she took a seat facing me at the front of the cabin in preparation for takeoff. Soon after, the jets began to roar and I felt the pull of gravity push me back against my seat as the plane lifted off the runway. When the attendant made eye contact with me momentarily, I fantasized that it was *her* pressing against me instead of the pull of the aircraft.

As she politely glanced around the cabin, I couldn't take my eyes off her. Whenever our eyes met, I looked away, embarrassed at my invasion of her personal space. As the heat between my legs began to build and the dampness in my panties spread, I peered up at the seatbelt sign, impatient to go to the restroom to relieve my pent-up tension. Watching this sexy goddess had gotten me thoroughly worked up and I knew it wouldn't take much to get me off. Even though it wouldn't be as glamorous as the usual in-flight fantasy, I'd have my own fun envisioning the two of us intertwined in the close confines of the tight water closet.

But when the bell chimed signaling that we'd reached cruising altitude and could remove our seatbelts, I found myself wanting to stay in my seat when I saw her getting up to begin the meal service. As she moved down the aisle offering a choice of beverages, I leered at her firm ass whenever she leaned over to hand a glass to one of the passengers. I was happy to be seated in the last row of the first-class cabin, with the relative privacy of the partition separating me from the coach compartment.

While I pretended to flip through the inflight magazine resting on my lap, my right hand began to inch between my legs in desperate need of stimulation for the aching nub underneath my jeans. The closer the cute attendant got to my seat, the more excited I got caressing myself under my magazine. By the time she reached my row, my eyes had already glazed over as I needed all my strength to contain the pleasure beginning to consume my body.

"Champagne?" she said, turning to me with a tray filled with tall goblets.

"Um, yes, thank you," I stammered, gripping the sides of my magazine tightly with two hands.

When she leaned over to hand me the glass, I couldn't help staring at her ample breasts spilling out over the top of her tight vest. A silver name tag dangled from her blouse reading Elsa.

"Can I get you anything else?" she said, smiling at me as I blushed shyly.

"What else are you offering?" I asked, my mind racing ahead with fantasies of her jumping into my lap while I ravished her in my quiet little alcove.

"Coffee, tea, juice," she offered. "Or would you prefer another cocktail?"

There was only *one* kind of tail I was thinking about at this particular moment.

"This will be fine for now, thank you Elsa," I said, biting my lip at the temptation to flirt with her further.

"I'll return in a little while with your meal service," she said. "Would you like the salmon or the filet mignon?"

I smiled, happy that I'd chosen to fly first-class for a change. Not only was the food and service a notch above normal, but I had a far better view of the pretty flight attendants in the smaller confines of the forward cabin.

"I'll have the salmon, thank you," I said, fixing my gaze on her brilliant blue eyes.

When she began walking back to the front of the plane, my eyes locked again on her firm ass.

*That's not the only thing I'd like to eat right now,* I thought, imagining my face buried between her thighs while she sat facing me on the sink in the lavatory.

While I continued undressing her with my eyes, my clit throbbed painfully under my tight jeans. After a few more minutes of anguished frustration, I finally stood up and bee-lined my way to the washroom. When I opened the door next to Elsa working in the galley, she turned around and glanced down at my midsection. I smiled at her, then closed the door and looked at myself in the mirror in shock.

*Was she just checking me out?* I thought. *What would be the chances of getting her to join me in here? Maybe if I leave the door slightly ajar...*

I shook my head, realizing the absurdity of my fantasy.

*These kinds of things only happen in Penthouse Forum letters. There's no way a professional flight attendant would risk this kind of impropriety while on duty.*

As I started unzipping my jeans to free my burning jewel, I noticed they were wet in the front. Peering down in the mirror, I saw that a large wet spot had formed in the crotch.

*"Fuck!"* I cursed out loud. *"That's* why she was looking at me that way."

I blushed in embarrassment at being found out, wondering how many other passengers had used this hiding place for release after watching these vixens go about their work. But at this point, the stain on the front of my pants was the last thing I was worried about. Right now, I just needed to get off, and quickly. I pulled off my jeans and underwear and hung them on the back of the door, then placed my right foot on top of the vanity. My slit stretched open as my flaming clit protruded out of its hood.

*Gawd how I'd like to grind my pussy against Elsa's face right now,* I thought.

I washed my hands under the sink then thrust two fingers deep into my pussy as I began to fuck myself, watching my reflection in the mirror.

If Elsa could only see me now, I dreamed. I had a pretty good figure for a thirty-six-year-old woman, and my looks were nothing to sneeze at either. Would she be able to resist keeping her hands off me, watching me fuck myself like this mere inches away?

As I began to feel the pleasure rising within me, I started to moan, pretending that Elsa was peering back at me in the mirror instead of my own reflection. I was happy for the background drone of the jet engines so that no one could hear me.

"Fuck me, Elsa," I panted. "Rub your beautiful body against me while we grind our pussies together and enjoy our own inflight entertainment."

While I imagined Elsa moaning in my ear and rubbing her tits against mine, my climax suddenly washed over me like a tidal wave as I grunted and spasmed over the sink. With my fingers embedded deeply in my hole, I jerked my hand up firmly against my mound while I gushed all over my palm. I was glad that I'd had the foresight to remove my jeans completely, because by the time I finished cumming, I'd produced quite a puddle on the floor underneath me.

*Damn—I needed that,* I panted, nodding at my reflection in the mirror.

I grabbed a few towelettes from the dispenser and wiped the floor, then washed my hands thoroughly and put my clothes back on. Realizing that I'd be revealing the stain on the front of my jeans for the entire cabin to see on my return trip to my seat, I loosened my blouse and draped it over the front of my crotch. Thankfully, it hung just low enough to cover the wet spot without looking too conspicuous. Then I brushed my hair and reapplied my lipstick to make myself presentable and opened the door. Elsa was still working in the galley, and she smiled at me as her eyes drifted down my body.

*Had my ruffled blouse given away what I was up to in the lavatory?* I wondered. *Or had she heard my moans over the noise of the jet engines?* At this point I hardly cared, and I smiled back at her with a flush in my cheeks as I walked back to my seat.

For the next hour or so, the cabin was fairly busy with the movement of the two first-class flight attendants serving and collecting the main meal service. I made small talk with Elsa whenever she passed by my seat, introducing myself and sharing my plans while I stayed in Sweden. When I told her that I intended to get in some snowboarding during my stay, she told me about the best resorts to visit in the northern part of the country. I was tempted to invite her to join me on my excursion, but my shyness got the better of me.

When things settled down after the meal service, she took a seat for a brief rest in one of the jump seats next to the main door. As she opened a magazine, I took the opportunity to study her body from head to toe. Her legs were crossed while she read the magazine, and the swelling of her calf resting on her knee amplified the sexy curviness of her long legs. I could see her dark leggings running up the underside of her skirt and wondered if they were full-height pantyhose or mid-thigh stockings with garters. It didn't take long for me to begin fantasizing once again about fucking her as she sat quietly reading her magazine.

Only this time I wanted freer access to my pussy, where I could feel my slippery slit directly and rub my burning button without any impediments. I reached up and pressed the overhead call button, and Elsa looked up when she heard the chime. She peered down the aisle and noticing the light illuminated next to my console, she put down her magazine and walked toward me.

*Damn*, I thought to myself as I watched her glide down the aisle. *She even walks like a supermodel.* With her narrow foot placement down the cramped aisle, her hips swayed from side to side as her calves flexed with each step. I felt sorry disturbing her from her well-earned rest, but I needed one more thing from her.

"Yes, Jade," she said when she reached my seat. "What can I get you?"

"I was wondering if you had a blanket I could use to keep warm?" I said, peering up at her innocently. "It's a bit chilly in the cabin and I didn't bring a shawl in my carry-on bag."

"Yes, of course," she said. "I'll be back in a moment."

Elsa strolled back to the front of the cabin and opened a storage locker, pulling out plastic-covered packet. Then she walked back down the aisle and handed me the folded blanket.

"Was there anything else I can get to make your flight more comfortable?"

I paused for a moment raising an eyebrow, then shook my head.

"This should be fine for now," I said with a knowing smile. "I'm sure this will make the rest of my flight much more relaxing."

Little did she know what I *really* needed the blanket for. I just wanted some cover while I touched myself secretly in the privacy of my corner while I watched her from a distance.

"Just give me a ring if you need anything else," she said.

"I will, thank you Elsa."

As she began walking back up the aisle, I glanced at the woman sitting across the aisle from me and noticing that she had nodded off, I pulled my jeans and panties down below my knees. It felt exhilarating to feel the cool gust of the jet breeze rushing up between my bare thighs. When Elsa returned to her seat, I glanced up at her and smiled, then she picked up her magazine and lowered her head.

*Perfect*, I thought. *You lose yourself in your little distraction while I lose myself in you as I get distracted doing other things.*

I snaked my right hand under the blanket and moistened the tips of my fingers with my slippery juices, then pulled them up and began circling my throbbing gland. Watching Elsa's pretty face while she read her magazine was the perfect aphrodisiac while I enjoyed myself under my blanket. As I rubbed my hard nub, I looked at her lips covered in clear gloss, imagining what it would feel like to have them surrounding my pearl. It didn't take long for me to start squirming in my seat as the pleasurable feelings began spreading throughout my body. Elsa peered up over the top of her magazine, and I looked away in embarrassment realizing she'd caught me staring at her once again. But when I glanced back at her, I noticed that she was still looking in my direction as she darted her eyes between my face and the bump in the blanket between my legs.

*Did she sense what I was doing?* I wondered. *Had I been too obvious in my amateur subterfuge?*

Either way, there was no way I was going to stop, because I'd gotten far too worked up to abandon my solo entertainment. As I returned her gaze, I slowly resumed rubbing my clit under the covering. At first, I did it in such a way that she'd have a hard time recognizing any suspicious movement. The last thing I needed was to get arrested for lewd or inappropriate behavior. I knew airlines had a low tolerance for disruptive passengers, and I had nightmares of being carted off the airplane in handcuffs in front of my fellow passengers upon landing.

But far from ignoring me or raising the alarm to her colleagues, Elsa seemed just as interested in what I was doing as I was in her. While she shifted her eyes between the magazine and the other passengers to distract attention from her watching me, I became bolder and bolder in my actions. I spread my legs wider apart and began to move my hand more quickly over my mound.

When it became obvious to Elsa what I was doing under my blanket, she lifted her leg and swung her thigh on top of her other knee. This time, I could see the curvature of her exposed thigh as her skirt hiked half way up her leg. While my hand began to move more forcefully under my blanket, I saw the muscles in Elsa's legs flexing rhythmically as she squeezed her legs together on her chair.

*Is she stimulating herself while she watches me get off?* I wondered.

Her quiet act of self-pleasure ratcheted up the intensity of my feelings even more, as I moved my other hand under the blanket and began to play with my sopping slit while I rubbed my bean with my other hand. Seeing that I was getting more worked up watching her at the front of the cabin seemed to increase Elsa's courage in lockstep, as the flexing action of her legs increased in speed and intensity. Recognizing that she was stimulating herself in full view of the rest of the cabin was an insane turn-on for me, and I thrust my fingers deep into my snatch, pummeling myself as I watched the flush on Elsa's face begin to spread down her neck onto the top of her chest.

I was aching for release, and when I saw her suddenly hunch over and pretend to cough as her body began to spasm, I gushed all over my hand, cumming hard for the second time during the flight. When she sat back up and glanced in my direction, I was still jerking in my seat with my mouth agape. She tried not to stare at me to avoid drawing attention from the other passengers, but she couldn't help flitting her eyes back toward me until I finally collapsed in my seat in delirious exhaustion.

For the rest of the flight, the two of us pretended like nothing had happened, continuing to carry on casual conversation while she attended to the needs of rest of the passengers. When we began to descend into Arlanda airport, I pulled myself together and collected my belongings in preparation for deplaning.

But by now, the stain in the front of my jeans had spread to the size of a grapefruit from the puddle I'd been sitting on, and I waited for the rest of the first-class passengers to disembark before rising from my seat. Holding my purse strategically over the front of my pants to hide the wet spot, I collected my bag from the overhead bin then made my way to the front exit door. Elsa was standing beside the exit wishing everyone well, and I paused for a moment before heading out onto the jetway.

"Thank you for such a memorable flight," I said, taking her hand and clasping it warmly between mine. "That was the most exceptional customer service I've ever experienced."

"The pleasure was all mine," Elsa smiled, placing her other hand over top of mine. "Enjoy your stay in our lovely country. Perhaps I'll see you on the return leg of your journey."

"I'll look forward to that," I said, realizing that I was holding up the rest of the passengers from exiting the plane. "Bye for now."

As our hands began to separate, Elsa pressed her fingers into the palm of my hand and I felt a strip of paper fall into my palm. I looked at her inquisitively, and she simply smiled and nodded. The moment I got through the jet bridge into the relative privacy of the main terminal, I stopped and unfolded the strip of paper she'd handed me.

*Hope you enjoyed your inflight experience,* the message read. *Drop me a line when you get settled in Stockholm. Perhaps we can enjoy a few more rides together on the slopes of the interior. Elsaflygirl@gmail.com*

I smiled a silly grin as I pulled my carry-on bag toward the exit door.

That wasn't the *only* kind of riding I had in mind for the remainder of my trip.

## 2

After I checked into my hotel room, I started up my laptop and opened a new email message. As my hands hovered over the keyboard, I pondered how best to respond to Elsa's invitation. Had she been thinking the same thing I was when she mentioned taking a few more 'rides' together? Was her choice of the words 'slopes of the interior' code for getting undressed and touching each other's naked bodies? Or was she just referring to snowboarding on the mountains of the north country?

*Fuck it*, I thought as I began to tap the keys. Either way, I wanted to see more of her—any way I could. We'd already shared an undeniably erotic moment together. There'd be plenty of other opportunities to get to know each other better during a few days of snowboarding together.

*Hi Elsa,* I typed.

*Thank you for your lovely note. It was a pleasure meeting you on my flight to Stockholm, even if it was quicker than I hoped. I'd love to have a chance to get to know you better. Do you have some free time to do some snowboarding before your next flight? I'll be in Sweden for a week and I've got an open itinerary. Let me know if you'd like to get together,*

*Best wishes,*

*Jade.*

For a few moments, I sat in front of my computer hoping she'd reply right away to my message. But after a few minutes, I realized how foolish it was of me to expect her to pause her normal routine just because we'd shared a passing moment on the transatlantic flight. I wondered how many *other* passengers had been equally obsessed by her and made similar passes. Surely, she'd have her choice of the most successful and prettiest travelers if she really wanted to strike up a more serious relationship.

I slammed my laptop shut and got up to distract myself from my single-minded infatuation. After all, I'd come to Sweden for a lot more reasons than just to meet new people. Between exploring the fjords, seeing the northern lights, and shopping the old city of Stockholm, there was plenty to do during my one-week stay. I'd even thought about staying one night at the famous ice hotel in Jukkasjarvi. But mostly I just wanted to recharge my batteries from my boring life in Chicago. I'd been flitting from one shallow relationship to another and needed a change. I figured the further I got away from home, the easier it would be for me to forget about my troubles. I hadn't planned on being gobsmacked by the most beautiful woman I'd seen in a long time.

After I unpacked my clothes and arranged my toiletries, I couldn't help checking my computer for new messages. To my surprise, I had a letter from Elsa marked only a few minutes after I'd sent my note. As I clicked to open the message, my stomach fluttered in excitement wondering what new adventures awaited me.

*Jade*, her message began.

*How nice to hear from you so soon after our flight. I've been thinking of you too, and was wondering if you'd like to join me and a few friends for a little ski trip. My parents have a cabin near the resort town of Are, and I'm traveling there tomorrow with a couple of girls from the airline for a few days of R&R. The easiest way to get there is by train from the central station in Stockholm. There's a departure around 9 p.m. tonight that will get you in to the village early in the morning. If it's not too quick a turn-around for you, I can pick you up when you arrive and we'll all head out to the hill together. You're welcome to stay with us at my parents' place until you're scheduled to leave.*

*Looking forward to more adventures together,*

*Elsa*

While I read the message, I could feel my heart beating in my chest as I imagined spending more time with the pretty stewardess. But now I'd have to share her with her friends, and I wondered if that would get in the way of our having some more intimate moments together. But she'd already demonstrated that she was attracted to women, and it didn't take long for me to imagine the bunch of us enjoying some quality après-ski time in the cosy confines of her alpine cabin. Besides, if the *girls* she was referring to were the other attendants on the flight from Chicago, the more the merrier. I'd have my very own fantasy bikini team to play with for a few days.

I quickly accepted her invitation, then packed up my things and checked out of the hotel, grabbing a cab to the downtown train station. I was surprised how packed it was for a Saturday evening, and after purchasing my ticket to Åre, it took a while to get my bearings and find my way to the right departure track. When the train pulled up, I was impressed at how sleek and clean it looked. So far, I'd found everything about this country to be beautiful, polished, and efficient. Even my round-trip fare for the six-hundred-kilometer trip was thrifty, costing less than a hundred bucks.

When I stepped inside the train, I placed my snowboard gear and travel bag in the overhead rack then settled into a seat next to the window. Everything about the train was first-class, from the spotless upholstery and gleaming handrails to the crystal-clear panoramic windows. Even the *people* on the train looked stylish, dressed in fashionable parkas and fur-lined hats.

When the train began to exit the station, I peered outside the window and watched the passing streetscape flash by. I marveled at the pretty architecture of the multi-colored townhomes and plentiful canals running through the city. Within thirty minutes, the train was hurtling through the snowy forest of the interior, and I soon nodded off with my head resting against the glass.

Three hours later, I woke to the feeling of the chilly window pressing against my head, and I looked outside to see a strange glow moving in the night sky. Realizing this was the fabled northern lights I'd read so much about, I craned my neck to take in the eerie spectacle. The luminous bands swirled and morphed into ever-changing shapes and patterns, like a giant fluorescent ghost dancing in the sky. Now I understood why the indigenous people of the arctic gave such spiritual meaning to this supernatural light show. The swaying bands of color almost looked like a living organism, undulating in perpetual rhythm in the northern atmosphere.

*There's another thing I can knock off my bucket list*, I thought, staring up at the sky with my eyes agape in wonder.

But as the train continued north, the skies began to fill with clouds, and I checked my watch to see what time it was. The nights were over sixteen hours long at this latitude at this time of year, and I didn't want to arrive at my final destination unprepared. Even though it was approaching 8 a.m., it was still pitch-black outside and the train would be arriving into Are within thirty minutes. I went into the onboard lavatory to check my makeup and have a quick pee, then wrapped a scarf around my neck under my snow jacket, wondering if I'd prepared sufficiently for the cold Nordic weather.

When the train stopped, I gathered up my gear and headed for the station exit. Elsa hadn't been very specific about how we'd find one another at the train station, so when I got outside I stood on top of the steps surveying the parking area. There were a lot of passengers milling about with cars pulling up into the pick-up zone, so I pulled off my woolen cap and began waving in the general area of the logjam.

A few seconds later I heard a car horn beeping and a late-model Volvo SUV pulled up in front of me with the headlights flashing. The passenger window rolled down and a familiar face smiled at me, motioning for me to approach the car. The rear latch swung open and Elsa stepped out of the driver's seat waving back at me. I smiled at her and threw my board over my shoulder as I walked in their direction. When I got to the car, she gave me a big hug and threw my gear in the rear compartment on top of a bunch of other boots and snowboards.

"Did you have any trouble finding your way here?" she asked.

"No," I smiled. "It was pretty uneventful, other than the spectacular pyrotechnics in the evening sky."

"Ah yes," she said. "The aurora borealis. Was that the first time you'd seen the northern lights?"

"Yes—and it was even more beautiful than I imagined."

"We'll have lots more opportunities to view it over the next couple of nights from my cabin."

She opened the rear driver's side door and motioned me inside.

"But first, let's have a bit of fun on the slopes. I think you'll find the *daytime* views can be almost as pretty in this part of the country."

When I stepped inside the vehicle, two familiar-looking blonde girls turned toward me and smiled. I recognized both of them instantly as the other flight attendants on my inbound trip, and dressed in their pastel snowboard outfits they looked even prettier close-up.

"Do you remember Astrid and Inga from the flight?" Elsa said.

"Of course," I said, thinking I'd died and gone to heaven, surrounded by the three gorgeous women. "How could I forget?"

On the way from the station to the ski resort, we made small talk about my plans while in Sweden and what my life was like back in Chicago. The girls said they traveled there frequently, and I immediately returned the invitation, inviting them to stay with me the next time they were in town. But the whole conversation was a blur as I kept flitting my eyes between the three striking Vikings sitting next to me in the car.

When we got to the ski hill, we all carried our gear up to the lodge then went inside for a quick breakfast and coffee. The girls ordered cereal composed of muesli, fermented milk, and strawberries, and I followed along, trying to sample the local cuisine. It wasn't as bad as it sounded, and I soon gobbled down the crunchy yogurt-tasting concoction on my empty stomach. Then we wolfed down some strong coffee and went downstairs to the locker room to change into our snowboard gear. The three girls all seemed quite adapt at getting into their heavy boots, and when they pulled their goggles over their toques in preparation to exit the cabin a couple of minutes ahead of me, I shook my head in wonderment.

"You girls look like you've done this a few times before," I said, gazing up at their pretty two-piece parkas.

Elsa smiled, kneeling down to help me lace up my boots.

"There's not a lot to do during long winters here in the hinterland," she said. "It's pretty much a choice between hockey or snow skiing. And the airline frowns upon our taking part in contact sports. Something about keeping ourselves in top condition for our guests."

"I can see why," I said, peering at the Swedish beauties. "I wouldn't want to mess with perfection either if I had your looks."

"You know," Elsa said, holding a hand out to help me off the bench. "With your fair skin and light hair, you could easily pass for a Swede too. And I think you're selling yourself short. You're just as pretty as any Scandinavian girl. Speaking of, let's get out there while we still have good light. The rides close in a few hours and it looks like we've had some good powder overnight."

When we got outside, the girls snapped on their boards then shuffled their hips forward as they began to glide to the base of the nearest lift. When we neared the front of the line, we positioned ourselves four abreast and sat down on the wide chair as it swung around to pick us up. As it picked up momentum and lifted us off the ground, my pussy pulsed in excitement feeling the hips of the other girls pressing up against my sides.

"So what brings you to Sweden?" Astrid asked, puffing a cloud of condensed air into the chilly breeze as she spoke.

"Besides the beautiful people and the gorgeous scenery?" I said, peering out over the mountainous landscape. "I guess I was just looking for something new. I was getting kind of bored with my usual routine in Chicago. It's been a while since I've been on a trip outside the country."

"Well if you're looking for something different," Inga said, smiling at the other girls. "Stick with us. We'll be happy to introduce you to some of our more interesting Swedish customs. The après-ski scene can be just as much fun as the daytime opportunities."

Elsa noticed my hands gripping the safety bar in front of me tightly as I shivered under my light snowboard ensemble.

"Are you warm enough?" she said, placing her mittens over mine on the bar. "I noticed you weren't wearing as many layers as the rest of us under that thin parka."

"I'm used to dressing for the mild midwestern winters back home. I guess I wasn't quite ready for the temperatures up here."

"You'll warm up once we get out on the slopes," she said. "All you need is a little exercise to get the blood flowing."

She peered forward as our chair neared the top of the mountain.

"What kind of trails do you like to take? How experienced a snowboarder are you?"

"I don't get out as often as I'd like," I said, glancing down the steep slope underneath our lift. "I used to be pretty decent when I was younger, but it's been a couple of years since I've hit the slopes. Maybe something intermediate to start?"

"No problem," Elsa said. "Just head to the left when we get off the lift. We can start out on the blue trail. It's wide and gently sloping, with lots of room for us to carve wide unobstructed turns."

When the chair reached the crest of the hill, we all pushed off while I struggled to stay balanced as it thrust me forward. The other girls seemed far more composed and confident, shifting their weight expertly backwards as they dug their edges into the soft corn while I wobbled unsteadily, trying to keep my board from getting away from me.

"Ready?" Elsa said, flashing me a brilliant smile.

"I think so," I hesitated.

Seconds later, the girls pointed their boards down the hill and began carving up the light powder in tight serpentine patterns, three abreast. I watched them for a few moments, marveling at how effortless they made it seem, but also how pretty their tight asses looked twisting and swaying as they kicked up light sprays of powder, schussing their way down the meandering slope. Not wanting to get left too far behind, I shifted my weight forward and tentatively pointed my board on a diagonal line across the slope.

At first, I was reluctant to commit myself fully into the fall line, but as I began to shift my weight forward and back on my board, I was pleasantly surprised by how easy I could turn in the freshly fallen snow. Before long, I was carving figure eight patterns overtop the trails left by the other girls and smiling with a giant grin as I began to find my groove. About halfway down the hill, I noticed the they'd pulled up on a flat section of the slope and I skidded to a halt a few feet in front of them.

"*Damn*, Jade," Elsa said as I huffed a stream of fog into the cold air, trying to recover my breath. "You know how to *ride*, girl. That's some pretty sweet carving you were doing down the trail. We're going to have to step up our game to keep up with you."

"Hardly," I smiled. "You're the ones making it look easy. I'm already starting to feel the burn in my legs. You might need to give me a couple of days to ease into this, or else I might need a wheelchair to get back onto the plane for the ride back. Something tells me you guys have had a bit more practice at this than me."

"Maybe," Elsa said. "But you sure aren't any slouch. Why don't you go first this time and we'll follow. Show us your best Lindsey Vonn moves."

I thought it ironic that they'd likened me to the pretty American downhill champion who'd recently turned the European circuit on its ear.

"I'm not *that* good," I said. "I'll just be happy if I can make it down the rest of the way without wiping out."

This time I flipped my board forward and headed straight down the fall line, rapidly picking up speed as I arched my body from side to side, reveling in the soft champagne powder of the Swedish resort. When I got to the bottom of the hill and stopped at the base of the lift, the three other girls followed close behind and skidded to a stop beside me.

"It looks like you've found your legs," Elsa said. "You can carve, girl. I was admiring your form all the way down."

"Are you referring to my ski technique or my skimpy little outfit?" I smiled.

"Both. I had a hard time staying on the course with such a pretty distraction in front of me."

"Glad I was able to keep you distracted," I smiled. "I'm hoping there'll be lots of other opportunities to divert your attention over the next couple of days."

The four of us spent the next couple of hours carving the hills, taking increasingly steep and exciting trails before we decided we need a rest. When we stopped near the bottom of one of the trails, Elsa looked over toward me and smiled in a heavy plume of mist.

"Are you ready for some fika?" she said.

Not knowing exactly what that was, but sounding pretty close to fucking, I nodded eagerly, happy to have a different kind of alonetime with the girls.

"Let's head into the lodge," Elsa said. "I don't know about you guys, but I could eat a moose after a hard morning of riding."

"Count me in," Astrid said.

"I could use a warm cup of coffee right about now," Inga nodded.

"Is that what fika is?" I said, pinching my eyebrows in disappointment.

"Yes," Elsa said. "In Sweden, coffeetime is more of a social gathering opportunity than just an excuse to get charged up on caffeine. Let's go inside and rest up for a bit while we get warmed up. We don't want to turn your body into rubber on the first day."

We trudged into the lodge and found an open spot next to a large wood-burning fireplace. As the girls began to take off their heavy parkas and outerwear, I couldn't stop scanning their shapely figures in their tight, form-fitting sweaters. The cute reindeer motifs reminded me of Pippi Longstocking, but their swelling breasts and hourglass figures reminded me more of that other Swedish meme. There was something about the warmth of the roaring fire and the sweat dripping down the back of my neck from the exertion on the slopes that was quickly getting me worked up. As I continued undressing the girls with my eyes, my mind began to wander to the possible après-ski activities that Elsa had mentioned.

"Shall we get a bite to eat?" she said, catching me eyeing up her body.

"Absolutely," I said, trying to quell my churning insides. My stomach wasn't the *only* body part that needed attention right now. I needed a distraction quickly before I peeled off their clothes right then and there and jumped their bodies in my mind's imagination.

As we strolled up to the food line, I once again followed the girls' lead. Everybody was ordering hot pea soup or oven-cooked pancakes with ligonberry jam and maple syrup. But when it came time to order coffee, they all looked at me with a strange expression when I ordered a latte with extra cream and sugar.

"What?" I said, looking at the girls with a puzzled expression. "You guys are looking at me like I just ordered *antifreeze*."

"We don't put all that extra stuff in our coffee in Sweden," Elsa said. "We like to take it straight-up, where we can enjoy its natural goodness."

"Mmm, I get that," I said, glancing at her shapely ass in her tight leggings. "Straight up it is."

When we returned to our table next to the fire, I was surprised how good the pancakes and soup tasted. I was so used to the typical American brunch of bacon and eggs that I'd almost forgotten about the pleasures of a foreign diet. Even the plain coffee tasted unusually good, as I savored the natural flavor of the north African bean.

While we made small talk about our favorite trails at the resort, I couldn't help staring at the girls' shapely figures in their tight sweaters as their chests expanded and contracted while they ate their food. The orange flames from the fireplace cast a warm glow on their faces, accenting their natural beauty. By the time we'd finished our meal, my entire body was burning and flushed in excitement.

"So what do you guys do for fun after playing on the hills all day?" I said, hoping to plant the seeds for some more adventurous après-ski activities.

Elsa looked at her friends for a moment then peered at me with a devilish grin.

"Have you ever participated in a polar bear plunge?" she asked.

"Isn't that where people jump into freezing cold water in the middle of winter?" I said, shaking my head in bewilderment. "Isn't that kind of painful and dangerous?"

"Not the way we do it. We only stay in for a short time then head into the sauna to warm up. It's actually quite refreshing. After a hard day of snowboarding, the cold water actually reduces muscle inflammation and speeds up your recovery time."

"Do you guys wear some kind of special insulation?" I said, not quite buying Elsa's dubious explanation.

"Actually, the best way to do it is in the nude. The less clothing, the better. You don't want any cold clothing clinging to you when you get out of the water. We'll have terrycloth robes ready for you to warm up quickly. But the best part about it is the sauna afterward. Feeling the warm steam all over your newly cleansed skin is absolutely heavenly. It's is a tradition we Swedes have been practicing for centuries."

The idea of seeing the three pretty flight attendants in the buff quickly eliminated my concerns about the discomfort of the procedure. It actually sounded like a lot of fun, and my mind was already racing ahead to all the possibilities once we got in the sauna.

"When in Sweden..." I smiled, cocking my head playfully. "You guys certainly aren't holding back giving me the full immersion experience. I'm eager to learn *all* about your special customs."

"Good," Elsa said, reaching down to lace up her boots. "Let's get back out on the slopes while we've still got some good light. It'll turn dark in a couple of hours and we haven't even tried the most challenging trails."

I smiled nervously, feeling the burn in my thighs when I stood to zip up my jacket.

Hopefully the *rest* of my body will still be able to function by the time these girls are ready to stop torturing me, I thought.

**3**

___

By three o'clock, the shadows were beginning to lengthen over the mountain, and the four of us headed back into the lodge to collect our belongings. I was actually looking forward to the dip in the cold water to help relieve my aching muscles. As we drove through the dense forest on the way to Elsa's cabin, I marveled at the natural beauty of the Scandinavian landscape. Heavy pillows of snow hung over the roofs of quaint chalets nestled among the tall evergreen trees, like icing on gingerbread houses. The woods got thicker and thicker, until we emerged onto a clearing with a small wooden cabin at the edge of an ice-covered lake.

"Here we are," Elsa said, pulling her car up next to a broad porch at the front of the structure. The setting reminded me of a prototypical arctic winter scene, like something out of a Christmas fairy tale.

"Let's go inside and get the fireplace going," she said. "You'll need to get warmed up before taking a dip in the lake."

When we stepped through the front door, I was surprised how cold the cabin was as I rubbed my hands over my shoulders trying to increase the circulation.

"Sorry about the chilly temperature," Elsa said. "We normally keep the furnace set just high enough to keep the pipes from freezing." She nodded toward a giant stone fireplace with tall stacks of wood framing the opening. "We prefer to heat our houses the natural way. There's nothing like the sound and smell of freshly cut birch cackling in the open hearth."

She kneeled down in front of the fireplace and rolled some newspaper into little balls then placed some kindling over top of them and struck a match. The material quickly burst into flame, and as she stacked the silver logs over the iron grate, the fire soon began roaring, throwing pretty sparks against the safety screen.

"*That's* what I'm talking about," I said, taking a seat on the mantle next to the fire, rubbing my cold fingers together.

"Can I get you something to drink while you warm up?" Elsa said. "Maybe a hot chocolate or a black coffee?"

"If it's not against the rules trying something a little sweet," I smiled. "A hot chocolate would be lovely."

Elsa disappeared into the kitchen and reemerged a few minutes later with a platter holding four steaming cups. She handed one to each of us, then the girls sat down on heavy armchairs facing me. I could feel my cheeks begin to flush as I gazed at them with the orange glow from the fire dancing over their pretty faces.

"So what do you think of our country so far?" Elsa said.

"It's a little chillier than I imagined," I said, clasping my mug between my palms to warm up my still-tingling hands. "But everything about it certainly is beautiful."

"We'll get you warmed up soon enough," she smiled. "Would you like a little tour of my chalet? We've got the place all to ourselves for the next few days, and you'll need to know where to find the water closet and other amenities. Besides, I need to stoke the coals in the sauna to heat it up in preparation for our polar bear plunge."

"Oh yeah," I said, huddling closer to the fire. "I'd almost forgotten about that."

As I followed Elsa through the different rooms of the cabin, I was struck by how small the place was. With only two bedrooms and one washroom, I wondered how four girls would comfortably share the space for more than a few days. But I hesitated asking about the sleeping arrangements, hoping we'd be able to at least double-up in the small space. I was already beginning to plan how I'd nestle up against Elsa on the pretense of getting warm as a prelude to more intimate exploration.

When we reached the back of the cabin, Elsa opened a heavy door and the smoky scent of fresh cedar filled my nostrils as I peered into a large wood-paneled room. Every surface of the interior was lined in reddish-brown planks of wood, with wraparound wooden benches on two levels surrounding a small metal stove topped with gray rocks.

"Wow," I said, inhaling the smoky scent. "This room is even bigger than the bedrooms. You must spend a lot of time in here."

"Having a daily sauna is like a spiritual experience for us Swedes," Elsa nodded. "It's part of our DNA. There's no better way to relax and wind down after a busy day."

She stepped toward the little stove and placed a large ladle into a wooden bucket of water. As she spilled the liquid gently over the glowing rocks, a hot steam began to fill the room with a pleasant eucalyptus aroma.

"That's an interesting way to warm up a room," I said, my heart racing at the thought of soon lying in the heavenly space next to the three beauties.

"Radiant heat is the cleanest type of heat," Elsa nodded. "Plus, the humidity does wonders for cleaning out your lungs and your pores. You'll feel like a new woman after spending a couple of hours in here."

"I can imagine," I said, beginning to feel my pussy perspire at the thought.

"Are you ready for a bracing swim first?" Elsa said, flashing me a sly grin.

"I guess so," I murmured, preferring to stay in the comfortable and aromatic environment of the steam room.

"Let's get changed out of our outerwear," she said, opening an adjacent closet. "I've got some heavy robes to keep you warm before and after the swim."

We all returned to the living room, where the three girls began to disrobe. I hesitated at first, nervous to reveal my naked body among a group of strangers. But as they peeled off their layers showing more and more skin, I slowly began to undress. Their firm breasts bounced on their chests as they pulled off their undershirts and I couldn't help gasping when they finally removed all their clothes. All three of them had creamy pale skin and Playmate-perfect figures. With nary a hair to be found anywhere on their bodies below their flowing blonde locks, my pussy pulsed in excitement as I stared at them unashamedly.

"Jesus," I said, shaking my head in amazement. "Is *everybody* in Sweden in this good shape? You guys all look like somebody straight out of a beer commercial."

"Yeah—we get that Swedish Bikini Team thing all the time," Elsa said, shaking her head. "I'm not sure Budweiser did us any favors creating that image of Scandinavian girls for North American consumption."

She gave my body a quick going over as I pulled off the last of my underclothes.

"But you're no slouch either, Jade. With your blonde locks and athletic figure, you could pass for a Swedish girl any day."

I stood awkwardly facing the three girls, feeling the heat of the nearby fire burning the back my naked body.

"I'm just happy to be mentioned in the same *sentence* with you guys, let alone be thought of as one of your countrymen," I said, hoping to deflect everyone's attention from my naked figure. "Are we going to do this or what?"

"Of course," Elsa said, handing out terrycloth robes and slippers to each of us. "But be careful as you walk down the path toward the water. There's plenty of ice, and the rocks are quite slippery. You might want to hold my hand as you make your way over the flagstones."

We all put on our gowns, then Elsa opened the front door as I felt a rush of cold air enter the cabin.

"Come on, scaredy-cat," she said, holding out her arm for me. "We don't want to let the cabin get cold again. Let's take a dip before you lose your nerve."

I wrinkled my forehead, then took Elsa's hand as the four of us scampered down the frozen flagstone path to a small dock extending out over the water. When we got to the end of pier, I noticed a ten-foot-diameter hole cut into the ice covering of the pond and I looked at Elsa with an incredulous expression.

"You want me to go in *there*?" I said with my eyes agape.

"Just for a few moments," she said. "I promise you'll enjoy it. There's nothing so invigorating as a brief plunge into freezing-cold water to charge up your adrenaline. Are you ready?"

"I don't know..." I said, pulling back on Elsa's hand.

Suddenly, Astrid and Inga threw off their robes and jumped into the black pool, emerging from the frigid surface hollering in delight.

"Come on in, Jade," Inga said, flinging her wet hair behind her head. "The water's lovely. Come experience the crystal-clear water of our natural habitat."

"Natural habitat?" I scoffed. "Maybe for a *polar bear*."

Elsa turned to face me and squeezed my hand.

"Come on Jade, you're just torturing yourself standing out here in the cold air. We'll jump in together and it'll be over before you know it. Then we can all get nice and cozy in the warm sauna."

There was something about the way she said *nice and cozy* that encouraged me to get this over with.

"Ready?" she said, dropping her robe onto the dock.

I looked at her sexy body shining in the bright moonlight and pulled off my frock.

"One–two–THREE!" she shouted, then she leaped off the dock pulling me into the pitch-black lake.

It took a moment to register the feeling of the cold water surrounding my body as my mind was still in shock at the audacity of what we were doing. But within seconds, I could feel the painful burn of the freezing depths as my teeth began to clatter while I treaded water.

"Isn't it *fabulous*?" Elsa said, smiling at me with a big toothy grin.

"Ye-yes," I stuttered, trying to block out the numb feeling rapidly spreading over my body. "That's one thing you could call it."

"Look, up at the sky," she said, peering upward. "The northern lights are even more beautiful this far away from the city."

"It's stunning," I said, recognizing the swirling green clouds. "But I think I could appreciate it better dressed up in a warm sweater from your front porch with a warm cup of coffee resting on my lap."

"Okay," Elsa nodded. "I think we've exposed you long enough to the natural elements for one night. Let's get out of here and warmed up."

She swam to the front of the dock and climbed up a small wooden ladder then held out her hand to me as she bent down over the edge.

"Give me your hand so you don't slip getting up."

As I kicked my way to the ladder and placed my hands on the rungs, I could feel my muscles shaking as I tried to pull myself up. Elsa grabbed one of my hands and lurched me out of the water, then wrapped one of the robes around my shivering body. As she held me close trying to share her body heat, I watched the other two girls emerge from the pool with beads of water running over their sexy figures. Their areolas contracted with deep goose bumps as their hard nipples extended out from their breasts almost a full inch. For a moment, I forgot that I was standing near-naked in subfreezing temperatures soaking wet while I admired their sexy bodies.

"Come on," Elsa said. "Let's get back into the cabin and warm up in the sauna. I think you're ready for a new kind of Swedish experience."

The four of us scurried up the path, then Elsa opened the front door and we scampered over the hardwood floor into the sauna. While Elsa poured three ladles of water over the steaming coals, the room soon filled with the soothing sensation of the humid heat. I sat down next to the stove, with the other three girls sitting on the two levels directly opposite me.

"There," Elsa purred. "Doesn't that feel a little better?"

"Yes," I said. "But not enough to take off my clothes quite yet. I'm still warming up in this nice cozy robe."

"Feel free to keep it on for a little longer," Elsa said. "But we normally like to take our saunas in the nude. Soon you'll begin to sweat and you'll want to give your pores a chance to open up and let your body cleanse yourself."

As if on cue, Astrid and Inga unfastened their belts and pulled their robes open, revealing their glistening breasts.

"Yes," I panted. "I want to experience *everything* here in Sweden the same way you native girls do."

"You know," Elsa smiled. "I kind of like watching you covered up. It reminds me of our little affair on the plane."

"Oh?" I said. "You remember that still?"

"How could I forget?" Elsa grinned. "That was the most interesting flight I've had in a long time."

"You seemed to be enjoying yourself almost as much as I was."

"I have a little secret to confess," she said. "I had a little help of my own while I watched you."

"Really?" I said, pinching my eyebrows together in confusion. "I saw you flexing your thighs, but–"

"There was a little more than that going on. I had something *inside* while I was rubbing myself."

"Inside?"

"Ben-wa balls. Have you ever tried those before?"

"I've heard of them but never tried it. How do they work?"

"You gently rock your hips or squeeze your legs together, and they roll around inside your pussy providing a very erotic sensation. It's quite an exquisite feeling. I have them inside me right now."

"*You do?*" I said, widening my eyes in surprise. "How do you keep them from falling out?"

"It's not hard to keep them in using your Kegel muscles. In fact, it's considered a good way to exercise those muscles to maintain optimal sexual function."

Elsa paused for a moment, as she began to spread her legs apart.

"Can you do me a favor and play with yourself under your robe while I replay our little erotic encounter on the plane?"

"*Hell* yes," I said, happy to see that Elsa and the other girls were just as interested as I was moving our relationship to the next level of intimacy.

As I slipped my hand under my robe, I felt my still cold and clammy skin over the front of my hairless mound. But as I moved my fingers over my slit, I felt my warm natural juices beginning to lubricate my vulva.

"Mmm," I purred, watching Astrid and Inga spread their legs further apart as they watched me. "I *like* seeing you in your natural habitat."

"Yes," Elsa groaned, rocking her hips gently on the wooden bench. "You're very pretty, Jade. I've been dreaming about watching you up close ever since our flight ended."

"I was so happy when I read your note," I smiled. "I've pleasured myself many times replaying that moment over and over."

"As have I," Elsa said, rubbing her thighs together as she opened her robe wider for me to see her juggling tits. "And I wasn't the *only* one who enjoyed that memory," she said motioning to the other girls sitting on the bench beside her.

Astrid and Inga nodded as they moved their hands between their legs and began to circle their nubs.

"You *told* them?" I said, feigning surprise.

"Of course. We share everything together. You're not the *only* one who likes a little play time between girls every now and then."

I smiled at the revelation that they were all bisexual like me.

"It looks like the only person missing from your troop is the hot flight attendant who reminds me of Tarzan," I said

"You mean *Erik*?" Elsa said. "He's quite a dish to be sure, but I think he prefers to bat for the other team as much as we do."

"You mean he's gay?" I said. "What a shame. I was undressing him on the plane almost as much as I was you girls."

"Not to worry," Elsa smiled. "I'm pretty sure between the three of us that we'll be able to keep you properly entertained during your stay."

"I hope so," I panted, watching Astrid and Inga place their fingers inside their pussies while they jilled themselves watching me play with myself.

"Open your robe now," Elsa ordered. "Let me see exactly what you were doing under that blanket on the plane. I want to watch your pretty body while you pleasure yourself. It's just us girls this time and nobody else is watching."

I didn't need any more encouragement as I began to feel the pleasurable sensations spreading throughout my body. The rising steam from the coal stove had increased the room temperature to well over one hundred degrees and I didn't need any more excuses to fully disrobe. I took my gown off my shoulders and threw it on the bench beside me and spread my legs wide apart to let the girls see my glistening lips.

"Yes," Elsa said. "Show us what you were doing with your fingers under that blanket."

By now, I was burning up inside from the rising passion as I watched the three goddesses touching themselves while they watched me. I plunged my middle two fingers into my snatch and pulled my palm against my throbbing button, stroking myself with increasing intensity as the three women writhed on the wooded benches in front of me. Elsa spread her legs further apart, rocking her hips forward and back while she rubbed her clit in tight little circles.

"Yes, Jade," she purred. "Fuck that sweet pussy with your pretty fingers. I want to watch your body heaving and shaking again when you come."

"Damn, Elsa," I said, feeling the wall of pleasure rapidly building inside my body. "This is a feast for my eyes. I'm going to come soon."

"Yes, my pretty American," she said. "Let us watch you satisfy yourself while we pleasure our bodies. I'm close too."

As I watched the three beauties rocking their bodies on the warm planks, I felt my body fall over the precipice as I clamped down over my fingers, hunching over in a series of rhythmic spasms. With the pressure built up inside my pussy from my fingers damming the flow of my juices, I pulled my fingers out of my hole and began spraying long streams of fluid over the steaming wooden floor. Seeing me squirting my juices while racked in pleasure soon pushed the other girls over the edge, and within seconds all four of us were shaking and groaning in the steamy fog of the sauna.

"Now I see why you were covering yourself up when you left the plane," Elsa sighed when she came down from her climax. "That's one part of the experience I definitely missed. You are one talented and sexy lady, Jade."

"Not nearly as sexy as the three of you," I said, catching my breath. "That was the hottest show I've seen in a long time."

"I have to agree," Elsa smiled, peering at her colleagues. "What do you think girls? Is this the sexiest passenger we've ever had on our transatlantic flight?"

"Definitely," Astrid nodded. "I've seen a lot of fuckable passengers in my day, but nobody I've wanted to get down and dirty with as much as this one."

"And we're just getting started," Elsa grinned. "There's so many other ways we can have fun together now that we're free of all the limitations on the plane. What's your ultimate fantasy, Jade? What would you like to do now that you have the three of us all to yourself?"

"Oh my God," I said, realizing all my dreams were about to come true. "My mind is racing with so many possibilities right now. But honestly, I'd just like to watch you three do your thing together. This is the like the ultimate erotic video, watching three gorgeous girls touching each other. I'll be happy to get in on the action soon enough. For now, let me just soak up your fabulous figures a little longer while I watch you get a little more interactive."

Elsa smiled as she peered over at Astrid and Inga.

"What do you say, girls? Shall we indulge our guest in her little fantasy?"

"I thought she'd never ask," Inga smiled, shifting her body closer to Elsa.

"If you're just going to *watch*," Elsa said, pinching a little string between her legs and pulling two glistening chrome balls out of her slit. "Would you like to try my little toy? I think you might find it makes for a more engaging experience."

"Absolutely," I said, raising my eyebrows as I peered at the intriguing balls.

Elsa stood up and walked across the floor then handed me the slippery orbs. I could smell the musk of her scent on the globes and I looked up at her, grinning a broad smile.

"Just be sure to leave some of the string hanging out your opening," she said. "They can get pretty far up inside you in the heat of the moment and you don't want to lose them up there. Once you place them inside, you'll find plenty of ways to stimulate yourself. Enjoy."

Elsa returned to the other side of the room, sitting on the upper bunk while Astrid stood on the lower bench facing her with her back toward me. As she lowered her face toward Elsa's pussy, Inga sat between her legs and tilted her head up as Astrid planted her mound over her chin. Within seconds, all three girls were rolling their hips in a three-way ménage as they began to grunt and moan in unison.

Watching them pleasuring themselves just a few feet in front of me soon got my juices flowing again as I awkwardly pressed the two chrome balls into my slit. They slipped inside easier than I imagined, but it felt unusual to have such a strangely shaped object inside me other than the usual dildos and vibrators I was accustomed to.

But as I began to rock my hips slowly on the bench, I could feel them sliding forward and back against the walls of my pussy, and I soon began to mew and groan along with the other girls. It didn't take long for me to get comfortable with the pleasurable feeling of the slippery balls stroking the walls of my pussy, and when I placed my fingers against my dripping clit, I felt a jolt of electricity running through me.

*This is a little different,* I thought. *Why haven't I tried this before?*

Now I understood why Elsa brought them with her wherever she flew. With their unobtrusive form factor and concealed placement, no one would be any the wiser as she went about her duties receiving gentle, sensuous stimulation whenever she moved.

As I watched Elsa spread her legs wide apart and Astrid humping Inga's face while they ate each other out, I began to rock my hips faster and faster watching the girls bucking and moaning in front of me. With Inga's legs splayed far apart as she rubbed her bald pussy with her glistening fingers, and seeing the base of her chin planted firmly against Astrid's mound, watching the three girls fucking themselves in the superheated environment of the aromatic sauna was the most erotic thing I'd seen in a long time.

When Elsa placed her hands beside Astrid's head and pulled her face harder against her pussy as she locked eyes on me, I suddenly felt a surge of pleasure engulfing me. With our mouths yawning wider and wider apart in shared ecstasy, I couldn't hold back any longer.

"Oh *fuckkk,*" I groaned in pleasure, my body beginning to shake once again in another intense orgasm. I could feel the Ben-wa balls rolling around inside as my pussy walls contracting rhythmically against them, sending me into new paroxysms of pleasure.

Watching me shaking uncontrollably on the steamy wooden planks seemed to bring Elsa to a new level of pleasure, and soon she also began jerking spasmodically as she held Astrid's face tightly against her pussy. Like a chain reaction, Astrid suddenly became weak at the knees as she slumped forward against Inga's chin with her buttocks shaking like a bowl of water. Feeling Astrid coming all over her face, Inga raised her hips off the bench and began flapping her thighs in and out in mutual ecstasy. Realizing that all three girls were coming together took me to another level, and within seconds I was having my third powerful orgasm of the afternoon.

After we all come down from our climaxes, I suddenly became aware of the ache in my quads from my hard day of snowboarding. I'd been so lost in the moment watching the other girls having fun and pleasuring myself that I'd forgotten I'd just had the most intense exercise in months.

*I'll have to take it easier on the slopes tomorrow*, I thought, *if I'm going to keep up with these girls and enjoy some more off-piste action.* The après-ski experience had been even more exciting and adventurous than the vigorous snowboarding exercise. I wanted to save myself for the next step in my Swedish immersion.

## 4

Over the course of the next few days, Elsa, Inga, Astrid and I made love many more times between our snowboarding, polar plunge, and sauna escapades. By the end of the week, I'd experienced every erotic entanglement with the three girls that I'd fantasized about on my initial flight to Sweden. When it finally came time to say our goodbyes, I was sad to leave but thrilled to have had the opportunity to spend so much quality time with the three Scandinavian beauties.

As the four of us drove back to Stockholm in preparation for my return flight to Chicago, we talked about reconnecting stateside, but I never expected to see the girls again. We'd had our moment of glory together, and that was enough for me. I'd cherish the experience forever and carry enough memories to keep me entertained for quite some time into the future.

But I still had one last flight with the girls, and I planned to make the best of it. Elsa and I had talked over the last couple of days about how we might be able to arrange a *real* mile-high liaison, and my body was tingling all over in anticipation of the trip. After I passed through airport security and collected my boarding pass, I smiled at Elsa and Astrid as I boarded the plane and took my seat near the back of the first-class cabin. The same woman I'd met on my inbound flight was sitting across the aisle from me again, and I smiled politely before pretending to check my email messages.

While the rest of the passengers shuffled onto the plane, I tried to keep myself distracted reading a magazine while I squirmed uncomfortably in my seat. Watching Elsa do the safety demonstration drove me crazy knowing she was receiving internal stimulation the whole time from her Ben-wa balls. I cursed myself for not remembering to buy some of my own to keep me entertained during the long flight.

But when the demonstration was over and the girls took their seats in preparation for take-off, Elsa winked at me, giving me a sly smile. Within thirty minutes, we reached cruising altitude and Astrid and Elsa began delivering the meal service. It was difficult restraining myself from interacting with the girls in a more familiar manner, but I continued playing the role of naive first-time traveler to maintain their professional demeanor. Besides, I knew that very soon we'd be able to dispense with the charade and have one last chance at resuming our special relationship.

When the meal service was over, Elsa and Astrid seemed more generous than usual offering the passengers their choice of alcoholic beverage. Before long, most of the early-morning travelers had nodded off in their seats from the combined effects of full stomachs and the alcohol-induced sedative. The girls took their seats at the front of the cabin for a brief rest, and after briefly scanning the attentiveness of the passengers, Elsa nodded toward me and tilted her head in the direction of the forward lavatory.

I carefully glanced around the cabin and when I saw that everybody was either sleeping or absorbed in their reading material, I rose from my seat and slowly made my way up the aisle. As I opened the door to the lavatory, I smiled at the two flight attendants and they winked back at me. When I closed the door behind me, my heart began racing a million miles an hour thinking about what we were about to do. Whether it was from the danger of being exposed or from the excitement of soon reconnecting with my Swedish lovers, I wasn't sure. But either way, my panties were already soaked from the rush.

It seemed to take forever for Elsa to join me in the lavatory, and after a few minutes I began to wonder if some of the passengers had woken up or requested additional aid. Not knowing what to do with myself, I began to disrobe and hung my clothes on the peg over the door. Looking at my fully naked body in the mirror, I began to play with myself imagining her touching me in the private cubicle. Just as I was about to come remembering the sight of the three sexy stewardesses in the sauna, suddenly the door swung open and Elsa stepped inside. She looked at me hunched over the sink with my hands between my legs and smiled as she shut the door quietly behind her.

"It looks like you've gotten started without me," she said. "That's my girl. We won't have too much time to do this while Astrid is keeping watch."

She stepped toward me then reached up to the paper towel dispenser above the sink and laid a protective layer of towels over the vanity.

"Get up on the sink and spread your legs for me," she instructed. "I need to fuck you right now. I've been dreaming about this ever since I saw you."

"That makes *two* of us," I sighed, turning around to face her while I lifted myself up onto the sink, splaying my knees against my naked breasts.

Elsa took one look at my glistening pussy and hiked up her skirt, revealing her bald pussy framed between black garter stockings.

"I *knew* you were naked under there," I smiled, feeling my juices beginning to run over my perineum all the way down to my throbbing rosebud.

"Would I have it any other way?" she said, pressing her mound against mine as she locked lips with me and pressed my back against the cold glass mirror.

"Mmm," I hummed, feeling her wetness touching mine. "Fuck me, Elsa. I've been waiting for this a long time."

Elsa lifted her knee and extended her right leg, placing her foot against the mirror beside me. Her legs were separated like a pair of open scissors, with our pussies grinding together as we moaned in each other's mouths. For a moment, my mind reeled at the audacity of what we were doing, but it didn't take long for me to begin feeling the rising tide of pleasure spreading throughout my body. Elsa had already revealed her incredible flexibility to me in our prior erotic encounters, but this new technique with her fucking me in a perfect split took me to a whole new level of sexual intensity.

"*Oh God*," I panted as I listened to our wet labia smacking together while we ground our pussies against one another. "Are you still carrying those love balls inside you?"

"You tell *me*," Elsa grunted as I felt her buttock muscles contract against my sweaty palms.

Suddenly, I felt the slippery balls pass out of her pussy into mine as her pussy began contracting in the initial stages of orgasm.

"Come with me, Jade," she panted. "I want to feel you spray all over me like you did in the sauna."

"*Fuck* yes," I hissed, feeling my climax suddenly overtake me from the feeling of Elsa's balls swirling around inside me. "I'm cumming, Elsa!" I groaned. "I'm cumming so hard!"

As my walls contracted tightly over the steel balls and I began squirting all over Elsa's pussy, the balls suddenly spurt back out as we grunted in unison from the feeling of the slippery orbs rubbing between our slits. We tried to remain as quiet as I could in the narrow confines of the lavatory, but it was difficult to stifle our screams of mutual ecstasy as we ground our hips together on the shaking vanity.

When the two of us came down from our powerful climaxes, I peered down, noticing that I'd soaked Elsa's black stockings with my juices.

"Sorry, sweetie," I said, shaking my head. "But I couldn't help myself. When you passed me the balls, I had the hardest climax I've had in a long time."

"Not to worry, babe," Elsa smiled, reaching into her purse beside the counter. "We flight attendants come prepared for every emergency."

As she began to pull out a new pair of stockings, we heard a tap on the door. Fearing we'd be caught by a passenger wanting to use the lavatory, my heart began thumping wildly as my eyes widened in fright. Elsa held a finger to her lips then tapped back twice on our side of the door, and the person on the other side tapped back quickly three times in succession. She smiled back at me then opened the door as Astrid squeezed in next to us.

"*What the...?*" I said, pinching my eyebrows in surprise. "Who'll be our lookout in case another passenger needs to use the washroom?"

"Everybody's completely passed out and sleeping peacefully," Astrid said. "We've got a few more minutes to have a little fun. I couldn't resist. Listening to you guys has gotten me all worked up."

"We were *that* obvious?" I asked.

"Only if you were standing next to the door. The sound of the jet engines drowned out most of the noise."

"Okay," Elsa said. "But we'll have to act fast. Let's let Jade take the driver's seat this time. I'll listen for any passenger pings next to the door."

Astrid hiked up her skirt and leaned back against the sink, pulling me toward her, rubbing her mound against my slippery pubis.

"Who's wearing the balls *this* time?" she smiled, peering toward Elsa.

Elsa passed Astrid the glistening balls and she slipped them inside her pussy, then she pulled me closer and began kissing me hard on the lips. Although we were standing in an upright missionary position this time, we were able to angle our hips just enough to touch our clits as we ground our pussies together. As I began to feel my pleasure rapidly escalating, thinking our little tryst couldn't possibly get any more erotic, suddenly Elsa stepped behind me and thrust her fingers into my snatch as she began finger-fucking me from behind.

"*Yes, Jade!*" Astrid panted, feeling Elsa rocking our hips together. "I want to feel you cream all over me when you cum. Fuck me with your pretty American pussy."

Feeling Astrid's pussy grinding against mine with Elsa finger-fucking me from behind as she squeezed my tits was a sensory over-load. Within seconds, I began climaxing once again as I squirted a stream of powerful jets inside Astrid's hole while we moaned into each other's mouths, gripping each other tightly. Elsa pressed her own mound hard against my quivering buttocks as the three of us groaned in simultaneous ecstasy with the cabin full of passengers just outside the door seeming a million miles away.

When we all recovered from our climaxes and realized what a mess we'd made, the girls quickly changed stockings while I cleaned up the room. When we finally collected ourselves and prepared to leave, Elsa placed her ear to the door and nodded.

"I'll go first to make sure the way is clear," she said. "If everything looks good, I'll tap twice then you can both come out."

Astrid and I nodded, then Elsa opened the door and closed it quickly behind us. Within a few seconds, we heard a soft double-tap and the two of us exited the washroom as I made my way back to my seat past the still-sleeping passengers. But when I got to my chair, I peered over at the woman sitting next to me and she opened one eyelid, smiling at me.

*Fuck*, I thought. *We've been made.*

But seeing that she wasn't overly perturbed by the incident, I settled back into my seat, feeling the dampness of Astrid's and Elsa's juices clinging to my pussy pressing up against my moist panties. I glanced toward the front of the cabin and saw the girls sitting quietly beside one another in their jump seats with a sexy glow still on their cheeks. I smiled at them and mouthed the words *Thank You*, blowing each of them a kiss.

Seconds later, the woman sitting next to me pressed her call button and when Astrid walked down the aisle to attend to her, she asked for a blanket. When Astrid returned with the cover, the woman placed it over her lap and moments later I noticed her hand slip underneath it as she began to stroke herself between her legs. Sitting in the middle row of seats, she wasn't able to make direct eye contact with Astrid or Elsa, so she turned her head and smiled at me. As I saw her eyes begin to glaze over in self pleasure, I smiled back at her with our shared secret.

It looked like I wasn't going to be the *only* one enjoying a little mile-high thrill on our trip back from Sweden.

# VOLUME TWO

## NUDE CRUISE

1
———

## EXOTIC VOYAGE

My exhilarating encounters at the dinner party, the dark room, and naked yoga had whet my appetite for new adventures. But each of these experiences, as stimulating and fulfilling as they were in their own right, were one-time affairs. In each case, it hadn't taken long for me to yearn for something new, something more. I wanted an *all-in-one* adventure, where I could move from one new experience to another without having to search for the next one. I wanted my own erotic *Disneyland*.

I knew if I could find such diverse activities online, there must be a whole underworld of swingers looking for something similar. Surely some enterprising operator would see the potential in putting together some kind of package deal. I sat down in front of my computer, opened up my browser, and typed in the words 'all-inclusive erotic adventure.'

A surprising number of 'clothing-optional' resort listings came up. I clicked on the first one, but it just showed the usual pictures of pretty pools, beaches, and guests suites, with a vague description of an 'upscale retreat for an adventurous lifestyle experience'. A little further down the page, I saw a blog article titled *Inside a nudist sex resort*. The article described an adventure traveler's experience at a resort where couples romped on nude beaches, swam in nude pools, and 'hooked up' in private cabins.

*Definitely a little too tame-sounding for me.*

I clicked on the next page of search results, where I saw a link titled *Nude Cruise — Explore Your Erotic Fantasies.*

*This looks interesting.*

I clicked on the link and a webpage opened showing pictures of naked people climbing walls, dancing in water fountains, and wrestling in a muddy pit.

*That looks a little different,* I thought.

At the top of the webpage, there was a tab titled *Fantasy Menu.* I clicked on the link, and a list of sexy-sounding shipboard activities appeared:

> Peak Sensation
> House of Holes
> Fantasy Fountain
> Sensuous Steam Room
> Masquerade Ball
> Sexy Games Room
> Get Down Disco
> Cybersex Rules
> Private View Rooms
> Intimate Massage
> FourPlay

I clicked on the first one and a photo appeared showing naked men and women scaling a climbing wall with unusual foot and hand holds. Instead of the usual jug and pocket holds, the 'grips' were in the shape of dildos and artificial vaginas, where climbers could pause to 'rest' and 'recharge their batteries' as they scaled the wall. A description under the photo read:

*Challenge yourself to a climbing wall like no other. The higher you go, the more stimulating the experience becomes. Reward yourself at each new level, where you'll find a new wall feature to stimulate and excite every part of your body, as you seek the peak experience at the top of the mountain. All while safely strapped into a comfortable harness that permits a maximum range of movement and accessibility.*

*That sounds like an incredible turn on,* I thought.

The idea of fucking a dildo strapped to a wall while people watched me from below sounded insanely sexy. My pussy began to twitch as I imagined the idea.

What's this next one—*House of Holes*?

I clicked on the next listed activity, and a picture appeared showing various nude men and women pressing their hips and buttocks against a wall with scattered holes. The look of ecstasy on their faces left little doubt as to what was happening on the other side. The description read:

*Hook up with a stranger on the other side of a wall through your own personal intimate portal. You can choose to 'give', 'receive', or 'merge' with a partner of either sex in an erotic and completely anonymous connection. Or you can choose to simply watch, as other couples get their groove on in this sensuous and erotic House of Holes.*

*Damn, that sounds dirty. And fun.*

I'd heard of glory holes before, but I'd always thought of them as skanky places where gay men went to get an anonymous blow job. The idea of engaging in heterosexual sex or touching pussies with another woman through my own private portal was different. And highly stimulating. My left hand dropped down between my legs and I began to rub my clit as I continued exploring the website.

*What happens in the Sexy Games Room?*

I clicked on the next activity, which displayed a photo of naked men and women in contorted positions atop a polka-dot-covered mat. Their hips and asses were pressed together while they stretched their arms and legs around each other. The caption read:

*Play interactive nude games with your fellow guests where the rules and rewards are wide open. With Naked Twister, stretch into increasingly difficult and erotic positions as you try to reach around, over, and under your naked partners. Or try Naked Poker where the 'loser' must engage in increasingly erotic situations in full view of their playing partners. Or jump into the Naked Mud Wrestling pit and try to wrestle your partner into submission, all while surrounded in sensuous mud.*

*Fuck, yes!* I thought. *These guys know how to organize an erotic party.*

I didn't need to click any more of the fantasy activities to know this was the sort of erotic travel destination that I had in mind. It promised to be an immersive, stimulating experience with multiple partners and exciting activities. As always though, I needed to be sure it would be clean and safe. I searched the page and found a tab marked *Conditions*, which read:

*Every Nude Cruise guest must provide a certified report from a verified medical testing lab, indicating negative for sexually communicated diseases. The report must be dated within one week of your ship's departure date. Clothing is optional for all activities. Security staff are available at all venues to ensure the safety of guests and to ensure that all interaction occurs only with express consent.*

*Fair enough,* I thought. *The medical test requirement shows this is a class act. You can't be too careful about these things.*

I clicked the Booking tab and viewed the calendar for available dates. The next cruise departed from Miami in two weeks' time. I'd have to move a few things around and schedule a two-hour flight, but one of the joys of my job as a freelance graphic designer meant I could choose my own vacation days. I booked a private cabin with a Queen-size bed, then I tore my panties off and plunged my fingers into my pussy as I fantasized about all the shipboard activities I'd soon be participating in.

2

———

## SETTING SAIL

On the scheduled day of my departure, my whole body was buzzing with excitement. This was my first cruise, and I didn't know what to expect. Besides my fear of seasickness, I was a little nervous about the idea of parading around nude in public. I'd picked up some anti-nausea pills at the pharmacy, but I had butterflies in my stomach for an entirely different reason.

So far, my excursions into the realm of public sex and nudity had been fairly anonymous. At the dinner party, I could hide behind my masquerade mask. In the dark room, the special light effects concealed my identity. Even at my naked yoga class, everybody was so busy concentrating on their poses that it was really only my partner who had a close-up view of me.

But on this 'clothing-optional' cruise, I'd be going about my everyday routines in plain view of hundreds of strangers. Granted, some of the activities sounded highly erotic and fun. But the idea of sitting down for dinner or even just sunbathing in the nude gave me the willies. I'd packed some skimpy bikinis in case I got cold feet, but I didn't want to be the only one wearing clothes if everyone else was naked.

When I arrived at the cruise terminal, it was a hive of activity.

There were hundreds of people waiting to go through security, and the building was buzzing with chatter and public announcements. I pulled out my boarding pass and looked for the sign directing me to my designated gate. Just like at airport security, there were multiple lines of people placing their bags on conveyor belts going through an X-ray machine. When it was my turn, I took off my shoes and opened my roller-bag to remove my liquids.

"That won't be necessary, ma'am," a handsome security attendant said.

"Oh?" I murmured, confused.

"No need to remove your shoes or any items from your bag," he said. "Security procedures for cruise ships aren't as stringent as they are for air travel."

I smiled and nodded sheepishly as I pulled my sandals back on.

"Unless you're carrying something metal, of course. That'll set our machine off."

"No, of course not," I said, blushing from all the attention I was getting holding up the line. But now I was worried about the vibrator I'd packed in my luggage.

*Who needs to bring a vibrator on a naked sex cruise, anyway?* I chided myself.

"I'll just need to see your boarding pass," the security agent said.

I showed him my pass, and he directed me to stand in line behind the pass-through body scanner. As I waited for my turn, I looked around at my fellow boarding passengers. Most of them were fairly young, in their 20s and 30s, but there were also some older couples who were apparently looking for a little adventure to spice up their marriages. I noticed a few people checking each other out. Most of them didn't make eye contact for very long, but I wasn't the only one undressing some of the hot passengers with my eyes.

I caught a tanned gentleman in the adjacent line running his eyes up and down my body. I'd intentionally worn skinny jeans and a tight blouse for the first day to show off my best assets. I stood up tall and lifted my chest to display my cleavage. He had a nice ass, strong arms, and beautiful skin. When our eyes met, he smiled at me, and I could feel the blood rushing to my face again.

*Come on, Jade,* I admonished myself. *Get a hold of yourself. If you're going to be this self-conscious fully clothed, how are you ever going to be comfortable walking around in the nude?*

I returned my attention to the X-ray machine as my bag disappeared under the cover. I watched the face of the security agent as he scanned the monitor for any suspicious contents, then breathed a sigh of relief when I saw my bag pop out the other end.

"Ma'am?" the agent at the opposite side of the body scanner said, motioning for me to step through.

I'd been so worried my vibrator would set off the X-ray machine, that I hadn't realized I was holding up the line again. I nodded self-consciously, then walked through the pass-through stand, making eye contact with the security agent to ensure I wouldn't set off any other alarms. After he nodded that I was clear, I picked my bag off the X-ray belt and looked for the sign to the check-in area. By now, I was sure that half the passengers in the security area were cursing in bewilderment at my awkward travel etiquette, and I was glad to find a respite at the end of a new line.

"That's a pretty big bag for a short cruise," a woman's voice said, as I heard someone step up behind me.

I turned around and looked into the eyes of a stunning brunette about my same height.

"Um, well, you know," I stammered. "It's mostly makeup and toiletries and that sort of thing. We women can't be shorthanded about these things."

I could feel the flush in my cheeks again, caught off guard by her disarming beauty.

"No, I suppose not," she said, smiling at my innocence. "Although something tells me *makeup* will be the least of our concerns on this trip."

Her confidence and bold manner was rapidly sending blood flowing to another part of my body.

"Is this your first time with this cruise operator?" I asked, not wanting to state the obvious.

"This is my third Fantasy Cruise. Once you dip your toes in, it's kind of addicting." Her eyes darted across my face, appraising my demeanor. "How about you?"

"It's my first time. I'm a bit nervous, to be honest. You know, about all the..."

"Yeah, there's a lot of that," she said. "But there's nothing to worry about. We're all in the same boat, so to speak. You get used to it pretty fast. It's actually quite liberating. Not having to dress up and put on airs. Nudity is a great equalizer."

I took a quick glance at her tight and tanned body. She was wearing loose fitting linen shorts and a tight T-shirt displaying a cruise ship sailing into the sunset. Her legs were long and shapely, and her firm breasts sat up high on her chest.

"Some of us are a little more equal than others, I'm afraid."

She scanned my figure and smiled.

"I don't think you have anything to worry about. You're gorgeous. As long as you don't mind being the center of attention with a body like that."

I puffed out my cheeks and exhaled heavily.

"That's exactly what I'm worried about. I'm not used to being the center of attention. At least not in a public setting with all my clothes off."

"What deck is your cabin on?" she asked.

I fumbled for my travel papers and pulled out my boarding pass.

"E deck," I said. "They told me that if I chose a cabin nearer the water line, I have a better chance of avoiding seasickness."

"That's my deck too. Stick with me girl, and I'll show you around. There are plenty of ways to take your mind off the motion of the boat. The key is to not stay in one place too long. With so many interesting shipboard activities, your stomach will be the *last* thing you'll be thinking about."

She held out her hand and smiled at me.

"My name's Heather."

"Jade," I said, shaking her hand softly. "Thanks, Heather. I could use a wing woman, or shipmate, or whatever you're supposed to call your cruise partner these days."

"It's a deal," Heather said, winking at me. "We'll be *partners in crime.*"

I reached the front of the line and saw one of the check-in agents motioning for me to come to her station.

"I'll wait for you past check-in," I said, suddenly mindful of the increasing dampness building between my legs.

3
___________

# RECEPTION

After clearing through Check-in, Heather guided me through the final boarding process then we walked together toward our rooms on E deck. We agreed to meet thirty minutes later when we'd go to the guest reception in the main lounge on the top deck. Our rooms were in the same hall, so after saying temporary goodbyes, I continued down the hall toward my stateroom.

When I opened my door, I was surprised by how small my room was. The Queen-size bed seemed to take up almost all of the space, with a tiny adjoining closet and small desk beside the wall-mounted TV. I went into the bathroom and was disappointed to see a stand-up shower with no tub. I knew that space aboard a cruise ship was at a premium, but I wasn't expecting it to feel so claustrophobic.

I unpacked my toiletries and placed them on the tiny sink, then carried my small carry-on case and placed it on the bed. There was a small sliding window beside my bed, and I immediately walked over and slid it open to breathe in some fresh air. I could see a flotilla of small boats moving about the bay opposite our ship, and I immediately regretted not upgrading to a larger room with balcony.

*I bet Heather has a bigger room,* I thought. *I'm such a lightweight at this cruise thing.*

I was looking forward to picking her brain for other tips about optimizing my shipboard experience. Not to mention picking over the *rest* of her body. I couldn't wait to see her naked and run my hands over her tight ass and breasts.

The porter had taken my larger roller case, and I didn't have much of a change of clothes in my carry-on bag. Heather had said not to worry too much about what to wear for the reception since most first-time guests chose not to go fully nude at the first activity. Nevertheless, I wanted to get with the program and ease myself into the idea of being naked on board, so I removed my bra and unbuttoned my silk blouse three buttons to reveal my cleavage.

I went into the washroom and looked at myself in the small mirror. The soft silk rubbing against my nipples had already stimulated them to an aroused state, and they protruded against the thin fabric, creating two conspicuous nodes. I smiled at how full and firm my breasts looked in my revealing blouse and hoped they'd attract Heather's attention too. I put on a new coat of light red lipstick and touched up my mascara, then grabbed my purse and headed down the hall toward Heather's room.

When she opened her door and I saw what she was wearing, it took my breath away. She wore a see-through gauzy top that barely concealed her large breasts through the sheer material. I stared shamelessly at her figure, wanting to flip her loose top up over her waist and devour her firm, round tits. To top it off, she'd let her long brown hair down and it shone with iridescent hues of amber and gold. She looked absolutely ravishing, and I was already regretting my wardrobe choice.

"Damn, girl," I said. "You're a feast for sore eyes. Who needs hors d'oeuvres when the main course is standing right here in front of me."

"That can be arranged," she said. "Come on in. Let's freshen up before heading over to the reception."

Heather motioned me into her room and I stepped inside. As I suspected, her room was larger than mine, with a small sitting room next to her bed and French doors leading out to a balcony.

"I knew I should have upgraded to a suite," I frowned. "I'm already beginning to feel claustrophobic in my tiny little cabin."

I looked out her French doors toward the open bay.

"Do you mind if I check out your view?"

"Of course. Make yourself comfortable. You're welcome to hang at my place anytime you're feeling closed in. I'll just be a couple more minutes."

Heather disappeared into the washroom, and I slid the side doors open and stepped out onto her balcony. I could smell the fresh salty air from the sea and I closed my eyes as I breathed it in.

*This is definitely the way to travel,* I thought. *Next time,* I reminded myself, *remember to get a full-size suite with balcony.*

After a few minutes, Heather emerged from the washroom looking even more beautiful than before, and I couldn't help shaking my head.

"I'm feeling terribly overdressed. You look like you're getting in the swing of this nude cruise thing already. Should I find something skimpier to wear?"

"Nonsense," Heather said. "You look perfect." Her eyes traced a line down to my aroused nipples protruding against my blouse. "You're revealing just the right amount for the meet and greet. I guarantee you'll be getting a lot of attention in that tight outfit."

I glanced down at her tanned legs and sandals.

"But you're showing a lot more...skin. Am I going to be the only one covering up my whole body?"

"Not at all. Most first-timers come to the initial reception dressed pretty conservative. It takes a couple of days for people to get comfortable being in the buff around their fellow passengers. By the second or third day, everybody will be strolling around buck naked. After the reception there's a dance, where the lights get turned down. You'll have plenty of opportunity to shed some of your clothes then."

As Heather walked toward me, I watched her breasts jiggle under her sheer blouse. When she stood in front of me, I stared at her tits and soft brown nipples. I couldn't stop myself.

"May I?" I said, looking gently into her eyes.

"I thought you'd never ask," she smiled.

I lifted her top and cupped her breasts in my hands and squeezed them softly. They were full and firm, and perfectly shaped, straight out of a centerfold. I noticed her areolas contract and her nipples begin to extend. I rolled them gently between my thumbs and forefingers, and she leaned in to kiss me. When our lips met, I pushed my body toward hers and pressed my hips against hers. She grabbed the back of my head and pulled me closer as our tongues danced around each other's mouths. I could have fucked her right then and there, but after a long lingering kiss, she pulled away.

"There'll be plenty of time for this later," she said. "Let's go meet some new people at the reception. This is a *nude cruise*, remember? We don't want to be holed up in our cabin the whole time, do we?"

"I suppose not," I said, slightly disappointed. My head knew she was right, but the ache in my pussy disagreed. I wanted her right now, and I didn't feel like sharing her with anybody else.

"Come on," she said, grabbing my hand, pulling me toward the door. "Let's go trip the night fantastic."

---

When we got to the top deck, Heather led me to a large open lounge with floor-to-ceiling windows offering a commanding view of the bay. I hadn't realized the ship had already left the pier, and I saw that we were steaming past South Pointe Park toward the open sea.

There were hundreds of people milling around the room, and Heather clasped my hand as she led me toward the bar. I was glad almost everybody was fully clothed, ranging from shorts and T-shirts to camisoles and bikini bottoms. A few veteran Fantasy Cruise travelers had been bold enough to go topless, but for the most part, it was a fairly low-key affair.

"What'll you have, ladies?" a handsome bartender wearing a white dress shirt and bowtie asked.

"I'll have a watermelon vodka," I said.

"I'd like some sex on the beach please," Heather said.

"Coming right up," the bartender smiled.

"You're so naughty," I teased Heather.

"Hey, when in Rome..." she said.

I turned and looked around the room. Heather had given me good advice about what to wear, and I began to feel more relaxed.

"You were right about the dress code tonight," I said. "Though the bartender seems a little formal. Are the staff always dressed so prim and proper?"

"They're always *dressed*, if that's what you mean. It's company policy that staff always must wear clothes, even on a nude cruise. Something about maintaining their professionalism, I suppose. It kind of helps to separate the staff from the guests, especially when you need something. The officers dress in navy whites, and the servers typically wear black pants, vests, and bow ties."

I watched the bartender approach us as he returned from the other end of the bar.

"Are they allowed to...you know...*hook up* with guests?" I asked.

"Officially it's a no-no, but whatever enterprising staff chooses to do when they're off duty, is nobody's business. If they get caught cavorting with passengers they can technically be fired, but it's pretty hard not to dip your toe in the water every now and then with so many flirty naked passengers floating around."

"I see your point," I said, as a pretty topless girl walked past us.

"Here you go, ladies," the bartender said, placing our drinks in front of us.

"Come on," Heather said, picking up her glass. "Let's go mingle."

For the next hour or so, Heather and I stuck together as we wandered from one cluster of passengers to another, making small talk. Nobody seemed to want to address the elephant in the room, mostly sticking with safe subjects like where we were from, what we did for a living, and if we'd been on a Fantasy Cruise before.

But everybody was definitely checking each other out. Although most of us were technically fully 'dressed', there was plenty enough skin showing to get a good idea of what we'd look like naked. Most of the men wore tight T-shirts or open shirts, revealing plenty of chiseled pecs and abs. The women wore skimpy bikinis, or flimsy camisoles and miniskirts. It was a feast for the eyes, and I soaked it all in. After a little while, I spotted the tall gentleman who I'd made eye contact with in the security line, and I gently steered Heather in his direction.

"I see you managed to survive the security gauntlet," he said to me, as I shimmied up next to him.

"Barely," I laughed. "I wasn't sure who was going to arrest me first—the security guards for my smuggled contraband or the passengers who were steaming about me holding up the line."

"It wasn't so bad," he smiled. "Traveling on a ship is easier than a plane. Is this your first time?"

"Yes," I said. "How about you?"

"This is my second trip. I guess I had some unfinished business from my first time around. There's so much to do on this big ship—one week hardly seems to be enough time to take it all in."

I paused for a moment as I appraised his body. He was wearing creme-colored linen pants and sandals, with a loose-fitting short-sleeved Bermuda shirt. But it was unbuttoned enough to show the cleft rippling between his chiseled pecs as he motioned with his powerful arms. His dark eyes beckoned to me, as I began to fantasize about falling into his arms.

"I'm Marc," he said, extending his hand.

"Jade," I said, feeling his large fingers envelop me. I turned toward Heather. "And this is my partner in crime, Heather."

Marc smiled as he looked at Heather, trying to keep his gaze concentrated above her barely concealed breasts.

"Are you two sisters?" he said. "Because I have seen such a lovely pair since Giselle and Patricia Bundchen."

"If you're talking about Jade and me," Heather teased, "no." Then she grabbed her breasts and shook them provocatively. "But if you're talking about my girls here, I'll take that as a compliment."

"Either way," Marc said, "I mean it as a compliment."

A woman's voice suddenly came over the room's public address system to break the sexual tension. The three of us turned toward the stage, where a woman wearing white shorts and a pressed shirt was standing holding a mic.

"Good evening, Fantasy Cruise travelers!" she said, raising her voice in welcome.

A loud cheer filled the room from the attending guests.

"My name's Ashley, and I'll be your cruise director. For those of you who are traveling on your maiden voyage with Fantasy Cruise, welcome. And for those of you returning for more fun and games, I promise you won't be disappointed. We've added even more fantasy activities to uplift and stimulate you.

"All of you should have found the brochure with our full Fantasy Menu on your nightstand when you checked into your staterooms, but we have lots more here on the desk beside the stage. Whenever you have any questions, just come see me any time. I'll be here the rest of the evening, and you can find my office mid-ship next to the Poseidon Restaurant on Deck B. Or just ring me at triple-two on your in-room phone.

"But now, let's get this party started with our first Fantasy Dance!" she hollered.

The suddenly lights dimmed and flashing lights began circulating the room. The sound of Marvin Gaye's *Let's Get it On* began booming over the speakers, and Heather, Marc and I began swaying our hips together in unison. Heather turned toward me and began shaking her ass suggestively in Marc's direction.

*He's dreamy!* she mouthed to me.

*Damn straight*, I returned, widening my eyes in agreement.

Marc simply smiled at me as he pretended to grind his hips against Heather's ass.

*My first fantasy cruise was off to a promising start.*

## 4

## GETTING DOWN

For the next hour or so, Heather, Marc and I got our groove on as the swirling lights from the disco ball flashed over the writhing crowd. With the sun beginning to set over the horizon, the room became increasingly dark, and some brave passengers began shedding their clothes. Heather was the first to take off her skimpy top, and after another ten minutes of bumping and grinding with her and Marc, I soon followed suit. Not long after, Marc ripped off his shirt and threw it on a growing pile beside the stage.

It felt fabulous to be semi-nude, and we shamelessly rubbed our bodies together as the sexy music played in the background. It didn't take long for us to remove our clothes completely as we got more and more worked up by the suggestive lyrics. When Donna Summer's *Love to Love You Baby* came over the speakers, we moved in close and rolled our hips and chests together, our passion rising in tandem with the singer's orgiastic moans. I could feel Marc's cock hardening against our bodies as my wetness commingled with Heather's on our skin. As usual, Heather made the first move.

"Let's get out of here," she panted in our ears, and we didn't even bother to pick up our clothes as the three of us pranced out of the lounge. Bypassing the elevator, Heather led the way down the closest stairwell while we raced down the three flights to E deck. We giggled our way down the hall past a few other half-dressed passengers as we headed toward Heather's room. When we got to her door, I looked at her blankly, wondering how we were going to get in. We were all stark naked, and none of us were carrying a room key.

"Shit!" I said to Heather. "What now? Maybe we can find a secluded spot on the deck—"

"Not to worry," she said. "I've been in this predicament before, and I've taken precautions."

She kneeled down on the floor and peered through the small crack under the base of her door. Then she reached into the space with her fingers and pulled a credit-card-sized room key out across the carpet.

"Shazam!" she said, standing up and displaying her room key triumphantly. "A lady is prepared for every contingency."

She fumbled with the key in the lock then pushed open the door, and the three of us scrambled into her room. As soon as the door closed, Heather jumped up onto Marc and threw her legs around his hips. He turned and pinned her against the door, and they started kissing passionately. I rubbed my breasts against his sweaty back and moved my hand between his legs. I could feel his hard cock pointing down between Heather's legs, and I rubbed it against her soaking pussy. It didn't take long for the three of us to be coated in her slippery juices.

I squeezed Marc's balls gently as he contracted his glutes and pressed harder against Heather. All three of us were panting, wanting a piece of his meat. Suddenly, he swung around and carried Heather toward the bed with her still clinging to his hips. He placed one knee on the bed and lowered her onto its surface, then pressed his body against hers. Not wanting to interrupt their rhythm, I stood and watched as my sticky hand moved between my legs.

At this point, I was so turned on I could have come just watching Heather and Marc make love. But Heather had other plans, and she twisted her body and flipped Marc over, straddling his hips. She motioned for me to join them on the bed and I kneeled down beside her and kissed her on her lips. I could feel her body writhing over Marc's midsection, and I ran my hands down her stomach to feel their connection. Marc's hard cock was flat against his stomach as Heather rolled back and forth over it with her wet pussy. I played with her clit and she began to moan in my mouth.

Then she began lowering herself until our mouths were inches away from Marc's throbbing phallus. She swung her leg over to Marc's opposite side and his penis popped up into an acute sixty-degree angle, pointing toward his head. In the soft moonlight streaming through Heather's balcony doors, I could see that it was large, straight, and magnificent. The head glistened with a mixture of pre-cum and Heather's juices, and we both wrapped our fingers around it.

While we gave him a slow, two-handed massage, Marc sighed and thrust his manhood into our pliant hands. After a couple of minutes, Heather lowered her head and took him into her mouth, as I cupped his balls and played with the space between his testicles and anus. Marc moaned and began to roll his hips more aggressively, obviously enjoying Heather's attention on his cock. I could hear his passion rising and I began to feel his balls tighten and rise up. I knew it wouldn't take long for him to come with the combined effect of two beautiful women attending to his erogenous area.

Heather must have sensed it too because she lifted her head off his dick and leaned over and kissed me. Marc began to raise himself up wanting to get in on the action, but Heather extended her right hand and pushed him back onto the bed. He quickly got the message and watched the two of us while we explored each other's bodies. I cupped Heather's tits again and rolled her nipples between my fingers, then we pressed our chests together and tribbed our nipples while we fucked each other's mouths with our tongues.

By this time, all three of us were ready for some direct stimulation, and I hesitated, unsure where to go next. It was my first time in a threesome—at least one where I had this degree of control—and I didn't want to leave anyone hanging. Heather suddenly lifted her right leg and swung it over Marc's stomach, then did the same with her other leg until she was straddling his hips from the side. She motioned for me to do the same, then we pulled each other forward until our vulvas touched Marc's throbbing member on opposite sides. It was an incredible sensation feeling the heat of his hard cock sandwiched between our two pussies. Heather and I wasted no time moving our hips up and down, giving Marc an entirely new type of erotic massage.

The three of us were now getting direct stimulation, and Heather and I moaned in each other's mouths as we rubbed our soaking pussies together against Marc's pointed cock. I could feel our combined wetness running between my legs, as I pushed harder against Marc's warm and wonderful joystick. I wrapped my arms around Heather's waist and pulled her closer toward me. By now, we were all moaning in abandon and nearing the tipping point. I tilted my hips downward a bit and pressed my clit against the side of Marc's cock. Heather and I were humping him hard now, and our tits rubbed together as sweat streamed down our stomachs. This was an entirely new kind of tribbing that I'd never experienced before, and the image of the three of us joined together soon put me over the edge.

I threw my head back and let out a primal scream as Heather and I thrashed our hips together and gushed all over Marc's throbbing hard-on. We kissed for another minute as we came down from our high, then we separated and peered at Marc. He had a silly smile on his face, but his cock was still pointing up, bobbing gently over his stomach from the pulse flowing through its veins. I ran my hand over my stomach to see if I could detect any sign of semen on me, then I looked at Heather and shook my head to signal that he hadn't come yet.

"Good boy," she said, leaning over to give him a long, lingering kiss.

Then she shifted her body until her hips were behind his head, and she looked at me, silently nodding. I knew her intent immediately, and I swung my legs over Marc's midsection, straddling his hips in her direction. She lifted herself up, placing her pussy over his face, then lowered herself onto his eager mouth. I could see her eyes roll back in her head as he took her swollen clit between his lips and began to suck her, and she began to grind her hips into his face.

I didn't need any more encouragement. I grabbed Marc's thick schlong and directed the tip toward my quivering opening. I teased him for just a second, rubbing his sticky head against my clit and vulva, then I lowered myself onto him until his mound pressed firmly against my clit. As Heather and I locked eyes, I convulsed in a mini-orgasm.

It was an unbelievably hot sight watching each other fuck this adonis from opposite ends as we watched our passion rising. I began to rock my hips in unison with Heather, and I could feel Marc's hips answering the call. I loved the feeling of his big cock filling me up, and he knew how to move his hips to give my clit direct stimulation. The combined feeling of my clit grinding into his mound and the head of his cock rubbing against my G-spot was driving me crazy. I began moaning more loudly as I stepped up the pace of my humping action, while Heather and I clasped hands.

I wanted to make this last as long as I could, but the sights and sounds of three beautiful people joining together in an erotic union was too much. I could feel my orgasm welling deep inside me and I made one final push down hard onto Marc's cock as I squeezed Heather's hands like a vice. When I finally came, I grunted like a wild animal as my body spasmed over Marc's hips while I looked Heather straight in her eyes.

I guess that was too much for Marc too, because he grabbed my hips with two hands and thrust his hips into the air, lifting me off the mattress as I felt his cock throbbing in rhythmic contractions inside my pussy. With him moaning into her pussy and her seeing me have a powerful orgasm, it soon put Heather over the edge. Just as I was beginning to feel the last of my contractions subside, her hands squeezed mine hard and her eyelids narrowed as she clamped her thighs around Marc's head. She growled like a dog in heat as I watched the pleasure roll over her pretty face. The whole time we never took our eyes off one another.

When she finally collected her breath and came down from her orgasm, she smiled at me. We were both thinking the same thing. My new partner in crime and I had found our first accomplice.

**5**

---

## WATER SPORTS

Later that evening, Marc returned to his room and Heather and I continued to make love into the wee hours. By 3:00 a.m., we were both spent, and we fell asleep sprawled naked atop the bed sheets, as a cool breeze from the ocean wafted over our sweaty bodies. When the morning sun streamed through her balcony door, Heather rolled over and caressed my breast.

"Morning, Sunshine," she said, as my eyes slowly flitted open.

"Morning, Beautiful," I said, moving in closer to give her a kiss.

"That was quite a first night we had together."

"Mmmm, yes," I said, tasting her sweet tongue in my mouth. "Hopefully the first of many."

"I hope so too. But I don't want to steal all your time and attention on this cruise. The main idea is to mix it up and take advantage of as many activities as you can in the limited time you have available."

"Can't we do that together?" I asked.

"Some of them, for sure. But I think some of the other activities you might enjoy more on your own."

"What about our new friend Marc?"

"I'm pretty sure he'll want to get out there on his own and sow some more of his oats. But he left his room number on my nightstand, so we might have a chance to hook up with him again before the cruise is over."

I looked out the open balcony doors at the sun shimmering over the open sea.

"You've done this before. What activity do you recommend we try next?"

"Most people like to ease into this whole nudity thing. Let's head up to the pool and do some people watching while we work on our tans. There's also a cool fountain on the top deck that's quite fun and refreshing. But first, I think we should get something to eat. I don't know about you, but I'm famished!"

"Me too. I think we burned enough calories last night for *three* meals. But first I'd like to return to my cabin to freshen up. What do you recommend I wear to breakfast?"

"It'll be pretty hot up top. A bikini and sandals should be enough. You'll just be taking it all off pretty soon anyway. You don't want to have to carry a bunch of clothes around with you."

"That reminds me," I suddenly remembered. "I've still got to retrieve my stuff from last night in the lounge."

"Something tells me you're not going to need jeans and a blouse for a while. We can pick that up on our return to our cabins later in the day. Did you want to borrow my shawl to get back to your room?"

I smiled at Heather's thoughtfulness.

"I'm just a few doors down. Judging by last night, half the people on the ship are already nude, so a little more streaking down the hall shouldn't hurt me."

"You're going to need a key to get in though. I'm guessing you didn't think of my trick."

Heather leaned over and picked up her room phone then tapped some numbers on the dial.

"Yes," she spoke into the phone, "my friend's lost her key for room E48. Can you send someone down with a replacement? She's in my room, E32. Thank you."

Ten minutes later, there was a soft tap on Heather's door.

"Maybe I'll take you up on that shawl offer after all," I said.

Heather smiled and went to her closet and held the garment open for me as I slid my arms into it.

"Meet you in the Poseidon Restaurant in an hour?" she said.

"Deal," I said, giving her a quick kiss.

I opened the door, gave Heather a playful shake of my ass, then followed the porter back to my room.

---

After breakfast, Heather led me to the main pool on the top deck, where scores of people were lounging naked on deck chairs and playing in the water. A series of interconnected pools simulated the look of a tropical lagoon, complete with life-size palm trees and small cabanas. We found a couple of open lounge chairs not far from the bar, and Heather asked me to mind them for us while she went to get a couple of drinks.

While she was gone, I made a quick scan of the scene. Virtually everybody was already naked, and it was a busy hive of activity. On one end of the lagoon, a large waterslide deposited screaming guests into the splashing water. In an adjacent basin, a small group of people were playing water polo. On the other side of the patio, a few passengers were skipping through a water fountain like a bunch of playful toddlers. It was all pretty surreal, and I paused to take it all in.

"Checking out all the action?" Heather said, returning from the bar and handing me a drink.

"Mmm, yes," I said, taking a sip of my pina colada. "There's certainly a lot of...*diversions*."

"Are you referring to all the naked people or the activities?"

"Both," I said, scanning the bodies of some of the men walking around the pool. "It's strange, though. Everybody seems so...*asexual*. I would have thought more people would be, you know, *aroused*, seeing each other naked."

"That's the thing about us all being in the same boat, so to speak. Like I said earlier, nudity is the great equalizer. Everybody gets used to it pretty quickly, and before you know it they're walking around like it's a normal walk in the park." Heather paused as she appraised my demeanor. "Are you disappointed?"

"Not really. I just expected the men in particular would be showing more sign of, you know, *interest*. The cruise operator billed this as more of a sex cruise than a nude cruise."

Heather smiled, as she lay back on her lounge chair.

"Believe me, there'll be plenty of opportunity for you to get down and dirty on this cruise. There's more going on than might first appear. For instance, take a look at that woman standing in the fountain on the other side of the patio."

I peered across the pool and saw a naked woman in her twenties standing over some jets of water spraying up from the surface. She had a strange look on her face as she spread her legs and squatted over the stream.

"It looks like she's having an enema," I laughed.

"I think she's directing the spray to a *different* part of her body," Heather said.

The look on the woman's face changed to one of pleasure as she began to shimmy her hips over the water stream. Suddenly the spray started pulsing like a shower head, and she let out a low moan.

I crossed my legs, beginning to feel a tingle in my pussy.

"I see what you mean," I said. "Now I see why they call it the Fantasy Fountain."

Heather noticed me squirming on my chair.

"Do you feel like giving it a try?"

"In a sec. Let me enjoy her experience first."

The woman suddenly grabbed her tits with her hands and pushed them up, as the spray from the patio surface gushed up over her abdomen and washed over her face. She was grunting and groaning now and moving her hips more rhythmically over the jet.

"Fuck, that's hot," I said.

"Kind of a nice way to cool off on a hot day like this."

"It looks like it might take the edge off in more ways than one."

Suddenly, the woman began screaming, as her body convulsed and her hips shook in rhythmic spasms. There was no doubt to us or any of the many other spectators that she had just enjoyed a powerful orgasm. When she staggered out of the fountain back toward her lounge chair, a small round of applause rose from around the pool.

"What do you think?" Heather said. "Are you up for it?"

"Now that I know I'm going to have an audience, I wouldn't mind some company. Will you come with me?"

"I think I will," Heather said, winking at me. "Let's toss these bikinis first. We don't want anything getting in the way of all the fun."

Heather nonchalantly unclasped her bikini top behind her back then stepped out of her bottoms. I'd almost forgotten how beautiful she was, and her tanned body looked magnificent in the bright sunshine. Her shaved pussy left nothing to the imagination, and I could see her nub poking out of her labia at the top of her pussy.

"Damn girl," I said, opening my eyes wide. "You're never afraid to let it all hang out."

"It's called a *fantasy cruise*, right? Let's live out our fantasies. Get those clothes off and let's go have some fun!"

I pulled off my top and bottom and threw them on my lounge chair, then Heather and I scampered around the pool past a throng of curious onlookers. When we got in the fountain, it was actually quite refreshing. The water was warm, but it felt cool against my hot skin in the blazing sun. The water jets were spread a few feet apart, facing different directions with alternating pulsing patterns. Some were a constant stream and some stopped and started periodically, while others pulsed at different speeds like an overhead shower faucet.

Heather and I stepped into the sprays and danced around for a minute, laughing and holding hands. Then we came together and kissed, rubbing our bodies together as the spray shot up between us, soaking our faces. Suddenly, I no longer cared about being naked in full view of the other pool guests. I was lost in the deluge of sensations I felt from the water jets spraying against my ass and Heather rubbing her body against mine.

We shifted position until we found a spot in the fountain where a steady stream directed toward our pussies. Then we pushed our mounds together so the stream sprayed directly against our touching clits. I opened my mouth and gasped as Heather smiled at me. This was a once-in-a-lifetime experience, and I wanted to enjoy every moment of it with her.

Suddenly, two more sprays began jetting at a forty-five-degree angle from behind each of us, and we bent our knees to give the spray direct access to our rosebuds.

"Oh my God!" I said to Heather, as my eyes flew open.

"Is this *arousing* enough for you?" she said, grinding her clit against mine.

"Fuck, yes!"

Just when I thought it couldn't get any more intense, the steady spray directed toward our clits began pulsing in strong, flickering streams.

"Uhnn," I moaned, closing my eyes at the intense feeling of pleasure I was experiencing from every part of my body.

"Enjoy, Baby," Heather said, as she thrust her tongue into my mouth, swaying her hips in tandem with mine.

I could feel the passion rising quickly inside me, and there was no way I could hold it back any longer.

"Fuck, I'm coming!" I said, as my pussy clenched inside me and I became weak in the knees. "Ohh, Ohh, Ohh," I panted into Heather's mouth, feeling the waves roll over me. Heather grunted into my mouth and I felt her hips shudder against mine as she reached her own peak. We moaned out loud together as the warm water from the jets sprayed all over our ecstatic faces.

When we finally came down from our orgasms, we held each other over the gentle spray, leaning against one another in exhaustion. When we separated, a loud cheer rose from around the pool from the appreciative crowd.

*I guess this won't to be so hard getting used to after all,* I thought.

## 6

## PEAK SENSATIONS

**H**eather and I spent the rest of the day lounging around the pool, people watching. We made a few new friends and got some more cabin numbers, but mostly we just wanted to relax and scope out our next move. Heather said if we didn't pace ourselves, we'd either be too sore or exhausted to partake in some of the more adventurous shipboard activities. After perusing the ship's Fantasy Menu, we both agreed our next rendezvous would be at the climbing wall.

I went back to my cabin alone that night planning to get a good night's sleep, with visions of naked climbers exposing themselves as they scaled the cliff. I woke up refreshed the next morning, eager to try out the next erotic challenge. When I met Heather at the breakfast buffet, the room was filled with naked passengers filling their plates with hardly a sideways glance. I guess she'd been right about everybody getting comfortable being in the nude by the third day.

As she explained to me what to expect at the climbing wall, my eyes widened in anticipation. It sounded terrifying and exciting at the same time.

"Do people ever *fall*?" I asked.

"Everyone's strapped into a harness and they have spotters to maintain tension on the rope holding you up, so even if you do slip, it's perfectly safe."

I frowned at the thought of other people watching my naked body from below.

"So I'll have some stranger watching my bare ass as I stretch my legs and move up the wall?"

"Yes, but that's part of the fun of it. Knowing other people are watching you as you get higher and higher is quite titillating, for both you and the observers. Plus, the staff doing the rope work are usually pretty buff, so it's kind of hot."

The idea of exposing my body while I stimulated myself on the wall reminded me of my Dinner Party experience. I squirmed in my seat reflecting back on the memory of Jasmine playing with me under the table while my fellow diners looked on.

"Tell me more about the unique 'features' on the wall."

"Besides the usual cup and lip-shaped ledges for gaining a comfortable hand and foot hold, there are other more *erotic* holds to clasp onto along the way."

"Such as?"

"For starters, some of the lips vibrate, so you can pause and get a little extra stimulation whenever you're feeling in the mood."

I pictured the idea of being in a harness clinging to a wall while sex toys stimulated my private parts.

"Now I see why they strap you in," I said. "I could barely maintain my balance on solid ground at the fountain yesterday, the more worked up I got. I can imagine how weak in the knees people might get, stimulated in a similar manner while climbing a challenging wall."

"Exactly," Heather said. "Especially the higher you go. The stimulation gets more and more intense the higher you climb."

"How so?"

"The features start out pretty tame at the bottom, just little nodules to rub against. But then they start vibrating, like little magic bullets. They get progressively larger and more animated the higher you go. If you make it all the way to the top, they've got some full-size dildos that twist and rotate to really give you a ride."

"Mmm," I said, feeling the moisture beginning to build inside my pussy. "Just like my favorite rabbit vibrator."

"Kind of like that. Except this time, you're suspended twenty-five feet off the ground in full view of your spotter and any other spectators while you get off."

Suddenly I had a burning need to have something inside me.

"That sounds pretty hot."

Heather raised her eyebrows and nodded.

"There's something about the whole idea that's very arousing. I think you'll find it's quite a different experience."

I wrinkled my forehead as I pondered the possibilities.

"What about the guys? Are there similar erotic features for *them* to enjoy on the wall?"

"Definitely. The wall holds alternate between 'innies' and 'outies', so everybody has a chance to enjoy. Many of them are fashioned in the form of flexible lips, pussies, and anuses, where men can insert their dongs along the way and get a similar thrill. Near the top, they become animated with internal vibrators, just like the bullets and dildos for the ladies. It's quite arousing to watch the men and women stop and fuck the life-like features along the way."

I shook my head and grimaced at a new thought.

"What about all the...*by-products* deposited along the way? It must get pretty slippery and gross before long. I wouldn't want to place my hands or my pussy anywhere near some dude's day-old cum."

Heather scrunched her nose and laughed.

"Not to worry. The ship operators have got it all figured out. After every new climber comes down from the wall, they cover the wall in a tarp and wash it down with high-powered steam water jets. They keep it all very antiseptic."

I clenched my legs together, trying to stimulate my burning clit. I couldn't wait to give it a try.

"What do you say?" Heather said. "Are you up for it?"

"Definitely. My pussy's ready to climb on just about anything right now!"

---

When we got to the wall, I was surprised by how tall it was. It towered at least thirty feet straight up, with foot and hand holds separated a few feet apart. It was odd but strangely arousing to see the artificial vulvas and dildos sticking out from its surface. Two naked people were already strapped into hip harnesses at the base of the wall, a man and a woman both appearing to be in their mid-20s.

They spoke with familiarity to one another, so I assumed they were a couple. What a thrill I thought it must be for the pair to experience this together. A small crowd of friends and onlookers were gathered a few feet further back from the wall, egging the couple on. As Heather had described, two buff staff members held thick ropes in their hands, which looped up over an extended wheel at the top of the structure. The other end dangled down the front of the facade and clasped securely to the front of their harnesses.

"Are you ready?" the man said, looking at his partner.

She nodded silently, then reached up for the first handhold and placed her foot onto a lip at the base of the wall. Heather looked at me and smiled. The idea of doing this in tandem appealed to me, and I hoped that the two of us would have our turn soon. It was strange watching the climbers spread their legs and bend their asses as they stretched to reach the next higher holds. I could see the man's balls hanging between his thighs and his penis wobbling back and forth as he swung from one placement to the other. They both seemed so focused on figuring out their path of ascent that they barely paused to rest.

But about half way up, the woman suddenly paused and pushed her hips against the wall. I could see a small ball-shaped object resting between her thighs, nestled against her vulva. A gentle vibrating noise emanated from the area. She looked over at her partner and smiled, encouraging him to find a similar place to rest.

He glanced to his left and saw an orange ring protruding from the wall. He stepped up and over until his cock was level with the ring then he positioned his flaccid member inside the hole. Suddenly the ring started vibrating, and the man threw his head back. I could see his cock hardening and lengthening as he positioned the vibrating ring around the glans of his penis. He turned toward his partner and they giggled while they gently humped the wall together.

"Higher! Higher!" their friends urged them on from the bottom of the wall.

The two reluctantly disengaged from their fixed positions and resumed their climb up the wall. About five feet higher up, the woman came upon a curved rubber dildo protruding about three inches from the surface, and she paused over it then lowered her pussy until it disappeared inside her hole. She started humping the small dildo to cheers from the crowd. I was glad everybody's attention was focused on the wall, because my fingers had already begun circling my clit as I matched the woman's hip movements.

The man noticed a new feature on his side of the wall, this time mimicking the lips and tongue of a woman. He didn't hesitate to slip his now fully erect cock inside the orifice and begin to moan as he deep-throated his artificial lover. Both he and his partner began speeding up the movement of their hips and it looked like one or both of them might come soon. But the crowd at the base of the wall weren't quite ready.

"Get to the pussy and the dick at the top!" someone shouted. "You're almost there!"

The couple glanced at one another then looked down and shook their heads in mock frustration. Then they peered up the wall and resumed their climb. All the while, the two staff members holding the ropes held the lines taut while pretending to be uninterested in the actions of the climbers. But I noticed the telltale bulge in their pants that belied their disinterest. I looked over at Heather and saw that her hand had slipped between her legs too.

The couple picked up their climbing speed with new determination, and it didn't take long for them to near the top of the wall, where the woman was presented with a large purple dildo and the man with a gaping artificial pussy. The woman placed her lips around the dildo and pretended to give it blowjob while the man pushed his face into the artificial vulva and shook his head playfully. The crowd below erupted in a loud cheer.

"Fuck it! Fuck it! Fuck it!" they chanted in unison.

The woman climbed a few feet higher, then placed the big dildo inside her pussy, and relaxed her legs. The staff member holding her rope bent his knees, clasping the end of the rope tightly with two hands. He'd obviously been in this situation before, and he braced himself for the shifting load. Just a few feet away on the other side of the wall, the man positioned himself adjacent to the artificial vulva and inserted his dick into the hole.

"Whomp! Whomp! Whomp!" chanted their friends down below, in encouragement.

With everybody's attention focused on the wall, Heather suddenly moved behind me and squeezed my breast with one hand, while she slipped her fingers inside my cunny from behind. I could hear vibrating sounds emanating from the artificial pussy and dildo, and the man and the woman clenched their buttocks as they began to fuck their sex toys more vigorously. They peered over at one another and mouthed something, and I could hear their breathing escalating in urgency.

Heather began to speed up the pace of her ministrations, and I fucked her fingers as I pretended it was me on the wall. Within a minute or so, the couple's bodies began convulsing, and their arms and legs suddenly became rigid. Heather held me tightly while I clamped down hard on her hand as I came at the same time with the couple on the wall.

The handlers held the couple's lines firmly until they pushed away from the edifice and were gently lowered. When they got to the bottom and removed their harnesses, their friends surrounded them in a group hug, jumping up and down in celebration. The staff ordered everybody to step ten feet back from the wall, then a canvas tarp descended from the top and hot jets began cleaning the surface.

I could feel the steam rising above the tarp as a rivulet of water began pooling at the base of the structure, draining into a grated hole beside the podium.

I turned around and looked at Heather. She raised her eyebrows to signal if I was game to try it next. I simply nodded my head and smiled. I could feel my own rivulet of warm liquid running down my legs.

## 7

## HOUSE OF HOLES

After they finished sanitizing the wall, Heather and I took our turn on it. Most of the spectators had moved on after the previous couple came down, but it was still unnerving being watched so closely by our rope handlers. As usual, Heather took the lead sitting over the erotic extrusions, and the look of delight on her face soon encouraged me to do the same. We came multiple times grinding our pussies into the various devices, culminating with two powerful orgasms on the large dildos at the top of the wall.

We spent a few more hours lounging around the pool, then Heather encouraged me to strike out on my own. I protested briefly, still not entirely comfortable with the idea of engaging in public sex by myself, but she suggested a few venues that might provide an opportunity for more privacy. After a quick lunch, I reluctantly began exploring the ship.

My first stop was the Sexy Games Room. It was filled with various contraptions, where solo men and women were getting fucked by automated machines. At one station, a woman bent over on all fours, while a large plastic dildo pounded in and out of her pussy. At another one, a man sat on a chair humping a life-like silicone doll, while he squeezed her fake tits and thrust his tongue into her fellatio-shaped mouth. In the corner of the room, a pretty co-ed straddled a device that looked like a pommel horse, as she bucked and writhed atop its vibrating saddle.

It all seemed so surreal and impersonal for me. I wanted a *human* connection, like the one Heather and I shared at the fantasy fountain. I scanned the activity menu and considered going for an Intimate Massage, thinking at least this way I'd have some human touch, and then I remembered one of Heather's recommendations. The description for the House of Holes sounded intriguing:

*Hook up with a stranger on the other side of a wall through your own personal intimate portal. You can choose to 'give', 'receive', or 'merge' with a partner of either sex in an erotic and completely anonymous connection. Or you can choose to simply watch, as other couples get their groove on in this sensuous and erotic 'House of Holes'.*

*Yes,* I thought, *'merging' with a partner is exactly what I need.* The notion of engaging with someone through my own personal 'glory hole', reminded me of the fun I'd had playing with hidden strangers in the Dark Room.

When I got to the venue and opened the door, the first thing I noticed was the sound. A cacophony of moans and grunts greeted me, as a variety of naked men and women shimmied their hips, asses, and mouths against the vinyl-coated walls. The lights were dimmed, but I could see the unmistakable shape of erect penises and vulvas poking through various small holes scattered around the room.

People on the other side were shaking their hips trying to get the attention of someone from inside the room, but everybody was already engaged in some form of coupling. One man was humping the wall, being serviced by someone from the other side. Another one kneeled on the floor giving head to a well-endowed fellow who thrust his cock vigorously into his consort's eager mouth. Not far away, a woman bent over rubbing her ass against the wall, where another man plunged his cock through the hole into her pussy.

But the whole scene somehow left me cold. It struck me as cheap and dirty. Medical clearance or not, I couldn't get on board with the idea of connecting with some other stranger's private parts in such an impersonal way. Just as I was about to leave the room, I noticed a neon sign in the corner reading 'Private View Rooms'.

*Private* definitely sounded more appealing. And being able to *see* my partner was more along my lines.

I opened the door and entered a dimmed hall with closed doors lining both sides. Most of them were locked with a sign reading 'Occupied', but a little further down the hall I found one marked 'Vacant'. I turned the handle and stepped into a small room. It had a single vinyl chair facing a floor-to-ceiling glass wall with a one-foot diameter hole cut in the middle. On the other side of the glass was a similar room with an empty chair.

I turned and locked my door, then checked the chair to see if it was clean. There were no visible marks or residue, but I ran my hand over its smooth surface just to be sure. Even the vinyl floor looked like it had just been cleaned, reflecting the light from the single over-head incandescent lamp.

*At least they clean up after themselves pretty well*, I nodded, as I sat down on the chair and waited for someone to enter the adjacent room.

I expected a man looking for a simulated adult video store glory hole experience, but I was pleasantly surprised when a slim young Asian girl opened the door. She paused for a moment and appraised me seated in my chair with my legs slightly ajar, then she turned around and locked her door from the inside. She was carrying something but she kept it hidden from my view as she turned around.

We could have easily talked if we'd wanted to, with a large enough hole in the glass to carry on a private conversation. But we both seemed to want to just *look* for the time being. She sat down on her chair and placed the hidden object behind her, then spread her legs apart. She had a petite figure with firm B-cup breasts and a small V-shaped patch of pubic hair on her mound that pointed toward a protruding nub at the top of her labia. She had large eyes with long lashes, and she smiled at me as she began to run her hands over her body.

I watched her for a moment, as I felt the juices from my pussy puddle on the chair in front of me. She placed her hands on the inside of her thighs and pulled them slowly toward her apex, then continued moving them up toward her chest. She squeezed her tits then pushed them up and tilted her head down, sucking each of her nipples.

I wanted a piece of her so badly, but I was enjoying her little strip-tease. I cupped my left breast with one hand and I began to play with my clit with my other, spreading my legs further apart. She did the same and pointed her toes, as she opened her mouth, signaling her pleasure. I could hear a soft moan emanating through the hole in the glass as she flitted her eyes and began to rock her hips on her chair.

By now I was thoroughly soaked, feeling the intensity rising in my loins. I slipped the fingers from my other hand into my pussy as I rubbed my clit more forcefully. The Asian girl suddenly thrust both of her hands into her love box and began fucking herself with a two-handed motion, rocking her chest in tandem with her hips. The sound of her juices sloshing around as she finger-fucked herself with both hands ratcheted my excitement up another level.

I could feel my orgasm beginning to build as I let out a low moan. The girl spread her legs wider until they were virtually straight out to her sides. I marveled at her flexibility, reminding me of my naked yoga experience with Kayla and Neve. We were groaning in tandem as we each fucked our own pussies, alternating our line of sight between our sopping pussies and our glazed-over eyes. Suddenly the girl's chest began to heave, and she grunted a staccato burst of moans as she hunched over in orgasmic spasms. That was enough to put me over the edge, and I growled like a wild animal as I gushed all over the chair in front of me. It was incredibly erotic watching each other come with only a few feet separating us between the clear pane of glass.

But now I was ready for a more personal connection. After I came down from my high, I stood up and walked toward the glass and motioned for her to do the same. She walked slowly toward the hole in the partition, then placed her palms flat against the glass at shoulder height. She was even prettier up close, with big brown eyes, high cheekbones, and full pouty lips. I placed my hands over hers and we moved our faces toward the glass until our lips touched on the cool surface. There was something about being this close to another naked woman and not being able to touch her that I found highly arousing.

Our opposite hands traced a path down the side of the glass and we reached through the hole to touch each other's pussies. I groaned when I felt the heat of her box and her fingers touching my clit. We lowered our bodies a few more inches to gain better access to our midsections while still peering into one another's eyes. I stuck out my tongue and began to lick the glass, showing that I was ready for a more personal touch.

I bent my knees a little further and her fingers slipped out of me as I squatted down over the hole in front of her pussy. She pushed her hips into the glass to try to give me better access, but it felt awkward tilting my head through the hole trying to get to her clit with my tongue. Sensing my frustration, she suddenly stepped back from the glass then lifted her right leg straight up and placed her heel against the glass beside her shoulder. Then she pushed her body forward until her legs were pressed flat against the glass in a perfect split.

Her open vulva was now pushing through the hole directly toward my face. I didn't hesitate to take her little button into my mouth and roll it around my tongue like a peppermint candy. Her lubrication coated my face as she ground her pussy against my cheeks. I reached through the hole and wrapped my arm around her hips, pulling her harder toward me. She moaned softly and whimpered as she fucked my face. I inserted two fingers into her love canal as I sucked and flicked her little cocklet in my mouth. Then I curled my fingers in a come-hither motion against her G-spot and she bent her knees, pressing her pussy harder against my face and fingers. Her moans were growing in intensity and my heart raced at the idea of her coming on my face. I pushed my fingers deeper inside and circled her clit more quickly with my tongue. Suddenly, she howled as her pussy clamped over my fingers in a long series of hard contractions. I held my face still while she gushed all over me.

If I could have squeezed my whole body through the narrow opening in the glass, I would have pounced on her right then and there and tribbed her hard until we both came together. Instead, I slowly raised myself up until my face was at the same level as hers and kissed her gently against the glass. She smiled at me and blinked twice as if to say 'thank you'. Then she turned around and walked toward the chair and picked up the object which she'd gone to such pains to hide from me. She held it up in the dim light and smiled. It was a long two-sided flexible dildo, anatomically correct on both ends, shaped like a two-headed penis.

*Fuck, yes,* I thought. *That's what I'm talking about.*

I wanted to fuck this girl so badly, and the two-sided dildo was just what the doctor ordered. She walked up to the glass and held it up in front of me, then licked it up and down the shaft. Then she placed one end in her mouth and simulated fellatio over the silicone glans.

*Please,* I mouthed through the glass. *I need it inside of me now.*

Demonstrating my urgency, I turned around and placed my ass against the open hole, then bent over to present my open pussy to her. She pushed the dildo through the hole and rubbed it back and forth across my vulva, and I shuddered in pleasure. I bucked my hips against the phallus and pressed my ass harder against the glass, signaling that I wanted her to place it inside me.

When she finally did, I almost fainted in pleasure. The feeling of the thick dildo pushing inside me from behind was exquisite. She pushed it as far as it would go, then I felt some slack on the device as she turned around and faced her ass toward me. I didn't need to look to know what she was doing, as I felt the pressure of the dildo when she pushed the other end inside her own pussy.

When our buttocks touched through the open glass, we groaned as we began to simultaneously fuck the giant phallus. I could feel her juices coating the dildo on the other end as our pussies sloshed and bucked against our imaginary partner. The girl began to whimper as we ground our asses together, trying to come over the thick joystick between our legs. It didn't take long for us to reach our peak as we screamed and shook in simultaneous orgasms on the writhing snake embedded inside us.

It took us over a minute before we were ready to disengage, when the girl finally separated herself from the two-headed dildo and pulled it out of my throbbing pussy. I turned around and placed my lips against the glass, and we kissed one last time before she silently picked up the dildo and exited the room. No words had been necessary the entire time we shared our intimate connection.

Just as I was turning to leave, a buff young man entered the room the girl had just left. I took one look at his large swinging cock and shook my head.

*I wouldn't mind a taste of the real thing,* I thought.

## STRAIGHT FLUSH

After I had another go with my new partner in the private view room, I staggered back to my room, sore and exhausted. I slept like a log that night, dreaming of animated cocks and pussies attached to life-like trees, as I walked through a magical forest. When I woke up in the morning, I lay in a giant wet spot atop my leaking cunny and rubbed another one out before showering and heading upstairs to meet Heather for breakfast.

She laughed when I told her about my strange dream, and we entertained each other over lox and pineapple with stories of our experiences from the previous day. She seemed interested in my private view room encounter, but when I told her about my disappointment with the games room, her ears perked up.

"You didn't explore the *other* games rooms?" she said.

"What other games rooms? I only found the one with the holes in the wall."

"There are lots of others that you might find interesting. One of my favorites is the Card Lounge."

"What happens there?"

"It's where groups of people meet to play card games."

"That doesn't sound very interesting."

"It *is* when everybody's naked and they play by different rules."

Heather noticed Marc heading back from the buffet and motioned for him to join them. Virtually everybody was now walking around the ship completely naked, paying little mind to the jiggling breasts and penises as people went about their daily routines.

"Good morning, ladies," Marc said, as he approached our table. "How have you found your shipboard experience so far?"

I took a good long look at Marc's body before he sat down, refreshing my memory from our first night together. Standing well over six feet tall, his well-muscled torso and arms rippled in the bright light streaming through the windows on the top deck. His penis was flaccid, but still hanging a healthy five to six inches as it swung gently above his nicely shaved balls. I picked a thick piece of pineapple from my plate, remembering what his dick felt like standing straight up.

"I think the word is...*eclectic*," I said, sucking the dripping fruit between my lips.

Marc sat down quickly on the other side of our booth to hide his growing erection and smiled.

"There's certainly no shortage of diversions," he said, scooping a large forkful of scrambled eggs into his mouth. "Have you had a favorite experience?"

"You mean besides our little tryst with you?" Heather said, grabbing a sausage from his plate and biting it in half.

"Of course I knew that would be your highlight," Marc said, continued the tease. "I was referring to the venues."

"The climbing wall was fun," Heather said. "But I think Jade may have experienced a different kind of high in one of the private view rooms yesterday."

"Oh? You like those sexy holes, do you?"

"Some holes were a little sexier than others," I said.

"Jade found the rest of the games room a bit underwhelming. I was suggesting she try her hand at a little strip poker. Care to join us after breakfast?"

"Just the three of us?" Marc said.

"I think we need a plus-one to balance things out. Maybe we can persuade one of the guys from the House of Holes to take his dick out of the wall and find a more interesting use for it."

Marc stretched his lips and nodded.

"Game on," he said, finishing his sausage and eggs.

When we got to the card room, we saw an empty round glass table with a pack of playing cards and four trays of betting chips. Heather excused herself for a moment, then returned a few minutes later holding a college-age boy's hand. He looked a little perplexed as he stared at the three of us and the empty table.

"*Three's* a lot more fun than one, don't you think?" she said to the young man. "Plus, there's no barriers here to limit your engagement. Are you ready to play some sexy games?"

He paused for a moment, then stuck out his hand.

"I'm Liam," he said, signaling his assent.

After we all introduced ourselves, we took alternating seats at the table and Heather cracked open the pack of cards.

"What are we playing?" Liam enquired.

"Five card stud," Heather said, winking at me. "With two *real* studs. You *do* know how to play poker, Liam?"

"Yes, but what are the stakes? I didn't bring any money..."

"You're so cute," Heather said. "We're not playing for money. We're playing for *favors*. The rule is that whoever wins each hand, gets to command one or more of us to perform some kind of act. Whoever ends up with the most chips at the end of the hour gets to propose a special group activity. The only limitation is that no one is allowed to come until the very end."

"That makes it a little more interesting," Marc said.

"And challenging," Liam said, crossing his legs to hide his growing erection under the table.

"Right then," Heather said, pulling two red chips from her tray. "The ante is ten dinars."

"Dinars?" Liam said.

"It's just *play* money, remember? They gain *real* value a little later."

Heather dealt one card face down to each player then one more face up. We each looked at our hole cards and placed our bets. Liam placed the largest stake in the pile, then Heather dealt another set of cards face up. Liam showed two Kings and threw in one of his three black chips.

"Too steep for me," Marc huffed, pushing his cards into the waste pile.

Heather displayed two tens, and I had a Jack-high.

Heather matched Liam's bet, and I decided to fold. She dealt the fourth card to herself and Liam. Heather got a Queen, while Liam showed an Ace.

"Hooo!" Marc cheered, as he rubbed his hands together. "Now it's getting interesting. Think hard about what you want the ladies to do for you, Liam."

"I'm *already* hard," Liam said.

I looked through the table top between his legs and saw his good-sized cock pointing straight up on his belly.

Marc reached into his tray and tossed another black marker on the table. Heather paused trying to read his face, then she glanced beneath the table at his throbbing cock.

"I think he's bluffing," she said. "I'll match your bet and raise you one hundred." She threw down her last two black chips then dealt the last card face up. She got another ten and Liam got a six.

Liam didn't hesitate to throw his last black chip in the pot.

"I call," he said, then he turned over his hole card and revealed three Kings.

"Whoa," Heather said, opening her eyes wide in surprise. She turned over her card and revealed a two. Liam had won the hand.

"Well played, young man," Heather said. "Your wish is our command. What would you like us to do?"

Liam ran his eyes up and down Heather's figure and smiled.

"I want you to spread your legs and play with yourself."

Heather pushed her chair back from the table to give everyone a commanding view of her crotch, then she spread her legs apart. She began to circle her clit, while she stared Liam directly in the eyes. His breathing increased as his gaze wandered between her legs. She began to move her hips on the chair, and Liam's hand dropped down to his lap where he began rubbing his cock.

"Hey!" Heather admonished. "That's not allowed. You get to watch only."

"But you said as long as we don't cum—"

"There'll be plenty of time for that later. I want you boys to save those nice big hard-ons for the main event."

Heather sat back up and handed the remaining pack of cards to Liam.

"Your turn to deal," she said.

"That's it?" Liam said. "That was hardly worth three hundred dinars!"

Heather placed her moist fingers in her mouth and licked off her juices.

"You better play your hand wisely the rest of the way, then. Now you've got some extra cash to up the ante. We're just getting started."

Liam collected the pot from the middle of the table, then we all threw in two blue chips for the next round. Liam dealt the cards, and I won the next round with a full house.

I looked at Marc and Liam and licked my lips. I noticed that Liam's dick had lost some of its firmness, but Marc's was rapidly elongating under the table. I wondered how far he'd be willing to go with this game.

"I want Liam to suck Marc's cock," I said.

"What?" Liam said, his eyes flying open. "But I'm not...*gay.*"

"It's just a game," Heather said. "No one's going to cum in your mouth, right Marc? At least not yet. Besides, how do you know if you don't like it until you try? Now get down there and suck that bratwurst."

Marc swung his chair out, and I noticed his cock was standing at full mast. Apparently at least *one* of the boys liked the idea of sucking another guy. Liam walked around the table and kneeled down in front of Marc. He stared at the tip of Marc's manhood, unsure what to do.

"Go on," Heather said. "It won't bite you. Just think of it as a popsicle. A very large warm popsicle."

Marc pulled his arms around behind his chair and clasped his hands together to give Liam freer access.

Liam opened his mouth and slowly lowered himself over the head of Marc's joystick. At first he just held it there, but after a few seconds he began to bob his head as Marc slowly swung his hips. They both seemed to be enjoying it, and I had to fight hard to keep my hands away from my steaming pussy. The sight of seeing two hetero men going at it was incredibly erotic. I wanted to see if I could push it a little further.

"Now play with his balls," I ordered.

Liam paused and peered up at me out of the corner of his eyes, and I simply nodded. Marc pushed his hips toward the end of his seat until his tight balls poked over the edge. Liam reached up and cupped them then rolled them gently between his fingers. His own cock had resumed its full length and was bobbing against his flat stomach. It was obvious that he was getting turned on by the experience, and I saw his tongue begin to roll around in his mouth as he circled the head of Marc's cock. Marc let out a groan and lifted his hips higher. I would have happily forfeited the game at that moment to watch Marc cum in Liam's mouth, but Heather interjected to remind us of the rules.

"Okay, I think that's enough for this round," she said. "You boys seem to be having a little bit too much fun."

Liam sheepishly disengaged from Marc and returned to his seat at the other side of the table. We resumed the game, with each round ratcheted up the degree of engagement between the players. Marc won the next round and asked Heather to sit in my lap while we tribbed each other for a couple of minutes. Then Heather won the next round and asked the men to do the same as we watched them jack their two cocks together between their bellies. By the time our hour was up, all four of us were worked up enough to jump each other bones. When we counted our chips, Heather had eked out Liam for the largest residual.

"What now?" Liam said, his cock bobbing on his stomach, already leaking pre-cum.

"I ended up with the highest winnings," Heather said, "so I get to decide on the final group activity. And I think we should all come back to my cabin."

We didn't bother to clean up the table as we quickly found the nearest exit. Unlike our first night together when we'd scurried down the stairs to her stateroom, this time we took the elevator down the three levels to her floor. But the tension in the lift was palpable as none of us said a word to one another, holding our collective breath in anticipation of what would come next.

## 9

## FOUR PLAY

When we got to Heather's room, nobody was sure who should make the first move. When it was just the three of us, Heather hadn't hesitated to jump the only man in the room, but this time we had to figure out what to do with Liam. The obvious thing would have been for us to pair up as two hetero couples, but Heather had seen enough in the games room to have other ideas.

"You boys lie down on the bed with your feet facing each other," she ordered.

Marc and Liam dutifully lay on the mattress as Heather instructed.

"Now bend your knees and move together until your cock and balls are touching one another."

I looked at Heather inquisitively, wondering what she had planned. We'd already seen the men frotting their cocks together in the games room, and I was eager for some of my own touching.

She glanced at Marc and Liam's glistening cocks throbbing against each other and smiled at me.

"Do you want to go first or me?"

I pinched my eyebrows for a second, then gasped when I understood her intention. The idea of having two cocks inside me was something I hadn't yet experienced. I moved toward the bed and kneeled on the mattress straddling the two men, facing Liam. I'd already watched Marc come inside me, this time I wanted to picture a younger man's reaction.

The men paused for a moment, unsure what I wanted. They were probably thinking of the classic DP maneuver, where one would fuck me in my pussy while the other fucked me up the ass. But I had a better idea. Ever since I saw them rubbing their cocks together in the game room, I'd fantasized about grasping them both inside my pussy. Both men were well hung, measuring together at least three times the girth of an average man's erect penis, but I figured if my anatomy could accommodate a baby's head during childbirth, surely it could take the equivalent of two good sized English cucumbers.

I reached around behind my ass and clasped their two penises together then slowly lowered my pussy until it touched the wet heads of their joined hard-ons. Marc's was a little bit longer, so it pushed its way through first, as I felt my lips widen to accommodate his large organ. Slowly sitting down another inch, I could feel Liam's cockhead pressing me apart still further, and I moaned as I felt my pussy stretch to take them both inside me. With both of them lying flat on their backs on the mattress, there was little they could do with the full weight of my body pressing down over their hips. I relished the feeling of control, watching Liam's face contorting in pleasure as my love tunnel squeezed over their joined cocks.

I slowly lowered myself until I felt my vulva resting on Liam's stubbly pubis. I was glad I'd placed Marc in the posterior position, where he had a little more room to sheath his larger cock. I began to use my thigh muscles to move up and down over their connected meat and reflected back on the Asian girl's two-headed cock from the view room the previous day. Two double pricks in as many days was a new milestone for me.

It seemed as if every nook and crevice of my pussy was filled up by the hot, throbbing manhood of these two virile men. I humped them faster, knowing it wouldn't to take long for all of us to come after the long buildup in the game room. Before long, Heather decided she wanted a piece of the action, and I could hear Marc's muffled moans behind me as she sat over his face. The look on Liam's face was priceless. I wasn't sure which he was enjoying more—the feeling of having his cock deeply embedded in my wet pussy, or the feeling of having Marc's throbbing member next to his.

His mouth was wide open as he moaned loudly in pleasure, and I knew he wouldn't be long to this world. I placed my hands over his tight pecs and squeezed the two-headed python inside me as I felt a powerful urge welling inside me. Heather suddenly reached around my back and squeezed my tits and we all howled in unison. When I came, I bucked wildly over the two men as I felt their cocks pulsing together, flooding me inside with their honey.

I sat there for a minute savoring the feeling of having two hard dicks inside me, as I peered out Heather's balcony window at the sun setting over the ocean. This cruise had been one hell of an adventure, and I didn't know if or when I'd have another chance like this again. I wanted to make it last as long as possible.

# VOLUME THREE

## THE HAREM

1

———

As I walked through the open-air market in Marrakesh, I could feel my heart pounding in my chest. I'd never been to Morocco before, and the hustle and bustle of the *Souk Semmarine* was a feast for the senses. With so many tourists and locals crammed into the narrow laneways, my eyes darted from one distraction to another. While I strolled past their stalls, shopkeepers noisily hawked their wares, begging me to make an offer on everything from cheap jewelry to handbags. The pungent aroma of grilled kebabs, fresh hummus, and fried snails permeated my nose. Everywhere I looked, women in long, full-body burkas or face-concealing niqabs passed calmly by, seemingly unperturbed by the chaos of the teeming bazaar. With my long blonde hair and tight jeans, I definitely stood out like a sore thumb in this conservative muslim metropolis.

After a half hour or so, I grew tired of the peddlers confronting me, and I ducked into one of the shops to try on some head scarves, hoping to distract attention from my obvious Western appearance. When I tried a pretty pink and teal colored one on and looked at myself in the tiny mirror on the wall, the owner came up behind me, smiling at my reflection.

"Very pretty," he said. "You like?"

"Maybe," I said, mindful of the hard-sell personality of local merchants that I'd been forewarned about. "How much is it?"

"For you, pretty lady, only five hundred dirham!"

Knowing the local exchange rate was roughly ten dirham for one U.S. dollar, fifty bucks for a scarf didn't seem out of line. But I also knew that shop owners in North African bazaars were notorious for fleecing unaware tourists and that haggling was an expected and necessary condition of purchase.

"That's more than I can afford," I said, placing the garment back on the rack.

"Perhaps we can make an accommodation," he said, lifting the scarf off the shelf and placing it back on my head. "Since the colors match your eyes so perfectly."

"Um-hmm," I smiled, knowing full well he was just buttering me up for a sale.

"How about two-fifty?" I said, placing my hands on my hips defiantly.

"Ps-shaw!" the merchant scoffed. "That is well below my cost. This is an authentic Moroccan hijab. Other merchants sell this style for much more."

"Well, I guess I'll just have to go check *them* out then," I said, placing the scarf in his hands and turning to exit the stall.

"Ok, ok!" he backpedaled, catching up with me and blocking my exit. "New price, only for you. Four-fifty. But that's as low as I can go."

"That's not much of a discount," I huffed. "Other vendors have offered far better. Three hundred is the best I can do."

The man threw up his hands, wrinkling his brow with a sad puppy dog face.

"My lady, I wish I could help you, but I'm just a poor merchant with high overhead. Don't you expect me to make a profit?"

"Of course," I said. "But I know most of these items have a high markup. I think you've still got plenty of profit to work with here. Perhaps I'll come back after comparing prices with some of the other sellers."

"Wait, wait," the man said, stepping in front of me again. "I can't have you leave without purchasing something. Four hundred is my best offer. But at that price, you're practically *stealing* it from me."

I picked up the scarf again, turning it over to look for some kind of label.

"How do I know this is even made here? There's no tag."

"Oh please," the man said, crossing his arms. "Now you *insult* me. We only sell authentic textiles manufactured in this country. Look at the intricate stitching. This is hand-embroidered right here in Morocco."

"And the fabric?" I said, rolling the cloth between my fingers. "Is it genuine silk?"

The man placed the garment under an overhead ceiling light, slowly tilting it from side to side.

"Can't you see how the patina changes color when you bend the fabric? I would never sell cheap polyester at my store. This is where all the local muslim women come to purchase authentic Arab clothing."

"Okay," I said, shaking my head in surrender. "I'll offer a little more since I can tell it's a quality product. "I will pay three hundred and fifty dirham, cash. That is all I have on my person."

The merchant paused for a moment, scanning my face with a stern expression as if trying to divine my thoughts. Then he burst into a broad smile, nodding enthusiastically.

"Only for you, my pretty American," he said. "And only because I don't want to see you walking around the bazaar in a cheap knock-off sold by the other vendors."

"Good," I said, turning back toward the mirror. "Do you mind showing me the proper way to wear it? The way the local women do?"

"Of course," he said, draping the scarf over the top of my head and pulling the ends softly under my chin, tying them in a gentle knot. "The idea is to cover your hair and tie it so it covers as much of your face as possible. Our culture requires women to express their modesty by covering their bodies when they are out in public."

"Thank you," I said, pulling some bills out of my pocket and handing him the agreed-upon amount.

"Please, come again," the man said, bowing with his palms centered over his chest. "I have many more items of clothing that you would look beautiful in."

"I'll try to come back before I leave your beautiful country," I nodded. "Thank you for your time."

"Safe travels," he said, waving goodbye to me as I exited the stall.

While I continued down the main thoroughfare jostled by distracted tourists, aggressive shopkeepers, and beguiling snake charmers, I realized the thin head covering provided limited camouflage from my fair skin and Western clothing. By the time I exited the packed marketplace, I was visibly sweating and exhausted. I found a nearby cafe and ordered a strong coffee, then found a vacant table in the corner and sat down, nursing my drink.

Most of the patrons appeared to be Westerners, but on the far side of the room sat a lone man in long white robes wearing a traditional headdress, sipping a beverage. I'd always been fascinated by the clothing and customs of native Arabs, and as he appraised the boisterous tourists gathering in the cafe, he peered at them bemused. The man had dark, weathered skin and a closely cropped beard with soft brown eyes and a square jawline. Appearing to be in his late thirties or early forties, he was quite handsome, with the juxtaposition of his flowing cream-colored kaftan and his golden-brown skin making him look like a young Omar Sharif.

As he casually glanced around the cafe, he caught me staring at him, and I quickly looked away. Moments later, my gaze was drawn back to him and this time he smiled when our eyes met. When I looked away again, he stood up from his table and went to the front counter where he placed an order for something. A few minutes later, the clerk handed him two steaming cups and the man began walking in my direction.

"Excuse me," he said, approaching my table. "I noticed you were sitting alone and wondered if you'd like some company. I brought you a cup of mint tea if you'd like to sample some of our local fare."

"Um..." I hesitated, looking around the room to make sure it was safe to be seen in the company of a stranger.

Normally, I'd quickly rebuff someone who made such a bold and unsolicited advance, but there was something about his quiet demeanor and warm eyes that put me at ease.

"Thank you," I said, shifting my chair back a few inches. "That would be lovely."

"My name's Amir," he said, handing me the cup of steaming tea.

"Jade," I said, nodding politely toward him.

"That's a lovely name. It sounds Asian or Moorish, but you look much *fairer* than that."

"Yes," I laughed. "I suppose my light skin gives me away. I'm from Chicago actually, in the United States."

"I know it well," he nodded. "The Sears Tower, Navy Pier, Millennium Park..."

"You've *been* to the United States?" I said, surprised by his fluent English and knowledge of my local landmarks.

"I spent four years studying law at Columbia University and traveled throughout the country during my summers off."

"I *wondered* where your perfect English came from," I said, smiling at his handsome face. "I never would have guessed–"

"That a sheep-herder like me might be so worldly?" he joked.

"No," I stammered. "I meant–"

"It's okay," he laughed. "It's a common reaction I get from Westerners. They either expect me to be some kind of sultan or a terrorist wearing these clothes."

"I'd never judge a person simply on the basis of what they're wearing," I said, furrowing my brow in sympathy.

"That's very wise," he said, peering up at my scarf. "What about you? You seem to be a little more...*restrained* compared to your fellow countrymen."

I lifted my hand self-consciously to my scarf and chuckled.

"I felt a little exposed walking around the markets with my long blonde hair. I think I was too easy a mark for your local merchants."

The man took a sip of his tea and chuckled.

"They can be a little overbearing at times when it comes to

approaching tourists. There's something to be said for exercising a little decorum and good manners."

"I couldn't agree more," I said, lifting my cup in agreement.

"So, what brings you so far from home?"

"Just looking for a change of pace, I guess. I've never been to this part of the world and I wanted to experience the unique culture of North Africa."

"Where have you been so far?"

"Just the medina and a few of the museums. But I'd love to see more of the countryside."

"You mean the *desert*? There's really only two climate zones in the Mediterranean crescent–the fertile orchards near the sea and the barren plains of the Sahara."

"I guess I'm more drawn to the desert. Maybe it's from watching all those romantic films like Lawrence of Arabia and The Wind and the Lion. There's something about the natural beauty of the red sand and the windswept dunes that seems so peaceful and alluring. It seems to be about as far away from the hustle and bustle of the urban jungle as you could possibly get."

"Have you ever ridden a camel?"

"It's on my bucket list."

"Would you like to join my caravan for a little excursion?"

"Caravan?" I said, widening my eyes. "You're traveling in a *caravan*?"

"Yes," he nodded. "It's a modest group. A few camels, some livestock, and my small coterie."

"Is that how you get around?" I asked, suddenly intrigued by this mysterious stranger. "Where are you from originally?"

"I was born in Jordan, but I come from a Bedouin family. We're nomads, moving from country to country, buying and selling livestock and living off the land."

"So you really are a–"

"Goat herder?" he laughed. "In a manner of speaking. But as the leader of my tribe, I'm officially considered a *sheikh*."

"But what about Columbia...?"

"My wealthy parents sent me there hoping for bigger things for me. But I prefer this simple life. There's something to be said for the freedom and stress-free life of a traveling vagabond. I get to meet interesting people in all the countries along the North African peninsula."

"Just like Sean Connery in the movie The Wind and the Lion," I smiled.

"I suppose, insofar as being the king of my domain and living a nomadic lifestyle. So what do you say? Do you feel as brave as Candice Bergen?"

"As I recall, she didn't exactly go *willingly* into the Sahara wilderness with her would-be captor. And I don't have any romantic intentions..."

"No worries," the man said. "You can stay as long or as short as you prefer, or even just for a day trip through the edge of the desert on one of my camels. I assure you that I have plenty of *other* distractions at my disposal."

I pinched my eyebrows, appraising the mysterious man in luxurious robes. I had no doubt that he had little trouble attracting beautiful women wherever he traveled.

"How would this work exactly?" I said, crossing my arms. "I've never run off with a strange man into the desert before."

"I understand your hesitation," he said. "My camp is just outside the city limits. You can join my troupe for an authentic Bedouin dinner while you stay with my other wives in a separate tent. If you feel so-inclined, you're free to join us on the next leg of our journey toward Algiers. I'll be happy to pay for your safe passage back to Morocco if that's where you've made return travel arrangements."

I paused for a moment, scanning his face for any sign of ill intent. I'd heard about the legal practice of polygamy in certain Arab countries, and far from turning me off, the idea of being surrounded by other women who could satisfy his sexual needs gave me a certain degree of comfort.

"That won't be necessary," I said. "It shouldn't be too difficult to change my airfare if necessary. But how can I be sure you don't intend to steal me away like Sean Connery and add me to your stable of harem girls?"

"That's not the way we operate," he laughed. "As you probably learned from watching that movie. Honor is the most important character trait among we Bedouin. But of course, I would encourage you to leave a message with your friends and family before you leave."

The man took a menu scrap from the table and scribbled something on the paper.

"This is my full name. I'm well known in most towns along the coast. The last thing I need is the American cavalry hunting me down like in the movie. I assure you, this is an honorable offer between friends. You have my word on that."

"Can you give me a day to think it over?" I asked, still not convinced this was a good idea. But the lure of joining a real caravan through the Sahara Desert was awfully tempting.

"Absolutely," Amir said. "If you decide to join me, let's meet in this cafe at the same time tomorrow. If you're not here, I'll understand and there will be no hard feelings. But if you do decide to come, we can take a taxi to the outskirts of the city where my aide will meet us and escort us by camel to my camp at the edge of the desert."

"How will I keep from falling off?" I smiled.

"It's not as scary as it looks to ride a camel," he said. "There are comfortable and secure saddles, and they walk quite slowly. But if you're still worried, you can always ride tandem with me."

"I'm sure I'll be fine," I smiled, turning my wrist to check the time. "Thank you for your kind offer, Amir. I look forward to meeting you again tomorrow at five p.m. And thank you for the tea."

As I rose to leave, he stood along with me, extending his hand.

"I hope to see you again, lovely Jade," he said, clasping my hand softly. "And keep an eye out for those carnival barkers. Best to keep your hijab on while you're walking about town."

"Will do," I said, heading toward the exit door.

After I left the cafe, I closed my eyes, inhaling the warm arid air of the Moroccan town square. Something told me that my North African adventure was about to take an interesting new turn.

**2**

———

For the next twenty-four hours, I vacillated back and forth on whether to entertain the handsome sheikh's offer. On the one hand, I'd always dreamed about trekking through the Sahara Desert on a camel. But I knew that traveling into the wilderness with a total stranger was not without its risks. He could easily abduct or molest me, with no guarantee that the local police would make any effort to find me or hold him to account. I knew that muslim law was highly skewed in favor of the man's rights and that women were often ostracized or worse for any kind of perceived sexual indiscretion.

The following morning after enjoying a light breakfast, I approached the front desk of my riad to enquire about the mysterious man. If he was as important and well-traveled as he claimed to be, I figured the staff of one of the best hotels in Marrakesh would have heard of him. But if he was an unknown or persona non grata, I'd simply ignore his invitation and remain in the relative safety of the downtown tourist areas.

"Excuse me," I said, slipping Amir's handwritten note across the counter towards the attending clerk. "Can you tell me if you've heard of this man?"

The clerk squinted at the writing then looked up at me and smiled.

"Of course," he said. "Mr. Haddad is one of our frequent guests. Would you like me to see if he's staying at the hotel?"

"Um, no, thank you," I said. "It's just that he invited me to take a tour with his caravan and I wondered if this was, you know–*safe* or irregular."

"I can't vouch for how often he entertains Westerners in his cavalcade, but he is often seen in the company of attractive young women such as yourself, and I've never heard of any complaints or misconduct. The Sheikh is widely respected as a man of honor and prestige in these parts. I'm quite sure that you would not only be safe, but indeed well-protected while under his guardianship."

"Thank you," I said, placing the note back in my pocket.

As the hour approached for our planned reconnection, I packed a light duffel bag of overnight clothes and sent an email to my best friend Hannah from back home.

*Han,*

*Enjoying my trip to Morocco so far. Will send more pics soon. I've accepted an invitation to go on a private caravan tour of the local desert with a prominent bedouin leader. His name is Amir Haddad. Apparently his family is quite prominent in Jordan.*

*If you don't hear back from me in a few days, contact the local embassy to see if they can track my whereabouts. I know this sounds crazy, but I've always dreamed of traveling the Sahara on camelback, and you only live once!*

*Talk soon,*

*Jade*

I knotted my silk scarf under my chin, then placed a wide-brimmed straw hat on my head and headed back towards the cafe where I'd met the sheikh the previous day. With my heart beating a million miles an hour, I strolled past the bustling souks wondering what I'd gotten myself into.

When I entered the cafe and saw Amir sitting in the corner with his legs crossed sipping a cup of tea, he smiled and stood as I approached his table.

"I'm glad you decided to join me again, Jade," he said, holding out his hand as he supported me while I lowered myself onto the adjoining chair. "I was afraid that I might have scared you away with my rather direct proposition."

"I went back and forth considering it, to be honest," I said. "But I asked around, and you were truthful about your reputation. Apparently, I'm not the *first* tourist you've entertained in this manner. But I left your credentials with the U.S. Embassy just in case."

"I would expect no less from such a wise and pretty lady," he smiled. "May I order you a cup of tea?"

I looked at my watch and glanced outside at the lengthening afternoon shadows.

"I'm already pretty charged up about this adventure," I said, concerned about traveling at night deep into the outback. "Shouldn't we head out to your camp while there's still good light?"

"As you wish," he said, standing up and extending his hand as he surveyed my wardrobe. "I see you've come well prepared for the elements. Though I'm not sure about that hat. You look more like *Audrey Hepburn* in Breakfast at Tiffany's than Candice Bergen in The Wind and the Lion."

I smiled at his genteel manners while he opened the cafe exit door for me then hailed a passing taxi. After we got in the cab and he gave the driver directions in arabic, he glanced down at my overnight bag.

"It looks like you're intending to stay for a while," he smiled. "I must not have scared you *too* much with my abrupt proposition."

"I've heard it's a pretty big desert," I said, pulling my handbag closer toward me. Unbeknownst to my host, I'd included a can of pepper spray under my belongings in case he got the wrong idea. "A girl can never be too prepared on these kinds of expeditions."

"Indeed it is," he smiled. "Did you know that the entirety of the Sahara Desert is even bigger than the continental United States? But never fear–my caravan has enough provisions to keep us comfortable for as long as you choose to stay."

As the taxi sped towards the outskirts of the city, I watched the passing scenery as it became progressively less populated and more barren. Within twenty minutes, the dusty streets soon gave way to grassy hillsides. When we crested the final ridge and I saw the open expanse of the desert stretching out in every direction, I gasped. The late afternoon sun cast long shadows over the undulating red sand dunes, making it look like a different *planet*.

"Is this your first time seeing the desert?" Amir asked, noticing my wide eyes surveying the eerie landscape.

"First time up close and for *real*," I nodded in a daze. "It's even more magnificent than I imagined."

"It has a way of transporting you," he nodded. "There's something about the open vistas and the way the sun reflects over the shifting sands that's quite captivating. Perhaps now you can begin to appreciate how I'm are attracted by its allure."

"It *is* mesmerizing, I grant you," I said. "But how do you navigate your way across this moonscape? There are no roads or landmarks to know which way you're headed?"

"We navigate by the shadows of the sun during the day and the stars in the evening. Plus, the desert isn't all sand. There are bluffs and oases and mountain ridges that point our way. We bedouin have traveled the deserts of North Africa for thousands of years. We know it as well as the back of our hands, as you Americans say."

"I'll have to take your word for it," I said, suddenly feeling the dryness in my mouth. "But something tells me I should have packed more bottles of water in my overnight case. How far away is your camp?"

"It's only twenty or thirty minutes by camel ride," Amir said as the taxi skidded to a stop at the end of the road. Nestled in a shaded dale of the hillside, I noticed a dark-skinned Arab man in a long tunic tending to three camels. "My aide brought an extra ride for you. Don't worry about the water. We've long-since learned how to manage our scarce resources in the parched desert."

Amir paid the taxi driver then escorted me to the dale where he introduced me to his servant.

"This is Ali," Amir said, motioning toward the other man. "He'll look after all of your needs during your stay with us."

The man bowed slightly at the waist, acknowledging me as Amir's guest. I found it a bit strange that Amir didn't introduce me by name, but I assumed it had something to do with the customs of his tribe and his status as leader of the clan.

I glanced at the three oddly shaped animals nibbling on grass besides us. With their long knobby legs, U-shaped neck, and large hump in the middle of their back, they looked like a cross between a llama and an oversized donkey. Towering at least two feet over the top of my head, I was already starting to get vertigo imagining myself trying to balance on top of their precarious mounds.

"These are a lot *taller* than I imagined," I said, noticing an absence of stirrups hanging from their woven cloth saddles. "How will I ever get on top of it?"

"You don't climb up on a camel like you would a horse," Amir said. "They kneel down for you to get on top of them."

He mentioned something to his aide in arabic and Ali pulled on the long hair on the side of one of the camels, then the animal knelt down on the ground with its front knees and lowered its back end until its belly was lying flat on the ground.

"Wow," I said. "That's certainly convenient. Have you trained them this way only for your guests, or is this the way *everybody* mounts a camel?"

"They're very domesticated," Amir said. "It's easy enough to climb atop a standing camel if you know how, but this certainly makes it a lot easier."

"I'll say," I nodded, seeing the top of the cloth saddle now resting at hip height.

"But you still need to be careful to hold on to the pommel at the front of the camel's saddle to make sure you don't get bucked off when it stands. It jerks forward and back as it rises, and if you're not used to it, you can easily be thrown."

Amir said something to Ali and he held out his hand, motioning for me to climb atop the saddle of the resting camel, and I swung my leg up over his hump and sat down on the surprisingly comfortable seat. Although the frame appeared to be made entirely of wood, I noticed a padding of straw and palm leaves under the thick woven blankets draped over its flanks.

"Okay," Amir said. "Now grasp the knob on the front of the saddle tightly and clamp your legs against the side of the camel as he rises."

I did as Amir instructed, then Ali tapped the side of the animal and it lurched forward lifting its back end, then it stepped forward with both front legs until it was fully erect. My body swung wildly as it see-sawed up to a standing position, and I could feel my heart beating as I stared down at the ground ten feet below me.

"Are you good?" Amir called up to me, seeing the fright in my eyes.

"Yes, as long as I don't fall off," I grunted. "But how do I *steer* this thing?"

"Don't worry about that," he laughed. "Ali will lead your camel with a tether behind his animal. But watch out as he begins to walk. They have a bit of a jerky gait. Try to relax your body and let it sway with the animal's movements. Are you ready to head out to our camp?"

I nodded my head then Amir and Ali mounted their camels, heading out in a straight line toward the open desert with Amir in the lead. It didn't take long for me to get used to my camel's rhythmic up-and-down gait, and as I began to relax, I looked out over the vast expanse of russet-colored dunes at the exquisite beauty of the desert. Looking like a giant Rothko painting, all I could see was an endless sea of golden waves juxtaposed against the brilliant blue sky.

The air was hot and dry, and I blinked as sprinkles of sand dusted up into my eyes from the strong wind sweeping across the dunes. More than once I had to grab my hat from falling off my head from the gusts shooting overtop the crescent-shaped hillocks. As I watched the long shadows of our three camels traipse across the soft turf, I smiled at the serene beauty and solitude of the glittering landscape. I wasn't sure what awaited me at Amir's camp, but for the time being, the gentle loping of my camel and the whisper of the warm Saharan breeze lulled me into a blissful, trancelike state.

**3**

______

Thirty minutes later, I noticed a clump of trees on the horizon, and I squinted through the shimmering haze wondering if it was a mirage. But as we got closer, I saw a small collection of tents nestled among the palms and a flock of livestock grazing on the grass surrounding the perimeter of the encampment. Hardly believing my eyes, I called ahead to Amir, wondering how anything could grow in this barren wasteland.

"Is this your camp?" I shouted over the howling wind.

"Yes," he said, pulling his camel up beside mine so I could hear him better.

"I thought my eyes were playing tricks on me at first," I said, shaking my head in astonishment. "How does any vegetation survive out here without any water?"

"The desert is riddled with a labyrinth of underground aquifers," he said. "In certain places, natural springs bring the water to the surface, feeding the surrounding vegetation. At other oases, manmade wells tap the aquifers, supplying much needed water to traveling caravans such as my own."

"I thought oases were just a figment of Western movies. I had no idea they actually existed in the middle of the desert."

"There are actually quite a few scattered across the Sahara," he nodded. "But because of the vast size of the desert, it can take many days on camel to travel between them. They've been the lifeblood of we bedouin for centuries."

As we got closer to the camp, I noticed a large herd of camels and scores of sheep and goats grazing quietly in the grass.

"And there's enough water to feed all those *animals* too?"

"Yes," Amir said. "The aquifers are practically endless. There's a veritable ocean of water underneath this arid surface. Did you know that the Sahara was once an enormous sea before the Earth's shifting plates separated the large continents of Eurasia and Africa?"

"I had no idea," I said, growing increasingly impressed with Amir's knowledge of world history and geology. "But why do you have so many camels and livestock? You must have quite a large entourage."

"Actually, it's mostly just me and Ali and my stable of wives. The animals are primarily used to transport our gear and provide food for our band."

"Wow, you really *are* a self-contained entity out here in the middle of the wilderness, aren't you?"

"Everything we need is supplied by the animals and the desert," he nodded.

"And your *wives*," I smiled, peering ahead toward Ali plodding along in front of us, wondering how he satisfied some of *his* more primal needs.

"Yes," Amir smiled. "And my wives."

When we reached the edge of the trees, I noticed a group of women kneeling in the sand preparing food. They all wore loose-fitting tunics and cotton headdresses that wrapped tightly around their heads and faces, providing protection from the overhead sun and the dusty wind. As our retinue approached the center of the camp, the women looked up and stared at me like I was from another planet. They all seemed young and strikingly beautiful.

*Maybe Amir doesn't need to entertain Western women after all,* I thought.

The two men dismounted their camels, then Amir tapped my

animal and he knelt onto the ground, where Amir offered his hand to help me dismount. Then he led me into one of the two large tents in the campground where an attractive dark-haired woman roughly my age was folding clothes in the corner of the enclosure.

"This is my wife, Laila," he said, introducing me to the woman. "Laila, Jade will be joining us for dinner this evening, so please make sure she has everything she needs."

She turned around and smiled at me with her piercing eyes. I was surprised how beautiful she looked bereft of any makeup or other embellishments. Her wraparound headdress framed her pretty face, highlighting her high cheekbones and golden-brown skin.

"Pleased to meet you," Laila said, bowing slightly at the waist.

It was hard to discern her figure under her layered cloak, but my pussy fluttered when I saw her face flush slightly in modesty.

"You speak *English*?" I said, surprised by her absence of any discernible accent.

"Yes," she said. "My family is from Cairo and we learned English in elementary school. I'm a bit rusty, so it will be nice to have a native speaker to help me brush up on my skills."

"We'll be having dinner when the sun goes down," Amir interrupted. "Then I'll be providing some special entertainment in my tent later on. You may wish to put on some warmer clothes, as it can get quite chilly outside after dark. I'll see you in another hour or so."

After Amir exited the tent, I peered at Laila with a quizzical look. "*Entertainment*?"

"Never fear," she chuckled. "He often entertains visitors with a traditional arab dance. Though it's usually for the benefit of other men. This is the first time he's brought a Western *woman* into his camp."

"I guess I should be honored then," I shrugged, wondering exactly what kind of dance he had in mind.

Laila peered at my cut-off capri pants and light linen blouse and smiled.

"Would you like to change into something more comfortable? As

Amir said, it gets quite cold at night and you'll want a bit more protection against the blowing wind."

"Sure," I said, happy to adopt the local customs during my brief visit with the group.

"If you'd like to remove your clothing, I can store them in a safe location while you stay with us."

"*Everything*?" I said, wondering what arab men and women wore underneath their long garments.

"It's more comfortable that way," she said. "Unless you need to wear something because it's that time of the month...?"

"No, thankfully," I chuckled, curious how they also managed *that* aspect of their personal hygiene.

As I began to remove my clothing, Laila peered at me, noticing the strange tan lines around my bra and upper arms. I paused for a moment before pulling off my panties, and her eyes widened when she saw my shaved pubis. I felt like a bit of a freak, realizing that she and the rest of the women rarely went outside with any exposed skin and almost certainly abstained from any kind of intimate grooming.

Laila fetched a neatly folded garment from the corner of the tent then opened it up to reveal an ankle-length tunic with long sleeves and an opening at the top. I held up my arms and she draped it over my body, stepping in close to me as she peered into my eyes. She smelled of jasmine and lemongrass, and my heart fluttered as her full lips neared my mouth when the garment fell over my shoulders. Then she wrapped a long cotton scarf over my head and under my chin, fastening it with a bobby pin at the ends to hold it in place.

*I guess they're not completely bereft of Western conveniences*, I smiled.

When she finished, she stepped back and nodded approvingly, smiling at the unusual appearance of a Western woman dressed in traditional arabian garb.

"Do you have a mirror or something to view myself in?" I asked, intrigued to see what I looked like.

"I'm afraid we don't," she said. "It is not part of our culture for women to primp over their external appearance. But I assure you that you look quite beautiful."

"Thank you," I said, reaching into my bag to retrieve my phone. I tapped the screen a few times then handed the device to Laila. "I know this must sound terribly touristy of me, but would you mind taking a picture of me? My friends back home will never believe that I got myself into this arrangement, and I'd love to have a keepsake of my visit to your camp."

"Okay," Laila said, squinting her eyes at the phone. "But this is a little different from the phones I remember using in my youth. How does it work?"

"Just step back and angle the phone until you see my entire body on the screen, then tap the red button at the bottom to capture the image."

Laila did as I requested and I heard the familiar shutter sound when the phone took the picture. She handed it back to me and I tapped the thumbnail image in the lower corner of the screen to view the full-size image. I laughed when I saw myself encased in the flowing robes, with only my pale face peering through the wrap-around fabric.

"That's certainly a different look for me," I said, feeling the soft fabric brushing against my hardening nipples and bare mound. "But I have to admit, it's a lot more comfortable than my usual attire. Is it comfortable to wear in the heat of the day?"

Laila pulled the fabric up over my shoulders and I felt a puff of air press up from the floor toward my exposed pussy.

"The cotton fabric breathes nicely, and the loose fit permits the wind to flow over our bare bodies underneath," Laila smiled.

"Yes, I can see that," I said. "I'm *already* beginning to appreciate the extra freedom of movement in this dress. Although I don't imagine you call it that in your native language."

"We women refer to it as a *thawb*, but when men wear similar robes, they call it a kaftan."

I nodded, beginning to understand the various ways arab culture subjugated women under the control of men. I crossed my arms, beginning to feel the chill as the sun began to set over the horizon.

"Do you think this will this be warm enough in the evening?"

Laila pulled a wool blanket off the pile of clothes in the corner and placed it over my shoulders.

"This shawl will help keep you warm," she smiled. "And it can also be used as a bed covering later on at night."

"Speaking of," I said. "I see you don't have any traditional beds in the tent..."

"We bedouin can't afford such luxuries," Laila laughed. "Everything has to be light enough to pack onto the backs of our camels when we move from one location to the next. We sleep on woven blankets on the soft sand. I think you'll find it's quite comfortable, actually."

"Does everyone sleep in this one tent?" I said, peering at the limited amount of floor space in the twenty-by-twenty-foot enclosure.

"All of the *women*, yes," Laila nodded. "The men have separate tents, of course. Everything is tightly controlled in our caravan. Nothing goes to waste."

"So I'm beginning to learn," I smiled, imagining myself lying on the soft desert sand next to the covey of beautiful women at night.

"Are you hungry?" she asked.

The mention of food made my stomach grumble. I suddenly realized that I hadn't eaten since early in the morning.

"Oh yes, very."

"Come, let's show you how we prepare our traditional bedouin meals."

Laila led me outside, where a large open fire cackled in a sand pit with a wooden frame erected overtop of its perimeter. The women sat in a large circle around the flame, hunched over in their long robes, kneading their hands into large porcelain bowls.

"It smells heavenly," I said, breathing in the fresh scent of milk and spices. "May I ask what the women are preparing?"

"It's a rice dish infused with fresh goat milk, lentils, and chopped onions, seasoned with saffron and turmeric."

"So you're all *vegetarians*?"

"Oh no," Laila said. "We also eat goat meat and lamb. But that's usually reserved for special occasions, like when we have a guest such as yourself."

"I see," I said, noticing Amir flipping open the canvas door of his tent and walking in our direction.

"I see that Laila has gotten you into some more comfortable clothes," he nodded approvingly. "Are you ready to enjoy our traditional bedouin dinner?"

"Absolutely," I said. "I don't know if it's this desert heat or the long camel ride, but I'm famished!"

"Well, we won't delay any longer then," he said, brandishing a curved knife from under his kaftan. He walked up to one of the younger sheep grazing quietly at the edge of the pasture and he grabbed the animal by the back of its head, calmly slicing its throat. The lamb staggered for a moment in shock, then fell to the ground twitching its legs for a few seconds, then lay still as the blood from its neck coated the desert sand. Seconds later, Ali approached the dead animal, and using a longer knife proceeded to slice open its belly, pulling out its entrails.

"Oh my God," I dry-heaved, turning away from the scene of the gory slaughter.

"You've never seen a live animal killed before?" Amir said, seeing my discomfort.

"Never up close and in person like this," I coughed, trying to keep myself from retching.

"But you eat meat?"

"Yes, it's just that–"

"You Westerners are insulated by your supermarkets and hidden slaughterhouses from the act of killing and preparing the animal."

"Yes," I said, realizing how hypocritical it was of me to be offended by the practice of killing live animals for consumption.

"A halal slaughter is considered the most humane way of killing an animal in our culture," he said. "The animal hardly feels a thing before it loses consciousness and quickly bleeds out."

"I'll take your word for it," I said, watching Ali skin the animal and thread a stake through its mouth as he placed it over the fire pit.

"I hope this won't diminish your appetite for the meal. Everything should be ready in another half hour or so."

"I'm sure I'll be fine," I said, smelling the scent of the fresh meat cooking over the pit. "I just need a moment to collect myself."

"Come join me then by the fire while the women make the final preparations."

Amir motioned to a blanket spread out on the sand about ten feet away from the fire, and he held my hand while I sat down on the mat.

"So, what do you think of our little caravan so far?" he said, sitting down cross-legged beside me.

"It's certainly *authentic*," I said, peering at the group of young women preparing the dishes in the circle around the fire. "But I'm wondering about the ratio of men to women in your troupe. Are all of these women your wives?"

"Not in the *legal* sense," he said. "I prefer to think of them as my courtesans."

"They're all so young and pretty. How did they come to join your caravan?"

"I bought them," Amir said nonchalantly.

"You *what*?"

"I know this is a custom frowned upon in the West. But it is quite common in conservative muslim cultures, especially among we bedouin. Families consider it an honor for their daughters to be indentured to a prominent sheikh such as myself."

"And when they get *older*? Do you simply dispose of them when they no longer suit your fancy?"

"They're sold off to other prominent men as maids, nannies, and cooks. The women are always treated well, generally enjoying lives far more comfortable and secure than in their own impoverished families."

"And in the meantime, they travel in your caravan for your own amusement?"

"Well, as you can see, they perform many *other* useful functions. Nobody goes for want in my troupe. Everyone's needs are fully satisfied."

"What about *Ali's* needs?" I said, noticing his servant dutifully turning the roast lamb on the fire spit. "Does he also enjoy the company of these attractive ladies?"

"He would never dare *touch* one of my women for fear of instant execution," Amir said, suddenly clenching his jaw. "But he's well compensated for his service to the caravan. He satisfies his more primal needs in the many small towns along our route."

"I see," I said, watching him remove the charred carcass from the spit then carving it up into smaller chunks and passing them around the circle. Each of the women took a piece and sliced it up into bite-sized portions, mixing them in with their bowls of rice.

"Come," Amir said, taking two bowls and placing them in front of us. "Let's not be concerned about such indelicate matters over dinner. Let's enjoy our feast under the stars of this magnificent canopy."

He picked up his bowl and dipped his hand into the dish, pinching skewers of meat and rice between his fingers and bringing it to his mouth. Looking around the circle, I saw the rest of the entourage doing the same, and I picked up my bowl not wanting to be rude, following their lead. The food was surprisingly moist and tender, with the milk-infused rice keeping all the ingredients bound together, making it easier to take bite-sized chunks in my fingers. I hummed appreciatively at the piquant taste of the freshly prepared ingredients, soon forgetting about the unsettling scene that I'd witnessed with the young lamb moments before.

As we all ate quietly around the circle, my eyes scanned the faces of the pretty young women peering at me curiously across the dancing flames of the bonfire. It didn't take long for my mind to wander to what *other* forms of entertainment they used to keep themselves amused when Amir was otherwise occupied. Surely, he couldn't keep *all* of them satisfied at one time, I thought. As my pussy twitched from the cool desert breeze wafting up under my fluttering robe, I began to look forward to sleeping on the soft desert sand later in the evening.

**4**

———

After dinner, Amir invited Laila and me to his tent to enjoy the planned entertainment. He motioned for two of the girls to prepare for the event, and they left the circle while the rest of the women cleaned up the dishes. When I entered his enclosure, I was surprised at how large it was for one person. More than twice the size of the women's shelter, it was bedecked with persian rugs, beautiful tapestries, and a large wood-frame bed with luxury linens.

*Wow*, I thought, shaking my head in dismay. *Arab men really do enjoy all the advantages in this culture.*

Amir invited the two of us to sit on the plush carpet in the center of the tent, then he fetched a heart-shaped guitar from the corner and sat down between us with the instrument cradled between his legs. A few moments later, I heard two women's voices outside the front door of his tent and Amir replied to them in arabic. When they pulled back the flap and entered the room, my eyes flew open in shock. Instead of their usual long robes and wraparound headdresses, they wore a skimpy ornamental bikini costume.

Their long black hair was held in place by a beaded headband with long tassels hanging down over their eyes, festooned with little silver bells. Dangling from their tasseled bikini bottom hung a knee-length black cloth that provided a modicum of modesty to cover their crotch area. But the rest of the costume left little to the imagination, showing the deep cleavage between their tightly compressed breasts and their exposed bellies and thighs glistening in the soft candlelight of Amir's tent.

Shifting from the ultra-conservative full-body covering of their traditional frocks to this bawdy costume was a shock to my system, and I soaked up the women's taut, sexy figures like I hadn't seen a near-naked body in weeks. Which I damn near *hadn't*. Suddenly realizing that I hadn't felt the touch of another woman's body since I left home, my pussy throbbed while I ogled the sexy girls standing only a few feet in front of me.

"Are you ready to watch a real arabian belly dance?" Amir said, noticing my pupils dilated in excitement.

"Definitely," I smiled, eager to see the two women gyrate their bodies next to me.

He nodded toward the two girls and they stepped back a few feet, then he picked up the guitar and began strumming a rhythmic folk tune. As the melody filled the cabin, the two women began to undulate their hips in unison, matching the beat of the song. My eyes flickered over their bodies, absorbing the sensuous spectacle while their stomach muscles flexed and their navels swayed from side to side like two winking eyes. As they stepped forward and back in perfect harmony, they snapped the castanets on the tips of their fingers together, providing a rhythmic accompaniment to Amir's lilting melody.

*Just when I thought this guy couldn't get any more suave and sophisticated*, I thought. *He even plays the guitar perfectly.*

In another place and time, I might have fallen for his seductive demeanor, but for the time being I was utterly hypnotized by the sensual moves of the two beautiful women dancing before me. As I watched their eyes gazing at us behind their swinging ringlets, I tried to place how old they were. Their bodies hardly had an ounce of fat, and their skin was as soft and supple as a teenager's. Knowing many arab countries had few restrictions against marrying much younger women, I wondered if they were even of legal age. As if that actually mattered out here in the middle of the desert.

Amir softened the strumming of his guitar and the girls eventually slowed their movement to a stop, then he turned toward me and smiled.

"What do you think of our traditional arab music and dance?" he said to me.

"It's beautiful," I said, shifting my position on the warm carpet, suddenly realizing how wet I'd become watching the two girls. "And very sensuous."

"Yes, it is," he said. "Do you have a particular request?"

I shook my head, unsure what he meant at first, then I cleared my throat when I realized he was talking about the music and not what I wanted to do with the girls.

"You mean like a Western *song*?"

"Yes," he nodded. "I always like to satisfy my guests' preferences."

I thought for a moment about a song that resonated with me that was also slow enough to fit with the girls' style of performance.

"Do you know the Bob Marley song Waiting in Vain, but played in the style of Annie Lennox?"

"Of course," he said. "It's one of my favorites."

He began strumming his guitar again, and the familiar melody of the song filled the tent while the two girls swayed their hips in harmony with the rhythm, clapping their castanets softly to provide gentle background accompaniment. A few moments later, Laila began humming the tune and Amir turned toward her, encouraging her to join him.

*From the very first time I laid my eyes on you, girl,* she sang with an angelic voice. *My heart said follow through. But I know, now, that I'm way down on your line...*

I turned to face her, amazed that she knew the lyrics to the song and enthralled by her gorgeous tone.

*But the waiting feeling's fine,* she cooed, meeting my gaze. *So don't treat me like a puppet on a string. 'Cause I know how to do my thing...*

Suddenly my thoughts echoed back to earlier in the day when she slipped my robe over my naked body, and the way she peered at me as she leaned in toward me.

Had she felt the same sexual attraction I'd had for her when we first met?

As she sang the words, she looked into my eyes and smiled while I tapped my feet rhythmically against the soft carpet.

*I don't want to wait in vain for your love*, she sang, gazing at me directly as my mouth parted in a spellbinding stupor. Suddenly, I couldn't wait to get out of Amir's tent and back into the women's enclosure where I could lie next to her on the warm desert sand under my soft wool cape.

As the song wound down and the girls' movement slowed to a stop, Amir placed his guitar to one side and reached around behind him, placing two odd-looking drums on the mat in front of him. Made of different-sized hollowed-out ceramic bowls with dried animal skins stretched over top, they looked like homemade bongo drums. As if on cue, Laila reached beside her and picked up a wooden reed instrument fashioned in the manner of a flared flute.

"That was beautiful," I said, peering at the two of them. "I don't think I've enjoyed that song as much as I did just now. This whole experience has been a feast for the senses."

Amir smiled as he pulled the drums in closer toward his knees.

"I'd like to finish with song I wrote myself for this kind of occasion," he said. "Unfortunately, I can't sing as well as Laila and her mouth will be otherwise occupied during this tune, so you'll just have to enjoy the *other* elements of the performance," he said, nodding toward the two belly dancers.

As he began beating on the drums with two hands, Laila picked up the flute-shaped instrument and began humming another arabic tune, tapping her fingers rhythmically over the holes on top of the shaft. The girls began swinging their hips slowly at first, but as Amir began increasing the pace of his tapping, they gyrated their hips faster and faster, turning their bodies around as I watched their buttock muscles flexing and shaking under the silk tassels hanging down from their tight bikini bottoms. As Laila matched Amir's escalating backbeat in pace and volume, the girls grew increasingly animated with the shaking of their bodies, looking like they were building up to some kind of climax.

While they shook their bodies with increasing passion and fervor in the form of a simulated sex act, I found myself shifting my weight again on the warm carpet underneath me, growing progressively wetter from their suggestive body movements and facial expressions. Amir became increasingly energetic pounding his drums with his two hands, and I noticed that he was staring at the girls with a lustful look in his eyes. The sexual tension in the room was now at a fever pitch, and as he banged out the last part of the performance, I saw a light sweat dripping over his brow. When he finished the song with two loud bangs on the drums, for a few moments everything in the tent became still as I listened to the sound of everyone's heavy breathing.

"Did you enjoy our little performance this evening?" he said, turning to face me after a long pause.

"Yes, very much," I panted, suddenly realizing how much the performance had raised my *own* heartbeat.

"If you'll excuse me now," he said, looking at the two scantily clad girls in front of him and motioning for them to stay behind. "I think it's time for me to turn in now. Laila will look after your sleeping arrangements. I'll see you again in the morning."

"Thank you," I said, as Laila and I stood to leave. "I'm sure I'll sleep very soundly this evening."

When I followed Laila out the front flap of Amir's tent, I noticed a dark shadow moving away from the perimeter and I recognized Ali's shape in the flickering moonlight. I shook my head realizing that he'd been spying on the erotic performance through a hole in the tent and picked up my pace to catch up with Laila.

"It's as simple as *that*, is it?" I said, referring to Amir's unbridled control over the girls. "He only has to nod, and the women submit to whatever his request?"

"Unfortunately, yes," she said, peering at me with sad eyes. "He's bought and paid for us, and we have to do whatever he says."

"Even if that means sleeping with him whenever he demands?"

"*Especially* that," she said.

"You seem somewhat less eager than the other girls," I said.

"He's had his way plenty enough times with me," she shrugged. "Thankfully, he now prefers the younger girls. Did you at least enjoy the performance?"

"Yes," I said. "It was very–*stimulating*. But honestly, I enjoyed your singing more than anything else. You have a gorgeous voice. Even when you played the wind instrument, I couldn't take my eyes off of you."

"Thank you," she said, noticing me pull my wool shawl over my shoulders to protect against the biting desert wind. "You have a very intoxicating manner about you as well. Come, let's get out of this cold desert air and bundled underneath something warmer."

When we entered the women's tent, all the other girls were already lying fast asleep on their blankets on the sand, with only one small open spot left in the corner of the enclosure. Laila laid a large blanket down over the space, then nonchalantly pulled her dress up over her shoulders, folding the robe and headdress on the ground next to the blanket. I couldn't help staring at her voluptuous body, highlighted by the lone flickering candle next to the makeshift bed. Her breasts were full and firm, resting high on her chest with dark medallions encircling her thick, pointed nipples. Her bare hips curved sensuously around the dark patch of pubic hair on her mound, tapering to long but muscular legs. In the dark shadows of the enclosed pavilion, she looked to me like some kind of sexy Amazon.

Then she picked up a large woolen blanket and threw it over her shoulders, lying down on the carpet peering up at me.

"Are you just going to stand there, or are you going to get under the covers and help keep me warm?"

"In the *buff*?" I said, unsure what the proper protocol was for women sleeping together in the tight confines of the communal tent.

"It's more comfortable that way," she said. "The less washing of our clothes that we have to do, the better. We prefer to air them out overnight. Besides, the sheepskin feels so much better against your bare skin. Come join me if you feel brave enough."

I pulled off my shawl and lifted my thawb over my shoulders, placing them gently on the sand on the other side of the blanket, then lifted the fluffy duvet and nestled in next to her.

"Oh, I'm feeling brave enough," I said, turning to face her.

"Good," she said. "Because those dancing girls weren't the *only* thing distracting my attention this evening."

# 5

Laila turned her body toward me, then shifted her weight closer, wrapping her legs around my hips. I could feel her soft bush caressing my bare mound as she pressed her breasts firmly against my chest. I placed my hand against the side of her head and leaned in to kiss her, and our tongues melded together in a different kind of erotic dance.

"Laila," I whispered. "I'm so happy we have a chance to sleep together. I've wanted you from the moment I laid eyes on you."

"Why do you think I joined the two of you in Amir's tent?" she said, smiling into my eyes. "I wanted you all to myself."

"Weren't you worried that I might have stayed with *him* instead?"

"Possibly," she cooed. "He certainly knows how to put on the charm when he wants something."

"I already made it clear to him that I didn't come here for *romantic* reasons," I said. "Besides, men don't really do it for me any longer."

"Oh?" she said. "You prefer the company of women?"

"Only *certain* ones," I purred, grinding my pussy against hers.

"Do you mind if I examine you more closely?" she said. "I've never seen a Western woman up close and naked before. You're very–*different*."

"Absolutely," I said. "I've been fantasizing about you strumming your fingers over something other than that *flute* for the last half hour."

"Mmm," she groaned, moving further under the blanket.

As she nibbled her way down my body, I felt her hard nipples etching a line over my trembling stomach. When her mouth reached my breasts, she circled my teats with her warm tongue then sucked them hard into her mouth as she squeezed my mounds with both hands. Unlike the tender manner of most new lovers, I reveled in her rough and dominant style of lovemaking. If this was the way arab women made love to one another, I was ready to be taken.

I placed my hands on the back of her head and pulled her harder against my chest, burying her face between my cleavage. Then I lifted my right knee and pressed it between her splayed legs until it stopped against her wet vulva. She sighed as I began to rock my hips forward and back, stretching the skin of my thigh over her burning pussy.

"Lick me down below," I panted, rolling my hips frantically against her belly. "I need to feel your hot lips on my pussy before I explode."

"Soon enough," she said, blowing softly on my belly as she inched her way down toward my aching snatch.

But when her face reached my shaved mound she paused, feeling my bare skin while she rolled the sides of her cheeks against my soft flesh, kissing me softly at the apex of my slit where my labia merged together at the top of my clit.

"Oh *God* yes," I panted, feeling her warm lips touching my sensitive organ for the first time. "Lick my slit and taste my juices. See how wet you've made me."

She pressed her head a few inches lower, then ran her flat tongue over the length of my folds, lapping up my dripping juices.

"Yes, I can see that," she purred. "You taste much better than goat's milk over rice."

"Yes," I gasped. "Suck on me like a tender lamb. I want to feel your tongue probing every part of me."

Laila curled her tongue as she mashed her face between my legs, pressing it deep into my hole. I grabbed her head, pulling her harder against my cunt, rubbing her face up and down my dripping crease. There was something about the raw act of fucking her naked on the desert sand that I found incredibly arousing. Seeing her wrapped up in her full body covering and suddenly feeling her naked body writhing next to mine took me to new heights of pleasure.

"Mmm," I groaned. "I need you to suck my button now. I want to feel your tongue on my clit. Suck me, Laila."

"Hmm," she purred, moving her head higher up on my slit.

When she surrounded my jewel with her lips I almost came right away, but she seemed to sense my heightened state of arousal and for a long moment she held her head still between my legs while she felt my clit pulsing in her mouth. But when she began rolling her tongue over my nub in slow sensuous arcs, bathing me with her warm saliva, I couldn't help moaning out loud.

"God, yes," I panted. "That feels so good. I needed this so badly."

"Mmm-hmm," Laila nodded, feeling my juices running down her chin and neck.

I could feel my passion beginning to rise and I could have come quite easily from the action of her tongue alone on my raging clit, but what she did next took me to an entirely new level of ecstasy. She slipped two fingers of her right hand into my hole and buried them knuckle deep while stretching her little finger further down my perineum and circling it over my tender anus.

*Fuck me*, I thought. *This girl really knows how to make love to a woman.* I wondered just how much extra-curricular activity went on at night in the privacy of the women's tent while the other men were sleeping. I had no idea, but I was certainly interested in finding out.

When she began curling the two fingers inside me toward my G-spot, I arched my back and began grunting like a wild animal. I couldn't hold back the floodgate of pleasure any longer as my orgasm suddenly overtook me like a freight train.

"Yes, Laila!" I wailed. "I'm going to come, baby. I'm going to come all over your pretty face."

Part of me wanted to warn Laila about my tendency to squirt when I was this wet and worked up, but there wasn't any time. I suddenly felt the muscles of my pussy begin to clench uncontrollably, gushing my pent-up juices all over her slippery face and the soft blanket below us.

"Uhnn," she groaned, seeming to enjoy my orgasm almost as much as I was while she felt the walls of my pussy contracting powerfully on her fingers still deeply embedded inside me.

It must have taken over a full minute for me to stop coming in her arms with the most powerful orgasm I'd had in months. When I finally began to calm down, I collapsed onto the moist blanket and turned to kiss her softly on her lips.

"Thank you," I said, running my fingers through her hair. "I really needed that."

"You seemed to be already pretty worked up. Did you get that excited watching the two girls performing their special dance?"

"I have to admit that I did," I nodded. "I don't know if it was because I was so surprised to see their almost naked figures or because of the way they were moving their bodies, but it didn't just put *Amir* in the mood for some extra nighttime fun."

"So you're attracted to women also?"

"Definitely," I said. "I find women are more adept at satisfying my sexual needs, just as you were a few moments ago. In fact, your special expertise suggests this wasn't the first time you've made love to a woman either."

"Of course not," she smiled. "What do you think we girls do with ourselves in this tent when we're left to our own devices?"

"*All* of you?" I asked, feeling my juices dripping out of my slit once again at the thought of the pretty girls having a group orgy in their little pleasure dome.

"Um-hm," Laila nodded. "There are twenty women but only one penis in our traveling caravan. How *else* do you think we satisfy our needs?"

"What about poor Ali?" I said. "Isn't he ever allowed to get in on the action?"

"Amir would never share the women he's bought and paid for with another man. It would be considered a violation punishable by death if he so much as *looked* at one of us the wrong way. Besides, with his hooked nose and foul-smelling breath, none of us would ever be interested in him that way."

"Well I'm certainly interested in *you* that way," I smiled, threading my thigh again between her legs toward her steaming pussy. "It's my turn to give you the kind of pleasure you just administered to me."

As I began to move my body lower under the blanket, Laila suddenly stopped me, flipping me over onto my back.

"Why don't we *both* share the pleasure this time?" she said, rolling her body on top of me and lifting my left leg while she pressed her wet vulva against my pussy.

"If you insist," I said, smiling up at her.

"I want to watch you this time while I make love to you," she said. "I've never made love to a white girl before."

I smiled at her reference to me as a white girl, even though we were both technically caucasian. But there was no denying that she was considerably darker than me, and I felt a similar sexual attraction to her exotic appearance.

"I'm sure it's not so different from the *other* girls you've fucked," I said, feeling her thick bush pressing against my bald pubis. "Other than being *bare* down there."

"Like a little girl," she grunted, beginning to grind her twat against mine.

"Does that turn you on?" I said, reaching up to pinch her thick nipples as her large breasts swayed overtop my chest.

"Maybe," she said. "I've never felt a woman's bare *kus* before."

"Not even when you experimented when you were younger?"

"Never like *this*," she panted, rocking her hips more rapidly against mine as the sound of our wet pussies slapping together filled the cabin.

"Fuck my girly pussy, Laila," I teased her, recognizing that she was getting turned on by the naughty imagery. "I want to gush all over your furry snatch when we come this time."

"Yes," she huffed, throwing her head back in pleasure as we squeezed each other's breasts tightly with both hands. "You're so wet and slippery down there. I like the feeling of your bare sex against me."

"Would you like to try it yourself sometime?" I said, lifting my hand to her face as she sucked my thumb into her mouth. "Perhaps I can groom you myself while I'm here."

"I'm not sure Amir would appreciate me defiling my body in a way that's not in accordance with muslim custom."

"But you already said he rarely shows interest in you that way. This can just be between the two of us. It will grow back within a few weeks after I leave."

"I'm not sure I'm going to *want* you to leave after this," she said, pulling my leg up higher as she wrapped her arms around it, pulling it tightly between her sweating breasts. "Come with me, Jade. I want to feel your juices mingling with mine when you climax this time."

"*Fuck* yes," I panted, just waiting for her signal. "Grind your pussy against mine. I'm going to cum all over your hairy bush. Here it comes, baby."

"Uhnnn!" Laila suddenly grunted, throwing her head back in rapture, and for the second time that evening, I felt my body pushing over the precipice as another powerful orgasm washed over me and I began squirting jets of liquid all over Laila's twitching pussy.

As we watched each other's bodies convulsing atop one another in the dim light of the tent, I suddenly heard the soft squealing sounds of the other women around us while they pleasured themselves listening to the two of us. Something told me my little caravan excursion was about to stretch out into a longer adventure than I'd planned.

**6**

———

The following morning, Laila and I rose at the break of dawn and got dressed, heading outside for breakfast. Amir was already sitting around the fire pit with a scattering of women preparing the meal. He smiled when he recognized me wearing my thawb and invited the two of us to sit beside him.

"Did you sleep well last night?" he asked me.

"Yes, thank you," I said. "I found it surprisingly comfortable sleeping on the desert sand."

"It's fine as long as you have a thick blanket underneath you. The grains have a way of finding their way into every nook and cranny of your body if you're not careful out here. I prefer to sleep a few inches off the surface myself."

I peered around the circle and recognized the two girls from last night's belly dance performance back in their long robes and head-dresses, baking flatbread atop a curved metal hotplate.

"That smells wonderful, whatever it is you're making," I said, choosing to ignore his none-too-subtle intimation about our sleeping arrangements.

"Fresh flatbread and yogurt," he said, motioning to the tall trees surrounding the encampment. "With a side portion of dates, harvested directly from these palm trees."

I shook my head in awe at the simplicity of their nomadic lifestyle.

"I'm amazed how self-sufficient you can be simply from what you carry with you across the desert."

"Yes," he nodded. "Our goats provide milk, cheese, and yogurt, and the sheep provide all the meat we need. Everything else is supplied by the markets we visit along the fringe of the desert on our caravan route."

"If you don't mind my asking," I said, watching the women flipping the sizzling flatbread over the metal hotplate. "How do you pay for the extra materials? I mean, how do you earn hard *currency* while traveling across the desert?"

"Primarily from our livestock," Amir said. "Our animals are quite prolific, and there's a strong demand for these animals wherever we go. The camels in particular are very valuable commodities since they live for so long and can travel long distances without any water."

I glanced at the herd of camels grazing on the sparse grass and drinking from a wooden trough next to the well.

"And they're able to carry your entire entourage with all of its regalia across the open desert?"

"Yes, they're very strong and hardy animals. We'd never be able to survive out here in the middle of the desert without them."

The girls placed some of the fresh flatbread on individual plates along with bowls of yoghurt and chopped dates, then passed them around the circle to the now fully assembled group.

"Please—eat up," Amir said. "You'll need your strength if you plan to stay with us a little longer. The desert provides, but it also takes away. Your body burns a lot more calories in this sweltering heat."

I watched him dip his flatbread into the bowl of yogurt and pick up the dates with his fingers, and I followed his lead. Everything tasted incredibly fresh and delicious and when I finished my plate, I licked my fingers clean like the rest of the group.

"Oh my God," I sighed. "I could get used to this way of life. Everything is so simple and easy out here. Even the food tastes better than what I'm used to at many five-star restaurants. Talk about farm to table!"

"Are you enjoying it enough to *join* us on the next leg of trip to Algiers?" Amir smiled.

I paused for a moment, remembering what I'd told Hannah before I left my hotel in Marrakesh.

"How far away is it? I told my friends they should expect to hear back from me in a few days."

"It six or seven days by camel ride. But we'll be sleeping out in the open most nights under the stars. We only set up camp when we stop near towns or at the few oases along our route."

"I think I can manage that," I nodded, smiling at Laila remembering how much I enjoyed sleeping next to her on the warm sand last night. "But only if you let me help clean and pack up like everyone else. If I'm going to join your troupe for a few days, I want to feel like a productive member of the tribe."

"If that's what you wish," Amir nodded. "Laila and Ali can look after whatever you need. Will you have any trouble making return travel arrangements from Algiers?"

"It shouldn't be a problem," I said. "As long as it has an international airport."

"Indeed it does," he said, standing to leave. "I'm going to collect my things while Ali begins dismantling the tents. We'll be setting out within the next hour."

I was surprised how quickly the group broke down the camp, neatly arranging all the tent poles, coverings, and contents atop the backs of the camels. When we were ready to leave, we filled our saddlebags with enough water to last us for a few days, then we headed east two-abreast atop the remaining camels. It was quite a sight watching the long train of animals traipsing through the pretty sand ripples lining the undulating desert with nothing to keep us occupied but the shifting shadows of the sun and the howling desert wind.

At nighttime, we circled the camels and livestock around us to provide a modicum of cover from the blowing breeze, then laid down on our individual blankets and woolen duvets to keep ourselves warm. I missed sleeping with Laila and more than once thought about sneaking under the covers to join her, but I dared not risk disturbing Amir and Ali who were sleeping nearby.

After three days, we came upon another small oasis and set up the tents once again to provide a respite against the searing overhead sun. I was thrilled to have another chance to make love to Laila in the relative privacy of our own tent, and after the girls fell asleep, she let me shave her mound with the travel razor I'd packed in my bag, using goat's milk and yogurt as an improvised shaving cream. Afterwards, I licked her clean as she knelt over my face writhing in pleasure while I sucked her bare vulva and clit into my mouth.

But the following morning, something happened that forever changed the course of my dreamlike desert adventure. As I flipped open the flap of our tent to fetch some water from the well, I noticed Fatima, one of the girls who'd performed the belly dance a few nights earlier, lifting a pail out of the well while Ali snuck up behind her, trying to lift her robe while he pulled his erect penis out from under his kaftan. When she ducked aside to evade his unwanted advance, he suddenly lost his balance and tumbled head over heels into the well, screaming all the way down until I heard a loud splash when he fell unconscious at the bottom of the pit. Fatima looked around her with frightened eyes and we she saw me watching, she rushed toward me crying, throwing her arms around me wailing in arabic.

Not wanting her to be discovered, I ushered her quickly into our tent and explained to Laila what had happened. A few seconds later, Amir emerged from his tent alarmed by the commotion, calling out Ali's name. Suspicious when he didn't immediately hear his reply, Amir went back into his tent and came out carrying a flashlight, pointing it down into the well. When he saw Ali's body floating face-down in the pool of water, he turned toward our tent and stormed toward it, angrily flipping open the door covering.

He glared at Laila with steely eyes and a red face, speaking loudly to her in arabic. She said something back to him and shrugged her shoulders, feigning ignorance at what had just transpired. He then approached each of the girls separately, asking them if they knew what had happened. But we got to Fatima, he noticed that she was shaking and he placed his hand under her chin, raising her face to meet his angry gaze. She shook her head, afraid to admit any involvement in the incident, but when he saw her dried tear tracks, he grabbed her hair, dragging her outside.

I looked at Laila bewildered and asked what was going on.

"It's not good," she said, following Amir outside. "Just stay close to me and don't say anything."

"Why don't we just tell him the *truth*?" I said. "That it was an innocent mistake, and that she was just trying to protect herself from Ali's unwanted advance?"

"It doesn't work that way," Laila said, shaking her head. "The scales of justice are tipped greatly in favor of the men in our culture. If she were discovered to have been involved in his death, even incidentally, it wouldn't end well for her."

"So what happens if nobody's willing to talk?"

Laila gritted her teeth as she watched Amir remove his long curved knife from under his belt and place it over the fire. I watched the steel grow red-hot in the flame, then he pulled Fatima's head back and placed the hot blade next to her face. He said something angrily to her and she shook her head frighteningly. Then he forced her mouth open as she slowly extended her tongue. He placed the flat side of the knife on it and she screamed as the blade made a horrible sizzling sound against her flesh.

"What the *fuck*..." I said, stepping toward her trying to intercede.

"Don't," Laila said, grabbing my arm.

"But what he's doing to her in *inhuman*," I protested. "She's just an innocent bystander–"

"This is the way justice is administered in the bedouin culture. When there's a dispute involving a serious crime and no one comes forward to admit guilt, the men administer what is called a *bisha'a*, which is a type of trial by ordeal. The accused person is forced to lick a hot piece of metal and if the tongue shows any sign of a burn or a scar, this is considered a sign of guilt."

"Of *course* her tongue will burn!" I exclaimed. "He just placed a red-hot *knife* against her flesh!"

Amir removed the knife from Fatima's mouth, then doused her tongue with a ladle of fresh water. Then he peered closely at it and threw her down on the sand, cursing at her in their native tongue.

"So what happens now?" I said to Laila.

"If a woman is convicted of this type of crime, she's usually sentenced to death, often by public stoning. But Amir won't do it himself. He'll have to take her to a local tribal court where judgement will be formally handed down and administered by the muslim council."

"You've got to be kidding me," I said, hardly believing what I'd just seen and heard.

Amir turned around noticing that Laila and I had witnessed the entire scene, and walked toward us with flaring nostrils.

"I'm sorry you had to see that," he said to me. "But what Fatima did was a serious crime that cannot be ignored. She will have to face the consequences of her actions. Laila, I want you to coordinate with the other women so we can pack up the camp immediately. We'll be heading out to Algiers as soon as possible to have Fatima's fate decided."

"Wait!" I said, stepping toward Amir in desperation. "I saw the whole thing. She didn't do anything wrong. Ali assaulted her and she was simply trying to defend herself. It was just an accident when he tripped and fell into the well."

Amir paused for a moment as his eyes flashed over my beseeching face, then he shook his head dismissively.

"She must have done something to provoke him," he said. "He couldn't have fallen so easily into the well. We will see what the tribal council decides in Algiers."

"And if she's found guilty?" I said.

"She'll be put to death immediately," Amir said, turning to head back to his tent.

I tried to follow after him, but Laila grabbed my robe, holding me back.

"He can't get away with that!" I said, turning toward her. "It's barbaric!"

"Unfortunately, this is the way of our culture. If a muslim woman is even *suspected* of fraternizing inappropriately with a man other than her husband, Sharia law dictates that she be summarily executed."

"By public *stoning*? What about the guilt of the *man*? What if it's simply one person's word over another?"

"In our culture, the man is always presumed innocent since they have free rein over the women and females are instructed to refrain from fraternizing with anyone other than their husbands."

"I'd hardly refer to what they were doing at the well as *fraternizing*. There's only one place for everybody to collect water out here. It's inevitable that there'll be some form of close contact among such a small group in close quarters. Surely something can be done–"

"I'm afraid we have no control over the situation," Laila said, looking at me sadly. "It's out of our hands now."

----

Later that evening, we stopped in the middle of the desert to rest for the night and grab a bite to eat, and everybody sat around the campfire looking sadly at each other. Nobody dared say a thing, knowing full well what Amir's intentions were. I peered at Fatima, shivering next to the fire as Laila wrapped her arms around her, trying to provide a modicum of comfort. When we dispersed after the meal to make our individual beds in the sand, I took Laila aside and peered into her eyes.

"We can't just let this poor girl be unjustly punished for a crime she didn't commit," I pleaded.

"What would you have us do?" she said. "*He's* the one with all the power and the control. We can't just overpower him and run away."

I crossed my arms and shook my head at the absurdity of the situation.

Laila paused for a long moment, then looked up at me through narrowed eyelids.

"There might be *another* way we can extricate ourselves from this unfortunate situation," she said. "What if we steal away in the middle of the night and take all the camels with us? He won't be able to follow us, and he'll run out of water long before he gets to Algiers."

"But he'd *die* out here in the middle of the desert without any food or water!" I said.

"It's either him or Fatima," she said. "Who do you think is more deserving to live? The innocent girl who did nothing other than try to protect herself from a violent rape, or the man who summarily judges her based on his ludicrous code of honor?"

"But he seemed to be so–"

"Sophisticated, and a man of the world?" Laila said. "There are two sides to every man, and this one is no different. He may have been educated in your country, but I assure you that his morals and underlying character have been indelibly shaped by his family affiliations and the culture of his tribe. Are you prepared to do what has to be done?"

I paused for a moment, trying to think of any other conceivable options, then I grudgingly nodded. I couldn't believe that my exciting desert adventure had suddenly turned into a deadly serious conspiracy where two people's lives lay in the balance.

**7**

─────────

Laila and I waited until we heard Amir snoring under his blanket, then she roused each of the girls, telling them about our escape plan. Everybody got up and tiptoed through the sand toward the camels, then we tethered them together and mounted them carefully, slowly leading them away from the rest of the livestock herd.

"What about the goats and the sheep?" I whispered into Laila's ear, who I'd paired up with on the lead camel.

"We haven't got time to gather them together and we can't risk disturbing Amir–"

Suddenly I heard a man's voice yelling in the darkness, and I turned to see Amir rising from his sleep and begin chasing after us. Laila kicked the sides of her camel and the whole train burst into a gallop, creating a dusty trail behind us. Amir screamed and shook his fists as he tried to catch up with us, but he was no match for the fleet group of camels, and within seconds he disappeared behind us in the thick cloud of dust.

"*Jesus*," I said to Laila after we'd put a few hundred meters between us. "Are you sure this is going to work? Now we're *all* unwitting accomplices in this sordid affair."

"We're at least three days' camel ride to the nearest village on the outskirts of the desert," she said. "It would take three times as long to cover that distance on foot. There's no way he can survive in this stifling heat for that long without water."

"And the *rest* of the animals?"

"They're a bit more hardy. We can come back for them a little later when the coast is clear."

I peered behind me to see the other girls following behind Laila's camel in single file.

"What will you and the others do now that you're no longer part of Amir's caravan?"

"I plan to send them back home to their families when we get to Algiers. This many camels will fetch more than enough money to arrange safe transit to their home ports."

"What about *you*? Won't people be looking for Amir at some point if he doesn't show up? Surely his family–"

"I plan to be long gone before anyone raises any suspicions. I've got some extended family in the Andalusia region of Spain where I can lay low for a while. I'm more worried about you. Did you tell anyone that you were going to join Amir's caravan? The local authorities won't take kindly to finding out you might have been involved somehow in his disappearance."

I paused for a moment trying to remember the details of the message I'd sent Hannah before I set off to see Amir at the cafe.

"Just my best friend back home," I said. "I gave her Amir's name and told her to alert the U.S. Embassy in Morocco if she didn't hear from me in a week or so."

"You'd best clear out of this region at your earliest opportunity then," she said. "It will be difficult for the local police to hold you to account once you're out of the country."

"But I didn't do anything–" I began to protest.

"We're *all* implicated now. If they find Amir's dead body, they could trace any one of us to the deed. Technically, we'd all be considered accessories to the crime."

"Christ," I sighed, feeling my heart suddenly racing at the implications of what we'd done. "What the hell have I gotten myself into?"

"Don't worry," Laila said, patting my thigh reassuringly. "The desert soon buries anything that doesn't move. He'll never be found, and we'll all be long gone before anyone raises any suspicions."

"What about *Ali*?" I said. "Won't another caravan eventually find his dead body at the bottom of the well?"

"Perhaps, but with any luck it should be pretty decomposed by then. Whoever finds him will have difficulty connecting him to Amir's disappearance."

Suddenly I had a queasy feeling in the pit of my stomach, and I wrapped my arms around Laila's midsection, resting my head against her back as I peered at the never-ending hills of red sand dunes.

"How will you find your way through this wasteland all the way to Algiers?" I asked.

"The shadows of our camels will guide the way. It shows which way the sun is pointed, and all we have to do is head east and north until we reach the Mediterranean coast. From there, it should be easy to track our way to the city."

"You're a pretty smart cookie," I smiled, clutching her closely. "These girls were pretty lucky to have such a strong leader to get them out of this predicament."

"I hope they'll be happier now that they're freed from Amir's grip," she nodded. "But I'll be sad to see some of them go. I've grown quite attached to these girls after all this time we've spent together in the desert."

---

Twelve hours later, the sun began to fade over the horizon and Laila stopped the group to set up camp, laying out our bedrolls amongst the circle of resting camels. Most of our food was still packed in the saddlebags and we enjoyed a peaceful dinner of rice, cooked legumes, and sweet dates. Everybody seemed much more relaxed around the campfire, chatting and giggling amongst them-selves in their native arabic.

When we finished eating, we retired to our beds but soon discov-ered in our haste to leave the previous camp that we hadn't brought enough bedrolls and blankets for everybody to sleep on separately. Taking charge of the situation as always, Laila nestled the blankets together then we lay down as a group, not bothering to take off our robes to protect ourselves against the encroaching desert chill. It didn't take long for everyone to snuggle together for extra warmth, and before long I felt the telltale sensation of someone's fingers sliding up the bottom of my smock.

I turned around and saw Fatima smiling at me in the soft moon-light, and she leaned in to kiss me. Whether she was trying to express her gratitude for my helping to save her or she was just curious about feeling my fair skin, I couldn't be sure. But either way, I was happy to accommodate her newfound intimate interest in me. As we began to kiss more passionately, intertwining our tongues and pressing our bodies together, she pulled my robe up over my hips, caressing the outside of my thighs and my round buttocks.

But when her hand curved around to my bald pubis, she gasped and uttered something in arabic. I heard Laila reply to her in the darkness on my other side, and Fatima giggled as Laila rolled over to sandwich me between the two of them. Suddenly I had two pairs of hands caressing my body from both sides, and I moaned as they slipped their fingers between my thighs, caressing my vulva from two ends. I pulled Fatima's smock higher, feeling her fluffy bush caressing my bare mound, and I groaned in her mouth as her fingers found my pleasure spot and she began rubbing my clit in soft circular motions. But when I felt Laila's fingers press inside my slit and begin finger-fucking me from behind, I began rocking my hips, moaning more loudly.

When the rest of the girls began to realize what the three of us were up to, it didn't take long for the entire group to devolve into a moaning, slithering mass of naked bodies writhing under the thick jumble of cotton robes and woolen blankets. I pulled Fatima's dress all the way over her shoulders and squeezed her bare tits while she played with my clit and moaned into my mouth. It didn't take long for the combined action of her manipulation of my clit and Laila's caressing of my vulva to bring me to the brink of pleasure. As the two women pressed their bodies tightly against mine, I felt my orgasm overtake me and I jerked my body spastically, gushing all over the two girl's hands.

Fatima said something again to Laila, and she responded in arabic, then Fatima moved her body down closer to my midsection, apparently fascinated by my unusual bare mound and my propensity to squirt when I came. When she spread my legs apart, the other girls stopped what they were doing to peer at my dripping bald pussy glistening in the moonlight. Before I knew it, I had a clutch of pretty young girls kissing and probing every part of my body as Laila propped her head up on her elbow, smiling at me.

"Holy shit," I said to her. "You weren't kidding about how these girls like to stay entertained when the men aren't around. I think I've died and gone to *heaven*!"

"Welcome to the club, baby," Laila said, leaning in to kiss me as I felt a deluge of tongues and fingers converging on me while they sucked and nibbled on every square inch of my body. The multitude of erotic sensations soon brought me to the edge again, and I screamed in ecstasy as my whole body convulsed in another intense orgasm. Fatima suddenly pulled away from licking me while the whole group watched my pussy twitching and squirting my juices all over her face and my bare legs.

"Oh my God," I purred to Laila, after I came down from my high. "I could seriously get used to this. Are you *sure* you want to disband this group of horny young vixens?"

"Not for a couple more *days* at least," she smiled, rolling her body on top of me, grinding her dripping mound into my pliant face.

As I began to eat her pussy, the girls swarmed over top of me like a bunch of buzzing bees, rubbing their wet pussies and hairy bushes over whatever open flesh they could find on my pinned body. One of them positioned herself between my legs, pulling her pussy tight against mine and began scissoring me in a prone 'X' position while some of the other girls sucked my nipples and toes. Before we all fell asleep in a steaming pile of sweaty flesh, I must have come at least a dozen more times sucking, caressing, and fucking every one of the girls in one position or another.

As I lay on the soft desert sand surrounded by the bevy of beautiful women, I looked up toward the sky at the cloud of stars shimmering above me like a blanket of sparkling sequins. Suddenly the troubles at the previous camp seemed a hundred miles away, and I smiled at one of Amir's last comments to me. *The desert gives and takes away indeed*, I thought, as I drifted off to sleep.

8

For the next couple of days, we rode slowly through the desert, stopping periodically to relieve ourselves and snack on dried dates and flatbread. At night we reassembled the blankets in one large group and resumed our wild orgy under the stars until we all fell asleep, completely spent and satiated. I almost regretted seeing the dusty buildings on the edge of Algiers as we approached the city from the west, and I squeezed Laila's tummy softly to express how much I dreaded the thought of leaving her.

She parked me and the rest of the girls out of sight behind a tall dune so as not to arouse suspicion, then she led the camels three at a time into the local trading market, where she sold them at a relative bargain. It was approaching dusk by the time she returned to fetch all of us, then she took us down to the docks to arrange clandestine travel for each of the girls to return to their original towns. She gave each of them enough money to pay for the remainder of their passage, then the two of us walked along the waterfront while we talked about our next steps.

"That looked easier than I *thought* it would be," I said after all of the girls had boarded their individual ships to head home.

"These merchant seamen will transport anything for the right amount of money," she nodded.

"What about the harbormaster? How did you manage to bypass all the usual paperwork and document controls?"

"The protocols for onboarding and offboarding passengers on cargo ships are far looser on the North African coast than in Europe or America," she said, sliding her fingers and her thumb together to indicate the payment of a bribe. "Nobody seems to have a problem looking the other way as long as you grease their palms a little bit."

"How can you be sure the ships' captains will *complete* the transaction now that they've already been paid?"

"Because I promised to have them paid an *equivalent* amount once the girls safely complete their journey on the other end."

"All of this is made possible from the selling of a few *camels*?"

"Um-hm," Laila nodded. "Amir paid to take us *away* from our homes, now he's indirectly arranged to pay for them to get back."

"I'm not sure this was exactly the way he envisioned it," I frowned, trying not to think about how much he was suffering in the middle of the desert without any food or water.

"I suppose not," she chuckled. "Though I don't think *any* of this went down the way he imagined."

"So what now?" I said, peering over the Mediterranean as the sun began to set on the horizon.

"We pretend like none of this ever happened," she said. "You go back home to America, and I slip across the sea to start a new life in Spain. It shouldn't take long for us to put all of this unpleasantness behind us."

"It hasn't *all* been unpleasant," I said, grabbing her hand and pulling her into an alley to give her a long, passionate kiss. "I'll have far more *happy* memories to hold onto than this one unfortunate affair."

"Mmm," she nodded, pressing her body up tightly against me.

"Well isn't *this* a happy little reunion," a familiar man's voice suddenly cackled from the shadows.

Laila and I swung around to see Amir blocking the exit to the alley, brandishing his glinty curved knife.

"I knew the two of you were up to no good the moment I saw you ogling each other during the belly dance performance in my tent. And now it's time for the lot of you to be held to account for your transgressions. Right after you tell me what you've done with the other girls."

I stared at Amir with my mouth agape in a mix of shock and confusion.

"How–"

"Did I manage to get all this way on foot?" he said. "Your first mistake was leaving me with all the livestock. Their milk and meat can sustain a man for a long time in the desert. Plus, I was lucky enough to catch another passing caravan after a couple of days. If you two hadn't dawdled taking your time crossing the desert, you might have made a clean getaway by now." He paused, running his eyes up and down our bodies. "Of course, I didn't have any *other* distractions encouraging me to pause for a little entertainment in the evenings."

"So I suppose you've alerted the elders by now and arranged for us to be taken before the council to be properly punished?" Laila said, stepping in front of me and placing her arm around me protectively.

"In due course," he said. "First I needed to *find* you before you slipped away. I'm afraid your fate, along with the rest of my little harem, has already been sealed, Laila." Then he turned toward me, clucking his tongue. "As for my pretty Western friend, I'm sure we can find a dark prison somewhere in the bowels of this medieval city to let her rot away the rest of her miserable life."

Amir lurched forward, placing the knife under Laila's neck.

"Now *tell* me where the rest of the girls are!" he sneered.

Suddenly, Laila reared back, kicking Amir as hard as she could between his legs and he hunched over, dropping the knife onto the ground. She quickly picked it up and before he could regain his composure, she sliced it across the front of his neck in one quick and silent motion. He clutched his throat, looking at us with wild eyes, then he fell to his knees, collapsing onto the cobblestone pavement. As a thick pool of blood seeped out of his jugular vein onto the darkened stones, the life slowly drained out of his eyes, and he suddenly became still.

"Holy *fuck*, Laila," I gasped. "You *killed* him!"

"It was either him or us," she said nonchalantly. "He got what was coming to him."

"What the hell do we do now?" I said, looking around frantically to see if anyone else had witnessed the scene. "We can't just *leave* him here. He can be traced back to us."

Laila paused for a moment as she peered around the wharf to get her bearings, then she nodded toward a nearby dock.

"We'll have to drag him to the edge of the jetty and dump him into the water. There's no one around and it's dark enough for us to dispose of the body. Grab a leg and help me pull him toward the pier."

I shook my head, hardly believing how fast our plan had unraveled and wondering what would happen if anyone saw us. But I knew Laila was right. Between the front desk attendant at my hotel in Morocco and my email trail to Hannah, there was more than enough circumstantial evidence to connect me to Amir's disappearance. The best chance for both of us to get away before the police caught wind of any malfeasance was to dispose of the body and exit as quickly as possible.

We each grabbed one of Amir's legs and after checking to make sure the coast was clear, we carefully dragged his body the thirty feet or so across the narrow roadway lining the wharf and dropped his lifeless body into the murky water at the edge of the pier. We watched his body slowly sink into the deep water, then we ducked into another alley to decide what to do next.

"So what do we do now?" I said, shivering from a combination of shock and the encroaching chill.

"You've still got your travel bag and papers," she said, nodding toward my clutch case. "You need to get changed back into your Western clothes as soon as possible and catch the earliest flight out of the country. With any luck, you'll be long gone before anyone finds any evidence of foul play. I'll pay for safe passage to the continent and try to slip into Spain undetected. Right now, we both have to get the hell out of here."

"Okay," I said, wrapping my arms around my body to keep myself from shaking. "But will I ever see you again? I hate leaving you this way..."

"It's best we make a clean break," she said, pulling me close against her breast. "We don't want anyone connecting us together after this. You'll be fine. I'll think of you whenever I'm sleeping alone under my woolen blanket."

I paused for a moment, darting my eyes across her pretty face. I hated the idea of leaving so abruptly, but I knew we didn't have any other choice. I opened my travel bag and scribbled my address on a piece of paper.

"This is my address back home in America," I said, handing her the paper. "Just do me one favor. Write me once you get situated in Spain and send me your address. It'll be safe to see you again once this all settles down. I'd love to be able to stay in touch."

"Okay," Laila said, folding the paper and tucking it away into her robe. "But you need to go now. I want you to catch the earliest flight out in the morning. I'll contact you once I get settled."

She leaned in towards me, clasping the sides of my head with both hands.

"This has been the most amazing adventure of my life," she said. "I'll never forget these few days we've shared together, my beautiful sweet, American girl. Safe travels, my love. We'll talk again soon."

Then she turned and walked briskly down the wharf into the inky darkness without looking back. I watched her robes billowing in the cool evening breeze until she disappeared in the mist, then I changed out of my thawb in the darkness of the alley and put my Western clothes back on, hailing a cab to the airport. I was lucky enough to catch the seven a.m. flight to Paris with a connecting flight to Chicago later that day. As my jet lifted off the runway and turned north over the Mediterranean Sea, I peered down at the wide expanse of sparking blue waves, smiling at how it reminded me of the golden sand ripples in the desert.

---

After I got home, a few months passed without hearing from Laila, and I began to fear that she might not have made it out of the North Africa. But when I received an airmail letter postmarked Seville, Spain, I tore it open and read the contents breathlessly.

> *Jade,*
>
> *I hope this letter finds you well and fully recovered from our little desert adventure. I've thought of you often since we departed so suddenly in Algiers and miss having your smooth, supple body snuggling up next to me. You may be happy to know that I've grown quite accustomed to your Western-style grooming habits and I always think of you whenever I touch myself on dark, lonely nights. If ever you find the time to come visit me, I've enclosed my new address below.*
>
> *Love always, Laila*

*Oh my God*, I exhaled, happy to hear that she'd made it out safely. And the fact that she still had fond memories of our time together and even thought of me whenever she touched herself intimately made my heart dance and my panties moisten. As I sat in my chair rereading her letter over and over again and smelling the delicate scent of jasmine and lemongrass infused in the paper, my fingers trailed a path down between my thighs as I separated my legs slowly.

*Maybe this won't be the end of my arabian adventure after all*, I smiled to myself.

# VOLUME FOUR

---

## THE ORIENT EXPRESS

**1**

———

Entering the Gare du Nord terminal in Paris, I peered up at the soaring glass ceiling enclosing the cavernous central hall. Knowing it was the busiest train station in Europe, I held my arms close to my sides to protect my valuables from ever-present pickpockets. Designed by the famous French architect Jacques Hittorff in the Beaux-Arts style of the mid-nineteenth century, I marveled at the ornate cast-iron pillars supporting the enormous structure. It was a clear sunny day, and bright beams of light angled through the windows, illuminating the shiny trains resting beside their platforms. I glanced at my ticket and headed toward gate eighteen, where I was about to embark on a five-day/four-night tour of Europe aboard the most famous train in history.

Passing through the pastoral countryside of southern France and the deep valleys of the Swiss Alps, the Orient Express wound its way through seven countries, terminating at the gateway to Asia in Istanbul. With its storied past and recently refurbished equipment, I was looking forward to being pampered in the five-star dining car and my own private cabin on the traveling caravan. I'd heard so much about the glamor and prestige of the famous line, and as I approached the black-and-gold vintage train cars sitting by the platform, my heart began to flutter in excitement.

Near the front of the train, a porter wearing a brass-buttoned uniform and white gloves checked my ticket then helped me up the steps into the forward compartment. When I stepped into the carriage, I was shocked at how opulent it looked. The main salon was decorated with sumptuous velour upholstery, polished cherry wood paneling, crystal lanterns, and giant windows framed with royal blue curtains. More beautiful than any luxury hotel I'd ever stayed in, the setting literally took my breath away.

"Oh my God," I muttered to the porter. "It's like I've entered a whole different world. This isn't like any train I've been on before."

"That's a common reaction from our first-time travelers," he said. "Our owners have spared no expense in recreating the feel and authenticity of the original train. If you like the main seating area, I think you'll be very pleased with your cabin. I see you've chosen the grand suite."

"Yes," I nodded. "I figured if I'm going to splurge on a luxury train ride, I might as well go all the way."

"I think you'll find the extra space is quite comfortable. You've got three large viewing windows, your own sitting area, and a large private washroom."

"Well if it's anything like the rest of the train," I said, tracing my fingers along the luxurious upholstery as we passed by the four-person seating booths, "I'm sure I'll be delighted."

We walked through two more carriages down a narrow passageway then he stopped by a polished wooden door with a brass handle.

"Here we are, madam," he said, opening the door and motioning for me to enter ahead of him with his gloved hand.

I stepped into the anteroom and gasped out loud. The entire chamber gleamed in a mixture of knurled walnut paneling, crystal light fixtures, and suede seat coverings. The king-size bed was festooned with plush Egyptian-cotton linens and blue-and-gold embroidered cushions, with outside light streaming in the huge viewing windows lining the entire side of the compartment."

"It's...*breathtaking*," I said, hardly believing my eyes. "It's the most beautifully bedroom I've ever seen. Is this all just for *me*?"

"Yes, ma'am," the porter said, opening another door next to the sitting area. "As is this private ensuite bathroom."

I peered inside the washroom, my eyes opening as wide as saucers.

Almost every surface was covered in polished alabaster marble. From the large, glass-enclosed walk-in shower to the brass taps on the vanity to the separately enclosed toilet, everything reeked of first class. It even had a separate, sit-down makeup table, replete with Lalique crystal lamps.

"If I ever get to heaven," I sighed. "This is what I hope it looks like."

"I'm glad you like it, ma'am," the porter said. "As part of your grand suite package, you also have twenty-four-hour butler service, private in-cabin dining, and free-flowing champagne for the duration of your trip."

"Okay, so *wait*," I chuckled. "Are you sure I'm not *already* in heaven?"

The porter set my bags down on the floor and backed up toward the entrance door.

"Please, make yourself comfortable," he said. "If you need anything at all, press this button and your butler will call upon you shortly. Dinner in the main cabin will be served starting at seven p.m. But the bar is open twenty-four-seven. I hope you enjoy your stay with us."

"I only wish it could be longer," I smiled, discreetly handing him a ten-Euro tip. "Are you sure this train doesn't go any further than Istanbul?"

"For now, at least," he said. "That's the end of the line. But I've heard rumors our operator is considering extending the service into the Middle East and beyond, following the path of the Silk Road used by Marco Polo."

"Now that would be a truly memorable journey," I nodded. "It *is* called the Orient Express, after all."

After the porter left, I unpacked my bags and changed into something more befitting the glamorous setting, then I went into the washroom to touch up my makeup. When I finished, I looked at myself in the full-length dressing mirror and nodded in satisfaction. I'd chosen to wear a form-fitting, mid-length red silk dress with black leather Christian Louboutin heels that showcased my long, well-toned legs. As the train began to pull out of the station, I pulled the door to my cabin closed behind me and headed toward the bar car.

*Let's see if the guests on this caravan are as interesting as the rest of the train,* I smiled.

When I reached the bar car, I noticed a scattering of passengers chatting in the plush velour booths beside the window. I peered up toward the bar and saw an elegant woman sitting alone on one of the stools with her back toward me. She was wearing a cream-colored lace embroidered dress, and I glanced down to see her slender and shapely legs crossed under the brass railing. I walked up to the counter and smiled at the bartender.

"Good evening, madam," he said. "Would you like something to drink?"

"Yes, thank you," I said, looking at the row of liquor bottles lining the wall behind him. I was about to order a Grey Goose martini when I noticed the woman was cradling a tall tulip glass filled with a pale yellow mixture with bubbles rising to the surface. "I think I'll have what the lady's having."

"Dom Perignon it *is*," he nodded. He pulled a magnum off the shelf and carefully loosened the cork to let out the air before tilting the bottle over a carved crystal glass and sliding it toward me.

"May I join you?" I said, glancing at the lady sitting next to me.

"By all means," she smiled, uncrossing her legs and lifting her knee over her opposite leg.

As I sat down and turned my stool to face her, I noticed for the first time her plunging neckline and deep cleavage pressing her plump breasts together. She had long auburn-colored hair, styled with curly ringlets framing her pretty face. She looked to be around my age, but with slightly darker skin. She had a vaguely European look to her, and as she peered at me with her smoldering eyes, I felt my panties beginning to moisten.

"Cheers," I said, holding up my glass.

"Santé," she replied, clinking her champagne flute against mine.

"This is quite the experience, isn't it?" I said, looking around me at the ornately decorated cabin.

"Is this your first time?" she said with a French accent.

"Aboard the Orient Express? Yes. How about you?"

"This is my third trip. I find the experience to be quite stimulating."

"Are you referring to the amazing views?" I said, peering outside the window behind her at the passing Paris streetscape.

"That, and you meet the most interesting people on this voyage," she nodded. "We're all captive on this little train while we're traveling, and you get to know everybody pretty well."

"I can imagine," I said, flittering my eyes downward to take in her voluptuous figure. Her nipples were pressing hard against the sheer lacy fabric, and I crossed my legs, feeling my pussy growing wetter by the moment.

"Where are you from?" she said, peering down at my exposed thighs as she took another sip of her champagne. "You don't have a British, Aussie, or Kiwi accent, so I'm guessing you're either American or Canadian."

"I'm from Chicago," I said, chuckling at her deductive powers. "How about you?"

"I'm from the Alsace region of France, near the German border."

"I thought I recognized some Continental genes in your appearance. You're very pretty."

"As are you," she said, placing her hand on my knee and sliding it softly up my thigh. "You American girls always take such good care of your bodies. I like how you're so toned and fit. We Europeans take a much more laissez-faire approach to our fitness."

"Thank you," I said, feeling the soft hairs on the top of my thighs standing erect as her hand caressed my skin. Suddenly I wished I'd remembered to shave the full length of my legs more recently.

"I'm Jade, by the way," I said, extending my hand to distract attention from the other passengers glancing at us nearby.

"Adele," she said, clasping my hand and squeezing it gently. Even the touch of her hand against mine sent a chill through my spine.

"So, what do people do to pass their time for five straight days on this little chugger?" I asked, trying to regain my composure.

"Besides eating and drinking most of the time?" she chuckled. "Most people curl up with a book next to the window to watch the passing scenery. But at meal time, everybody gets together in the dining car, where we can mingle a bit more comfortably."

"Speaking of drinking," I said, realizing the bartender had already replenished my glass three times while I'd been talking. "I'm already starting to feel a bit tipsy. If I don't get off this bar stool soon, I'm afraid I'll fall over. I think curling up in one of those comfortable booths by the window is just what I need about now. Would you care to join me?"

"Perhaps a little later," she said, rising up from her stool. "Right now I need to make a trip to the ladies' room. But I look forward to meeting you again soon, lovely Jade."

While I watched her head down the hall toward the public lavatory, I couldn't help staring at her tight ass in her form-fitting dress as her buttocks flexed sexily under the sheer lacy fabric. I staggered to the nearest seat a few feet from the bar and rested my head against the backrest as I peered out over the passing landscape of the French countryside. I felt surprisingly lightheaded for only having had three drinks. Whether it was from drinking on an empty stomach or from the passing vineyards rushing by my window or from the excitement of meeting this mysterious and sexy woman, I couldn't be sure. Either way, my trip aboard the Orient Express had gotten off to an exciting start.

As I rubbed my thighs together thinking of the way she'd touched me, Adele suddenly passed by me and took a seat four booths down, sitting on the edge of the aisle, facing toward me. At first, I was disappointed that she hadn't decided to join me in my section, and I wondered if she just hadn't noticed me with my back turned away from her. But when she peered up at me and smiled, I nodded to acknowledge her reaction. I didn't want to intrude on her personal space, but what she did next left little doubt that she was far from being done with me. She lifted her left leg and placed her foot on top of the seat cushion next to her and hiked up her dress a few inches, revealing her bare, glistening pussy. Then she placed her hand between her thighs and began circling her fingers over the top of her slit.

I looked around me to see if anyone else could see what she was doing, but fortunately all the other guests were sitting snugly against their windows, either reading a book or quietly gazing outside. Because we were the only two people in the compartment sitting on the outside edges of our booths, we had a direct view of each other. At first, I sat dumbfounded watching her play with herself, shocked at her audacious display of carnality, but as my panties grew wetter and wetter watching her, I looked around me to make sure the coast was clear, then I lifted my ass off my seat and pulled my panties down over my ankles and placed them inside my purse. Then I pushed my hand under my dress and slid my fingers up my thighs until they reached my sopping sex.

When they touched my burning clit, I gasped from how turned on I was, and Adele smiled at me from the other end of the cabin. I didn't have the courage to hike up my dress the way she had for fear that a passing porter or passenger might catch me in the act, but it certainly didn't stop me from fingering myself furiously while I watched the sexy French woman touching herself. Adele spread her legs further apart, exposing her bald, glistening snatch, then she thrust two fingers deep into her hole as she began finger-fucking herself with her flexing arm muscles.

I could hear the rumbling of the train as it passed speedily over the tracks, and the imagery of our pleasing ourselves in this strange but exciting public place elevated my passion even higher. As I felt my pleasure beginning to radiate throughout my body, I couldn't help squirming in my seat and pinching my nipples with my free hand. Apparently, Adele was equally turned on by the erotic scene, with her mouth beginning to part from her own rising pleasure while she stared back at me from across the aisle.

I could tell that she was nearing the crest of her pleasure as her face began to flush and her hand began moving more vigorously in and out of her dripping pussy. I began to feel my own orgasm rapidly approaching, and I pressed my hand harder up against my burning clit, unaware that my own dress was now hiked up near the top of my thighs, exposing my own bald and glistening vulva. Suddenly, a deep flush rolled over both of our faces as we began jerking spastically in our seats with our bodies consumed in a powerful simultaneous orgasm. We didn't take our eyes off each other the whole time while we gazed at one another with our mouths wide agape.

It must have taken a full thirty seconds for my contractions to subside, and when my orgasm finally receded, I slumped in my seat with my legs still spread wide apart. It was only then that I noticed in horror that someone *else* had been watching us the whole time. Just a few feet behind Adele in the next compartment sat a young teenage girl peering through the crack in the seats with wide eyes, staring directly toward me. I closed my legs immediately and pulled my dress down over my thighs, then squiggled over closer to the window, shocked and humiliated. As I looked out the glass with my heart beating a million miles an hour, I felt my juices slowly trickling out of my wet pussy while I reflected on the exciting moment Adele and I had shared in the open compartment of the famed transcontinental express.

**2**

———————

After I'd had a chance to calm down, I rested my head against my seat cushion and peered out over the passing landscape. The neatly spaced rows of vineyards provided a hypnotic counterpoint to the stimulating view of Adele playing with herself across the cabin, and before long I felt my eyelids grow heavy as I began to nod off. But just before I was about to pass out, I caught some movement from Adele's end of the carriage. The girl who'd been spying on us suddenly stood up and began sidestepping her way out of her cubicle.

She looked to be of middle eastern origin, with caramel-colored skin and large brown doe eyes. Her hair was pulled back into a pony-tail, and with her high cheekbones and puffy lips, I was immediately struck by how beautiful she was. She could have easily passed for a young fashion model, but when she stepped out into the aisle, I gasped. Wearing a mid-length plaid skirt and matching green blazer with bow tie, it was obvious that she was just a schoolgirl. I couldn't make out how old she was, but from the shape of her body barely concealed by the short skirt and her bulging white blouse under her blazer, she certainly looked all grown up to me.

When she caught me staring at her, she winked at me playfully, then turned away and began walking toward the opposite end of the compartment. She hesitated for a moment outside the door to the public lavatory, then hiked up one side of her skirt, revealing an exquisitely toned and completely bare ass. Before entering the restroom, she glanced back at me and tilted her head, beckoning for me to follow her.

*What the fuck?* I thought to myself, shaking my head at my incredible streak of luck. *Was everybody on this train oversexed and ready to jump on top of anyone they happened to bump into?*

I paused for a moment, contemplating my predicament. I didn't even know if the girl was of legal age to have sex. I took a closer look at her booth and saw a middle-aged man wearing a neatly pressed suit sitting close to the aisle. He had her same dark complexion and was reading a newspaper, seemingly oblivious to the sexually charged energy in the room. It seemed obvious to me that he was the girl's father or guardian, and I suspected he wouldn't look kindly upon my taking advantage of his daughter's youthful ardor.

But why was she dressed so provocatively, and why did she want me to join her in the lavatory? Had anyone *else* in the compartment noticed her libidinous display and was watching to see if I would join her? I glanced around the cabin and noticed that everyone was either staring outside their windows or had their heads bowed down tapping on their phones or laptop computers. If I was going to do something, I'd have to act soon before her father became suspicious of her extended absence.

Feeling the moisture beginning to accumulate once again between my thighs, I raised myself out of my seat and began walking in the direction of the lavatory. When I passed Adele's booth, she peered up at me and smiled. With her body facing away from the direction of the girl's booth immediately behind her, I had no idea if she was aware of the special connection I'd made with the other passenger. But from the look of her swelling nipples in her form-fitting dress, she still appeared to be charged up from our earlier encounter.

As I passed by the girl's cubicle, her father glanced up from his newspaper and we nodded politely toward each other. Not wanting him to catch onto my lascivious intent, when I reached the closed door of the lavatory, I ducked into the adjacent cubbyhole near the train's exit door and leaned against the side wall with my heart pounding in my chest.

*Holy shit!* I cursed under my breath. *Was I really contemplating going through with this? What if we were found out? What if someone else needed to use the washroom while we were both inside?* It would be impossible to extricate ourselves without the other person knowing what we were up to in there. What if her *father* needed to use the washroom while we were busy making love to each other inside?

For a moment, I contemplated returning to my seat and dispensing with the whole idea. But the streams of lubrication running down the inside of my thighs was giving me second thoughts. When would I ever have a chance like this again? It's not every day that you get propositioned by a comely young schoolgirl to have a secret tryst with her on board the most famous train in the world.

*Fuck it*, I hissed, stepping forward to the lavatory door and tapping on it gently. Seconds later, the door opened a few inches and the girl peered out at me. I hesitated, not knowing what to say, then she reached out and pulled me inside, locking the door behind us. I looked at her with wide eyes, wondering what I had gotten myself into.

"Are you sure you want to do this?" I mumbled. "What about your father? How old are–"

The girl suddenly pulled me toward her, thrusting her tongue into my mouth while she pressed her hips and breasts against mine. When I felt her warm body against me and her tongue sliding over my teeth, everything else melted away as my hands began roaming over her curvy body. She tried to hike up my dress over my hips and press her hand between my legs, but I knew we didn't much time for the usual foreplay. I placed my hands under her armpits and lifted her ass up onto the edge of the sink, pressing her torso against the mirror. Then I lifted her plaid skirt and buried my face in her moist pussy.

At this point I no longer cared if she was of legal age. I intended to give her the best head she'd ever had, if indeed she'd ever had oral sex of *any* kind before. She had a narrow patch of pubic hair on her otherwise hairless mound, and as I sucked her swollen clit into my mouth, she placed her heels on top of the vanity and pulled my head hard into her cunt as she began squirming and moaning in delight. I was tempted to lift my hand to her mouth to muffle her squeals, but I figured the clattering of the train's metal wheels on the tracks was sufficient to drown out our mutual sounds of ecstasy.

Instead, I reached up and began unbuttoning her blouse, threading my hand inside her placket and squeezing her firm tits. I was surprised how large they were for a girl her age, and as her gushing juices began to coat the front of my face while I ate her out, I hooked my thumbs under the bottom of her bra and forced it up over top of her bosom. When I felt her bare melons filling my hands, I moaned along with her in rising pleasure. My own clit was throbbing between my outspread legs in my squatted position, and I would have loved to have ground it against her tender pussy, but I knew it would be difficult in the tight confines of the train lavatory to find enough room to properly scissor our bodies together.

*Besides*, I was enjoying eating the young girl's pussy and listening to her squeals of pleasure as I ravished her dripping cunny like it was my last meal. As she squirmed wildly on the edge of the counter, she placed her hands over the back of my head and began to dig her nails into my scalp. It was becoming apparent to me that she was nearing the crest of her pleasure, and as her squeals turned to impassioned whimpering, I placed her teats between my thumbs and forefingers and pinched her nipples firmly as she dug her nails ever-harder into my flesh.

Just when I thought I wouldn't be able to stand the pain any longer, her body suddenly lurched and she humped forward, jerking spastically over my head while she uttered a deep guttural moan. I held her close as I felt her juices pouring out of her hole and down over the front of my chin until she stopped heaving overtop of me. When she finally stopped moving, I pulled my face away from her pussy and she pushed herself off the edge of the counter and turned toward the mirror to pull her bra back in place and button herself back up. Then she turned around and glanced at me, reaching for the lock on the door.

"Thank you," she said with a faint Arabic accent, then she opened the door a crack and peered outside to make sure the coast was clear.

"*Wait*," I said, grasping her hand. "Can I see you again?"

"I better return to my seat before my father gets suspicious. Maybe if you can find a way to pass me your room number..."

I smiled at the girl and squeezed her hand as she left the compartment, then I closed and latched the door behind her. I'd never felt such a thrill in all my life, and I had matters of my own that needed attending to. Whether it was the possibility of having had sex with an underage girl, or the fact that we'd done it only a few feet away from her waiting father or the sheer audacity of having sex with a stranger in the train's public lavatory, I still felt incredibly turned on. As I hiked my dress up over my knees and plunged my hand between my legs, trilling my clit furiously while I bent over the stainless steel sink, I began to plot how I might entice the girl into a more comfortable setting to properly make love to her.

**3**

———————

After cumming hard bent over the sink reliving my exciting liaison with the pretty schoolgirl, I returned to my seat in the main cabin and fell asleep with my head resting against the window. I awoke two hours later with a rumbling stomach, and noticing that the bar car had almost emptied out, I approached the bartender asking where I could get a bite to eat.

"Excuse me, sir," I said. "Which way is it to the dining car?"

"We have *two*, madam," he said. "The Cote D'Azur is the next car toward the front of the train, and the Hagia Sophia is the adjacent car to the rear."

"What's the difference?" I asked, wondering why in the world they would need two dining cars.

"The Cote D'Azur provides a continental menu, whereas the Hagia Sophia offers middle eastern fare."

"Wow, okay," I said, shaking my head at the continuing opulent array of choices on the luxury line.

I hesitated for a moment, then turned toward the aft section of the train, hoping to see another glimpse of the mysterious Arab girl. When I entered the adjoining carriage, my eyes widened at the sight that greeted me. The dining tables were immaculately set with neatly pressed white linen tablecloths, fine china, crystal drinking glasses, and sumptuous red velvet chairs. Most of the chairs were already occupied, but towards the rear of the compartment I noticed Adele sitting with the Arabian father and daughter pair, and I approached the table, motioning to the open seat.

"Do you have room for one more?" I asked, peering toward the gentleman.

"Of course," he said, rising politely and motioning for me to take the available seat.

I smiled toward the girl seated next to him at the window and nodded at Adele sitting next to me.

"I'm Jade," I said, extending my hand toward the gentleman.

"Omar," the man said. "And this is my daughter, Leila.

"And this lovely lady–" he said, motioning toward Adele.

"*Adele*–yes," I blushed. "We met earlier in the bar car."

"Perfect," he said, smiling toward his daughter. "I guess I'm the lucky one who'll be enjoying the company of three charming women over dinner this evening."

"Is this your first trip aboard the Orient Express?" I said, trying to break the awkward sexual tension at the table.

"Oh no," he said. "I make this trip often to visit my daughter in Paris. She's studying at the École Internationale."

"Oh?" I said, eager to hear more details about the mysterious girl. "What grade?"

"Lycée troisième," the girl said in a perfect French accent.

"My French is a little rusty," I smiled. "I'm not quite sure how that equates to our American education system."

"It's equivalent to grade 12 in the United States," Adele clarified.

"So you're a *senior* then," I nodded. "That would put you around seventeen–"

"I just turned eighteen," Leila replied matter-of-factly.

"You must be looking forward to graduating," I said, relieved to hear that she'd reached the age of majority. "I understand the Ecole Internationale is one of Europe's most exclusive private schools. Have you thought about where you'd like to go to college?"

"I've been accepted to Cambridge, La Sorbonne, and Harvard. But I'm leaning toward Harvard. I've never been to the United States–"

"I'd be happy to show you around if you'd like to visit. I have friends in the Boston area who I'm sure would be happy to put you up while you tour the campus."

"Really?" Leila said, her eyes perking up. "Where do you live in the States?"

"I'm from Chicago, but I do business in New England quite often. If you let me know when you'd like to come, I'm sure I could work my schedule around to accommodate you."

"That's very generous of you, Jade," Omar said, noticing the waiter approaching our table. "But we can talk about these matters later. Who's ready for something to eat?"

"I'm so hungry I could eat a horse, as we say in America," I said, winking at Leila.

"Well I don't know about *that*," Omar chuckled. "But I believe they serve lamb and Moroccan chicken if you prefer Arabian dishes."

"I'm definitely ready to sample more of your local fare," I smiled, feeling Leila tapping the outside of my foot under the table.

After we all ordered our meals, Adele excused herself to freshen up in the lavatory, and I took the opportunity to move over to the seat next to the window so I could be closer to Leila. When Adele returned, we talked about our travel plans and vocations. Omar ran an import-export business out of Istanbul and Adele was a finance executive with Commerzbank. The two of them struck up a conversation about foreign exchange rates, and before long Omar agreed to open an account at her bank. He then offered to let us stay at his villa on the Black Sea while we were in Turkey, to which both Adele and I readily agreed. Whether we were just happy to find any excuse to stay together during our layover or we were equally smitten by his beguiling daughter, was unclear. Either way, I was in no hurry to break up our happy little coterie.

When our meal service started with a shared plate of freshly baked pita and hummus, I noticed that Leila was growing increasingly frisky playing footsies with me under the table. By the time our main courses arrived, she'd already kicked off her shoes and was caressing the inside of my calves with her bare foot. Growing more emboldened by her father's seeming distraction with Adele's sexy lace dress and her continued efforts to solicit his banking business, she forced my knees apart and slowly began pressing her foot further up under my dress toward my bare crotch. When the ball of her foot began rubbing against my slippery vulva and twitching clit, I had a hard time concentrating on eating my meal. After a few minutes, Omar peered over at me, noticing my elevated breathing rate and soft moaning.

"Are you enjoying your lamb, Jade?" he said.

"Oh yes," I sighed, trying to keep my composure while his daughter foot-fucked me under the table. "It's quite...*succulent*."

"Shakriya is one of our most popular dishes in Turkey," he nodded. "But the chefs here seem to have a special knack for bringing out its unique flavors. I'll have to ask them what their secret ingredient is."

"Yes," I moaned. "They seem quite skilled. I haven't enjoyed a meal quite this stimulating in a long time."

As he and Adele continued chatting about their growing banking partnership, I dared not even *look* at Leila for fear of betraying what she was doing to me under the table. Just when I thought it couldn't possibly get any more awkward and titillating, she suddenly thrust her big toe inside my pussy, curling the rest of her foot against my burning clit. I gasped in surprise, and Omar peered over at me in alarm.

"Are you alright, Jade?" he said. "Are you choking on something?"

"No," I said, bringing my napkin to my mouth to distract attention from my rapidly escalating arousal. "A piece of lamb just went down the wrong way. I'll have to slow down a bit while I'm eating. I think I'm just getting a little carried away with this sumptuous dish."

"It's definitely meant to be savored," he said, smiling at me politely. "But watch out for those spices. There's quite a bit of garlic and paprika in there. It'll burn your mouth if you're not careful."

"Yes," I panted. "I can feel it burning already."

"How about *you*, dear?" Omar said, turning to look at his unusually quiet daughter. "Are you enjoying your meal equally as much?"

"Yes father," Leila said. "I'm just enjoying listening in on your conversation with Adele. I find the world of finance fascinating."

"I'm glad you find it interesting," he said. "I'm looking forward to placing you in an important position in my business when you graduate from Harvard."

"Yes father," Leila nodded obediently while flexing her toes inside my dripping cunt.

As Omar and Adele continued their conversation, Leila quietly picked away at her dish with her knife and fork clinking against the fine china while she pretended to be absorbed in their discussion. Before long, the combination of her deft toe-fucking and tickling of my clit with the rest of her foot brought me to the brink of climax, and I fought valiantly to maintain my composure as my orgasm quickly swept over me. Trying to remain still in my chair, I couldn't help expressing the joy in my face as a deep rash suddenly poured over my cheeks and my eyes began to water from the intense pleasure emanating within my body.

Noticing my discomfort once again, Omar turned toward me with a concerned expression.

"Too much garlic?" he said, offering me a glass of water.

"Too much *something*," I said, gulping down the water trying to keep his attention focused above the table. "But it's very stimulating. I think I just need to acclimate more to your customs and cuisine. I'm looking forward to enjoying more of these delicacies once I land in your country."

"I'm looking forward to sharing more of our culture with *both* of you as my guests," he nodded, turning toward his daughter. "Don't you agree, Leila? We'll have to show these women some proper Turkish hospitality."

"Absolutely father," Leila said, beaming at both Adele and me. "There's so much more I'd love to show these lovely ladies."

For the rest of the meal, the four of us talked about our past experiences and future plans, while Omar and Leila raved about the various attractions awaiting us in their home town. I was looking forward to exploring the ancient city of Istanbul, but I was much *more* interested in exploring what other secrets Leila might be hiding. If her expert massage of my private areas was any indication, I expected her to be quite a minx when she was freed from her father's oversight. But I also knew it would be difficult for me to wait the remaining four days for our train to reach its final destination before I could have more of her. While Omar graciously offered to pay for our meal and thanked the waiter for his excellent service, I quietly slipped a note under Leila's napkin with my room number.

With any luck, she'd be able to find some time to slip away later in the evening to join me in my private boudoir.

After dinner, the four of us returned to our individual staterooms to catch up on email and change out of our formal wear. By now, the train had reached the Swiss border, and I looked out the window peering up the soaring Alps. The juxtaposition of the lush green valleys and the snow-covered mountains provided a calming culmination to my exciting first day on the Orient Express, and I soon fell asleep from the soft rumbling of the train as it sliced its way through the deep canyons.

I awoke a few hours later to a soft tap on my door, and I threw on the plush terrycloth robe hanging in the bathroom while I approached the cabin door warily. In my still-groggy stupor, I'd temporarily forgotten about the note I left for Leila in the dining car, but when I saw her through the peephole, my pussy throbbed in excitement. I opened the door and noticed that she'd changed into skinny jeans and a tight t-shirt that hugged every inch of her curvy body.

"Leila," I said, peering into the hall to make sure she was alone. "I wasn't sure if you got my message..."

"I had to wait a few hours for my father to settle into his stateroom." she said. "I think maybe he has a visitor, so I've got a little time while he's distracted–"

"Come in," I said, practically yanking her out of the hallway into my bedroom. "*God*, you look so sexy. I haven't been able to stop thinking about you all day."

Without saying a word, Leila placed her thumbs under the bottom of my belt and pulled it apart, dropping my robe to the floor. For a moment, I stood stark naked in front of her, shocked at the boldness of her action for someone her age.

"Something tells me this isn't the first time you've done something like this," I panted, feeling my nipples hardening as she admired my yoga-studio-toned body.

"It's the first time I've done this with a *woman*," she said, running her hands softly around the sides of my heaving breasts.

"Not counting earlier today," I smiled.

"Right, but that hardly counts. It was far too quick and one-sided. I've been wanting to fuck you ever since I watched you touching your-self in the bar car."

"Let's get you out of those clothes," I said, pulling her toward the bed. "This time I want to touch *every* part of your magnificent body."

The two of us flopped down on top of the mattress while we unbuttoned and tugged off her clothes, until she lay nude beside me. We pulled each other close and intertwined our legs as we pressed our breasts together, kissing passionately.

"*Damn*, girl," I panted. "You sure don't act like a schoolgirl."

"No?" she said, gazing at me coyly. "How exactly are schoolgirls my age *supposed* to act?"

"Like *this*," I said, flipping her onto her back and leaning over her while I grabbed her firm tits in my palms and suckled her erect teats like a hungry calf.

"No fair," she panted, arching her back as I threaded my thigh between her legs toward her steaming pussy. "It's my turn to lick *you* this time."

"You'll have your chance soon enough," I said, placing my palm over her crotch and plunging two fingers inside her wet tunnel. "Right now, I just want to *look* at you while I caress you all over."

As I finger-fucked her with my hand, she squirmed on the bed and peered up at me with parted lips.

"Do you *like* that?" I taunted her. "Do you like being probed while you lie pinned on the mattress, only able to peer back at me?"

"You mean the same way I fucked you with my foot under the table in the restaurant?" she smirked.

"Exactly," I said. "That was very rude of you. You put me in an uncomfortable position sitting right next to your father."

"You didn't seem to mind it too much at the time. Besides, he seemed preoccupied with your lady friend. He had no clue what I was doing to you under the table."

"You're a very naughty girl," I said, pushing her over onto her side while I spread her legs into a scissor position. "Now it's my turn to have my way with *you*. I'm going to fuck your sweet pussy and watch you whimper and moan the same way you did with me."

I raised myself up into a kneeling position and straddled her thighs, pushing my pussy toward hers, then I tilted my hips until our vulvas merged, rocking my wet lips against hers. Leila groaned softly, reaching up to squeeze my tits, but I extended her upper leg and swung it between my breasts, pulling her harder against me.

"*Fuck* yes," Leila hissed, throwing her head back against the mattress. "Fuck my cunt with your wet pussy, Jade. That feels so good."

"Better than my *head* between your legs?" I smiled, humping her more vigorously.

"Yes," she grunted. "At least this time I can *see* what you're doing to me."

"That works *both* ways, young lady. I far prefer looking at your pretty face than having your tartan skirt pulled over my head."

"Oh?" she smirked. "You didn't enjoy eating out the innocent schoolgirl in the private lavatory?"

"Not as much as I did sucking on my lambchops while you fucked me with your foot under the table in full view of all the other restaurant patrons."

"You seem to have a predilection for dangerous public sex," she smiled.

"Maybe," I said. "But I also like having you all to myself, where I can live out *all* my fantasies in the privacy of my own bedroom."

"You better hurry up then," Leila panted, digging her nails into the side of my hips as our pussies slurped loudly over the background rumble of the train. "Before my father looks in on me and sees that I've disappeared from my cabin."

"Yes, baby," I groaned. "I'm going to cum all over your sweet pussy while I imagine all the dirty things I want to do to you. Come with me while I grind my cunt against yours."

"Yes, Jade," Leila panted. "I'm close. Fuck me harder. Let me feel your tits caressing my leg while I gush all over your twat."

"Holy *fuck*," I screamed, suddenly overcome with passion at her dirty talk and the look of pleasure on her face as her mouth widened approaching her climax. Suddenly, her body jerked violently, and I felt a gush of fluid spraying all over the inside of my thighs as a crimson flush spread over her upper chest and face.

"Oh God, Leila," I hissed. "I'm cumming baby. I'm cumming all over your sweet, slippery pussy."

While I wrapped both of my arms around her leg, now pointing straight up in the air between my bouncing tits, I felt my pussy clamp down hard as I emitted hard jets of my own all over her pulsing hole. Between the two of us, our juices were spraying in every direction, and I blinked as it squirted all the way up into my eyes. But I hardly cared, reveling in the sensation of our commingled love juices running down over the front of my face while she stared up at me.

After we both finished coming hard, I collapsed onto the bed beside Leila and we giggled as we spread our lubrication all over our breasts and stomachs.

"That was *insane!*" Leila panted, rolling over to kiss me. "Who knew having sex with a *woman* could be so much fun?"

"And *sticky*!" I said, rolling her nipples softly between my slippery fingers.

"I thought *I* was the only one who squirted like that," she said.

"So did I," I smiled. "You're the first one I've been with who could do it with me at the same time."

"What other firsts can you teach me before my daddy catches me breaking curfew?" Leila asked.

"Well," I said, reaching into my nightstand for the double-sided dildo I'd packed hoping for a moment precisely like this. "Have you ever tried one of *these*?"

"Not one as long and flexible as that one," she said, peering up at the silicone dildo as I shook it in the air. "Is that what I *think* it is?"

"That depends what you think it is," I smiled. "You can use this thing in so many interesting ways."

"*Show* me," Leila purred. "I think it's about time one of us got fucked with something bigger than a finger or a toe."

"I thought you'd never ask," I said. "Assume the position."

"Which position did you have in mind?" she grinned. "I mean, it looks like you could fuck me with that thing in all manner of positions."

"That's true," I nodded. "I've tried it with both of us on our backs, on our knees ass-to-ass, and even in the pile-driver position. But this time, I want to be close to you while we enjoy it together. Let's sit facing each other on the bed while we kiss and hold hands. It might be fun to watch each other while we're both humping this thing."

"You seem to have a lot of experience trying different things with women," Leila said.

"It wasn't always this way," I said. "But once you decide to go *femme*, you quickly learn there's no longer any need for men."

"Ha, ha," Leila chuckled. "Especially when we have our choice of giant phalluses. I'm in—fill me up with that thing. This time I'm going to watch you squirt all over my pussy while we come together."

"You're way ahead of me, girl," I smiled, positioning my hips in front of hers and spreading my knees apart as I inserted one end of the long dildo into Leila's box before pressing my hips forward and thrusting the other end in my hole while we clasped hands and moaned feeling the instrument filling us both up.

"Uhnn," Leila groaned, watching the pink appendage disappear into our slits as we began to rock our hips together, gazing excitedly into each other's eyes. It didn't take long for the sight and sensation of the double-sided dildo plowing in and out of our flapping pussies to have the desired effect, and within minutes we were both moaning and squirming on the bed, squeezing our hands tightly together as both of our mouths parted and we stared into each other's eyes nearing another mutual climax. When we both tipped over the edge, our eyes darted down between our legs, where we watched with joyful celebration as our pussies squirted powerful streams of lubrication over each other's stomachs.

It seemed to take forever for the two of us to stop cumming, but when our orgasms finally began to subside, we flopped down on the bed in opposite directions, peering outside the picture window at the snow-capped mountains passing by.

"Talk about a *peak experience*," Leila panted.

"You got *that* right, girl," I moaned contentedly.

Suddenly, we heard a loud tap on the cabin door and we both jerked upright, looking at each other with frightened eyes.

"You don't think that's–" Leila shuddered.

"Let's hope not," I said, thinking the same thing. "Why don't you lock yourself in the washroom just in case, while I check out who it is. Don't worry, if it's your father, I'll tell him I haven't seen you since dinner."

"Thanks," Leila said, scurrying into the washroom and closing the door behind her.

I straightened my hair, then pulled on my robe and approached the door cautiously. When I looked out the peephole, I was relieved to see Adele peering back at me. I opened the door a crack, not wanting her to invade Leila's privacy, and placed my face against the opening.

"Adele!" I said, pretending to be surprised. "What brings you back this way so late at night?"

"I was hoping you might be interested in picking up where we left off earlier in the day," she said. "I've been thinking about you ever since we shared that intimate moment together in the bar car."

"I've been thinking the same thing," I said. "But it's getting late and I'm kind of tired–"

"Who are you kidding?" she said, forcing my door open. "This room *reeks* of sex. Something tells me you haven't been alone in here all this time..."

"I don't know what you mean–" I protested, trying to block her ingress.

She took one look at my messy bed and smiled back at me.

"Just as I thought," she smiled. "You obviously haven't been alone. And by the look of that glistening sex toy on the bed, I suspect you've been mixing it up with that cute Arab girl once again."

"That wouldn't be appropriate..."

"Oh *please*," Adele huffed, barging past me. "Where *is* she? You didn't think I knew what you two were up to over dinner below her father's line of sight?"

"I don't know what you're talking about–"

"With all your moaning and fawning over your spicy curry? Remember, I was sitting right next to you. You practically gave me a charley horse knocking your legs against mine while Leila foot-fucked you under the table."

"Was it that obvious?" I said, resigning myself to the obvious.

"Only to *me*, apparently. Her father was too busy gaping at my tight bosom and trying to negotiate more favorable banking terms to realize what the two of you were doing right under his nose."

"Thanks for that," I sighed. "But I'm not sure Leila's quite ready to bring another partner into the picture just yet..."

Suddenly, the bathroom door parted open and Leila stuck her head out, peering at us with wide eyes.

"I *knew* it!" Adele said. "The *least* you guys can do is share in the spoils, since I've been the one keeping her dad occupied while the two of you were getting your groove on in here."

"So it was *you* who was in the room with him this evening," Leila said, stepping out from behind the door completely naked.

"I saw Jade passing the note to you over dinner and figured the two of you would be looking for some more quiet time together," Adele nodded. "I just hoped to get in on the fun while your father thinks you're still resting in your cabin."

"What do you say, Leila?" I said, peering at her with a coy smile. "Do you think you've got enough time for a little more girl-on-girl action?"

Leila paused for a moment appraising Adele's sexy body, still clad in her clingy lace dress.

"The more the merrier," she smiled. "Now that I've got a taste for women, I want to sample *all* the offerings before this trip is over."

"Come try a little *French* cuisine then," Adele said, clasping Leila's hand and leading her over to the ruffled bed.

I stuck my head outside the door to make sure no one else was spying, then I closed it softly behind me.

This luxury train ride was turning out to have a lot more extra amenities than I could have wished for. As I plopped down on the bed next to the two women, we all intertwined our legs and moaned as we began caressing and disrobing our new partner-in-crime.

# VOLUME FIVE

## POLYNESIAN PLEASURE

## 1

Peering over the prow of our fifty-foot schooner at the rising sun on the horizon, I closed my eyes and breathed in the fresh scent of the ocean breeze. After a series of short but intense one-night stands, I was beginning to feel cheap and demoralized. Even though I'd taken the initiative in most of the flings, at the end of the day I'd always come home alone feeling shallow and empty.

The affairs had helped free me from the bonds of my passionless marriage and opened my eyes to the pleasures of lesbian love, but somehow I'd never been able to make any of the relationships stick. Even calling them relationships was laughable, given the longest ones never lasted beyond the occasional overnight stay. I needed to clear my mind and get away from all the distractions and temptations of the big city.

This chartered cruise was the perfect balm for my aching heart. With a tiny crew of three sailors and eleven passengers, I had plenty of time and space to collect my thoughts and recharge my batteries. In the absence of the usual big ship amenities, our private yacht provided a much-needed respite from the hectic bustle of the urban jungle. The only sound I could hear was the rhythmic flapping of the boat's sails in the gentle breeze and the peaceful slapping of the waves against the hull as our sloop pierced through the cobalt-blue water.

As the sole uncoupled passenger on our month-long tour of the South Pacific Islands, I was happy to curl up with a good book on the forward deck and feel the wind flowing through my hair. Although everybody went out of their way trying to keep me engaged, I made it clear I was content to be left to my own devices. I'd paid a hefty sum for this cozy cruise, and I just wanted to have some alone time to cleanse my soul.

"Another beautiful day in paradise?" the ship's captain Ben said as he leaned his arms on the rail beside me.

"Yes," I said, gazing off into the distance. "It's so quiet and peaceful I can actually hear myself think."

Ben pinched his eyebrows as he glanced over at me briefly.

"Is that what you've been doing up here? I thought most people came on these cruises to get away from all those distractions. You know, to free their minds and commune with nature and all that."

I turned my head and peered into Ben's weathered eyes. His dark skin was prematurely wrinkled, but his salt-and-pepper beard and chiseled jaw revealed a handsome, sea-worn face. I wasn't sure if he was making a veiled pass or if he was genuinely concerned for my emotional state of mind.

"Never fear, Captain. I'm feeling the weight of the world fall off my shoulders with each new nautical mile we pass through these azure waters."

"Happy to hear," he said, straightening his arms on the handrail. "Is there anything I can get for you? Are you hungry? I've got some fresh halibut or pineapple if you're in the mood for a snack."

"Thanks," I said, shaking my head. "I'm still feeling pretty full from that full-course breakfast your chef prepared for us this morning. But in another hour or two, some fresh fruit and seafood will be just what I'm looking for."

"I'll see what we can scare up. You're going to need a little extra energy for our planned excursion later today."

He pointed toward the horizon on the port side of the ship.

"We'll be dropping anchor in another hour or so at that small island. There'll be lots of hiking trails with plenty of local flora and fauna to explore."

I squinted my eyes in the direction he was pointing and saw a tall green patch rising over the blue expanse of ocean. Up to this point in our cruise, most of the islands we'd visited had been little more than shallow reefs and sandy atolls.

"Judging by its elevation above sea level, it doesn't look so tiny from here. Is this another uninhabited island?"

"Actually, this is the first inhabited island we'll be visiting on our tour. But we're unlikely to encounter any natives. There's a small tribe on the opposite side of the island, but they're not very accommodating to visitors. They like their privacy. In fact, they're among the most isolated people you'll find anywhere on earth. With hundreds of miles to the next nearest inhabited island, they've learned to become quite self-sufficient."

I stared at the island as it slowly grew larger the nearer our vessel passed. It looked dense and lush, with thin silver waterfalls cascading through the thick jungle foliage.

"As long as they don't feed on *foreigners* to mix up their diet," I laughed nervously. "Are you sure we'll be safe there?"

The captain chuckled as he wiped a wash of sea spray from the bow of the boat off his forehead.

"Not to worry, m'lady. The whole cannibal myth is overblown. There are very few tribes that still practice that custom anywhere in the world. These people are reasonably enlightened, considering their remote location. Missionaries passed through here centuries ago, instilling a modicum of Western values. Some of them even speak English. But we'll be putting in on an isolated section of the island. In the unlikely event we encounter any natives, they shouldn't give us any trouble. Just be sure to stay close together and not stray off the beaten path."

"I wouldn't dream of going off on my own, Captain. My jungle survival skills are nonexistent—cannibals or no. I'll be happy to join up with the group for this expedition."

As Ben returned to the rear of the ship to navigate us around the encroaching shoals, I watched the beautiful island as we sailed closer. The lush foliage and turquoise water surrounding the sandy beaches reminded me of the stories of my youth. I fantasized about being marooned on the isle like Robinson Crusoe, building a fanciful fort in the trees and catching live fish to feed myself. Of course, having a hunky partner like Mel Gibson or Brooke Shields to keep me company in my little blue lagoon would make it even dreamier.

Suddenly I felt a stirring in my loins that reminded me how long it had been since I'd felt the tender touch of a lover.

2

When we put in on the secluded beach and carried our provisions onto dry land, I marveled at the surrounding landscape. Unlike the other remote islands we'd visited so far, this one looked tall and imposing. A dense blanket of trees carpeted the steeply sloped mountains, rising to a flat crater hundreds of feet above sea level. I could hear the harsh trill of birds screeching from behind the blind as thick, shiny leaves rustled in the distance. A small reef encapsulated our lagoon in a little crescent, creating a shallow pool to wade through. It would be the perfect spot to cool off after lunch and a hike through the humid jungle.

I watched with fascination as the captain and his crew caught some fish in the lagoon then cleaned and prepared the catch on a wooden plank on the beach. I don't think I'd enjoyed a seafood meal so much in my entire life. Whether it was simply the succulent taste of the freshly caught snapper or the exquisite scenery, I savored every bite as I soaked up the spectacular view.

I'd brought with me a minimum of provisions—just enough to fortify me for our planned excursions. Foam sandals for walking on the beach, hiking shoes for the trail hike, and a cloth handbag with a few bare essentials: a bikini for a swim in the lagoon, some sunscreen and lip balm to protect me against the sun, and my smartphone to read romance novels during quiet moments. After we all finished lunch, the captain stood up to address the group.

"I hope you all enjoyed our impromptu picnic lunch. We'll be spending the rest of the day on the island and setting anchor for the night. For those of you still finding your sea legs, a calm sleep in the lagoon under the stars should help quiet your stomach. In a few minutes, we're going to organize a little inland hike. If you prefer to stay on the beach and have a swim or collect shells, our first mate Mike will stay behind to keep watch on our belongings. The rest of you can join Will and me as we explore the amazing landscape of this island. There's some beautiful wildlife and waterfalls, and at the top of the island there's a dormant volcano from which you can see a spectacular view of the Pacific for miles around. Before we head out, does anyone have any questions?"

One of the young couples raised their hand.

"Yes, Tricia," Ben said, nodding at the couple.

"Do we need to bring any special protection with us? I mean, are there any dangerous animals like monkeys or bears? I heard there are some tribespeople on the island. What should we do if we encounter someone?"

Ben chuckled at the familiar question. It never failed to amuse him how ignorant city slickers were of local customs.

"The islands of the South Pacific are actually some of the safest places in the world in terms of wildlife. There are no mammals other than harmless fruit bats and the local tribespeople, who are far away on the other side of the island. The only creatures that might harm you are brown tree snakes and mosquitoes. Just keep your head away from overhanging branches and wear lots of insect repellant and you should be fine."

Ben and Will passed out some silver whistles connected to a key chain.

"In the unlikely event that we should encounter a native person in our travels, do not approach them unless they approach you. They generally like to keep to themselves and won't engage unless provoked. Keep us in sight at all times and don't stray too far off the path. If anybody should get separated from the group, just give us a tweet using these whistles so we can find you. If for whatever reason you get lost, just follow the trail down to the shore. We plan to be back to the boat around five p.m. local time."

After collecting our gear and fastening our whistles to our belt loops, we followed single-file behind Ben along a narrow trail into the woods, with Will taking up the rear. It didn't take long for the brush to thicken, and as I swatted the thick leaves aside, I kept glancing upward for any sign of slithering reptiles. The one thing I feared more than anything was snakes, and I could feel my heart beating in my chest as much from the fear of being bitten as from the exertion of the steep climb. I was glad when our path crossed the occasional stream, giving me a chance to soothe my hot and aching feet in the cool running water. After an hour or so, we passed another creek and I sat down on the bank to tighten a loose shoelace.

"Everything okay?" Will asked, pulling up behind me.

"Just a loose string," I said. "You go ahead, I'll catch up in a few seconds."

Will peered ahead, noticing our group turning a corner in the dense forest.

"Are you sure you'll just be a moment? We don't want to get too separated from the rest of the group."

"Yes, I'll be fine—I promise." I patted the whistle hanging from the belt loop on my cargo shorts. "Besides, I can always give you a ring if I can't find you, right?"

"Yes," he said. "But it's always best to maintain line-of-sight. The terrain up here is pretty steep and treacherous. We've had people fall and twist an ankle. Just be careful. I'll be walking slowly ahead."

As Will continued up the trail and turned around the corner out of sight, I paused to take in the peaceful sound of the forest. Besides the occasional call of a distant bird, the only sound I could hear was the soft gurgling of the water as it tumbled over the mossy rocks. After I finished tying my lace, I hesitated when I heard an unusual sound emanating from the forest a few hundred feet upstream. I turned my head and strained to listen, then my eyes widened in recognition.

It was the sound of a woman's voice. A sweet, lilting sound, like she was singing. I squinted through the dense thicket of trees, then my eyes grew wider as I recognized the familiar figure. She was standing under a waterfall, stark naked and rubbing her body like she was taking a shower. It was hard to tell how old she was from my distant location, but she had the slender, lithe figure of a young girl. I glanced up the path in the direction Will had headed then back toward the girl.

*What the hell,* I thought. *I'm on vacation. Everyone says the best way to enjoy a different culture is to go native. I can always catch up with the group later. If Will is really worried about me, he'll double back to find me. Worst-case scenario, I'll have to wait for them to return along the same path on their way down, or I return to our cove. But this is some local fauna definitely worth exploring.*

I followed the tributary upstream, picking my way carefully over the slippery rocks and boulders. As I got closer to the girl, her voice became louder and I found myself humming softly, mimicking her lilting tune. She was speaking a language I'd never heard before, but the melody was simple and rhythmic. I flashed back to another one of my favorite fairy tales from my youth, when the English explorer John Smith stumbled across Pocahontas by a waterfall in the forest. The closer I got to the girl, the more mesmerized I was by her. I could only catch fleeting glimpses of her through the breaks in the heavy brush, but it was quickly becoming apparent that she had the body of a goddess.

When I reached a clearing about fifty feet away from the waterfall, I stopped next to a tree and gently parted the branches blocking my vision. When I finally saw the girl close-up, I gasped. She couldn't have been much beyond her teens, but she was stunning. With thick, shiny black hair cascading over her shoulders and breasts, her pouty lips and high cheekbones reminded me of a young Halle Berry. Her body had all the same curves and swells of her Catwoman avatar, except in this case, she was completely naked.

As I watched the water splash over her full breasts and hourglass-shaped hips, I couldn't stop gawking at her like some kind of creepy peeping Tom. I didn't even know if she was of legal age, if that even mattered out here in the remote stretches of the Pacific Ocean. But when I saw her hand disappear under the triangle-shaped patch between her legs and she began moaning under the torrent of water, I couldn't help myself. It had been far too long since I'd had any kind of sexual contact, and here was the girl of my dreams putting on the sexiest live show I'd ever seen.

I thrust my hand down the front of my cargo shorts and began circling my slippery pearl, trying to stifle my own moans of pleasure. Within moments, I felt the rising swell of my passion beginning to overtake me and I rested my left arm on the tree trunk to support my quivering legs. Just as I was about to be overtaken by my climax, I felt a strange object slithering up my arm. As I turned my face in shock to see what was crawling on me, I stared directly into the eyes of a long brown tree snake.

I had just a moment to scream and flinch my arm away before the snake lunged forward and embedded its fangs deep into the flesh of my neck. Within seconds, I began to feel faint and numb as my legs suddenly collapsed beneath me. As I crumpled to the ground beside the tree, the last thing I remembered was the shocked look on the face of the pretty native girl as she watched me lose consciousness on the moss-covered ground.

**3**

———————

I woke up on the hard floor of a stick-frame hut, peering through bleary eyes at the interwoven leaves covering its thatched roof. An old native woman sat cross-legged beside me, holding a smoky bowl under my nose. The aroma was pungent, and I instinctively flinched my head to the side. The pretty girl I'd seen at the waterfall kneeled by my other side, holding a wet compress against my neck. I felt dizzy and weak, and my head throbbed with pain. When I tried to speak, I realized that the left side of my face was numb.

"Wh—where am I?" I said in a slurred drawl, trying to lift myself up on my elbows.

The girl smiled at me as she removed her hand from the side of my neck. I noticed a green paste on her palm, which she wiped off with a heavy cloth next to a wooden bowl containing what appeared to be a long animal bone.

"You're in our village," she said in a strange accent I'd never heard before. "You're safe now, but you need to rest. You're still weak from the after-effects of the *gata* bite."

She placed her other hand on my chest and gently pressed me down on top of a scratchy mat.

"Gata?" I said, pinching my eyebrows in confusion. "How did I get here?"

"It's our native snake. Normally, it doesn't cause this much trouble, but it struck you in the neck and the poison traveled quickly to your head. I had to carry you back to our village."

"*Carry me?*" I said, wondering how her small frame could support my weight. "How far?"

"I guess it would be more accurate to say I dragged you. I built a rough stretcher out of tree branches and vines. It took almost a full day to bring you back to our village."

I paused as I looked at the girl quizzically.

"Where are my travel mates? I came with a dozen other people—"

"If you're referring to the people on the sailboat, they stopped by our bay a few hours before we arrived asking if anyone had seen a yellow-haired European woman. The chief wasn't very happy with their intrusion, and when he said he hadn't seen any other foreigners, they sailed away."

"Away?" I said, shaking my head in dismay that they would abandon me so quickly. "Does that mean I'm *alone* on this island?"

The girl reached out and clasped my hand in hers as she smiled at me warmly. A group of young naked children suddenly rushed into the hut giggling, and the old lady shooed them away.

"You're hardly alone here," she said, glancing up at the woman who was still holding the smoking cup under my chin. "My family and tribe will care for you until your friends return."

The old woman said something to the girl in their native tongue and I flinched again, smelling the strong vapor rising from the bowl.

"What's this strange smoke you're having me inhale? It smells like incense—"

"It's burning hibiscus leaves. We've found that it helps neutralize the effects of the toxin. Since you were unconscious, it was the only way we could get the medicine inside you. But now that you're awake, there are some more potent herbs you can take internally."

The old woman reached down beside her and lifted a coconut

shell filled with a milky substance and raised it to my lips. She smiled at me softly and nodded for me to drink the elixir.

"What is that?" I said, frowning from the pungent smell of the mixture. "It smells like something died in there."

The girl chuckled as she squeezed my hand.

"It's made from the same natural ingredients that I've been using to neutralize the pain and swelling on the side of your neck. It's a mixture of plantain leaves, papaya bark, and turmeric, dissolved in coconut milk. You have to trust us. We've been administering this medicine for hundreds of years, and we know it works. I think you'll find the taste quite pleasant."

I reluctantly lifted my head and parted my lips as the old lady tilted the bowl toward my mouth. The potion was thick and grainy, like a soup broth, but it tasted more like chocolate milk. I swished it around in my mouth for a few seconds, then gulped it down nervously. The old lady looked into my eyes and nodded as she tilted the cup higher.

"*Sila atu*," she said in a heavy accent.

"Drink the rest," the native girl said. "It will help settle your stomach and ease the pain."

I slowly emptied the bowl, then the old lady got up and said something to the girl before she stepped out of the hut.

For the first time since I'd woken up, I began to feel a little less anxious about my situation, and I gazed up at the native girl, studying her face. She was even more breathtaking close-up than I'd remembered. Her large brown doe eyes, small slender nose, and spongy cheeks gave her the appearance of a girl far younger than her sexy figure would suggest. I glanced at her chest and was disappointed to see that she was fully covered with some kind of dyed dress. The cloth looked thick and dense, more like a mat than the woven cloth used to make our Western garments. I glanced down my own body and was relieved to see that I was still wearing the same clothes I'd left the boat with.

"How long have you and your family lived here?" I asked, interested as much to learn about the history of her culture as her actual age.

"Our family and those of our tribe have lived on this island for centuries. As best we can tell from the oral traditions passed down from our ancestors, the island was settled by Polynesians traveling from the larger islands around 300 AD. I myself have lived in this little hamlet my entire life, which I'm told is eighteen rainy seasons."

*So young*, I sighed. With her flawless brown skin and soft cheeks, she looked even younger than her chronological age. I flashed back and remembered what she looked like naked under the waterfall, and shifted uncomfortably on the mat beneath me. I could feel the wetness building between my legs and blushed suddenly, realizing how attracted I was to this island goddess.

"You look even younger than that," I said, glancing at her tight-fitting frock. "At least, from the neck up. You're very pretty."

The girl smiled at me as she leaned in closer and lowered her voice.

"I saw you watching me," she said. "And I saw what you were doing behind that tree."

"Um..." I stumbled, not knowing how to react at being found out.

"It's okay," she said. "We're very open about our sexuality in our tribe. It's perfectly healthy and normal. I'm glad that you saw me. I think you're very beautiful also."

I felt a sudden tingle between my legs as I squeezed my thighs together, unconsciously rubbing myself against my tight cargo shorts.

"Oh?" I said, fishing for more details. "Have you had a lot of experience in that area? Where I come from, girls don't usually become active until your age or later."

"Most of the boys and girls in our tribe become sexually active soon after they reach maturity. But since I'm the daughter of the chief, he expects me to save myself until marriage."

"Now I see why you needed to find another form of release under the waterfall."

The girl smiled at me as I began to feel the perspiration building between our palms.

"A woman can only go so long with unsatisfied needs—"

"I know the feeling all too well," I nodded. "It's been a long time for me too."

The girl's eyes widened in surprise as she rubbed my ring finger with her fingers.

"You're not married? I would have thought a pretty woman of your age would have plenty of suitors..."

"I was, once. But my interests seem to have gravitated more toward women these last few years..."

The girl shifted her weight off her knees and sat cross-legged beside me, pulling the heel of her foot under her dress against her crotch.

"So have mine lately."

I paused for a moment, wondering how far I should take our little flirtation.

"You've never even been *kissed*?" I said.

The girl chuckled as she looked towards the front door of her hut.

"Not unless you count all the pecks on my cheek by my *matua*. I'm expected to remain chaste until the day I'm given away."

"Given away?" I said, shaking my head in confusion.

"Any potential mate must first be approved by my father. Not many suitors have stepped forward in deference to his authority."

"How many men are there in your tribe of marrying age?" I asked. "I can't imagine *any* young man or woman not being attracted to your physical beauty."

"It would have to be a man," the girl frowned. "It's considered *tapu* for a woman to sleep with another woman after she's reached child-bearing age.

"That's a shame, because it's a singular pleasure to be properly kissed by a girl."

She paused for a moment as she looked longingly into my eyes.

"I suppose it wouldn't be a sin if we were to kiss briefly. My grand-mother says the exchange of saliva acts as a potion in the case of snakebite. Something about the built-in immunity I've acquired from so many of my own snake bites. In this case, it would be more medicinal—"

I pulled the girl's hand toward me as I lifted my head up to her face.

"What's your name?" I whispered in her ear.

"Teuila. It means red flower in our native language."

"My name's Jade. It means pretty green stone in my language. Kiss me, Teuila."

The girl leaned forward, and when our lips touched, it was like a lightning bolt passed through me. I could feel goose bumps on my arms as my heart pounded in my chest. As she pursed her lips awkwardly against mine, I felt the sweet taste of her wetness filling my mouth. But as I reached up with my hands to cradle her head, I heard the loud flap of the blanket covering the front door sweep aside and the thud of heavy footsteps on the wood lattice floor.

"*O le a lea?*" a gruff middle-aged man shouted in front of the doorway, flanked by the older woman who'd treated me earlier.

Teuila shot up into an erect position and said something in her native language to the man. He looked at me with an angry expression and continued talking to her in an agitated manner. It was apparent from her submissive body language that the man was her father and the chief of the village. He obviously disapproved of a foreigner in his house as he pointed at me and motioned with his finger in the direction of the beach. He continued berating Teuila for many minutes before storming out of the hut and down the front steps. The older woman said some gentle words, then followed the man out of the hut as I heard them talking some distance away.

"I'm guessing that was your father?" I said.

"Yes," the girl said. "I suppose it was a bit of a surprise to find a strange European woman lying in his house after he'd been out fishing all day."

"He seemed a little angry," I said. "Was it because of our kiss?"

"I explained to him that I was trying to administer *pulu*, but I don't think he was very convinced."

"What was all that gesturing about when he pointed at me and then toward the sea?"

Teuila exhaled heavily as her lips tightened into a frown.

"He said that he wants you off the island as soon as possible. If your friends don't return soon, there's a cargo ship that passes by here every month or so, where we exchange goods. He insists on your being on that ship by the latest."

I glanced up at Teuila, grunting as I tried to sit up.

"In the meantime, where do you want me to stay?"

"You're still weak and sore," she said, easing me back down onto the mat. "You're welcome to stay with us until you're fully recovered. I'm sorry to have put you through all this. My father can be a little hard-headed sometimes. I'm sure he'll come around once we explain the situation. How are you feeling?"

I smiled at the native girl and reached back out for her hand.

"I was feeling much better when you were administering your magic elixir. If the coast is clear, can I have another one of your healing kisses?"

Teuila turned her head as she watched her father and grandmother walking slowly toward the other end of the village.

"Maybe for just a few more minutes..."

She leaned down to kiss me, and I reached up and ran my fingers through her soft hair. When our lips touched, I gently probed her mouth and played with her tongue, tasting her sweet salve. Teuila moaned softly, as she rolled her hips over her splayed skirt on the floor.

*This won't be the only waterfall we'll soon be experiencing*, I thought, feeling my panties begin to rapidly moisten.

4
___________

Later that day, the chief returned to the hut, and he and
Teuila had a calmer discussion. His countenance seemed to
have changed completely toward both of us, and he nodded
as he made eye contact with me before leaving to attend to other
business. Not long after, the old lady entered the cabin carrying a
platter of food and some fresh water. She spoke with Teuila briefly,
then she kneeled down beside me and felt my forehead, encouraging
me to drink the cool water. I was beginning to feel stronger, and I was
able to sit up as the two women tended to me.

"Your father seems less angry," I said. "Should I thank your grandmother for that?"

"Probably," Teuila nodded. "When she explained the circumstances of your arrival and reminded him of our longstanding tradition of giving refuge to wayward travelers, he softened up. In fact, he
insisted on holding a ceremony this evening to celebrate the rapid
recovery of our honored guest. Do you think you'll feel well enough
to attend the festivities?"

"Will it require my active participation?" I said, still feeling a bit
sore and lightheaded.

"Not unless you want to. It mostly involves a lot of singing and dancing. My father has asked that we prepare a special feast for the occasion. There will be lots of local dishes for you to sample. All you really have to do is watch and eat. You haven't had anything in over twenty-four hours. It will be good for you to regain your strength."

I looked at the large platter of food that the old woman had placed on the floor beside me and smiled at her.

"I'm beginning to feel my appetite coming back. Is this all for me?"

"*Ai meaai*," the woman nodded, holding the platter up and motioning with her hand toward her mouth.

The tray was filled with pieces of sliced banana, papaya, fresh fish, and some kind of shaved gourd. In the corner of the board sat a hollowed out half-coconut shell filled with the same creamy brown fluid the woman had administered to me earlier.

I looked at the plate, inhaling the rich fragrance of aromas, then peered up at Teuila.

"Is it okay to eat it with my hands?" I asked, not seeing any utensils.

"Of course," she said. "That's the only proper way to enjoy good food. Dig in!"

I picked up a slice of papaya, and when I bit into it, I closed my eyes, humming in appreciation.

"Oh my God," I said. "That is *so* good. It's so much more flavorful than the fruit I buy at my local grocery store. Do you grow all of your food on the island?"

"Absolutely. We have a great variety of fruit, vegetables, and seafood. The gods have blessed us with an abundance of natural resources to allow us to be self-sufficient."

I picked up a piece of white fish and sucked it slowly into my mouth. It appeared to be raw and marinated in some kind of citrus seasoning. Unlike the fresh snapper our charter chef had cooked up on the beach yesterday, this seafood was far more tender and juicy.

"You're spoiling me," I said, purring as I savored the succulent flesh. "This is the most tender seafood I've ever tasted. What kind of fish is it? And what's the seasoning? It tastes so simple and pure."

"We call it *fa'aipoipo*, but I think you call it halibut. It was fresh-caught today by my father and his fishing crew. We've added nothing but fresh lime juice to season it."

I shook my head at the simplicity of the native diet. I'd always felt that the best food needed little extra embellishment if it was truly fresh. And you couldn't get much fresher than this—from sea to plate in a matter of hours.

I took a sip of the coconut milk, then picked up the large pear-shaped tuber and took a small bite off the tip. It tasted a bit like sweet potato, but I also detected traces of the fresh seafood and papaya juices that covered the wooden board.

"What's this interesting fruit? It's got a delicious texture and flavor. I've never seen it before."

"It's one of our staples," Teuila said. "The taro root is actually a vegetable, not a fruit. We use it in much the same way that Westerners use potatoes. It's a very nutritious side dish that soaks up the flavors of other foods it's paired with. Do you like it?"

Holding the curved tubular vegetable in my hand, it reminded me of one of my favorite sex toys that I'd use on lonely nights to stimulate my G-spot.

"Mmm," I said, sucking the rich seafood juice from the tip of the bulb while raising a suggestive eyebrow at Teuila. "I'll definitely have to try more of this. I can imagine *all sorts* of ways it can be paired with other delectable dishes."

After I devoured the rest of the food on the serving plate, the old lady smiled at me and said something to Teuila.

"We should probably start getting you ready for the celebration tonight," she said, glancing at my soiled hiking clothes. "You must be looking forward to a bath. Let's get you cleaned up and into some fresh clothes. There's a private section of the lagoon where I can take you if you're strong enough to walk. Then my matua and I will prepare you with our local costume for the festival."

My pussy suddenly pulsed at the thought of bathing privately with Teuila.

"You're really having me go native, aren't you?" I said. "I think a swim in the lagoon would be very refreshing. I shouldn't have any trouble walking as long as you stay close by my side."

"I wouldn't think of leaving you," Teuila smiled. "Besides, I saw the way some of our young tribesmen looked at you when you came into our village. I need to make sure they don't get any ideas about the sexy white girl in their midst."

5

As Teuila escorted me toward the bathing lagoon, women and children smiled at me from the open verandas of their huts flanking the main thoroughfare of the village. But a group of men carving a dugout canoe on the main beach eyed me suspiciously when we veered off onto a flagstone-lined path leading into the woods. When we reached the secluded lagoon, I peered around me at the natural splendor of the landscape.

"Your island is so beautiful," I said, inhaling the fresh onshore sea breeze. "Where I come from, people pay a small fortune to visit these tropical paradises. And here I am, being feted by my native hosts, with never a thought to any kind of compensation."

"At least for a few more weeks," Teuila frowned, reminding me of the cargo ship pickup that was scheduled to pick me up later this month.

"If not earlier, if my shipmates return before then." I glanced toward the thick canopy of trees lining the lagoon. "If I hide in the forest, will you tell them I'm still lost? I'm in no hurry to leave this Shangri-La."

"I'd be happy to, but I think my father will have other ideas. We have to be careful not to test his patience too much. He's very suspicious of European visitors overstaying their welcome. He's heard stories of the destruction they brought to some of the other Polynesian islands."

I nodded, recalling how the indigenous people of Easter Island were nearly wiped out by disease and infighting after Dutch settlers arrived.

"I can appreciate why he'd want your people to be left alone. But you'll have to stop referring to me as *European*. I'm actually from the United States. I'm technically an American."

Teuila chuckled as she shook her head.

"They're just another colonial oppressor as far as he's concerned. He doesn't trust anybody who travels to these islands on fancy boats and planes. He thinks you'll corrupt our simple and natural way of life."

"He's probably right," I said. "Lord knows, our so-called advanced civilization has plenty of shortcomings."

I looked at Teuila's simple one-piece toga and motioned to my soiled clothing.

"Shall I take these off and leave them on the beach? Will you be offended if I swim in the nude?"

"Not at all," Teuila smiled. "It will give me a chance to clean your garments while you cool off. We all swim naked when we're bathing in the lagoon."

I glanced around me to see if anyone else was stealing glances from the surrounding brush and slowly began to disrobe. I knew that if anyone wanted to gawk at the white woman while she bathed that they could easily hide undetected behind the thick blanket of foliage, but I didn't really care. There was something about this remote island that seemed so natural and carefree to me. I was far more mindful of the impression I'd leave with the pretty native girl.

I turned my back toward Teuila, then pulled down my cargo shorts and panties, and slipped off my sweaty t-shirt and bra. It felt good to be liberated from the vestiges of Western civilization, and for the first time in my week-long tour of the South Pacific, I slipped into the warm waters of the tropical lagoon completely naked. It felt exquisite to be immersed in the buoyant salt water, and for the longest time I just floated on the surface, watching the wispy white clouds pass slowly over the sky. When I caught sight of the thin contrails of a jet aircraft high up in the atmosphere, I couldn't help smiling.

*Those suckers have no idea what they're missing down here,* I thought. *They probably can only imagine what it must be like to be untethered from society, living on these remote islands.*

I hadn't even once thought of picking up my smartphone since I'd left the boat. Not that I could do much with it, hundreds of miles away from the nearest wi-fi signal. I glanced over at Teuila, who was rubbing my cargo shorts with a taro root amid a froth of white foam in the shallows near the beach. She looked up at me and smiled in my direction.

"Are you starting to feel better?" she called. "Don't stray too far from the beach. There are treacherous currents near the reef. The last thing we need is for you to drown after nursing you back to health."

"Not to worry," I shouted. "I'm just enjoying this little moment of bliss."

After five minutes or so, I began to walk out of the water in Teuila's direction. As I emerged from the surf, she eyed my body from top to bottom. She seemed particularly interested in my bare mound as her eyes danced over my pale white hips. As I approached her, she held open a painted native dress, and I stepped into it while she pulled it up over my breasts and fastened it with loose strings behind my shoulders.

"Do you mind my asking," she said, as I turned around to face her. "Why your *agava* is smooth like a young girl's? It seems strange to see a full-grown woman without any hair down there. Is this a particular custom of Euro—I mean *American*—women?"

"As a matter of fact," I chuckled. "It is. "It's become the norm for Western women to shave themselves down there. I'm not exactly sure how the practice started. Maybe it's because it makes us seem younger and more alluring to our sexual partners. Or maybe it's just easier to navigate around down there. I find it heightens the sensa-tion when I'm touched in that delicate area. But I can see how strange that must seem to someone who's used to living a natural lifestyle."

"Actually," Teuila said, thinning her eyelids as she peered at my deep cleavage atop the tight-fitting tunic. "I find it quite sexy. You look like a doll. A very curvy and *sexy* doll."

"I've never been called that before, but I'll take it as a compli-ment." I glanced in the direction of the village. "When does the festival start? What can I do to help you prepare?"

"First of all, we need to get you properly dressed for the festivities. The ceremony will start at dusk. Let's go back to my hut and see if we can make you look like a proper Anutian girl."

I paused for a moment, raising my eyebrows in curiosity.

"Is that the name of your island—*Anuta*?"

"Yes. It means slippery shore. Because our island is so small and far away from anybody, everything seems to just slide by us."

*That's not the only thing that's slippery right now,* I thought, feeling the cool sea breeze wafting over my bare vulva as I watched Teuila's sexy lips moving.

When we got back to her hut, Teuila and her grandmother fitted me with a grass skirt and decorated my hair with a garland of native flowers. The old lady pinched her eyebrows when she saw my bare pubis and she ran the back of her hand over my mound, making a comment to Teuila about my lack of *lauulu*. I wished it had been the young girl who had caressed me instead, but I hoped we'd soon have an opportunity to explore each other when we alone later.

I found it interesting that they left the upper half of my body exposed, draping it simply with the long floral lei that her grand-mother had brought into the hut earlier. The flower petals were bright and soft, and they tickled my nipples as they fell over the full-ness of my breasts. I smiled at the old woman and nodded in appreci-ation as she pulled it over my neck.

"What's your grandmother's name?" I asked Teuila.

"Her given name is *Tausa'afia*, meaning kind one, but we all call her Nona."

"You Anutians seem to prefer long and difficult-to-pronounce names. Does your grandmother have a pet name for you?"

"She calls me Te', like the French word for tea."

"That's perfect," I said, "because you're both so kind and calming."

I looked at the old woman and smiled, caressing the floral lei gently between my fingers.

"Thank you, Nona," I said, "for this lovely gift. You've both made me feel so welcome in your home. I'm looking forward to tonight's celebration."

**6**
———

Shortly after dusk, Teuila and her grandmother escorted me out to the main promenade of their village. A huge bonfire was burning at one end while her father sat on an elevated platform at the opposite end. Nona sat on the right side of the chief's platform along with his younger sons, while Te' and I sat on his left side with her sisters. This was the first time I'd seen her entire family assembled in one place, and I counted a grand total of eight siblings, all considerably younger than Teuila. Arrayed in front of us on a long serving plank were huge bowls and plates made of seashells festooned with a variety of fragrant foods. The rest of the villagers sat in family units on opposite rows lining the central esplanade, eyeing me curiously.

Further to the side of the chief's platform stood two men dressed in grass skirts with woven mats on their chests, wearing what looked to be war paint on the sides of their cheeks. In front of them rested hollowed-out logs with an animal skin pulled tightly over the top, while they held two large bones in each of their hands. When all the families had taken their designated seats, the chief raised his arm and a hush fell over the assembly.

"*Amata le pati!*" he hollered, nodding toward the two drummers flanking his platform.

The drummers started beating their drums rhythmically, and everyone began singing and chanting in their native dialect while the young women of each family stood to assemble in the central square. Teuila squeezed my hand, then stood up to join the other girls in the pit. As the older women began singing in their heavily accented intonation, the girls in the square began swinging and shaking their hips in rhythm with the beat. I watched in fascination as they swiveled their perfectly toned bodies to the music. Their grass skirts shimmied suggestively as their bare stomachs and breasts writhed under the skimpy covering of their flowery leis.

This was the first time I'd seen Teuila's pretty figure partially unclothed since the waterfall, and my eyes widened as I watched her sexy hips swaying to the music. She had virtually no fat on her immaculately toned stomach, and my mouth watered watching her abdominal muscles twitching and flexing on her tanned midriff. Knowing she was naked under her heavy straw skirt made the display all the more intoxicating, and I began to shake my own hips on the ground, as much in sympathy with the dancers as to produce some much-needed friction on my acting clit.

After a few minutes, Te' pointed at me and curled her finger in a come-hither manner, motioning for me to join the girls in their hula dance. I looked at her with a quizzical expression shaking my head, but she danced closer to me and held out her hand for me to stand up. I looked at the other women sitting around the square as they continued singing, and they smiled and nodded at me, encouraging me to join the group. I was still feeling a bit dizzy and sore, but I knew this was an opportunity I'd regret if I didn't take part.

I clasped Te's hand and walked with her toward the other dancers, trying to mimic the shaking of their hips like I did when I was a little girl trying to balance a hula hoop. It felt awkward trying to match the vigor and pace of their movements, and as I joined the line, the older women around the camp smiled at me with big grins. Whether they were simply trying to contain their mirth at the awkward attempts of the European woman attempting to mimic their native dance technique, or they were just happy to see me joining in with the rest of the locals in the celebration, was unclear. I looked up at the chief resting on the platform, and he nodded approvingly at my awkward attempt to dance an authentic tribal hula.

*At least I can blame my rubbery legs on the after-effects of the snake venom*, I thought.

After ten minutes or so, I began to feel wobbly, and I motioned to Teuila that I needed to sit down. She nodded and escorted me back to our resting position, holding my hand as she continued shimmying her hips to the music. When the song ended, the hula girls sat down with their families, and a group of young men carrying long spears stood to take opposite positions in two straight lines facing one another about five feet apart.

As the drummers began beating their drums more vigorously, the two men at the far end of the line moved into the center row and began dancing in a side-step fashion toward the front of the line, thrusting their spears forward and back in a menacing fashion. The combination of their fierce expressions and scary war paint, along with the waving of their stone-tipped spears, certainly looked convincing to me. I wondered what purpose these warrior actors could find for their threatening weapons in what appeared to be an otherwise peace-loving culture.

When the two men from the back of the line reached the front, they took positions beside their compatriots in the straight lines, stomping the bottom of their spears on the ground as the next pair at the end of the line copied their routine. In this manner, the line of warriors slowly but steadily approached closer to the chief's platform and our own position. As the drumming and chanting slowly built toward a crescendo, Teuila squeezed my hand as if to assure me that the spectacle was all for fun.

But I noticed as the final pair of dancers approached the front of the line that the tallest and most imposing one kept his eyes locked on Teuila the whole time. When he reached the end of the line, he bellowed some kind of war chant and glanced down at the two of us holding hands, then he took his position at the front of the formation, closest to the chief.

"That one seems to have a special interest in you," I whispered to Teuila, trying not to stare at his scary expression.

"I think he has designs on me," Te' nodded. "Manaia's been following me around the village the last few months. I've caught him and my father having private chats whenever I return from the women's lagoon."

"Well he certainly looks like a *capable* mate," I said, noticing the young man flexing his arm and leg muscles as he stared at us.

"That's exactly what I'm afraid of," Teuila said as she passed me some fresh plates of fish and manioc from the buffet table in front of us. "But for now, let's not fret about what may be. Let's enjoy the moment and savor all the good food and dancing."

# 7

After the ceremony ended, Teuila's family returned to their small hut, where we all slept shoulder-to-shoulder on the dusty floor. I wanted to reach out and touch her lying next to me, but her father's heavy breathing so close by soon squelched my desire. In the morning, we all shared a hearty breakfast of frigate eggs, yams, and fermented breadfruit paste on the porch overlooking the courtyard. As I gobbled up the savory mix of yolk-stained starch and sour mash, I marveled at how tasty the local cuisine was in the absence of our typical Western condiments.

Later that morning, Teuila led me on a private tour of the island. As we traipsed into the heavy brush along a stony path, I shook my head wondering how she could cover such rough ground in bare feet. The only thing she carried with her was a stone adze which she used to hack away the overhanging leaves, and the one-piece dress on her back made from pressed bark.

"Be careful with that thing," I said, following her a few feet behind. "We don't want to antagonize another one of those tree snakes. I'm not sure I could carry you back to the village like you did for me if you get bitten."

"Don't worry about me," Teuila said. "I've acquired a certain degree of immunity. Our people believe that all living things are endowed with supernatural powers—what we call *mana*. We've learned to live in harmony with our fellow island dwellers. As long as we leave them alone, they shouldn't cause us too much trouble."

"Tell that to the critter who bit me by the waterfall. I don't think he's recognized my mana yet."

"Never fear," Te' chuckled, "Worst-case scenario, I can always resuscitate you with my special potion."

"Mmm, yes," I said, remembering our last kiss. "In that case, bring on all the angry serpents you can find."

As I watched her scamper over the jagged rocks and thick brush lining the trail, I glanced at her soiled feet.

"How can you walk over all this rough terrain in bare feet?" I asked. "I'm wearing heavy hiking shoes, and I'm already feeling sore and all scratched up."

"The soles of our feet get pretty toughened up from all the coarse surfaces we walk on from the moment we're born. Between the sandy beaches, the rocks in the lagoon, and rough brush in the jungle, we soon develop a thick skin to protect us against most obstacles. But if you need to rest for a moment, there's a clearing up ahead where we can stop for a bite to eat."

"I could use a little respite," I nodded, breathing heavily from the steep uphill climb. "I'm a little out of shape from all the lounging around I've been doing since I began my tour of these Pacific islands."

We stopped at a small clearing surrounded by a copse of tall palm trees.

"Are you hungry?" Te' asked.

"I could do with a bite, but we didn't bring anything. What did you have in mind?"

"The island provides everything we need," she said, glancing up toward the canopy of trees. "How about some fresh pineapple?"

I looked up and saw a clump of spiny pods bunched together under the leafy umbrella of long green fronds at the top of the tree.

"I'd love some, but how can we get those down?"

Teuila smiled, as she rubbed the bottom of her feet.

"These tough soles are good for more than just *walking* over rough surfaces," she said.

She placed her adze on the ground, then approached one of the palm trees and grasped its cracked bark with two hands, placing the soles of her feet in perpendicular positions against the sides of the trunk. She pulled her body toward the trunk and lifted her feet a few inches higher, pointing her knees outward. Then she pressed upward with her legs, taking a higher handhold on the stem. After a series of similar shimmying maneuvers, it didn't take long for her to ascend halfway up the tree.

I shook my head, dumbfounded at how easily she could scale the timber using just her arms and legs. With her legs splayed apart, I could clearly see under her tunic, and my pussy began to water as I watched her buttocks and vulva flexing with each leapfrog up the tree. When she neared the crown, she looked down and called out to me.

"You might want to stand back a bit. I'm going to shake the tree now, which should drop a few pineapples. They're pretty sharp and prickly, so make sure you stay out of the way."

I nodded as I looked up at her, taking a few steps back. As she started shaking her body against the tree, the leaves began rustling and a few seconds later four or five pineapples plopped to the ground beside me. She descended the tree just as easily as she'd climbed it, and when she got to the bottom, she rubbed the loose bark off her hands then brushed the debris covering the front of her gown.

"Now I see why you native girls wear such thick clothing," I said, pinching her cloth between my fingers. It felt a bit like thin cardboard, though it clung to her curvy figure like a cotton dress.

"The bark of the mulberry tree is like papyrus," she said. "And it's easy to decorate using turmeric dye and volcanic mud. Nothing goes to waste on our island."

I picked up one of the spiny pineapples off the ground and held it in my hand, feeling its heavy weight.

"These look pretty nutritious. But how will we get to the flesh inside?"

"It's simple with the right tools," Teuila said, taking the fruit from my hand.

She placed the husk against the side of the tree, then deftly hacked the two ends off with her sharp adze. Then she chopped the shell in half across the middle and placed the two hollow rings against the trunk and cut each section into two semi-circular crescents. We sat down, leaning our backs against the tree, and bit into the juicy pulp like watermelon pieces. The yellow juice squirted all over my face as I bit into it, running down my chin. I drew the back of my hand across my mouth, then wiped the sticky juice on the blanket of leaves lining the forest floor.

"Be careful there," Teuila said, noticing the juice dribbling down my neck toward my T-shirt. "Or we'll have to do another load of wash."

She rubbed her fingers over my chest just above my cleavage then sucked her fingers into her mouth.

"Anything to get me out of my clothes again near you," I said, feeling my pussy throb from her seductive gesture. "Besides, I can always change into my new native garb," remembering how sexy I felt wearing just a grass skirt and floral lei around my neck.

"We might be able to get you out of those clothes and cleaned up sooner than you think," Te' said, motioning further up the trail. "There's another waterfall about twenty minutes up the slope, with a secluded swimming hole. It's one of my favorite places to go when I want to be alone."

"To convene with nature or to find some private play time?" I said, raising an eyebrow.

"Both. But this time, we won't just have to *watch* each other."

"Mmm, yes," I said, feeling my panties moistening with a different kind of juice. "I've been dreaming of touching you ever since I laid eyes on you two days ago."

"We better get a move on then," Te' said. "Because I'm definitely starting to feel hot under the collar."

Teuila and I quickly finished eating our pineapple slices, then we continued walking up the trail. As I watched her sexy hips rocking back and forth in her tight native smock, I reflected back to the ceremony last night and her extended family sleeping on the floor of their straw hut.

"Do you mind my asking," I said. "Whatever happened to your mother? Your grandmother is so sweet and helpful, but with such a large family, how do you and your father manage?"

"She died many years ago when she stepped on a rusty knife a European traveler had left on the beach and her foot became septic. The infection spread rapidly, and we had no way of saving her. I think this is one of the reasons why my father is so suspicious of Western visitors."

"I'm so sorry to hear that. Did your father ever remarry? I noticed that most of your siblings are quite a bit younger than you."

"He never quite recovered emotionally from her loss. But our tribe has a culture of sharing between families, and he's adopted many children whose mothers and fathers died during fishing expeditions and other natural disasters."

"So your Nona raised you from the time you were young? Where did you learn to speak such good English?"

"There was a period when my father welcomed the presence of Western visitors. We had a missionary school set up for many years where other children of my age studied many of the same subjects you learn in primary school. But my father became suspicious of their motivation after a period of time and banished them from our island, fearful they were stealing his *mana*. Ironically, they might have been able to save my mother if he'd allowed them to stay."

"It's a difficult proposition," I nodded, "melding two disparate cultures. Many other native people around the world have rejected Western help for the same reasons. It's never easy for men to relinquish the reins of power, no matter how much his subjects may welcome the change."

"My father can be a stubborn man," Te' said. "But his heart's in the right place. Even though our tribespeople defer to him, our culture of *aropa* dictates that all of our natural spoils be shared equally by the community. He's never tried to hoard resources or oppress our people in any direct way."

"What about this cargo ship that visits the island from time to time?" I said, reflecting back on his order that I leave the island as soon as practicable. "Why does he still permit the occasional outside intrusion?"

"We only exchange *goods* when the ship comes around," Teuila explained. "The markets in Honiara on the Solomon Islands are willing to pay a high price for the shark fins we harvest. We barter their equivalent value for things like nylon fishing line, cloth sails, and nets for catching fish in the lagoon."

"*Shark fins?*" I said, cringing at the thought of sharks flapping help-lessly in the sea without their essential means of navigation.

"Don't worry," Te' said. "We use every part of the fish we catch. Shark flesh is considered a delicacy in our tribe. We even use their teeth as cutting blades."

"Nothing goes to waste," I nodded, breathing a sigh of relief.

After another twenty more minutes of hiking, I began to hear the sound of a cataract in the distance, and before long we came upon a break in the forest with a small waterfall cascading into a shallow pool.

"Do you feel like cooling off?" Teuila said, smiling toward me.

"Do I ever," I said, practically tearing my clothes off.

As I watched Te' step out of her one-piece tunic, I studied her body carefully. I hadn't seen her fully naked since the last time we were near a waterfall, and I could feel my nipples hardening as I ran my eyes all over her athletic figure. Her breasts sat up firm and high on her chest, and her dark teats stood out prominently on her caramel-colored skin. As she wiggled out of her tight dress, I couldn't help staring at the triangle-shaped patch of dark pubic hair nestled between her exquisitely carved hips.

"You look like you've never seen a naked woman before," Te' laughed, noticing me soaking up her body.

"Just not one so naturally pretty," I said.

"Come on," she said, standing on the edge of an abutment overlooking the aquamarine pool. "How do you Americans say it? Last one in is a rotten egg!"

Teuila placed her arms over her head then executed a perfectly clean dive into the murky water. Before she could surface, I chickened out and jumped off the cliff, placing my hands between my legs to protect the slap of water against my private parts. When we both surfaced, we splashed and squirted water towards each other's faces, giggling like little girls. I swam toward her and wrapped my arms around her back, pressing our chests together as our mouths joined in blissful union. As we kicked our legs together under the surface to stay afloat, our hips bumped together and I could feel her bush rubbing against my bare mound. The more passionate our kiss became, the harder it became for the two of us to stay above the water.

"Come," Teuila smiled, motioning toward the waterfall. "Let's go somewhere more comfortable. I bet you've never experienced a true Anutian shower before."

We swam to the base of the waterfall, then climbed up over the slippery rocks and ducked our heads under the chute. As we pressed our bodies together under the torrent, I leaned down and sucked Te's nipples into my mouth. She placed her hands behind my head and pulled me closer, purring under the falling water. I slowly kissed my way back up her chest and thrust my tongue deep into her mouth, kissing her passionately.

As our tongues danced in each other's mouths, we ran our hands over each other's bodies. I reached behind Te's back and cupped her firm buttocks in my palms, and she pressed her mound tightly against mine. I pulled away just far enough to slip my hand between the front of her thighs and began to stroke her slippery lips, pressing my fingers gently inside her. She spread her legs further apart and I drew my hand over her soft bush, pinching her clit softly between my two fingers.

As Teuila began moaning in my mouth, I rubbed my fingers in gentle circles around her nub. It only took a few moments before her hips to begin shaking as she gasped into my ear. I held her tightly against me, rubbing our nipples together, as she experienced her first orgasm at the hand of another woman.

**8**

———————

Teuila and I made love on the grassy knoll overlooking the waterfall then slept under the late afternoon sun to dry off. By the time we woke up, it was already starting to get dark and we headed back to the village, walking hand-in-hand along a moonlit beach. It felt sublime to take my shoes off and feel the warm seawater lapping at our feet as we talked about our past experiences and future plans. But as we neared her village, Te' suddenly became quiet.

"Is everything alright?" I asked, fearing she was having second thoughts about our making love. "Are you angry with me for taking advantage of you at the waterfall?"

"No, Jade," she said, smiling warmly into my eyes. "It was beautiful. I'm so glad you were my first. I can't imagine a more tender and giving lover."

"You seem a little pensive. Was there something on your mind?"

"It's just—", Te' paused, as she looked out over the moonlight reflecting off the ocean. "I know you'll be leaving soon. I've grown fond of you in the short time we've been together. I can't imagine being alone on this island without you."

I paused and ran my hand softly through her hair.

"As you said earlier, you're hardly alone here. You've got a loving family and the support of your entire community. I've rarely seen the kind of mutual love and generosity practiced by your tribe. Your tradition of aropa is a rare and wonderful thing."

"It's true that we all get along and share everything communally," Teuila said. "But what you and I have is something personal and special. I've never felt this way with someone else before. You make my heart dance."

I placed my arms around Te's shoulders and held her gently as I watched the surf crash softly against the shore. I was surprised by how close I'd grown to her in the three days we'd been together. But I worried that her feelings were being influenced by her youth and inexperience. I remembered what it felt like to fall in love the first time and how fragile our relationship was as my high school sweetheart and I took our first steps into the adult world.

"Oh Te'," I said, cradling her face in my hands. "I feel the same way about you. But we have to be careful about letting our emotions get carried away. We have such a short time together. I think we should just live in the moment and enjoy this while it lasts."

Teuila looked at me with a pained expression as a tear rolled down her cheek.

"Why can't you take me *with* you?" she pleaded. "The missionaries have taught me so much about the outside world. I think it would be so exciting to live with you in America."

I paused for a long moment as my eyes traced back and forth across her pretty face. She'd broached a subject both of us had fantasized about, but up until now neither of us had had the courage to express.

"How would that work?" I said. "America is thousands of miles away, both geographically and culturally. It would be a huge adjustment for you. And besides—I'm not sure your father would allow it. You're his only natural child, and you've already told me how suspicious he is of Western people."

Even though I was trying to talk her out of the crazy idea, I was already thinking about how I might arrange her landed immigrant status. The island of Anuta had no sovereign status as an independent nation and there were no embassies or consulates to help prepare the necessary paperwork. How could I even prove that she'd reached the age of majority?

"I'm a grown woman!" Teuila shouted. "I'm old enough to make my own decisions. Some of the young men from our island have traveled aboard the cargo ship in the past to pick up provisions in Honiara. My father can't stop me if I want to explore the world. And there's no one I'd rather do it with than you."

I pulled her close to me and held her tightly, feeling her heart beating against mine. It was an audacious idea, but not an insurmountable one. Surely there must be a protocol in place for allowing people from unrecognized jurisdictions into the United States. Even if I had to *marry* her—"

I pulled myself back and placed my hands on Te's shoulders. I couldn't believe I was thinking the unthinkable.

"Let's sleep on this tonight and talk about it in the morning, okay? This is all happening so fast. I don't want you to do something you'll regret later. We've still got a couple of weeks to explore our feelings for one another and talk to your father to test his receptivity to this idea."

I glanced over in the direction of the village and noticed a billow of white smoke rising into the night sky.

"Let's head back to your hut. He's probably worried about you. Like you said, we shouldn't test his patience too quickly."

"Yes," Te' sighed. "He's probably thinking about sending out a search party if we don't return soon." She clasped my arms firmly, furrowing her brow. "Promise me that you'll think about this. I want to be with you forever."

I looked into her limpid brown eyes and smiled.

"I promise," I nodded.

As we continued strolling through the foamy surf, I suddenly felt my own heartbeat pounding strongly in my chest.

*Forever's a long time*, I thought.

When we returned to Te's village, everyone was already lying asleep on the floor of her hut. Her father was reclining in a rocking chair on the front veranda with his eyes closed, snoring loudly. We crept up the front stairs and passed by him as he snorted, then we took off our clothes and pulled a taro blanket over us, reclining in the far corner next to some of the young children. We tried to sleep, but we were both still too excited about what had happened at the waterfall and about our discussion on the beach.

Te' rolled over on her side and pressed her hips against mine, and we mashed our mounds together, sighing quietly in each other's mouths. It was difficult to remain quiet with the sound of our moving bodies on the crunchy mats underneath us, but once our clits joined together, we couldn't stop tribbing one another until we both reached a powerful climax together. Five minutes later, Te's father rose from his chair on the porch and paused in the doorway for a long time, watching the two of us lying peacefully next to one another. When he finally lay down on the other side of the cabin and began snoring, we giggled under the covers and fell asleep in each other's arms.

We woke up to the sound of Te's siblings chattering on the front porch and got dressed, finding Nona preparing breakfast. The chief was nowhere to be found, but a few minutes later I noticed him talking privately at the far end of the courtyard with the young man who'd shown such an intense interest in Te' at the feast two nights ago. When her father approached the hut, he looked at Te' with a serious expression and motioned with his head for her to join him in the courtyard.

I watched the two of them walk down the sandy esplanade together, then Teuila suddenly stopped as she confronted her father with a raised voice. I heard the chief mention something about Manaia, and Te' shook her head violently, gesturing wildly with her hands. Shortly after, she stomped up the path and grabbed my hand, leading me into the woods.

"What is it, Te'?" I asked. "Was your father angry that we returned so late last night?"

"Worse," she said as tears streamed down her cheeks. "Much worse. He heard us making love last night and disapproves of how close we've become. He intends to marry me to Manaia in a ceremony tomorrow night."

That night, neither one of us slept well. I kept replaying the image of Teuila being violated by her groom as she fought to resist his advances. I could feel her tossing and turning next to me, and whenever she cried out or whimpered in her sleep, I cradled her gently in my arms. My mind raced with crazy ideas of stealing one of the tribe's canoes and sailing to safety to the nearest neighboring island. But I no idea in which direction that might be, and neither Teuila nor I had any way of navigating our way through the open seas. Even if the charter boat crew returned for me, it wouldn't be easy to kidnap the chief's daughter from the clutches of her heavily armed tribe. After running every possible scenario through my head, I eventually fell asleep resigned to the idea that my precious island girl would soon be wrenched away from me.

In the morning, Nona began preparing a special meal for the evening's ceremony while some of Te's sisters braided her hair under the watchful eye of her father. We were both under virtual house arrest, with the chief posting an armed guard outside the front door of their hut. He wasn't taking any chances that the two of us might steal away again before his daughter was betrothed to Manaia. Te' put on a brave face as her sisters talked excitedly with her, but she kept glancing toward me with sad eyes. Fortunately, we were the only ones in her family who spoke English, so at least we were able to carry on a limited discussion.

"You look beautiful," I said, peering at her pretty face with her hair pulled back behind her head. "I like you in braids."

"The girls have lots of practice," Te' frowned. "With all the mats and baskets they've woven, they could probably do this with their eyes closed." She looked at her grandmother scraping some manioc shavings into a large wooden bowl. "That and cooking is pretty much all we women do around here."

I glanced at Teuila's father, who was sitting cross-legged on the other side of the hut, watching us with a stern expression.

"What about raising a *family*?" I said. "Isn't that something you're looking forward to? You and your sisters seem to have a close relationship."

"Jade," Te' said, shaking her head slowly. "I know you're trying to make me feel better, but it's no use. You're the only one I want. There's nothing else in the world that I need as long as I'm with you."

I tightened my lips, trying to hold back my emotions.

"It won't be so bad," I said. "Lots of marriages are arranged. Over time, I'm sure you'll grow to love your new husband. After I'm gone, you'll soon forget about me—"

"I could *never* forget you," she said, her eyes flaring. "And I'll never love that brute. As long as we're apart, I'll never be happy."

"Te'," I said, glancing in her father's direction. "We have to accept the reality of the situation. It's out of our hands now. You'll soon be married, we'll be separated from each other, and I'll be banished from the island. It's best that you get on with your life..."

"I've been thinking," she said. "There might be another way. All we have to do is find a way to get the two of us away from the clutches of my father for a few moments. Then we can slip into the forest and hide away until one of the boats comes to pick you up."

I glanced at the two burly men standing opposite the front steps of their hut holding sharp spears in their hands.

"How could we do that? Your father doesn't seem to want either one of us out of his sight, much less *both* of us at the same time."

"It shouldn't be too difficult to stretch your legs for a moment. It's me that he's primarily worried about. He knows you couldn't fend for yourself very long if you ran away. He'd probably be *happy* if something were to happen to you, so I'd stop pining for you. We just need to find a way to get you out of the hut. Then all I'd need to do is create a distraction and slip away. I know this island better than anyone. There are lots of places where we could hide out for a few weeks."

"I don't know, Te'," I said. "It sounds risky. What if we get caught? Your father doesn't seem like the kind of man to let that sort of challenge to his authority go unpunished. There's no rule of law on this island. It wouldn't take much for him to have me put down. I have a feeling he's already at the end of his patience."

Teuila paused for a long moment as her eyes studied my face. As much as I was concerned for my own safety, I was far more worried about the consequences to *her* if we got caught. The worst thing would be for her to see me tortured or killed for disrespecting the chief's power.

"Do you think you could find your way back to the waterfall we visited yesterday?" she asked.

"I don't know, maybe. I suppose if I followed the same path—"

"If you can find your way there, I'll meet you in a couple of hours. Worst-case scenario, you can hide out in the jungle and live off pineapples and taro root until your ship arrives. My father won't harm you with other Westerners around. He knows it would just bring more visitors to the island and threaten his position as chief."

I shook my head and sighed heavily.

"But on what pretense would he let me out of the hut? And what if he sends an armed guard with me? How would I escape?"

Te' paused as her eyes darted from side to side.

"We'll need to relieve ourselves eventually. My father isn't such a brute that he'd insist on our doing our business right here on the floor of the hut. You can ask to be escorted to the women's bathing lagoon, then ask the guard to let you take care of business behind a clump of palm trees. When his back is turned, do you think you could climb to the top of one of those trees like I showed you? He'll never expect you to do that, searching the trails and beach for your footprints, not looking up."

I closed my eyes, reflecting back on Te's technique climbing the pineapple tree. She'd made it look remarkably easy, and I was still in decent shape from my regular trips to the gym.

"I think so. But how long will I have to stay up there before it's safe to come down?"

"My guess is that if the guard can't find you within a few minutes, my father will tell everyone to forget about you. He'll be far more concerned about letting me out of his sight."

"And how will you manage that?"

"Let *me* worry about that," Te' smiled. "I'm very resourceful. Just make sure you find your way back to the waterfall. It's a big island, and it will be very difficult to find each other again if you get lost."

"I can't believe I'm considering this," I said, feeling my heart beginning to pound in my chest.

For the first time in many years, I'd never felt so alive. The idea of running away from an angry tribe on an isolated island with the girl of my dreams was beyond any fantasy I'd ever imagined. I could feel the adrenaline coursing through my veins and the hairs on the sides of my arms standing on end.

"I'm in," I said.

Teuila turned to speak with her father for a few moments, then he paused as he appraised my demeanor. I tried to remain as calm as possible, but I could feel the veins in my neck pulsing like crazy as he glared at me. Eventually, he gave a single nod of his head, then rose to give instructions to one of the guards standing outside the front door.

"*Alu*," he said to me, jerking his head towards the open door. "*Le maua manatu.*"

"What did he say?" I asked Teuila.

"Pretty much what we expected. He's going to send a guard with you who won't give you a lot of space to maneuver, so you'll have to choose your position carefully. Find one with enough cover to protect your modesty, but also close enough to a tree so that you can climb it without him noticing you. I'll come for you as soon as I can."

"Be careful," I said, standing to exit the cabin.

"You too."

I paused at the door of her hut and looked back at Teuila one last time. I didn't know if or when I'd see her again.

When I got to the base of the front steps, one of the guards looked sternly at me then motioned with his spear in the direction of the women's lagoon. As I walked down the same sandy path where all the tribespeople had welcomed me so warmly two nights ago, I noticed the women and children tracing my movement with vacant expressions.

*It looks like I'm on my own again*, I thought.

When we reached the edge of the lagoon, the guard motioned to a shallow depression at the edge of the brush.

"*Oe alu ai*," he ordered, pointing to the basin with his spear.

I glanced around the area, noticing there was little surrounding vegetation to provide privacy for someone taking care of such intimate business.

I shook my head as I pulled on my shorts, indicating that I needed more privacy. He looked around the edge of the lagoon and pointed to a more secluded spot about a hundred feet up the beach, next to a small clump of coconut trees. When we reached the spot, I climbed behind a small bush and began to squat, noticing the guard still watching me.

I motioned with my hand for him to look away, and he turned his back briefly. Knowing I'd only have a few seconds to act, I removed my hiking shoes and hid them in the brush. Then I crawled behind the sandy embankment toward the nearby palm trees. When I reached the furthest one, I stood and peered around the side of the trunk. The guard had turned around and was glancing curiously in the direction of the pit, tilting his head high in the air as he lifted his heels off the ground. He shouted something in his native language, and when I didn't respond, he rushed forward with a look of alarm, finding the pit empty.

He swiveled his head quickly from side to side, then peered at the stand of trees. As he began walking in my direction, I placed the soles of my feet against the side of the trunk as Teuila had shown me, then I grasped the crusty bark and pulled myself upward. As I heard the guard's footsteps nearing the stand, I began slowly shimming myself up the tree. With most of my weight borne by the inward pressure of my feet pressed against the trunk, it was easier than I expected to scale the thick stem. But as I pulled my knees inward, worrying he'd see them sticking out from the side of the tree, I ended up using more arm strength than I intended to move upward.

By the time I reached the crown of the tree and glanced down, I was sweating profusely. My feet were bleeding from the sharp crust pressing into my tender skin, but I was able to leverage my weight with tight handholds against the layered bark. As the guard peered frantically from side to side looking for me, I noticed the pod of coconuts under the palm fronds shaking precariously. Just as one of them snapped from its stem, I reached out and caught the husk as it fell into my open palm.

The guard cocked his head hearing the sound and started to look up. I threw the nut as far as I could in the direction of the bush, and when he heard it land in the dense thicket, he took chase into the forest. I sat in my cramped position breathing heavily as sweat poured down the front of my T-shirt, listening carefully for the sound of the guard's footsteps in the jungle. When the footfalls diminished into the distance, I quickly descended the tree, falling sharply to the ground. I looked around to make sure the way was clear, then I hobbled toward the far end of the beach and disappeared into the thick brush.

Half a mile away, Teuila sat patiently on the floor of her hut as her sisters finished decorating her hair with scented frangipani blossoms. She glanced toward her grandmother preparing the wedding ceremony dishes on the front veranda and asked her father if she could help. The chief nodded and followed Te' out onto the porch, taking a position in the rocking chair as he nodded toward the remaining guard.

Teuila sat next to her grandmother and Nona smiled, handing her a knife and a taro root to peel. Suddenly, the other guard came running up to the front of the hut, and when he told the chief that the white woman had escaped, her father summoned a group of young tribesmen and they ran off in the direction of the lagoon. Nona glanced at Teuila, pinching her eyebrows in suspicion, wondering what kind of trouble the girls were getting into now.

Te' picked up the taro root and smiled, remembering how Jade had teased her when she first bit into it. Suddenly, the vegetable slipped in her hand and the knife cut a deep diagonal gash along the side of her index finger. As her hand began spurting blood all over the white gourd, Nona dropped what she was doing and motioned for the guard to summon the village's medicine man. When the guard hesitated remembering the chief's orders to keep a close watch on his daughter, Nona screamed at him, warning that if Teuila was not attended to soon, she could suffer the same fate as her mother.

"Do you want to be responsible for the death of the chief's daughter on the eve of her wedding?" she shouted in their native language.

The guard mumbled something and took off scurrying down the path. Nona looked at Te's cut shaking her head, then she wrapped a banana leaf around the wound and peered into her granddaughter's eyes.

"This wasn't an accident, was it?" she said.

"Forgive me, Nona," Te' said. "I love her. This is the only way I can be with her. Can you help me?"

Nona glanced down the sandy courtyard, then escorted Teuila

toward the rear of their cabin, where she lifted a flap of leaves and pointed into the forest.

"*Lau manamea*," she said. "Be with your lover. I'll pray that you both find happiness. Go quickly now, before your father returns."

As Teuila scampered into the forest holding the green bandage tightly against her swollen finger, she yelped in glee, knowing she'd soon be in the arms of the only person she ever truly loved.

**10**

———

When I got far enough away from the cluster of palm trees, I ducked into the bush and paused to get my bearings. From my new location, it would be difficult to find my way back to the waterfall. All I could remember was that it was about an hour's hike uphill in a roughly forty-five-degree angle from the village. But from my vantage point in the women's lagoon, it would be almost impossible to pick up the trail through the thick jungle. My only chance would be to double-back towards the village and hope that nobody saw me.

To make matters worse, my feet were sore and bleeding from climbing the rough palm tree. I thought taking my shoes off would help me to climb the trunk more quietly, but I hadn't counted on puncturing my skin in multiple places. And it would be too risky to try to return to the pit to retrieve them. Like it or not, I'd have to make my way back up to the waterfall in bare feet.

I shook my head at the irony of my predicament.

*The only way to truly appreciate another culture is to immerse yourself in it,* I reminded myself. *Well now I'm really going native. Let's see how quickly I can develop tough Anutian soles.*

I peered over the top of my sand dune to see if the coast was clear.

I hadn't heard from the guard since he ran off into the jungle, but I knew it would be too risky to use the cover of the thick brush to find my way back to the village. The carpet of broken twigs and sharp rocks on the forest floor would just make my feet worse, and the rustling of leaves could draw attention to my position. My only chance would be to backtrack along the beach before he returned.

But just as I prepared to sprint down the beach, I noticed my guard running toward me from the direction of the village, along with the chief and a group of other young tribesmen. They paused at the location where I'd squatted, and it didn't take long for the chief to find my hiking shoes.

"*O a nei?*" he shouted, holding my shoes up in the air.

The guard shook his head in bewilderment, then pointed into the jungle in the direction where I'd thrown the coconut.

"*Ona mamao,*" the chief said, throwing my shoes far into the lagoon. "*Salalau solo!*" he said, gesturing into the jungle in multiple directions.

As the group fanned out into the thick brush, I waited for a few moments then dashed back along the beach in the direction of the village. Feeling my blistered feet burning in the hot sand, I hobbled my way across the lagoon, glancing into the bush for any sign of the tribesmen.

Maybe it wasn't such a bad idea taking my shoes off after all, I thought, watching the impressions my feet left in the sand. I'm the only one on this island with Western shoes. It would be a whole lot easier to track me from the unique tread they'd leave on the ground than with my bare feet.

I just hoped the blood from my soles wouldn't leave another type of trail.

When I got to the edge of the village, I crouched low behind the back of the huts lining the central promenade, trying to stay out of sight. Small children giggled as they ran across the courtyard, playing a game of tag. One of the boys ducked under the crawlspace of the cabin I was hiding behind, and I pulled myself up on the side of the hut, trying to conceal my legs. He glanced in both directions to see if the coast was clear, then scampered back across the courtyard behind another hut.

*Great,* I thought. *Just what I need right now. A bunch of kids playing hide and seek. At least they're showing me some good hiding spots.*

As I slowly made my way toward the far end of the courtyard, I paused when I saw the chief's hut. There was no armed guard outside the front door, and I peered inside the darkened interior for any sign of Teuila. Her grandmother was peeling vegetables on the front porch, and she glanced in my direction, noticing movement across the lane. We locked eyes and for a moment and I was afraid she'd call out. But instead, she placed her finger to her lips, then motioned with an open hand toward the trailhead at the end of the square.

*She made it!* I breathed a sigh of relief. *God bless that woman.* Maybe I had a friend in the village after all.

I crept past the remaining huts lining the square then dashed onto the trail and scampered up the familiar path leading to the waterfall. Once I was on the path, I recognized the familiar landmarks and made good time picking my way up the slope. Even though the brush was thick, I was far more worried about bumping into one of the chief's chase team than I was about encountering another tree snake. When I reached the pineapple tree clearing, I knew I was on the right track and I smiled remembering the sight of Te's pretty ass climbing the tree.

*Soon,* I thought, *I'll have her all to myself.*

Thirty minutes later, I heard the sound of the waterfall nearby, and I breathed in the fresh scent of the misty air wafting over the trees. I didn't know if it was because all my senses were on high alert being on the run, or if it was because my heart was pounding knowing I'd soon be back with Teuila, but everything around me suddenly seemed so much more *alive.* The flowers at the side of the trail looked prettier, the air smelled sweeter, and the birds chirping in the distance sounded happier.

For the first time in many years, I was madly, deliriously in love.

When I reached the waterfall, I looked around frantically for my island girl, but there was no sign of her. I furrowed my brow, puzzled why she'd have taken longer to reach our destination than I had. She appeared to have had a head start on me, and she should have been able to scale the uneven path much quicker than me, especially with my chafed feet. But seconds later, she broke through the heavy brush on the opposite side of the waterfall and rushed toward me.

"Thank God you made it!" she said, throwing her arms around me. "I was so worried about you."

"Our little trick worked," I nodded, tilting the underside of one foot up toward her. "Although it looks like it's going to take a little longer than we hoped for the soles of my feet to get properly toughened up."

Teuila looked at my scarred soles and shook her head.

"What happened to your shoes?"

"I thought it would be safer to climb the tree without them. But it didn't take long for your father to find where I'd hidden them. I guess I'll be walking around barefoot like a real Anutian sooner than we thought."

Teuila chuckled as she squeezed my hand.

"It's probably better this way anyhow," she smiled. "Those treads would be visible a mile away."

"Why did you come up the other way?" I said, pointing to the direction of the jungle where she'd emerged.

"I wanted to throw my father off the trail," she said, pointing to the imprint of my boots on the muddy embankment. "But it won't take long for them to find us. We have to get out of here as soon as possible."

I noticed that the leaf wrapped around Te's index finger was dripping blood down her hand.

"What happened?" I said. "You're hurt!"

"It's just a flesh wound," she said. "It looks worse than it is. We'll be able to patch up our wounds when we get to safety."

Suddenly we heard the shouting of men's voices approaching our position. I looked at Teuila with terrified eyes.

"What should we do?" I said. "In which direction should we head?"

"There's no time for that," Te' said. "We have to *hide*. There's too many of them. They'll catch us too quickly."

"Where?" I said, looking around the clearing. "In the brush?"

Te' glanced around the glade, then peered into a still section of the pool furthest from the waterfall.

"How long can you hold your breath?" she said.

I looked at the surface of the pond for a moment, then back towards her.

"Not long in my present state," I said, feeling my chest heaving up and down. "Between my elevated state of adrenaline and my fear of being caught, I can hardly catch my breath as it is."

"What if we fashioned some kind of breathing tube?" she said, peering at some bulrushes at the far end of the pond. "Do you think you could remain still under the water while our tribesmen search the area?"

"I suppose so. What did you have in mind?"

"Those reeds on the other side of the pond are hollow. Follow me, but try to step as much as possible on the rocks instead of the dirt. We don't want them to be able to trace where we're hiding."

Teuila took my hand and led me to a flattened section of the embankment where we tiptoed over the scattered rocks on the edge of the shore. Then she slipped into the water and pushed herself away from the shore.

"Be careful when you step into the pond," she said. "We don't want to make too much noise or stir up the mud around the bank where they could see where we entered the water. Quickly now—I can hear them getting closer."

I lowered myself into the water then I pushed myself gently away from the shore. Teuila led me to the other side of the pond, then she pulled a pocketknife out of a pouch on her tunic and cut two four-foot lengths of reed. She tested each tube by puffing through them, then handed one to me. I could hear the sounds of the men's voices rising in volume and the rustling of the brush very close by.

"Put this in your mouth then duck under the water about three feet. Don't go any lower than that or you'll choke if the other end dips beneath the surface. Then follow me toward the waterfall. The rippling current will help camouflage us in the depths."

I looked at Teuila with frightened eyes, then placed the tube in my mouth and submerged under the water. After a brief moment of panic, I realized it wasn't so different from using a snorkel. I was scared using one of those at first too, but once I learned that I could breathe comfortably underwater, it didn't take long for me to relax. After I dropped a few feet, I opened my eyes and saw Te' submerge beside me. Then she took my hand and pulled me toward the churning undercurrent next to the waterfall.

When we reached the base of the cataract, I glanced up through the foaming water and noticed a group of half-naked tribesmen walking around the base of the swimming hole, pointing toward footprints in the ground. I looked toward Teuila fearfully, and she pumped her palm up and down, motioning for me to remain calm. Her dress was billowing underneath her, spreading out to her sides, and I worried the white sheen of the fabric would be noticeable from above. But she placed her hands between her legs in a Marilyn Monroe manner and pressed the gown downwards as her long black hair floated upwards.

I shook my head, smiling at the improbability of the situation. Only Teuila could make almost suffocating under water while a bunch of savages circled around us menacingly look sexy.

Suddenly, I noticed Manaia standing on the edge of the embankment, looking intently into the water. He walked around the edge of the pond, thrusting the dull end of his spear into the water, as if searching for something under the surface. When he reached the clump of reeds, he paused for a moment, then moved closer to the edge of the waterfall. Teuila's eyes widened as he got closer, and she motioned for us to move closer to the base of the cataract. She pinched her fingers around the base of the tube in her mouth then pulled them away quickly as she puffed her cheeks.

I glanced at her for a moment, then nodded my head in understanding. One of the first things I'd learned when using a snorkel was how to purge the water from the tube whenever I ducked under water. I took a deep breath in, then we paddled under the falling water as I felt the reed vibrating from the pressure of the deluge above us. When the we finally reached a calmer section near the embankment, I blew heavily out the tube, feeling the water passing upward through the reed, then I breathed deeply in. There was still a bit of water in the cylinder and I coughed suddenly, but after a few more frantic purges, I was able to breathe comfortably again.

As we treaded water trying to remain in a fixed position, we looked up through the gurgling surface. Manaia stared in our direction for a long moment, then he finally stepped back from the shore and joined the rest of his team on the cliff. Teuila's father motioned in the direction of the brush where she'd emerged earlier, then the group quickly dispersed. I kicked my legs toward the surface, but Te' reached out and grabbed my arm, motioning for me to stay submerged a little longer. About a minute later, Manaia reemerged at the edge of the abutment and turned his head to scan the surface of the lagoon, then he took off again into the forest. Teuila waited another five minutes, then she signaled that it was safe to resurface.

"Oh my God!" I said, looking at her with wide eyes. "That was *intense*. I was sure that Manaia had seen us. That was smart of you to wait until he'd left the second time."

"It's still not entirely safe," Teuila said. "I think we should wait here for another half hour or so. Once we know that they're not coming back, we'll have to find another place to hide. I want to put as much distance between us and the village as possible."

I circled my hands gently underwater as my eyes darted over her face.

"What about the beach where my charter boat came in? You said that was a good day's hike from your village. That should be the first place my crew will look for me if they return."

"That might work," Te' nodded. "But we'll have to be careful about staying too close to the shore. My father will probably send out another search party following the perimeter of the island by canoe. We'll scope out the area when we get there."

I kicked my legs excitedly, realizing we'd soon be alone again.

"Teuila," I said, throwing my arms around her, almost pulling both of us underwater. "I'm so happy we're together again. I could live in a *cave* with you if I had to."

"Let's hope your friends return for you soon," she said, peering nervously around the edge of the waterfall. "That might be the only safe place for us to hide soon if they don't."

**11**

———————

Teuila dressed my wounds with the milky sap of a spongy plant, then she wrapped my feet in banana leaves to help quell the bleeding. After a few minutes, I could feel the pain and throbbing begin to subside, and I shook my head marveling at her ability to apply natural cures. But I was far more concerned about the cut on her finger, which was still dripping blood under her makeshift bandage.

"That feels better," I said, lifting her hand to take a closer look at her incision. "But your cut looks far worse. Will a couple of leaves will be enough to close that wound?"

"I missed the main artery," she said, squeezing her finger tenderly. "I just need to apply a tight compress to stem the bleeding and allow it to clot."

She glanced down at my wet T-shirt and smiled.

"Do you think you'd be willing to part with your shirt? If we tear it into strips, we can wrap it around both my finger and your feet. We've got a long walk ahead of us to get to the other side of the island and it will help keep the dirt out of your wounds."

"Why not?" I smiled. "I've done it once before already. Now that we're alone, I don't feel so self-conscious about protecting my modesty." I pulled my shirt over my head and handed it to her. "Do you want my bra too?"

Te' peered at my bosom pushed together with the constricting garment and shook her head.

"It's probably best that you keep that on for a little longer. There will be plenty of sharp objects poking out of the brush as we make our way through the jungle. We don't want to get those pretty breasts of yours all scratched up. Besides, we might be able to find a better use for it later."

She bit the bottom of my shirt to make a small incision, then tore it in half lengthwise down the front and the back before pulling off the sleeves. Then she hacked two narrow pieces of bark off a nearby tree with her adze and placed them under my feet, wrapping the long ends of my shirt around the husks and tying the ends firmly behind my ankle.

"Not quite as pretty as your Western shoes," she said, but hopefully they'll last at least until we get to the other side of the island.

I stood up and paced forward and back a few steps, testing my newly fashioned sandals.

"They're surprising comfortable," I nodded. "Especially with those leafy insoles. Maybe we can hook you up with Nike when we return to the States."

"Nike?"

"Just kidding," I laughed. "They're a big shoe manufacturer back home. You're a woman of many talents, Te'. I'm sure we can find you a more interesting job when the time comes."

Teuila looked up at me and smiled.

"I'm excited to learn all about your culture. But right now, I think we should head over to the other side of the island. We don't want to overstay our welcome here. My father may come back to search for us if he doesn't find us elsewhere."

Teuila tore up one of the sleeves into a spiral strip, then she wrapped and tied it tightly around her wounded finger.

"Come on," she said. "Let's go see if we can find a better hiding place."

It took most of the day to cross to the other side of the island. Te' wanted to stay off the marked trails to avoid running into our search party, so we walked along the side of narrow creeks and streams to stay out of sight. I was afraid the stony riverbeds would splinter my makeshift moccasins, but the flexible bark absorbed most of the brunt and the shirt-tie miraculously survived the entire trip. When we passed the same waterfall where I was bitten by the snake, I knew we were getting close to the beach.

"How can you navigate through this dense jungle so easily?" I said, amazed at how she'd found her way back to the same spot on such a large island.

"I've lived here my whole life," she said. "I know this island like the back of my hand. There's not much else to do for fun around here, so I've made lots of expeditions in my eighteen years."

"I hope your father and your boyfriend don't know the island as well as you do. Otherwise, there'll be nowhere safe to hide."

"Don't worry about that," Te' said, peering up at the darkening sky. "I've had lots of practice hiding out in the forest. It's starting to get dark, so we won't have time to build a more comfortable shelter until the morning. We'll have to make do with a camouflaged lean-to for this evening. I'm looking forward to showing you how easily we can live off the land. We'll try to make the most of our little exile until your friends return."

"I'm looking forward to it too," I said, recalling my Robinson Crusoe fantasy. "This should be quite the adventure."

When we reached the beach where our charter boat had set anchor, Teuila checked out the lagoon and nodded.

"This will work fine. It's nicely secluded, has shallow water and shoals to catch fish, and has a good lookout for approaching boats."

"Where will we sleep?" I said, wrapping my arms around my chest, feeling the cool onshore breeze.

"It's probably best not to sleep on the beach tonight. My father may be sending out a canoe patrol to search the perimeter of the island. We'll have to sleep inland this evening."

I peered into Te's brown eyes and smiled.

"As long as lying I'm next to you, I can sleep anywhere."

Teuila found a secluded spot behind a sand dune and hacked down some large palm leaves to provide cover and keep us warm. Then she harvested a few pineapples and coconuts from some nearby palm trees, and we enjoyed an impromptu dinner.

"You must be hungry after trekking all day," she said, noticing me shivering as she placed some leaves over my bare torso. "Tomorrow we'll catch and cook up some fresh fish. But it's too risky to build a fire right now. Will you be warm enough sleeping here tonight?"

We lay down in the pit and Te' snuggled up close to me, pulling the big leaves over our bodies.

"I am *now*," I said, feeling her warm skin pressed against mine.

As much as I wanted to make love to her again, after ten hours of hiking we both fell asleep within minutes. In the morning, I woke to the sound of seabirds chirping in the distance as the morning sun began to warm up our little nest of leaves. Te' rolled over when I began to stir, and I kissed her gently.

"Did you sleep well?" I asked, caressing her warm shoulders.

"Like a log. But I had a few nightmares. I dreamed that my father found us and dragged us back to the village where he tied you to a stake in the main square. As everybody celebrated my marriage to Manaia, he set you aflame while I watched helplessly from his arms."

"Jesus!" I said, flaring my eyes open. "Would he actually *do* that if he caught us?"

"Perhaps not quite so viciously. But he's had other tribespeople punished for far less an offense."

Te' began lifting herself up to get out of the pit.

"We need to begin building fortifications and a better hiding place."

"Can't it wait a few more minutes?" I said, clutching her wrist. "This is the first time we've been alone in almost two days. I was hoping we could have a little fun before we get to work. Besides, don't you need to let your finger rest a little longer to let it heal?"

Teuila lifted her hand and untied the strip of cloth around her finger then opened the leaves to peer at her cut. The bleeding had stopped, but she had a nasty inch-long scar on the side of her hand.

"It still looks tender," I said, lifting her finger to my mouth as I sucked on the tip gently. "Maybe it needs some of my special healing juices."

"I'm not sure it works that way," Te' chuckled. "But it feels good, just the same."

"Well if it feels good licking your *finger*, maybe I can make you feel even better licking you somewhere else."

I lifted Teuila's robe over her shoulders then lay her down on the leaves.

"Lie down while I give you some loving."

As I nibbled my way down the front of her chest, I cupped her firm breasts in my hands and sucked on her nipples. It felt sublime to be holding her in my arms for the first time, knowing she was truly mine. I swirled my tongue over her fleshy peaks, and she moaned in pleasure. I could feel her hips gyrating below me, and she gasped when I pressed my thigh against her opening.

While I continued to suck and nibble on her breasts, Teuila ground her pussy into my thigh, coating the front of my leg with her wetness. After a few minutes, I pulled away and drew my tongue over her quivering abdomen until I reached her furry mound. It had been eons since I'd seen or felt a full patch of pubic hair, and I paused as I caressed her soft fur.

"Mmm," I purred. "I love how soft you are down here. I could run my hands through your hair all day."

"I like the way you touch me, Jade," Te' panted. "Kiss my private areas. I want to feel your lips on my *agava*."

As I drew my face over her bush, I could feel the moisture from her pussy beading in her hairs. I closed my lips over her muff and lifted my head up a few inches, gently tugging her hair as I sucked her dew into my mouth. It might have just been my wild imagination channeling my Blue Lagoon fantasy, but her juice tasted sweeter and fresher than anything I remembered.

The closer I got to her jewel, the harder she pushed her hips up into my mouth, and when I finally encircled her clit with my lips, she gasped out loud. As she spread her thighs further apart and I began to circle my tongue around her button, she began to whimper and call my name.

"Oh Jade," she whispered. "That feels so good. Lick me with your beautiful mouth. I want to feel you kissing me everywhere."

Hearing her cry out my name in the throes of passion sent a shiver down my spine, and I began to feel my own panties sticking to my skin. I wanted to feel her trembling against my face and call out my name as the waves of pleasure rolled over her. As her hips began shaking with increasing fervor, I sucked her into my mouth, dancing my tongue over her nub. When her hips began to rise up off the ground, I cradled her buns in my hands as she pressed herself tighter against my face.

"Yes, Jade," she groaned. "I can feel it coming now. Hold me while I release my *pito*. It's coming now!"

Suddenly, Te' growled as her hips began bucking wildly against my face and her buttocks started quivering in my palms. I opened my eyes and watched her tummy cavitating as she thrashed her head from side to side. I held her tightly while she spasmed against my face, coating me with her sweet, pungent syrup. When she finally stopped shaking, I lowered her hips to the cool leaves and snuggled up next to her.

"Does my healing touch work better that way?" I smiled, grinding my hips against her wet mound.

"Yes," she purred. "But now I think there's *another* wound that needs my attention."

Te' and I made love for the rest of the morning, then our growling stomachs reminded us how little we'd eaten in the last twenty-four hours.

"Come," she said, pulling me out of the pit. "Let's catch ourselves a proper breakfast, then we need to begin preparing a safer resting place. No more sleeping on the beach. I don't want to take any chances that my father and his thugs will stumble across us while we're resting. Let me show you how to catch fish the Anutian way."

She led me into the brush until we came upon a small stand of seedlings. Te' hacked two of them off near the base with her adze, then whittled the ends of each shoot down until they had sharp pointed ends.

I looked at her quizzically, wondering what she had in mind.

"Were you planning on using those in case we get ambushed?

"No, I would never harm my own people. These are for another type of creature. We're going to use them to spear fish."

"Really?" I said with wide eyes. "You can do that too? You really are a woman of many talents."

"It's not so easy to spear a free-swimming fish," she said. "But it's a lot easier when there's a bunch of them trapped in a contained area. That's where you come in. You're going to push them toward me."

"How will I do that?"

"You're going to rake them into a trapping area."

I pinched my eyebrows with a confused expression, and she smiled at me as she began chopping down a taller seedling. After she felled it, she chopped off the top to about a fifteen-foot length, then hacked off the branches on three sides so that it looked like a giant comb.

"That's a pretty big rake," I said.

"You'll find it works remarkably well at herding schools of fish into shallow water," Teuila said.

"How am I supposed to use it? It barely looks like I'll be able to lift that thing."

"I'll help you carry it to the shore. Then all you need to do is place the branch atop the water and push it up and down to scare the fish forward. I'll look after the rest. Are you ready?"

"Lead on, Pocahontas," I chuckled. "Show me your ways."

Teuila and I carried the big branch to the edge of the water, then we floated it to the far corner of the lagoon where we saw some schools of iridescent fish darting underneath the clear water.

"Those critters sure can scamper around down there," I said. "Are you sure we'll be able to snare one of them with just a spear?"

"Watch and learn, city girl."

Te' escorted me to a spot waist deep about twenty feet from the shore.

"I'm going to wade a little closer to the shore," she said. "When I signal that I'm ready, I want you to pump the pole up and down on the surface of the water as you slowly walk toward me. The sound and motion of the spikes pointing underwater will scare the fish in my direction. As they begin accumulating in the shallow water, it will make it easier for me to catch one."

When she got into position, Te' nodded toward me and I began to churn the water as she had instructed. Sure enough, within seconds a group of fish began flapping in her direction as they twisted and turned, confused by the agitating water. Some of them slipped around the ends of the rake, but enough moved forward that they began to congregate in the shallower water. When I got to within five feet of Teuila, she pulled one of the spears high above the surface and paused for a moment, then thrust it rapidly down into the water. Seconds later, she pulled the pole out of the depths with a flapping striped fish impaled on the end of the spike.

"Holy crap!" I said, hardly believing my eyes. "Is it that easy?"

"It takes a bit of practice. But it's a whole lot easier when you've got them bunched up in a narrow space."

"Here," she said, holding out the other spear to me. "Do you want to give it a try?"

"Okay," I said, wincing momentarily at the idea of killing such a pretty fish. But I loved my seafood, and catching a fish this way looked a whole lot less messy than using a hook and bait.

"Make sure you wait until you see a bunch of fish swimming near your feet," Te' said. "You don't have to aim at a single fish necessarily. It's a bit hit and miss. It might take you a few attempts to hit one. Just be careful you don't spear your own foot."

"No," I said, peering down at my still bandaged feet. "I think I've had enough scratched up feet for a little while, thank you. Just don't laugh at me."

"I wouldn't dream of it," Te' said.

As we took up our respective positions and Te' began scaring the fish toward me, I could see them darting underwater closer and closer to me. When she got close enough, she looked up and nodded.

"Now, Jade!" she yelled, as she pumped the surface of the water into a foamy brine. "Get them before they escape around the sides of the rake."

I saw three or four striped fish darting about in front of me and I lurched back, flinging the pole into the water. It knifed into the surf and struck the sandy bottom. I pulled it out shaking my head, realizing this wasn't going to be as easy as Teuila made it look.

"Try again," she said. "You'll get it. But you have to act fast, before they escape."

I reared back and thrust the spear into the water a few more times, and on my third attempt it stopped half way underwater, shaking rapidly.

"Grab the stick!" Te' yelled. "Don't let it get away!"

The fish was twisting in a frenzy with the stick running through it, and I grabbed the pole as it slapped on top of the water, then lifted it above the surface to show my prized catch to Teuila.

"Not quite as big as yours," I said. "But not bad for a first time, what do you think?"

"You did great, Jade," Te' said, beaming at me. "Tomorrow, we'll build a retaining wall to funnel them toward us more easily. Then we'll have no trouble catching all the fish we can eat. Let's take a break to enjoy our catch."

As Teuila and I waded toward the shore, I looked around the lagoon and smiled. I knew I'd finally found my slice of paradise.

## 12

———

Teuila cleaned and filleted the fish we'd caught then we sat on the beach and enjoyed some fresh sushi marinated in pineapple juice and coconut cream. While we ate, she asked me about my life in the United States and I learned more about her culture on the island of Anuta. The more I listened to her, the more I began to envy her stress-free life in this tropical paradise. With each passing day, I was becoming less dependent on my Western comforts. For the first time in years, I didn't miss having my phone next to me.

When we finished eating, she examined our wounds and decided to keep the bandages on for one more day to let them fully heal. But there was no longer any need for me to wear my bra, and I happily threw it into the pit, symbolizing my liberation from the binds of Western civilization.

"So what's on our agenda for today?" I asked, bouncing up and down like a giddy schoolgirl. "Swimming in the crystalline waters of the lagoon and lounging on the beach?"

Te' ran her eyes over my pale breasts and smiled.

"As much as I'd like to rest and relax, I'm afraid we've got a fair amount of work to do. We don't know how long it will take for your friends to return. I want to build a more secure place for us to sleep, one that's better hidden from the lagoon and any foot patrols.

"Besides," she said, noticing the burn lines around my chest. "I think you need to be careful about getting too much sun too quickly. It's going to take a few more days for you to get a proper Anutian tan."

"Yes," I said. "Especially since I left all my sunscreen in my purse at your village. What kind of shelter did you have in mind?"

"One higher off the ground, in the trees. It might take us a couple of days to finish it. The most important material will be twine to hold the support beams in place. And that takes a bit of time to produce. But two people can do it twice as fast. Let me show you how to make organic rope."

Te' led me a few hundred feet into the forest until we came upon a clump of short, spiky bushes.

"This is the pandanus plant," she said. "Our tribe normally makes ties using bark, but the fewer trees we have to strip the better in case someone comes snooping around. The leaves of this plant are very fibrous and will be a good substitute."

"You can hold up a *house* with just a few leaves?" I said, bending the skinny stalks in my hand.

"With the right braiding, yes. Plant cellulose is an incredibly strong material, especially when it's properly twined."

She snapped one of the leaves off near the base, then ran her fingernail along its length to separate the fibers. She pulled a few of the stringy strands apart and lay them in her hand.

"Now they look even flimsier than before," I said, shaking my head. "How can those skinny fibers hold much of *anything* together?"

"For such an enlightened culture," Te' smiled, "you Americans sure lead a sheltered existence. Watch what happens when we combine the strands and weave them together."

Teuila bunched the strands together in her palm and folded them into a long U-shape, then she bent one end down, forming a small loop at the joined end. As she pinched the loop with the fingers of her left hand, she twisted the horizontal band of strands away from her with her other hand while using her middle finger to lift the end pointing down and pulling it toward her, wrapping the two shoots around one another. She repeated this process for a minute or two, until she'd formed a six-inch-long line of interlaced strands that looked just like a braided rope.

"That's pretty cool," I said, nodding at how quickly she'd fashioned a rope out of natural materials. "But that doesn't even look long enough to tie around my wrist. What do you do if we need to make a longer rope?"

"It's simple to join extra pieces together," she said. "Watch carefully."

Te' gathered another bunch of leaf strands and folded them in half, pinching them tightly together at the fold. Then she inserted the V-end of the folded shoots into the open end of the braided strands and repeated the wrapping sequence, twisting the two ends of the joined strands away from her while simultaneously pulling the other two loose ends toward her. Within seconds, the loose ends of the first set of strands disappeared into the lengthening braid until there were only the short ends of the new set of strands remaining at the end of the rope.

"Holy crap," I said, shaking my head at how easy it was to create any length of rope using just plant leaves. "But how *strong* is it? And how firmly connected are the two joined pieces?"

"Why don't you see for yourself?" Te' said, handing me the waxy twine. "Try to pull it apart."

I grasped the braid on each end and yanked it as hard as I could in opposite directions. Still not believing that a plant leaf could be so sturdy, I lifted my leg and wrapped the twine over my knee and pulled as hard as I could on each side. Still skeptical of its strength, I lifted it in front of me and bent it up and down a few times. When it began to splinter and crack, I looked up at Teuila triumphantly.

"Hold on, girl," she said, taking the leaf rope out of my hands.

"If you bend anything like that long enough, just about anything will break—even steel. But we're not going to use it that way. We're going to bend it around large poles and tie it in a fixed position. You saw how it's almost impossible to break with fixed tension. That's all we care about at this point. We're going to use it to *hold* things, not as a swing!"

"Okay," I sighed. "You've convinced me. How much of this stuff do we need to build our tree house?"

"A lot. A few hundred pieces of cord a couple of feet long should do it. If we separate the tasks and work together, it shouldn't take too long. Would you rather harvest the strands or braid them together?"

I held Te's bandaged hand and peered at the swelling around her finger.

"Which task will be easier on your hand? It looks like you still need a bit more rehabilitation time than me."

"The less twisting and bending, the better," she nodded, pinching her finger tenderly near the knuckle. "How about if I collect the leaves while you weave them together to start?"

"Sounds like a deal."

Teuila demonstrated one more time how to properly twist and join the shoots, then I sat down on a broken tree stump while she began to tear and separate the leaves. After a half hour or so, I'd assembled a decent pile of arms-length twine, and I shook my wrists trying to relieve the muscle cramps in my hands.

"That's a pretty impressive length of cordage," she said. "I think we're about halfway there. Would you like to switch positions for a while to rest your aching fingers?"

"If you think you're up for it," I nodded. "I'm not used to doing this amount of physical labor with my hands. I better pause for a while before I get repetitive stress syndrome."

"Repetitive *what*—?" Te' asked with a puzzled expression.

"It's another frailty of our Western culture. A lot of people sit around hammering away at computers all day long and develop sore wrists and hands. Something tells me this is not an affliction known to native Anutians."

"I've never seen anything like that," Te' said, shaking her head. "We tend to do most things around here in measured doses. There's plenty enough work to keep everybody busy doing different things at any one time. Between fishing, planting, cooking, swimming, and dancing, we keep our bodies fairly limber."

"I noticed," I said, watching Te's lean legs flexing as she stooped down to cut another bunch of leaves from the base of the plant. "I wouldn't mind switching positions for a while if you're up for it. I'd like to learn how to do everything your culture does. You never know when I might be stranded on another deserted island."

**13**

———

Te' and I worked for another hour or so splitting and weaving the leaves until we had an impressive pile of shiny green twine.

"That's a lot of rope," I said, wiping my brow with my forearm. "What do we do now?"

"Now for the *fun* part," she smiled. "We begin building our house in the clouds. Grab a pile of rope and let's see if we can find a suitable location."

As we began walking deeper into the forest, Teuila swiveled her head from side to side, scanning the thicket of trees.

"What are we looking for exactly?" I asked.

"Ideally, a tree that's not too far from the lagoon, but still out of sight from the beach. One with high, sturdy branches and a thick canopy to provide cover from the elements and any search parties. We can build the rest."

While we continued foraging through the forest, my mind wandered to the story of The Swiss Family Robinson, who built such a beautiful and intricate treehouse on their deserted island. But something Teuila mentioned bothered me.

"If we're going to be out of sight from the beach, how will my charter boat crew know where to look for me when they return?"

"I have an idea about that," Te' said. "The trick will be to build a marker that they can find, but my father won't so easily see. We'll focus on that tomorrow. Our priority today is to build a safe hiding place."

I glanced around the forest and noticed a tall mushroom-shaped tree standing in a clearing a few hundred feet away. It had a thick golden trunk and long stringy vines hanging down from its domed canopy. Broad horizontal branches radiated out in every direction about fifteen feet off the ground.

"How about that tree?" I said, pointing to the unusual specimen. "It looks pretty sturdy and well camouflaged."

Teuila turned in the direction of the tree and nodded when she caught sight of it.

"That's a banyan tree," she said. "It's perfect. It's even got a built-in elevator."

"If you're referring to those vines hanging down from the branches, that's not exactly what I'd call an *elevator*."

"Yes, but they're a lot less obvious than a ladder. If my father comes around, nothing will look out of place. He won't have any reason to believe we're hiding in the trees."

Te' walked up to the tree and grabbed one of the hanging vines, pulling herself up hand over hand until she reached the bottom of a branch. Then she grabbed the limb and flung her body upward in one quick motion, placing her feet on the branch and standing up.

"*Damn*, girl," I said, shaking my head at how nimble she was. "You make that look like Tarzan. You really do know your way around this jungle, don't you?"

"It's easy, once you get the hang of it," she said. "Now you try it."

I grabbed the vine with two hands, then wrapped my legs tightly around the cord and pushed up. It took me a minute to shimmy to the top, and when I reached the branch, I couldn't pull my body over it like Teuila had, so I flung one of my legs over the bough and awkwardly rolled myself on top.

"Not quite as elegant as your technique," I said, standing precariously on the limb, holding an adjacent vine for support.

"You'll get the hang of it soon enough," she said, brushing some loose debris off my bare breasts. "You just need to learn how to climb the vine with less rubbing. Otherwise, it won't just be the bottom of your *feet* that get scraped up."

I glanced above me and noticed some teardrop-shaped fruit dangling from the branches.

"Are those *figs*?" I said, widening my eyes in excitement.

"Yes," Te' nodded. "And they look nicely ripe. Have you ever tried one fresh off the tree?"

"If they're half as good as your fresh pineapple and mango, I can't wait."

Tequila picked one of the purple pods off a nearby branch then pinched the skin with her fingernails and separated it in half, placing it under my nose. The pulpy seeds glistened in the crimson-colored syrup of the berry.

"It smells heavenly," I said, closing my eyes as I savored the floral aroma. I cradled the dewy husk in my hands and bit into it softly.

"Mmm," I hummed. "This is almost as good as sex. Sweet, juicy, and succulent. Just like you."

Te' plucked another fig off the branch and bit it in half, squeezing the moist nectar over her hand.

"I see what you mean," she smiled. "This is definitely getting me in the mood. Let's hurry up and finish building our nest so we can have some more fun."

As I finished eating my fig, I looked up at the web of golden branches above us, marveling at how far the crown extended out in all directions.

"At least we've got pretty good protection from above. Will those leaves keep us dry when it rains?"

"Only during light showers. We'll have to build a thatch over our heads to channel heavier rainfalls away."

"What about *beneath* us?" I said, wobbling on the thin limb. "What will keep us from falling between the branches?"

"We'll have to put some additional support beams in place. We'll use the twine to hold them together. Come on, it's time to go gather some more supplies."

Teuila led me back into the brush and we hacked down a handful of ten-foot-long poles about three inches in diameter. We carried the poles back to the banyan tree where she tied three crossbeams between two overhanging branches about fifteen feet off the ground. Then she placed the longer poles over the crossbeams, creating a webbed floor in the shape of a fan spanning between the radiating branches. After she taught me how to wrap and tie the twine so that each connection was tight and secure, it only took us a little over an hour to secure the floor. When we were done, she stood on top of the latticework and held out her hand.

"What do you think?" she said, inviting me to join her on our newly installed deck. "Does this look more comfortable than lying in a pit for the evening?"

I stepped gingerly onto the web of poles and flexed my knees to see if it would support my weight. The poles bent slightly, like a firm mattress.

Te' sat down on the web and smiled.

"Lie down beside me and see how comfortable it is."

I lowered my body onto the lattice, then lay on my back. The hard poles pressed into my flesh, especially where we'd lashed the ties around the connections.

"Not quite as comfortable as my mattress back home, but at least it's less lumpy than lying on the ground."

"We're not finished yet," Te' said. "We still haven't laid the carpet for our new home."

"*Carpet?*" I said, pinching my eyebrows imagining how the rough surface of our jerry-rigged deck could be converted into something as smooth and comfortable as the broadloomed floor of my house back home.

Teuila took my hand and we shimmied down a nearby vine, then she led me a little deeper into the forest where she hacked off some wide strips of bark from a mulberry tree. Then she climbed a coconut tree and passed down a handful of long palm fronds. When we returned to the banyan tree, we cut and lay the thick pieces of bark horizontally across the webbed floor until all the gaps between the poles were covered, then we sat down again.

"Better?" Te' asked.

"Definitely," I said, surprised at how similar her construction technique was to the conventional wood-frame houses I'd seen built in the Midwest. "It's still a bit hard though. Will we sleep on it like this?"

"There's one last step," she said, handing me one of the palm fronds. "Now we're going to make the carpet."

She began tearing the leaves into one-inch-wide strips, laying the strips on the floor in neat parallel lines. Then she placed another strip perpendicular across the leaves and deftly wove it over and under each of the underlying strands. With each successive strand, the leaves began to form a beautiful two-foot-square mat of interlaced leaves that looked as pretty as any placemat I'd find at Crate & Barrel or Target. When she finished, Te' lay the mat over the bark and asked me to sit on it. The soft leaves absorbed my weight and felt as soft as carpet.

"This feels almost as comfortable as my broadloom back home," I said, running my hands over the cushiony mat. "But it's much *prettier*. The two of us might be able to find a whole new vocation when we return to the United States. People would pay big bucks for this kind of natural fabric. What *else* can you use this stuff for?"

"We use the same weaving technique to make baskets, handbags, fishnets, all kinds of useful objects," Te' said.

I shook my head at the myriad uses of the island's natural resources.

"You guys really are self-sufficient on this little island, aren't you?"

Te' smiled at me as she thinned her eyes.

"Are you sure you want to go back to America?"

"Ask me in another week or two. I'm growing more fond of this lifestyle with each passing day."

"Help me weave some more mats then," Te' said, happy to see me beginning to enjoy the crafts of her tribe. "We need to cover the whole floor and add a few more layers for extra cushioning."

"Our very own wall-to-wall carpet," I nodded.

As the two of us continued weaving our natural-fiber mats, I looked up at Te' and smiled with a silly grin.

"What are you thinking?" she asked. "You look like a child who's just discovered her first pearl shell."

"I'm just so happy to be with you," I said. "All this nesting makes me realize there's nowhere else I'd rather be in the entire world."

## 14

After we finished building our carpet of plant leaves, Te' and I made love until we fell asleep exhausted under the warm canopy of our new home. The last thing I remembered before my lids fell heavily over my eyes was the sight of the luminescent figs gleaming like Christmas tree ornaments in the fading light of the setting sun. In the morning, we picked some more fruit from the branches above us and playfully rubbed the sticky pulp all over our naked bodies before going for a cleansing dip in the lagoon.

As I emerged from the surf gazing at Te's sexy tanned body, I could hardly believe my luck. Fate, or happenstance, had landed me in a tropical paradise with the woman of my dreams. We spent the next half hour spearing fish for breakfast, then she placed the catch in a small holding pen we'd built out of large rocks near the shore.

"No fresh sushi for us this morning?" I asked, wondering why she wasn't filleting the fish right away as she had yesterday.

"I thought this might be a good time to teach you the next essential step in your survival skills. I need to teach you how to build a fire. You never know when you might need one. Besides, fresh fish tastes even better when it's grilled over an open flame."

"I was wondering when we were going to get around to that. But are you sure it's safe? I thought you wanted to keep a low profile in case your father came snooping around."

"There's an art to building a fire with a low smoke signature," Te' said. "Just as there is to building one with a *strong* smoke signal, which might come in handy later. Let me show you how to gather the necessary ingredients."

By now, the soles of my feet had fully healed and all the rubbing on the sandy beach and jungle floor had begun to form a thick, leathery second skin. I was surprised how comfortable it was to scamper across just about any surface without any external protection. More importantly, Teuila's cut had finally closed and she was able to remove her bandage and use her hand freely. Now the only items of clothing either one of us wore was my fading cargo shorts and her tapa-cloth dress, re-fashioned as a wrap-around loincloth. It felt exhilarating to traipse about our corner of the forest completely topless, unconcerned about the judging eyes of our neighbors.

Te' led me back into the forest where we began collecting dead twigs of varying thickness. When we had a handful, we returned to the edge of the beach where she dumped the pile in our old sleeping pit.

"There are three things to keep in mind when building a fire you don't want anybody to see," she instructed. "The first is the *smell* of burning material. We have an onshore breeze today, so at least we're protected from people approaching from the sea. The second is the appearance of the *flame*, which is why we're building this fire in a pit protected from surrounding lines of sight.

"But the biggest danger is from the *smoke*, which can be detected from further distances. The trick is to use the driest and smallest materials, so the fire burns more efficiently and doesn't smother. But first, we have to get it started, and for that we need some special materials."

Teuila grasped the shank of her adze and began scraping the blade along the edge of one of the longer branches, producing thin curly strands of dried pulp. Then she picked up the pile of filaments and rubbed them between her hands, breaking them into finer, shorter pieces.

"They look a bit like the strands we used yesterday to make cords," I said.

"You could use this to make rope also," she nodded. "But since this material is drier and more combustible, we're going to use it as a fire starter. But now that you mention it, we're going to need another three-foot long length of string. Do you think you could do that while I prepare the other elements? This time we'll need the rope to be a little thinner, so use about half the amount of strands for each side as before."

"No problem," I smiled. "After all the rope we created yesterday, that technique is indelibly imprinted on my brain."

While I lifted one of the fronds lying in the pit and began separating it into thin strands, Teuila chopped the long branch she'd shaved earlier into a two-foot length then chopped a small indent into the side of the branch on each end. Then she picked up a shorter dead branch about one inch in diameter and sharpened one end to a sharp point while rubbing the other end against a nearby rock to create a rounded stub.

"That doesn't look like a very efficient spear," I said, twisting the doubled ends of my palm strands into a thin rope.

"We're not going to use this as a spear," she said. "We're going to use it as a *drill*."

"A drill?" I said, raising my eyebrows. "But it doesn't have any thread."

My mind suddenly flooded with images of Tom Hanks' character in the movie Cast Away blistering his palms while he rolled a dry stick in his hands trying to build a fire.

"And what are you going to use to *turn* it? I'd hate for you to damage those pretty hands again."

"Don't worry," Te' said, smiling at me. "My hands aren't even going to touch it. We're going to build a *bow* to create the necessary friction."

While I looked at her with a puzzled expression, she picked up two pieces of flat driftwood and carved a small notch in the center of each board. When I finished splicing the strands of the palm leaf into a three-inch length of braided string, she took the cord and tied each end around the notches in the stick, bending it to create a tight bow.

"This is going to help us build a fire?" I said, shaking my head wondering how she could use the bow to generate any kind of friction.

"Oh ye of little faith," Te' smiled. "Watch and learn, my apprentice."

She took the short beveled stick and placed it against the inside edge of the string then twisted it a hundred and eighty degrees, creating a tight loop around the shaft. Then she positioned the rounded end of the stick into the notch of the larger piece of driftwood and placed the smaller piece of driftwood over the pointed end. Then she angled the bow parallel to the ground and began swiping it forward and back. As if by magic, the beveled stick began rotating rapidly in the shallow hole in the driftwood.

"Holy cats—you weren't kidding!" I said, amazed at the ingenuity of the device. "That way is so much more efficient than the way Tom Hanks did it!"

"Tom who—"

"It's just another one of our crazy Western stories that I'm sure you'd find amusing." I noticed Te' was pressing firmly on the top piece of driftwood as she sawed the bow. "Is there anything I can do to help?"

"When you begin to see smoke, place the shavings around the twisting piece of wood. We'll need to act fast to ensure the heat ignites."

I watched with fascination as Te' jerked the bow forward and back until the lower end of the stick started turning black and small wafts of smoke began rising from the fulcrum.

"Now, Jade!" she panted. "It needs fuel!"

I bunched the dry shavings around the edge of the stick, watching the smoke grow thicker and denser. When tiny orange embers appeared under the shavings, Te' bent down and cupped her hands around the pile, blowing gently into the nest. Within seconds, it erupted into flames as she began piling small twigs onto the pile. Eager to not have all her hard work go to waste in the fledgling fire, I began to throw a bunch of larger twigs and leaves onto the pile, throwing up a large plume of gray smoke.

"Be careful," she said, pulling the material off the flame. "We don't want to smother it. A fire needs plenty of oxygen to burn efficiently. If it has more fuel than it can burn at any one time, it just creates more smoke. The key is to feed it only as much as it needs to keep burning at the desired intensity."

Within seconds, the smoke began to dissipate as the fire steadily grew while she fed it increasingly large twigs and logs. When the flames reached a height of six inches or so, Te' looked up at me and nodded.

"We're almost ready to begin cooking our fish. Can you gather ten or fifteen small rocks so we can build a cradle for the grill?"

"Absolutely," I said, my mouth already watering at the idea of our eating warm food for the first time in three days.

When I returned to the pit with a handful of rocks, Te' placed them in a two-foot-wide circle around the fire then held some long branches above the top of the flame, charring them a dark brown color.

"I think we've got everything we need now," she nodded. "If you bring me two of the larger fish from the pen, I can cut them up and begin grilling them."

I went to the holding pen and snared two fish with a spear and carried them back to Teuila. She placed each one on the large piece of driftwood, cutting off its head and slicing it under its belly, removing the entrails and pulling the flesh away from the spiny skeleton. Then she spaced the charred poles about two inches apart over the top of our fire pit and placed the fillets on top of the makeshift grill. As the flesh began to sizzle, she fed the fire with medium-sized twigs, keeping the top of the flame a few inches below the slats.

"You're a master at this outdoorsy stuff, aren't you?" I said, shaking my head at how seamlessly she'd learned to live off the land.

"You get pretty handy at doing these things when you've been doing it your whole life," she said, turning the fillets over with her bare fingers. "Tonight, it'll be your turn. But for now, let's enjoy our new catch."

As we ate the perfectly charred fillets with our bare hands, I oohed and ahhed at how delicious the fish tasted.

"Ok," I said. "Scrap that basket-weaving idea I suggested earlier. I think your real calling is in the *kitchen*. I think we should open your own authentic Polynesian restaurant when we get back to the States."

**15**

———

After we finished eating, Te' and I strolled hand-in-hand along the shore of the lagoon while I stopped periodically to pick up pretty shells strewn along the beach. I marveled at the magnitude and diversity of the beautiful specimens, sprinkled like gleaming jewels across the pink-colored sand. Displaying in all kinds of shapes and colors, I felt like a kid in a candy store as I picked up the fascinating objects and turned them over in my hands.

"I've been to a lot of beaches in my life," I remarked. "But nothing like this. I've never seen such a huge variety and quantity of seashells ever. This is truly a magical island."

"Maybe it's because there's no other islands for hundreds of miles around," Te' nodded. "Or maybe it's just because there's fewer tourists picking them up."

"Is *that* what I seem like to you?" I said, pinching my eyebrows in disappointment.

"Well," she said, squeezing my hand playfully, "I suppose you're still technically a tourist since you aren't officially *living* here. But if you keep learning all of my native island secrets, we'll have to make you an honorary citizen soon enough."

As I continued picking up and examining one beautiful shell after another, Teuila suddenly became silent as she gazed out to sea.

"What's it like on the other side of the ocean, Jade?" she asked. "Will I be like a fish out of water in America?"

I stopped and placed my hands over Te's shoulders as I gazed into her eyes.

"Not as long as you're with me. You speak near-perfect English, and you have an amazing array of practical skills. I can teach you everything else you need to thrive in my country, just like you're showing me here."

"Does that mean you want to stay with me?" she asked with a pained face. "I don't know what I'd do if I lost you again."

I pulled her close to me, feeling her heart beating against my chest. For the first time since my first college affair, I felt that she was the only one for me.

"I will never leave you, Teuila," I said, squeezing her arms. "I've never felt such strong feelings for anybody my whole life. You're the only one I want to be with—forever and ever."

As we held each other close, I peered down at the warm water washing over our feet. Bobbing on top of the surf I saw a skinny threaded shell, shaped like the head of a spear.

"Look at that," I said, pulling away for a moment. "This one almost looks like a unicorn horn."

"A *what*?" Te' said, furrowing her brow.

"It's another one of our silly Western fairy tales. But it also reminds me a bit of your ingenious little fire drill. I think I'd like to keep this one as a memento of my trip to your island."

Te' rolled it around in her palm and nodded as she peered up at me.

"Would you like me to attach it to a wrist bracelet made out of palm twine? That way you won't lose it."

"I'd like that very much," I said, kissing Te' gently. "My very own Anutian charm bracelet."

Suddenly, a larger swell washed over our feet and I peered down seeing a shiny green stone. It was about an inch and a half in diameter and shaped like a heart, glistening in the morning sun. I picked it up and examined it carefully, shaking my head in amazement. Under its emerald-green coating, I could see tiny specks of black embedded in the rock.

"I can't believe," I said, shaking my head. "I think this is a natural Jade stone. What are the odds we'd find it on a remote beach like this?"

Teuila picked up the stone and turned it around in her hand, rubbing it gently with her fingers.

"It's smooth and soft, just like you. What a perfect name for such a pretty stone. Do you mind if I keep this one to remind me of you?"

"Of course not, baby," I said, my eyes tearing up in a swell of emotions. "Do you know what this unusual shape means?"

"Is it from another one of your American fairy tales?"

"In a roundabout way," I chuckled. "It's a powerful symbol of love where I come from, symbolizing the shape of our hearts that beat strongly when we feel especially close to someone. And I can't think of a more perfect memento for you to take away from your native island, because that's exactly how I feel about you."

I paused, as I gazed gently into her eyes.

"I love you, Teuila."

"If that's what all this pounding in my chest is that I'm feeling right now, then I guess I'm in love with you too, Jade. I think the Gods are trying to tell us something."

As I looked at Te' with tears of joy streaming down my face, I noticed some movement at the edge of the cape a few hundred feet offshore. I narrowed my eyes trying to focus on the object, then my eyes flung wide open when I realized it was the bow of a canoe slicing through the water. I grabbed Te's hand and pulled her behind one of the dunes.

"What is it?" she said, recognizing the fear in my eyes.

"It's a canoe," I said, pointing in the direction of the craft. "I think your father is getting closer than we hoped."

Te' poked her head carefully above the dune and peered in the direction I'd pointed, then ducked her head back down, her chest puffing up and down in frantic bursts.

"Is it from your tribe?" I asked.

"It looks like it," she said. "If we stay hidden, hopefully they won't come ashore. We haven't left any visible signs of habitation nearby. They're probably just searching the boundary of the island to see if they can find any sign of us."

As we lay flat against the side of the dune, I heard the sound of rhythmic singing emanating from the lagoon, growing progressively louder, then it began to diminish. After another minute or so, Teuila lifted her head again.

"What are you doing?!" I said, grabbing her hand. "They might see you!"

"It sounds like they're almost past the lagoon," she said. "I just want to see who they sent out to look for me."

Te' peered over the top of the sand for a long moment as her eyes grew wider and wider, then she ducked down again into the pit.

"What is it?" I said. "You look like you've seen a ghost."

"It might as well have been," she said. "Those men weren't from my tribe. They must be from the tribe on the other side of the island. And they weren't singing. Those were *war chants*. I think they have something far more sinister on their mind."

**16**

---

"There's another tribe on this island?" I asked. "Why didn't you mention this before?"

"I didn't think it was important," Te' said. "It's a big island and they usually stick to themselves, so I didn't think we'd cross them. But they're venturing further afield than usual and coming from the direction of my village, which worries me."

"Have the two tribes never had contact before?"

"Many years ago, we all lived together in peaceful harmony. But when a power struggle erupted between the chief and my grandfather, my *tama matua* was killed in battle and the chief banished the other faction to the other side of the island. My father became the chief of our clan and built fortifications to keep the other tribe away. Since then, everybody's been content to mind their own business. At least until now."

"What makes you think they mean to threaten your village?"

"It's unusual for them to venture so far from their side of the island. Their normal fishing grounds are to the north, not the west. And they were wearing war paint. But it was what they were *chanting* that worries me the most."

"What were they saying?"

"Something about taking back their land and reunifying their clan. I think they intend to recapture the women and children and kill off all the men. This was probably an advance reconnaissance mission to scope out our village's defenses before sending in their full war party."

"Oh my God!" I said, widening my eyes in horror. "What do you intend to do?"

Teuila paused for a moment as her gaze darted from side to side in thought. Then she looked up at me and frowned.

"I don't think I have any other choice. I've got to warn my father of their intentions before my tribe gets slaughtered. I'd never forgive myself if I didn't do everything in my power to save them."

I peered into Te's brown eyes, considering the implications of her plan.

"But aren't you risking your *own* freedom if you go back? After you've already disobeyed his wishes, he'll never let you out of his sight a second time."

"I can sneak in under cover of darkness and warn my nona. We can trust her to protect our safety. She'll tell my father, then we can retreat back to our hiding place."

"While you worry about the safety of your family? Do you really think you'll be able to stay here while there's a battle raging on the other side of the island?"

Te' looked at me with a pained expression. I could tell she was torn between the loyalty to her family and her love for me. My stomach sank, realizing I was putting her in an impossible situation.

She paused for a long moment as she considered her predicament.

"There might be another way," she finally said. "If I sneak into the other tribe's camp, maybe I can gather information about their plan. If there's still enough time, my father might be able to set up a meeting to defuse the tension. If the other tribe realizes that we know about their plan, hopefully they'll be less likely to attack."

"That sounds almost as dangerous as your *first* idea," I said, shaking my head in dismay. "What can I do to help?"

"I don't think you should go anywhere near either village. Your blonde hair and white skin will stick out like a sore thumb and be that much easier to detect. The best thing you can do is hide out here and wait for me to return. Now that you've learned the essential survival skills, you should be fine on your own for a couple of days."

"Screw that!" I said, fearing for Te's safety. "I'm not letting you go there alone. What if you get caught? At the very least, I can be a lookout and send for help if you get captured. You mean far too much to me. I'm not taking any chances that we'll get separated again."

Te' peered into my eyes and sighed in resignation.

"Okay. You can come with me—but only if you promise to stay further back while I scope out the situation. There's no point in both of us getting captured.

"Besides," she said, scanning my bare breasts, "there's no telling what they'd want to do with you if they got their hands on you."

"It's a deal."

"Come on then," she said, grabbing my hand. "There's no time to lose. We need to be there when the scouting team returns to their village so I can hear their plans."

Teuila picked up her adze and led me through the jungle, staying a few hundred yards away from shore to keep out of sight from the canoe team. Every now and then, a thin break in the brush revealed the wide expanse of blue surrounding the island, and she stopped to earmark the position of the passing boat.

"Do you know your way to their village?" I asked after she paused for another moment.

"Not as easily from this side of the island," she said. "But I've spied on them before on some of my longer hikes from my village. As long as we keep following the canoe, they should lead us directly there."

"Assuming they're heading to *their* village and not yours," I said, wondering if the angry tribesmen were already planning to attack.

"It's not a large enough team to overtake our village, even with the element of surprise. I'm ninety-nine percent sure this was just a scouting mission in preparation for the main invasion."

"It's that other one percent I'm worried about," I said, peering at

Te's primitive hatchet. "If it came to an armed conflict, how would you defend yourself? Shouldn't we have brought the fire bow with us just in case?"

"That wouldn't do much good against an army of hundreds. It's too small to function as a weapon. Besides," she smiled, "that's one skill I still haven't taught you."

I shook my head at how quickly everything had begun spiraling out of control

"And here I thought the people of Anuta were such a peace-loving tribe."

"We normally are," Teuila said. "But some men's egos are easily offended. It appears that this next generation of chiefs still have a bone to pick."

"I just hope it won't be *our* bones they're picking over in the end," I said, re-imagining scenes of cannibalism among the warring tribes.

**17**

———————

Dusk was beginning to set in as we approached a flickering light near the edge of the forest. Teuila held up her hand and crouched low as she peered through the trees. The team of canoeists were pulling their vessel up onto a sandy beach framed by thatch-roofed huts similar to those in her own village. A gray-haired man wearing a grass skirt approached the boatmen, flanked by a group of other young tribesmen. They paused to confer briefly on the beach, then they walked up the path and sat around a large fire burning in the center of their square.

Te' turned around and handed me her stone adze and small filleting knife.

"You stay here," she said. "I'm going to try getting closer to see if I can make out what they're saying."

I looked at the basic implements, batting my eyes wondering how they could possibly serve me better than her.

"What do you expect me to do with these?"

"Nothing, hopefully," she smiled. "They'll just slow me down. But you might need them if I get caught."

"What? To tomahawk the bad guys and cut you free?"

"Don't even think about trying that," she said. "If I don't return within the next hour, can you find your way back to my village to warn my father?"

I paused, looking up at the darkening sky.

"Not at dark, that's for sure."

"It will be easier if you double back to our lagoon, then try to pick up the trail from there. Worst-case scenario, just stay close to the beach and follow the island around until you get to our village. It might take a little longer, but at least that way you won't get lost."

"You're making this sound increasingly ominous," I said, wrinkling my brow. "Please be careful, Te'. Don't go any closer than you have to."

"Don't worry, my love," she smiled. "I've done this many times before. I should be back before the sun disappears over the horizon."

Teuila kissed me gently, then crept into the woods in the direction of the village. As I watched her tip-toeing through the trees, I marveled at how quietly she was able to pass through the dense brush hardly making a sound.

*That's my girl*, I nodded, peering up at the whispering canopy. *Don't even let the snakes know you're there.*

After a few minutes, she passed out of sight, and I squinted through the thicket, focusing on the circle of tribesmen seated around the fire.

*It's true*, I thought, remembering what she'd said to me earlier. *Why is it always the men who need to mix things up and create conflict?* I closed my eyes and imagined Teuila and me back in our little tree-house, living a peaceful life in our isolated stretch of paradise. I was in no hurry returning to all the stress and noise of Western civilization.

I picked up her adze and ran my finger gently over the edge of its blade. It was heavier than I imagined, and surprisingly sharp. I studied the head and shape of the handle, admiring how her people had fashioned such an effective tool out of basic materials. The stone head had been filed down to a sharp edge, with the butt of the blade supported by the extended arm of the ninety-degree handle. Tight cords of woven bark wrapped around the shank, securing it tightly to the frame. As I held it up wondering if it could be wielded as a weapon if the need arose, a deep masculine chant suddenly arose from the direction of the fire.

I peered through the copse of trees and saw that the men had raised to a standing position as they danced in a circle around the fire, flexing their spears and chanting loudly, just as I'd seen Manaia and the other young warriors from Teuila's tribe demonstrate a few nights earlier.

*Maybe they'll kill each other off and let the two of us live peacefully on our own,* I thought, shaking my head at their belligerent behavior.

I squinted my eyes, glancing from side to side to see any sign of Teuila. For the first time in days, I wished I'd had my phone or watch to keep track of time. It seemed like an eternity since she'd snuck off in the direction of the camp.

*Where are you?* I cursed under my breath, fearing she'd been discovered.

Seconds later, I heard some branches rustling behind me and I ducked defensively behind a bush.

"Jade!" Teuila whispered as I poked my head up.

"Thank heavens you're okay," I said, pulling her tightly against me. Her bare breasts were warmer than usual, toasted from the heat of the enormous fire in the village.

"I said I'd never leave you again," she said, kissing me sweetly on the lips.

I held her closely, feeling her heart beating against mine, then I pulled away and looked into her eyes.

"Did you hear anything?" Do you have any clearer sense about their plans for attacking your village?"

"Yes," she said, tightening her face in concern. "And it's even worse than I thought. They intend to attack two nights from now, during the next full moon. We haven't any time to lose. I have to get back to my village immediately to warn my father."

Teuila picked up the blades from the ground beside me and pulled me back through the forest in the opposite direction of the camp. As we scurried through the brush, I shook my head in dismay. I wasn't sure which posed the greater threat—her father, or this new tribe.

**18**

———

By the time we wound our way through the dark tangle of jungle to the other side of the island, the first glimmer of morning light had begun to appear over her village lagoon. Teuila paused at the edge of the forest overlooking the main square and peered in the direction of her hut. Everything appeared to be quiet and still, save the occasional squeal of a seabird returning from the surf with its morning catch of fish.

I glanced at Te', shaking more out of fear than from the cool onshore breeze.

"So what's your plan?" I said. "Everyone still appears to be sleeping."

"I'm going to sneak up behind my hut and try to get the attention of my nona. I want you to stay here and keep a lookout. If you see any unusual activity, whistle softly twice in succession."

"Won't that attract the suspicion of the tribespeople?"

"Not if they're still asleep. Just try to sound like one of those seabirds."

"Fat chance of that," I said, realizing I still had much to learn about her island. "What should I do if you get caught?"

"Same thing we talked about earlier. It'll be safer for you to return to our lagoon until things quiet down. I'll steal away when I can and find you."

I shook my head and furrowed my brow at the fragility of her plan.

"You might not have enough time. The other tribe is going to attack in two days."

"Once my father finds out about their plans, I'll be the least of his concerns. He won't be able to spare any extra tribesmen to watch over me. It shouldn't be too hard to break away during all the distraction."

I placed my hands around Te's arms and stared into her eyes.

"Just tell me no matter what happens that you won't stay and fight. I don't know what I'd do if I lost you."

Teuila smiled at me as she cupped my face and kissed me gently. Then she pulled the heart-shaped stone we'd found on the beach out of a pouch in her loincloth and patted her chest with the palm of her hand to symbolize the beating of her heart.

"You'll always be with me, Jade. *Forever and ever.*"

I pulled her close to me and squeezed her tightly against my chest.

"Please be careful."

Te' nodded, then crept quietly around the perimeter of the camp toward the chief's hut. As she disappeared behind the cabins, I glanced toward the beach and noticed Manaia stowing something in one of the village's outrigger canoes. It seemed odd that he'd be up alone at this early hour and I peered back toward Teuila, unsure if she'd seen him. For a moment, I pursed my lips preparing to send a warning signal. But he seemed unaware of her presence and I decided it was best not to risk any further distraction.

When I looked back in Manaia's direction, I noticed a flickering light emanating from inside the hull, as smoke began to rise above the gunwales.

*He's setting fire to their outrigger canoe!* I realized, pinching my eyebrows in confusion. *Why would he be doing that?*

Teuila had told me how important the village's few outrigger canoes were to their tribe and how long it took them to hollow them out from the thick trunks of the island's breadfruit trees. If they needed them as their sole method of navigation around the island and for deep sea fishing, what purpose would he have in destroying them?

Then it suddenly dawned on me. The timing of his act of sabotage was too coincidental. He must be a *spy* for the other tribe! By virtue of his status as Teuila's chosen mate, he'd have unique access to her father and his plans for protecting the village. He must have been offered some kind of preferential treatment by the other tribe for him to take such drastic action.

I turned back in Teuila's direction just as she slipped behind the rear of her family's hut. If I gave the warning signal now, she mightn't hear me and just attract the attention of Manaia. As I swiveled my head frantically back and forth between the two scenes at opposite ends of the village square, I heard some rustling coming from the chief's cabin. A few moments later, Te's grandmother appeared at the front entrance. She slowly swiped the door covering aside and tiptoed down the front steps toward the back of the cabin.

Te' pressed her finger to her lips when she saw her nona, and two women retreated further up the path away from their hut. I could see the two of them talking quietly at the edge of the forest, then her grandmother began gesticulating wildly with her hands, obviously upset about what Teuila had told her. When I turned back in the direction of the beach, I noticed two more canoes had been set aflame and there was no sign of Manaia.

I wasn't sure if he had escaped into the bush to rejoin his comrades, or if he'd retreated to his cabin to maintain the guise that the other tribe had sabotaged their canoes. Either way, Teuila needed to be warned so she could notify her grandmother of the betrayal within their ranks. I pursed my lips and strained to whistle as loudly as I dared.

It took longer than I hoped to attract Teuila's attention, and by the time she finally looked in my direction, the flap of her hut's front door swung open as her father stood in the entrance, peering from side to side. From her position many yards away from her family's hut, she was unaware that her father had been roused. I wanted to scream out loud to her and tell her to run, but by now many of the villagers had begun to stream out of their huts, attracted by the unusual smell of burning wood.

When the chief caught sight of the burning canoes, he hollered something in his native tongue and a swarm of tribesmen converged on the beach trying to put out the flames with baskets of seawater. But it was too little, too late. By the time they were finally extinguished and the gray smoke stopped pouring out of the hulls, all three of the village's outrigger canoes had been cut in half by the charred ruins of the fire.

When I looked back toward Teuila's hut, I was horrified to see that Manaia had found her and was holding her arms tightly behind her back as her father stormed back up the path in their direction. When he confronted his daughter, they hollered at each other for a few moments as Te' struggled helplessly against Manaia's hold. Her younger sisters and brothers began streaming out of the hut, and the chief muttered something to Manaia, motioning for him to take Teuila inside.

When they disappeared behind the door curtain, the chief castigated nona for helping his daughter then yelled to the tribesmen returning from the beach, pointing into the woods in my direction.

"*Saili latou!*" he shouted, as the angry warriors spread out into the jungle.

**19**

———

As the tribesmen darted toward me, my mind raced trying to devise an escape plan. All I could think about was Teuila's dream where her father tied me to a stake and burned me alive after he found us. It seemed like an extreme punishment for two lovers following their hearts, but from the crazed look in his eyes, I couldn't rule anything out right now. And with her jealous boyfriend demonstrating increasingly suspicious behavior, I'd have one more enemy wanting me out of the picture.

With the warriors fanning out in every direction, I knew running wasn't an option. I'd quickly be overtaken by their superior speed and familiarity with the terrain. And climbing another tree was out of the question. With so many eyes probing for the white girl, I'd stick out like a polar bear in the dark jungle. My biggest liability was my light skin and hair color. I needed to find a way to blend into the landscape —fast.

Picking up the stone adze Teuila had left behind, I hacked away at the ground, exposing the dark volcanic topsoil. I clawed at it with my fingertips and rubbed it all over my blonde hair and upper body, then shrunk behind a leafy bush as low to the ground as possible. Within seconds, I heard footsteps approaching my position with the sound of sticks beating the bushes.

Lying as still as possible not even daring to breathe, I closed my eyes praying that my clumsy camouflage job would keep me hidden for a few moments longer. The slapping sounds grew louder and louder until it seemed as if one of the searchers was standing right over top of me. Suddenly, something struck the ground next to me and I opened my eyes to see the sharp point of a stone-tipped spear plunging into the bush.

*Jesus!* I thought, realizing how serious these tribesmen were in apprehending their prey. My mind began to spin with all the possibilities. *Was it really me they were after? Had Teuila's father asked for me to be returned dead or alive? Maybe they thought I was the one who'd set fire to the canoes? Or were they looking for the saboteurs from the other tribe? Had Teuila even had a chance to tell her father about their plans to attack the village?*

While the tribesman continued jabbing his spear into the bush, I watched his dusty feet dancing over the ground not far from the gash I'd made with the adze. From my perspective inches away, it looked like an obvious mark inflicted by a recent intruder. As I lay on the ground with the sharp tool digging into my stomach, I wished I'd had the presence of mind to cover the fresh soil with some leaves.

But just as the tribesman stopped spearing the bush and I thought I was in the clear, I noticed some unusual movement sliding along the ground out of the corner of my eye. It was another three-foot-long snake winding through the brush! All the beating of the bushes in the surrounding area had scared it from its roost, and it was moving directly toward me. And this time, I knew that if it bit me, I couldn't count on Teuila and Nona to nurse me back to health.

As it slithered up over my arm toward my shoulder, I lay deathly still, holding my breath. At least I was aware of its presence this time. If I could just keep from flinching, maybe it would think I was another dead branch on the ground and leave me alone. I watched its forked tongue flickering in and out of its mouth like a divining rod.

When it got to within inches of my face, I closed my eyes and prayed it didn't view me as a threat.

*Why would it want to bite me?* I thought. *I'm too big for it to eat, and I'm not threatening it in any way.* I remembered my father telling me on family excursions into the cottage country of northern Wisconsin that rattlesnakes were threatened by the vibrations of the earth in their vicinity. *As long as I remain still, it should leave me alone.*

As the snake paused next to my ear, I clenched my neck muscles unconsciously, expecting it to strike. But after a few seconds that felt like an eternity, it continued winding its body over my back and down the side of my torso, until it slithered off into the brush. The moment it left contact with my body, I gasped in a breath of fresh air as slowly as possible, trying not to make any sounds that might alert the nearby posse. I'd been so focused on the serpentine intruder, that I hadn't even realized the tribesman who'd been searching in my area had moved on. As I strained to listen for any nearby activity, I heard the sound of shouting receding into the distance, and I finally began to relax my muscles, pulling the sharp axe from underneath my body.

*Now what?* I thought, realizing I was still in a dangerous position, surrounded by a small army of warriors on the lookout for any suspicious movement. *How long should I stay concealed in my precarious hiding place? Should I wait a little longer to see what the chief intends to do with Teuila? Will he stop looking for me when he realizes he needs to start preparing for the impending attack?*

I had no way of knowing what kind of arrangements Te's father had made to prevent her escape. She'd told me to return to our lagoon and wait for her to come back, but what if she was tied up or had a twenty-four-hour guard? Maybe I could create some kind of distraction and cut her free.

I looked at my small stone adze and shook my head. With my luck, I'll get myself caught too and be no good for either one of us. I'll just have to spend the night here and see if I could find an opening at first light. I peered up at the bright moon, noticing that it was almost perfectly round.

Either way, we've got less than forty-eight hours before the crap hits the fan and someone's going to get hurt.

## 20

Teuila sat against the knobby walls of her hut with her hands tied behind her back, staring angrily into Manaia's eyes. He returned her gaze with equal intensity, as his lips curled into a menacing sneer. His eyes darted over her exposed body, taking particular interest in her loincloth wrapped tightly around her hips and waist.

She lifted her knees and pressed them against her chest, folding her arms around her legs. The idea of Manaia violating her made her sick to her stomach. Beyond the fact that she was madly in love with Jade, there'd always been something sinister about him that gave her the creeps.

"What do you *want* with me?" she asked in her native Samoan tongue.

"What makes you think I need anything from you right now?" he said.

"The way you're looking at me, for one thing. I've seen that look on men's faces before. I'm never going to let you touch me like that."

"We'll see about that," Manaia snickered, glancing back down in the direction of her crotch. "We'll soon be married and you'll have no other choice. And this time you won't be able to run off with your girlfriend. We'll either find her soon or she'll perish in the jungle. Without you looking after her, she'll die of starvation or get bitten by another snake. Either way, there's no way you're going to escape this time."

Teuila huffed at Manaia, realizing he had no idea just how well equipped Jade was to survive in the jungle with her newfound skills. As long as she could evade the search dragnet currently underway, she should have no difficulty looking after herself until Te' could make her way back to their lagoon.

"You could *never* satisfy me like she does," Teuila taunted. "You men are only good for two things. Making war and making babies. And I have no interest in either of your plans. Her friends will soon come back for her and when they do, you'll never see me again."

"I wouldn't be so sure about that," Manaia said. "Her tiny crew will no match for our tribe of warriors. We'll be ready for them if they return, then remove any sign they'd ever been here."

Teuila thinned her eyes as she studied Manaia's face. Although her father was no fan of Western interlopers, she knew it wasn't his style to kill outside visitors. As chief of the village, Manaia and the others were still bound to follow his commands.

"My father would never do that," she said. "You know as well as he, that that would just invite more external aggression."

"Only if the outsiders have reason to suspect foul play. We have plenty of ways to conceal any evidence of visitation to our island. And besides, your father won't be chief for much longer. Soon, *I'll* be the one calling the shots."

Teuila squeezed her eyes together, unsure what he was alluding to. But right now, she had bigger concerns. She needed to warn her father of the impending attack and make sure Jade got to safety. She'd worry about Manaia later. The smirk on his face soon disappeared when the flap covering her hut's front door swung open and her father stormed into the hut.

"Where is she?!" he shouted angrily, standing over his daughter.

"Who?" Teuila said coyly.

"The Western woman! She can't have gotten far and you must know her hiding places. Tell me now!"

"I honestly don't know," Teuila said. "But you have more important matters to be concerned with right now. The *Tuange* tribe is planning to attack our village tomorrow night. You need to prepare our defenses or take preemptive action."

The chief stepped back, placing his fists on his hips.

"How do you know this?" he asked.

"I overheard their warriors discussing their plans when I followed one of their scouting missions back to their camp. They intend to steal the women and children and kill all of our men. You have to act quickly."

Manaia suddenly stood up and stepped toward me with an angry expression on his face.

"She's lying!" he said. "She's just making up this crazy story to distract our attention while she tries to escape again. We need to focus our manpower on making sure she doesn't get away. What she's been doing with that fair-skinned woman is an abomination."

"Shut up!" the chief said, turning toward Manaia, thrusting his hand against his chest. "*I* make the decisions around here, and we need to listen to Teuila's warning. I know what the *Tuange* is capable of, and we cannot take any chances at being ill-prepared."

Teuila's father swung back around and looked sternly into his daughter's eyes.

"Did they say if they planned to attack by land or sea? Were they the ones who burned our canoes?"

Teuila looked at her father with a confused expression and shook her head.

"They didn't mention anything about destroying our canoes. I got the impression they were going to wait for the full moon before they struck out for our camp. What do you intend to do, father?"

The chief stood for a long moment pondering his options, then motioned to Manaia.

"Gather the other tribesmen in the village square. We will need to organize our battle plans quickly. I will make sure my daughter doesn't escape again."

When Manaia rushed out of the hut, Te' struggled to stand. Her father placed his hand gently on her head and motioned for her to stay seated.

"I'm sorry to have to do this Teuila, but I can't afford to lose you again." He kneeled down and wrapped some thick strands of hibiscus twine around her binds then tied the new rope around a sturdy branch in the side wall. "You'll have to stay here until we sort this other matter out. And this time Nona won't be here to help you."

As her father stormed out of the hut and Te' struggled against the sharp twine digging into her wrists, a lone tear dribbled down the front of her cheek. It looked like regardless of the outcome of the looming war between the tribes, she'd soon be bound into the arms of one power-hungry man or another. She wiggled her leg and felt Jade's stone rubbing against her thigh.

*Stay safe, my love,* she thought. *Hopefully at least one of us can escape this madness.*

## 21

I woke up at first light the following morning with a growl in my stomach. It had been twenty-four hours since I'd eaten anything, and I swallowed hard realizing I was left to my own devices to feed myself. But I had more pressing immediate matters to attend to. I needed to see what had become of Teuila and find a way to extract the two of us safely from the village. We only had a little over thirty-six hours before all hell would break loose in the camp. The safest place for both of us would be as far away on the other side of the island as possible.

I slowly lifted myself up and parted the leaves of my bush, peering in the direction of the village. The square was busier than usual for this time of the morning, with sentries posted at opposite ends of the esplanade. A large group of tribesmen sat in the middle of the square sharpening stones, tying them carefully to the ends of long spears and arrows. Manaia paced around the circle, gesturing and barking orders like he was in command.

I glanced in the direction of Te's hut and saw that a guard was standing on all four sides of the structure. There was no sign of Nona or the chief, and from the stillness of the cabin, I assumed that Teuila and her family were still sleeping. After another twenty minutes or so, her father stepped through the front door and called to one of the tribesmen in the working group. He walked to the bottom of the steps, and as Nona and Teuila's siblings streamed out the front entrance, the chief motioned for them to follow the tribesman toward the lagoon. I took this to mean that Teuila had notified him of the other tribe's invasion plans and that he was taking no chances leaving the women or children unattended.

*At least he's aware of the danger now and is taking necessary precautions*, I nodded.

But where was Teuila? Why hadn't he sent her down to the lagoon with the rest of her family to attend to her morning ablutions? Was he going to leave her under armed guard in the hut all day, where she'd have to take care of her private affairs in a bowl?

I shook my head at the barbarity of his decision.

*He's not taking any chances with her,* I thought. *It's going to be next to impossible for her to escape with an armed guard surrounding her cabin and with her grandmother not allowed to go anywhere without an escort.*

I glanced toward Manaia again, wondering what he was up to. After destroying the village's only means of marine navigation, instead of slipping into the forest to join his comrades from the other clan, for some reason he'd chosen to stay behind and help his tribe prepare for the attack.

Was he going to join his tribe in battle, then turn on them at the last second? Or was he waiting for the right time to slip away and alert the other tribe that his village had been forewarned of their intentions?

I still wasn't sure if the chief intended to defend his village against the attack or if he planned to take preemptive action. Either way, Manaia couldn't be trusted. I needed to find a way to warn Teuila and her father before it was too late. The other tribe looked to be at least twice as large as Teuila's. The only chance her group would have to prevail in the looming battle was to maintain the element of surprise. Manaia surely would have already informed the other side of her village's defenses and battle readiness. If he were to switch sides in the heat of the fight, that could easily turn the tide in favor of the other clan.

But how could I get close enough to her hut to send her a signal? Trying to whistle again was out of the question. After my last pitiful attempt to mimic the local wildlife drew her father's attention, I couldn't risk betraying my position again. My only chance was to leave some kind of message with her grandmother. But how could I draw her attention when she was being watched so closely?

I paused to rack my brain with every possibility. Then it suddenly dawned on me. Teuila had told me she'd studied many of the same subjects as me during the time missionaries visited the island. What if she could *read* English as well as she spoke it? If I could get her grandmother to pass her a note, I could warn her about Manaia's intentions and see if her father might relax his restrictions.

But how could I write her a message? I didn't have any writing material, and I'd left my phone in my bag in her hut when we escaped three days ago. I looked around for any object that might serve as a writing tablet, then I noticed a mulberry tree like the ones Te' said her tribe used to make their skirts and dresses. I knew that the inner layer of its bark was thin and pale. If I could strip a piece off, maybe I could carve a message into its pulp-like skin.

I got up on all fours and crawled toward the tree, keeping a close eye on the village square to make sure nobody saw me. When I reached the tree, I used my small paring knife to cut a four-by-six-inch piece of bark off the trunk, then I lay it flat on the ground and found a small sharp stone nearby. Realizing I wouldn't have long before Nona and the rest of Te's family returned from the lagoon, I scrawled a rough message into the backside of the strip.

*Watching close by. Manaia burned the canoes. Warn chief. Will wait for you at our lagoon.*

I hid my adze and knife under the bush then stuffed the piece of bark in the back of my shorts and carefully circled around toward the lagoon. By now, I had a decent understanding of the layout of the village, and it didn't take long to wend my way through the woods near the trailhead to the bathing lagoon. When I got there, I saw

Nona and the children walking single-file up the path with the tribesman urging them on from the rear.

I waited until she was close to my position, then I shook the branch of a low-lying tree to get her attention. She glanced in my direction and when she saw me hiding in the brush, she paused as I tossed the piece of bark toward her. The guard yelled something to her, then she kneeled on the ground and leaned over, pretending to be sick. The tribesman hurried past her with the rest of the children as he grimaced in her direction. Nona picked up the piece of bark and noticing the strange writing symbols on it, tucking it under her tapa dress. Then she nodded toward me and joined the rest of the group while the guard waited impatiently.

As the group continued marching up the path toward Teuila's hut, I doubled back to my previous hiding place and waited for her grandmother to deliver the news. When they returned to the hut, the chief stood on the front porch with his arms crossed and ordered them all back inside. A few minutes later, Nona stepped through the front door carrying a large wooden bowl and the chief jerked his head in the direction of the jungle. She tiptoed down the steps cradling the bowl carefully, then disappeared behind the hut and returned a few minutes later, sprinkling some loose sand inside the container.

*So it's true,* I grimaced in disgust. *The chief is making her do her business in a pail. At least it's affording her a little privacy to receive my message.*

Nona disappeared back inside the hut for a few minutes, then she stepped out and spoke quietly with the chief as she glanced nervously in Manaia's direction. The chief shook his head angrily, then he flipped open the door flap and stormed back into the cabin. I could hear he and Teuila talking in strained voices, then her father stepped out onto the porch and motioned for Manaia to join them in the hut. For the next minute or two, the sound of angry voices emanated from the building as the rest of the tribesmen turned and looked at one another in confusion.

Finally, the two men stepped out of the cabin and the chief said something to Manaia as he pointed toward the men working in the square. Manaia scurried to join them, but this time he sat quietly among them, joining them in their labor. Then the chief sat on his chair on the porch, motioning for the four guardsmen guarding his hut to maintain their positions.

*That's it?* I thought. *He's letting Manaia off scot-free? What about Teuila? Is he just going to leave her in there? Didn't she tell him about Manaia's treacherous behavior?* He must have convinced the chief that she was making it all up to drive a wedge between them in the hope of rejoining her white girlfriend.

*It looks like we're on our own again babe,* I sighed.

At least it looked like her father had temporarily demoted Manaia and was going to keep him in his sights for the time being. However he chose to address the coming assault, I couldn't help much sitting here in the crossfire between the two tribes. Besides, my stomach was getting increasingly noisy, telling me I had to get something to eat soon. I decided to head back to our private lagoon and try to catch some fish while I planned my next steps.

## 22

————

It took me longer than expected to find my way back to our lagoon on the other side of the island. After getting lost a number of times, I had to retrace my steps more than once to get back on the trails that Te' had marked. By the time I saw the familiar shape of our crescent-shaped beach, the sun was almost setting over the horizon. I knew I wouldn't have long to catch some fish in the fading light, so I grabbed a spear from the treehouse and waded into the shallow waters of the lagoon.

Without Te' herding the fish toward me with the big rake, it was hit and miss trying to spear one, but I got lucky when a big grouper ambled nearby and I snared it on my second attempt. By this time, I was so hungry that I didn't bother trying to build a fire and instead tore open the flesh with my paring knife and dug into it like a grizzly bear eating fresh salmon.

When my stomach finally began to quiet down, I paused to consider my options. I knew that I could spend the night holed up in our treehouse in the hope that Teuila would find a way to steal away from her camp under the cover of darkness. But what if she couldn't escape? And what if her tribe lost the battle? What would the other tribe do to her? Even if her clan won, her father wouldn't be likely to let his guard down as long as I was on the lam.

I had to do something. I couldn't just wait here and pray that the odds rolled in our favor. There were far too many variables that could swing this in the wrong direction. With Manaia working to undermine his own tribe, there was no telling which way the battle could go. At the very least, I could keep an eye on the other tribe and send a warning to Nona and Teuila if I recognized any change in their plans.

I grabbed a few figs from our banyan tree to wash down the sushi, then I went for a quick swim in the lagoon to wash all the filth from my body. It felt refreshing to be clean again, and for a moment I thrust my hand down the front of my cargo shorts remembering the image of Teuila's naked body walking toward me in the lagoon. Then I quickly buried my leftovers and picked up my adze and pocket knife, following the trail toward the other tribe's camp.

With the light beginning to fade over the horizon, I struggled to remember the path Teuila had taken to make her way to the other village. After an hour or so, I became lost again and headed toward the shore to follow my way around the edge of the island. I knew the other tribe's camp was in a clockwise direction from our lagoon. If I just followed the shore, sooner or later it would lead me to their camp.

As I stumbled along the rocky shoreline, trying not to step on any sharp shells or sea urchins, I glanced up toward the sky. The moon was almost full, casting a bright glow over this side of the island. At least I could see what I was stepping on for the most part. The last thing I needed right now was to crack open the soles of my feet again. Whatever was going to go down over the next twenty-four hours, I knew I needed to remain fleet of foot and nimble.

As the moon continued rising over the shimmering sea, I began to hear the sound of men chanting in the distance. I peered to my right and saw the flicker of a fire burning in the distance. Recognizing I was getting close to the other tribe's camp, I stepped off the rocky shore and began to wind my way through the thick woods in the direction of the light. When I got to within a few hundred yards of the camp, I paused near a tree and crouched down low to get a closer look at the tribesmen assembled around the fire.

A large twig suddenly snapped underneath me, and I cursed under my breath for not being more careful where I stepped. Teuila had made it look so easy passing through the thick brush like a jungle cat, barely making a sound. Apparently, I still had a lot to learn about how to behave like a true Anutian.

When I looked back in the direction of the campfire, the number of tribesmen appeared to have thinned somewhat, and I wondered if they were sending out another reconnaissance mission to Teuila's side of the island. At least Manaia was nowhere to be seen, I thought. He's probably too afraid to try slipping away now that Teuila's father suspects him of foul play. He's undoubtedly waiting until the last moment to see which way the battle is going before he chooses which side to fight on. My lips curled into a sickening scowl imagining Te' wedded to that coward.

Suddenly, I heard some bushes rustling behind me and I twisted around to see what it was. Peering up in horror, I saw a band of painted warriors surrounding me with their spears raised over my head.

*Damn,* I thought, immediately recognizing I shouldn't have been so eager to bathe in the lagoon. My white skin and yellow hair were shining in the moonlight like a beacon atop a lighthouse.

**23**

As the tribesmen shouted at me, angrily stabbing their spears in my direction, I shrunk back against the tree, fearing for my life. I had no idea what they would make of a half-naked white woman spying on their camp. From Teuila's description of the rift between the clans, I wasn't even sure they'd seen a Westerner before. One thing was for certain—they were in no mood for a peaceful welcoming committee.

One of the warriors noticed my adze lying on the ground and he picked it up, shouting something at me. I shook my head indicating I didn't understand what he was saying. He motioned to two of the other tribesmen and they lifted me up, finding my steel paring knife tucked under the waistband of my cargo shorts. He ran his fingers over the sharp blade and flinched when it drew blood.

*Great,* I thought. *Their first exposure to a white person, and the first thing they find are two weapons of mass destruction.*

The lead warrior said something to the other tribesmen, and they grabbed my arms, dragging me in the direction of the village. As I stumbled to catch my footing, I peered toward the large bonfire burning in the center of their camp. All my fears of being burned alive and eaten by cannibals were suddenly rekindled. I twisted and screamed for them to let me go, but the two men just tightened their grip on my arms until they were throbbing in pain.

As we approached the main camp, the tribesmen sitting around the fire turned toward me with puzzled expressions on their faces. Everyone was wearing grass skirts with war paint streaked across their naked upper bodies and faces. An older man with a beaded vest and elaborate headdress stood to greet the search party. The two tribesmen holding me marched me within three feet of the old man, then they forced me to kneel on the ground in front of him. I peered up at him and they shouted at me, pushing my head back down. I shook my head, unsure what they wanted me to do and the guards puckered their lips, tilting their heads in the direction of the man's feet.

This must have been some strange island ritual that I'd been spared at the other camp because of my infirm condition. I knew based on the superior elevation of Teuila's father's hut that the Anutians placed a high value on the height difference between individuals as a reflection of their relative power standing. It was obvious that this was the other tribe's chief and that as an unwelcome outsider I'd have to pay homage by submitting myself to his lowest level.

I looked at his dusty feet and leaned forward slightly as the two warriors nodded. Pinching my lips tightly together, I bent down and touched my mouth to the top of each of the chief's feet. He then motioned to the two tribesmen to lift me up, but when he saw that I stood three inches taller than him, he instructed them to push me back down onto my knees.

"*O ai oe?*" he said, grabbing my jaw and thrusting my face up to look at him.

"I'm sorry," I said feebly, "I don't speak your language. I'm from America."

"Amerika?" he asked, with a puzzled expression, peering at my faded cotton shorts and bare chest. "*Uana oe lava?*"

He seemed confused by my unusual appearance. I was pretty sure that if he'd ever seen a Western woman before, she would have been fully clothed.

The lead warrior stepped forward and presented my knife and adze to the chief, mentioning something as he motioned to me. The chief pinched his thumb gently over the end of the knife then turned the adze slowly around in his hands, noticing that it was well worn.

"*O fea na mua?*" he said, jutting it toward me with a furrowed brow.

He must have wondered what a naked Western woman was doing so close to his camp carrying one of their local tools. I wanted to tell him that I meant no harm and that Te' and I had noticed his tribesmen while bathing in our lagoon, but it was obvious that no one among the group spoke English.

"English?" I said, swinging my fingers from my lips, feigning a speaking motion. "Does anyone here speak *English*?"

The chief paused for a moment, then motioned to one of the tribesmen to fetch someone from one of the huts overlooking the square. A few minutes later, he returned with a native woman walking a few paces behind.

The chief mentioned something about *iglisi* to the woman, then he jerked his head in my direction.

"Do you speak English?" she said, looking at me.

"Yes, thank God," I sighed. "I mean you no harm. I'm here alone—"

The chief yelled something at the woman and she turned back to face me.

"What are you doing here?" the woman asked. "How did you get on this island?"

"I came on a chartered cruise from New Zealand. When our crew stopped to visit your island, I got lost and they left without me. I've been here alone for the last week or so."

The chief shook the adze angrily as he shouted at the woman.

"*O fea na mua!*" he repeated.

"Where did you get this axe?" the woman said. "It looks like one of ours."

I paused as I peered at the chief unsteadily. I wasn't sure how much I should disclose about my knowledge of the other tribe with so much tension brewing between the two clans.

"I met a native girl from the other side of the island," I said. "She taught me how to use it."

The woman said something to the chief, then he looked at me suspiciously, trying to discern my intentions.

"*Oe sakina mo latou?*" he said.

"Were you spying for them just now?" the woman translated.

"No," I lied. "I was returning from my camp when I got lost. I meant you no harm—"

The woman repeated what I said to the chief and he paused for a long moment, studying my face. I knew my story sounded improbable, but I hoped that he would find a naked Western woman carrying a stone axe as no threat.

He reached down and ran his hands over my head, rubbing his fingers through my hair. Then he leaned over and caressed my face, running his hands over my shoulders onto the front of my chest. Suddenly I felt less afraid and more embarrassed with so many male eyes ogling my naked figure. The chief cupped my breasts and squeezed them with his hands.

"*Fata masali!*" he shouted, peering around the campfire at his fellow tribesmen. They all laughed as he continued running his hands down my body. When he reached my shorts, he paused, feeling an unusual object under the cloth. He reached into my right pocket and pulled out the spiral unicorn shell that I'd found on the beach with Teuila.

"That's mine!", I shouted, reaching out to take it back.

The chief peered up at the translator, and when she told him what I'd said, he scoffed and threw the shell far to the other side of the sandy courtyard. Then he motioned for the two guards who'd carried me down the hill to tie me to a large pole standing in the middle of the square. As they lashed my hands tightly behind my back around the pole, I squirmed, screaming at the top of my lungs.

"What are you doing with me?" I cried. "I'm innocent! I don't have anything to do with the other tribe. Let me go!"

As the tribesmen reassembled around the fire laughing amongst themselves, the native woman paused, looking at me.

"Why are you doing this?" I said to the woman. "Can't you see I mean you no harm?"

"You're aligned with the other tribe. Our chief will keep you here until our grievance with them is settled. It's best that you don't resist. It will just make things more difficult for you."

As she walked back to her hut, I glanced at the group of tribesmen leering at my bare breasts. I had no idea what they intended to do with me, but the look on their faces gave me a sickening feeling in the pit of my stomach. I wasn't sure which would be a worse—being burned at the stake or getting raped by these savages.

As I dropped my head to my chest in resignation, I caught a glimmer of light reflecting off the sand near the edge of the fire pit. It was my unicorn shell.

"I'm sorry Te'," I said, realizing she'd have no way of finding me if she managed to get herself free. "I wanted to be with you. Hold close my love if I never see you again."

**24**

---

Teuila shifted her weight uncomfortably on the woven mat covering the floor of her hut. It had been twenty-four hours since she'd last seen Jade, and the crunchy sound of the leafy fibers reminded her of the first time they made love after building their treehouse. But the tight twine digging into her wrists quickly dispelled the pleasant memory as she began to focus on their current predicament.

She was pleased that Jade had evaded her father's dragnet and managed to pass word that she was returning to their lagoon, but there were still too many immediate threats that placed them both in danger. Compounding her anxiety, she didn't have any idea what her father's plans were for defending the village. If he decided to dig in and try to hold off the other tribe's attack, there was no way of knowing which way the battle would go. And if he chose to make a preemptive attack against their village, she'd be left here alone awaiting the outcome.

And with her father not believing Jade's story about Manaia's suspicious behavior, it was looking increasingly likely that either way, she'd be tied to him as long as she remained on the island. Even worse, Jade would be left to her own devices, with no way of protecting herself if Manaia mounted another concentrated search. Although she was capable of feeding herself and knew how to build a fire to stay warm, Jade didn't have Teuila's knowledge of the island or her ability to blend into the terrain. It was only a matter of time before either her father or Manaia would find her.

Jade's only chance now was for her sailing crew to return to the island and find her before the others did. But how would they even know she was still alive or where to search for her? Teuila wished she'd taken the time to help Jade build a marker atop a nearby hill to draw the attention of passing vessels. And what if she was bitten by another snake or stepped on a sea urchin? she thought. Jade didn't have Te's knowledge of the local plants to heal herself back to health.

Things were looking increasingly bleak for a happy reunion. Either Jade would be rescued by her Western friends or she'd be recaptured and sent home on the next cargo ship. Or worse, if she was found by Manaia. There was no telling what he might do to dispose of her in a more expedient manner. As Teuila's face contorted into an anguished grimace, the flap covering the hut's entrance swung open and the chief stepped into the hut.

Thank God! Te' sighed, thankful to finally have another chance to talk to her father.

"Father," she pleaded, twisting against the ropes tied behind her back. "Why are you treating me like this?"

"I'm sorry, Teuila," he said, squatting down into a cross-legged seating position in front of her. "But I can't trust you to not try running away again."

"So what if I did?" Teuila said. "What's so wrong about wanting to be with the person you love?"

Her father sighed as he shook his head dismissively.

"It isn't right for a woman to be with another woman that way. It's your duty to marry a man when you become of age and produce children to keep our community alive. Besides, running off alone breaks with our longstanding custom of aropa, where we've always shared everything communally."

"But I *love* her, father! I don't want to be with anyone else. If you loved me, you should want me to be happy."

The chief paused for a long moment as his face tightened with anguish.

"What makes you think this Western woman would be happy staying on this island with you anyway? She's ignorant of our customs and would soon begin longing for her material things. Eventually, she would just pollute our culture like the missionaries before her."

Teuila sighed, hesitant to tell her father of Jade and her plans to leave the island when her friends returned. She knew he'd never permit her to leave her family and the island. Beyond the insult to his personal authority, it would set a dangerous precedent for other members of the tribe. If she was allowed to go west, what would stop others from wanting to experience the temptations and luxuries of more developed societies? But she knew her father was right that Jade would likely soon miss her life on the other side of the ocean if they tried to stay.

"We've had a very happy couple of days living on our own on the other side of the island. Jade is beginning to appreciate the quiet comforts of our life on Anuta. But even if we did decide to leave, our community is strong enough to survive without me. Aren't you interested to know what life might be like outside our sheltered little island?"

The chief slammed his fists angrily on the floor of the hut, shaking the entire structure.

"You're already betrothed to Manaia!" he said. "No one is leaving this island. Our tribe has lived here in peace and harmony for hundreds of years. You are my daughter. I simply won't allow it."

Teuila gritted her teeth as she peered at her father impassively. She suspected his decision was based far more on his desire to protect his authority over his clan than a desire to maintain internal peace and harmony.

"What about this new aggression by the other clan? The peace is soon to be violently disrupted. How can you continue to protect us without outside help?"

"I have a plan for dealing with these renegades. We will attack them when they least expect it. I'm preparing a team to advance on their camp this evening. They will be too busy making their own battle preparations to anticipate our preemptive strike."

Teuila squinted at her father with a worried expression.

"Will Manaia be going with you?"

"Of course. He's one of our most powerful warriors."

"Do you really think you can trust him based on what Jade saw him doing earlier this morning?"

"That's just lies!" the chief said, flaring his nostrils. "She's making this up to drive a wedge between the two of you. Why would he do this?"

"Maybe he's been talking to the other tribe. If he knew of their invasion plans, this act of espionage would help protect him if they win. How can you be so sure he's not working for the other side?"

"I'm not completely sure he isn't," her father said. "Which is why I'm keeping a close eye on him until we leave. We'll know soon enough if he's a traitor. In the heat of the battle, he'll have to choose sides. Either way, he won't have a chance to inform them that we're coming. We still have the advantage of surprise."

Teuila thought for a moment about her father's plan. There was something about the idea of including Manaia in the campaign that gave her pause.

"Let me come with you, father. I know the configuration of their camp and I'm skilled using a spear and arrow. You're going to need all the help you can muster against their superior numbers."

"This is a job for *tangata*," the chief said. "We can't afford to lose any more women from our tribe. Besides, I can't trust you to use this as another excuse to slip away."

Te' looked at her father with a painful expression.

"Father, you know I'd never abandon my tribe in a time of need such as this. Do you really think so little of me to believe that I would shrink from my duty to protect my village?"

The chief reached out his hands and cupped Teuila's face gently.

"I know you want to do what's best for your community. But leave this to us. I promise we will come back for you soon. I'm going to leave a small contingent behind to protect the village from any interlopers. When I return, we'll talk further about your plans. This will all be settled soon enough."

Te' twisted against the tight cords binding her hands.

"Can't you at least untie me while I'm under guard?"

"I'm sorry, Teuila. This is for your own safety. You're far too crafty. It's safer for you to remain in the village than be roaming over the island with so many dangerous elements on the prowl. We will celebrate our victory when we return with a wedding ceremony to join you and Manaia in marriage."

The chief kissed Teuila on her forehead then stood and exited the hut brusquely. Not long after, she heard the sound of warriors chanting war songs in the village courtyard. She peered through a gap in the wall of her cabin and noticed Manaia waving his spear menacingly as he glanced in her direction.

*You might possess me soon,* she thought, noticing the heart shape of Jade's stone pressing against her loincloth. *But you'll never own me.*

**25**

---

Teuila squinted through the narrow gap in the wall, watching the band of warriors dancing around the bonfire in the middle of the square. As their chanting progressively escalated in volume, her father exhorted them to be strong and brave. Whenever Manaia circled around and gazed in her direction, he seemed to have a crazed look in his eyes. Even though she knew he probably couldn't see her through the thin breaks in the wall, it seemed as though he was staring right at her. Then with a final flourish, the chief waved them forward, and they charged into the jungle.

Te' paused for a few moments, listening to the sound of silence, save the cackling of the fire outside her door. She couldn't see any further sign of movement through the slits in her cabin, and she wondered where the rest of the villagers were. She remembered that her father had said he would leave a few tribesmen behind to guard the village, but where was her nona and the rest of her family? Had they been sequestered to another hut to prevent her aiding Teuila's escape again? It was strange to see her village so eerily silent at this early hour.

"Hello?" she called out, checking to see if anyone was guarding her hut. "Is anyone there? Who's protecting our village?"

"Be quiet, Teuila!" a young tribesman replied from outside the front entrance to her hut. "We don't know if there are spies watching us. We don't want to betray the location of the remaining villagers."

*Okay, Te' nodded. So I know I have at least one guard. It was clever of father to concentrate the women and children in a few huts. That way if the other tribe attacks, the remaining defenses can be concentrated on protecting a smaller perimeter. I guess I'm on my own until the war party returns.*

"Is there anyone else with you?" Teuila whispered to the guard outside her gate, fishing for more information. "How many warriors are left to protect our village?"

"There are five of us," the tribesman replied. "But don't get any ideas about trying to escape again. We have every side of your cabin under surveillance, so even if you were able to untie your binds, you'll be unable to leave the hut. Now shut up and let us focus on keeping an eye out for other threats."

Teuila paused to consider her options. She could stay holed up here and wait until the battle was decided before she made her next move. There'd be plenty of other opportunities to steal away into the jungle after things quieted down. Her father couldn't keep her tied up forever. She could try to escape and rejoin Jade in their private lagoon and fortify their defenses to avoid detection from any further searches. Or she could unite with her father in the attack on the other village and keep an eye on Manaia to make sure he didn't stab the chief in the back.

The more she thought about it, the less appetizing the idea of waiting it out seemed to be. There were far too many variables at play for her to risk the lives of her loved ones. Besides the threat to her father and the rest of his war party, there was her family and the rest of the villagers to think about. If her father lost the battle, there was no way of knowing how the victors would treat the remaining women and children. She knew they intended to kill all the men, but did that mean the young *boys* as well? And would the remaining women be simply absorbed into the new tribe, or would they be treated as sex slaves for the enjoyment of the conquering heroes?

And what of Jade? Even if she was able to find her way back to their lagoon and remain hidden, how could Teuila be sure she hadn't left a trail back to their hiding place? Te' knew how to use the riverbeds to hide her footprints, but Manaia and the other tribesmen were excellent trackers and would sooner or later pick up Jade's trail. Whether it was her tribe or the other clan that eventually found her, neither could be trusted to keep her safe and protected.

She knew that one way or the other, she'd have to find a way to escape to make sure that Jade was safe, then join her father and do whatever she could to ensure the success of their mission. But how could she escape from her hut if it was being monitored on all sides? It wouldn't be as simple as slipping out the back with the help of her nona. The first order of business was finding a way to break her bonds. She wouldn't be much use to anybody if she couldn't free her hands.

Te' wiggled her body along the floor until she found a sharp spur on one of the posts supporting the wall. Then she began rubbing the cords binding her hands as quietly as possible against the knob, trying to splinter the twine. She could hear the fiber pulling and tearing, but it took fifteen minutes before they finally snapped and freed her hands.

*Now what?* she thought, rubbing her aching wrists. *How am I going to get out of here with five people watching me?*

She peered through a gap in the far wall of her hut and noticed the diminishing reflection of the moon on the water, indicating it was moving higher in the night sky. Time was running out if she was going to have any chance to help her father. She already knew where the weak spots were in her hut, and for a brief moment she considered wedging out the back and making a dash into the woods. But if she got the timing wrong and was caught, she wouldn't have a second chance at her escape.

As she peered down at the leafy mats covering her floor, she reflected back to when she and Jade had built their own improvised house in the trees. She knew the floor of her hut was built the same way, with lashed poles supporting the foundation. If she could get underneath the webbed floor, the guards might not be able to see her while she planned her escape route. Teuila peered in the direction of the front door, watching the guard swiveling his head from side to side as he looked up and down the courtyard for any sign of suspicious movement. Then she pulled back a few of the leafy mats to inspect the floor more closely.

Each of the poles was spaced about an inch apart with tight binding connecting them every foot in length to keep them from separating. She would have to remove the ties from at least a dozen joists for a distance of three or four feet to have any chance at bending them enough to give her space to wiggle through. At least the ties were made from flat strips of inner bark instead of braided leaf strands, which would make it easier for her to dig her nails into the fiber to loosen the knots. But each of the ties were made in the form of a double constrictor knot, which made them all the more difficult to untie.

Te' cursed, realizing it was going to take longer than she hoped to disentangle the posts. She chided herself for not keeping the small paring knife for herself, but she realized Jade needed it as much as she did.

*I guess we'll just have to do this the natural way,* she thought.

For the next half hour, she painstakingly pinched and pulled each of the ties until they fell away to the floor of the pit six feet below the raised platform. Then she pulled two of the poles in opposite directions until the posts bunched together, leaving a narrow hole to squeeze through. Taking one last glance in the direction of the front door to make sure she wasn't being watched, she squeezed her legs and upper body through the hole, then dropped silently to the ground below, flexing her knees to absorb the impact.

Fortunately, the foundation of her hut was surrounded in leafy thatch similar to the kind coating the walls, so she had a modicum of cover concealing her from prying eyes. She crept to the back corner of her hut and parted the leaves carefully, peering out the crack. There were two guards standing at opposite sides of the hut keeping a close watch on the edge of the jungle for any suspicious movement.

With a good twenty feet from the edge of her hut to the forest, there was a good chance she'd get tackled before she was able to reach the brush.

She'd have to create some kind of diversion to distract the guards, then slip over to the adjoining cabin from which she'd have a better chance to steal into the jungle. She looked around the base of her hut and found a large rock then picked it up and parted the curtain. She waited until both of the guards were looking in the opposite direction, then she threw the rock as far as she could straight into the opposite brush. The guards looked at one another, then one of them motioned for the other to check it out.

As the first guard stepped into the bush to investigate the disturbance, Te' pulled the leaves covering the side of her hut aside and sprinted across the lane, diving underneath the adjacent cabin. She waited a moment to catch her breath, then she parted the covering at the back of the new hut to see if the coast was clear. By this time, the other guard had returned to his position, shaking his head to indicate that it was likely just a bird rustling the leaves. From her new position, Te' could see that she was still too close to the guards to attempt a dash into the woods, so she crawled across the laneway separating the next two huts and took shelter one cabin further away.

But with each cabin further from the chief's signifying a lower status in the tribe, the floor of the third cabin was only a couple of feet off the ground, and she had to crawl on her elbows and knees to reach the furthest side away from the guards. As she rustled through the leaves, she could hear children's voices above her, so she knew this was one of the cabins that was being used to hide the remaining villagers.

But she didn't have any time to check on their wellbeing. She lifted the grass skirt at the far end of the cabin, then crawled out into the laneway, crouching low as she peered in the direction of the guards. She waited once again until they were looking in the opposite direction, then she prepared to sprint to the cover of the woods. Just as she was about to leap forward, she felt a hand touch her on the shoulder. Turning around fearing she'd been discovered by one of the guards, she was surprised to see the face of her grandmother peering through the slats in the wall, reaching out her arm toward Teuila.

Teuila squeezed her hand and Nona nodded silently toward her, blowing her a kiss with her other hand. No words needed to be spoken between the two women. They both knew where Teuila was going, and her grandmother simply wanted to wish her well. Te' looked up at Nona and lifted her finger to her lips, instructing her to keep the children quiet. Then she glanced in the direction of the tribesmen guarding her hut and leaped to the edge of the forest, disappearing quietly into the jungle.

**26**

___

Teuila knew she'd lost precious time fashioning her escape and that she'd be hard-pressed to catch up with her father. There was no time now to check up on Jade to make sure she was safe. She had to assume that she'd found her way back to the lagoon and that she would wait for Te' to return as she'd promised. There'd be plenty of time to attend to Jade later. Right now, her priority was to catch up with the war party and make sure Manaia didn't stab her father in the back.

The good news was that by now she was familiar with her way to the other tribe's camp and was able to cover the distance in half the time. Still, it took her almost three hours to traverse the island, and by the time she neared the other tribe's camp, the moon had risen almost directly overhead. As she neared their village, she heard the sound of tribesmen singing and chanting around a flickering light in the distance. Not wanting to set off any warnings in case her father was still preparing to attack, she found a point on top of a hill overlooking the village and peered around the woods trying to locate the position of the war party.

She couldn't see them on any of the high ground, but as she glanced down the slope, she saw the backs of warriors creeping through the jungle in a semi-circular formation, closing in on the tribesmen prancing around the fire. When she turned her head to make sure the other tribe was unaware of the encroaching invasion, her eyes suddenly flung open when she caught sight of a familiar blonde figure tied to a stake in the middle of the square.

*It was Jade! How had she managed to get captured by the other tribe? And what were they planning to do with her?*

Teuila could see logs and kindling spread around the base of the post she was tied to in the familiar shape of a fire starter.

*Oh my God!* Te' thought. *They're planning to burn her alive! Just as she'd feared in her wildest dreams!*

But as she watched her father's war party creep closer to the fire pit, she realized Jade was in grave danger of *another* threat, just as severe. Her position next to the band of targeted warriors placed her in the middle of the coming crossfire. Teuila had to get her out of there as quickly as possible. As she began sprinting down the hill in the direction of the camp, she heard the war party scream as they surged out of the woods, flinging arrows and spears in the direction of the tribesmen.

*Hold on, my love,* Te' thought as she crashed through the under-brush. *I'm coming for you!*

**27**

———

My legs trembled in fear as I watched the chanting tribesmen circling around the fire. I had no idea what they were saying, but judging from the brightly colored war paint adorning their faces and the intensity of their intonations, they must have been preparing for something big. But I knew their attack on Te's village wasn't due for another twenty-four hours. Was all this in preparation for the planned invasion, or were they getting worked up for something else?

I peered down toward my feet and got a sick feeling in my stomach. The twigs and logs assembled around the base of my stake looked threateningly similar to the type Teuila had used to start the fire in our lagoon.

*Were they really going to burn me alive? Simply for stumbling onto their camp carrying a few small tools?*

I'd always been reluctant to travel to third-world countries because I wanted to have the rule of law to protect me in case anything went wrong. But this was taking the abuse of human rights to an entirely new level. *What kind of barbarians would treat another human being in this way?*

*At least they haven't raped me,* I thought. *Yet.* Then I shuddered at another possibility. *Maybe they're planning to cook me in preparation for a special feast.* My charter captain had dismissed the notion of cannibalism being practiced in this region of the world, but Teuila hadn't explicitly denied it. Maybe these villagers looked at the odd stray Westerner who washed across their shores as a rare delicacy to be enjoyed in the same way we looked forward to the occasional roast turkey or rack of lamb.

I cursed at my stupidity for ever having strayed from the group hiking inland after we'd set ashore. But then I'd never have met Teuila, who was the most special person I'd ever known. I'd never have known a love as strong and pure as the kind I'd experienced in the short time we'd been together. There was something sweet and innocent about her, unvarnished and uncorrupted by Western civilization. The ironic thing was that we'd *both* stretched the boundaries of what we'd previously imagined possible by being thrown together in this unlikely place.

It was this clash of cultures that had brought me both the greatest joy in my life and the greatest despair. And now it was all about to end in the most horrifying way imaginable. Even worse, there'd be no way for Teuila to know what had become of me. She'd have to live the rest of her life thinking her lover had abandoned her without even saying goodbye after her friends returned to pick her up. There would literally not be a single human remain left of me for her to put the clues together. I closed my eyes and said a prayer, asking God to make the ending quick and to look after Teuila.

But just as I began my supplication, I heard the loud shouts of tribesmen approaching from the woods. I opened my eyes to see scores of painted warriors closing in on the men around the fire as they flung arrows and spears in their direction. The local group turned to face the attacking horde, hurling their own spears in self-defense. Within seconds, the attacking group had closed in on the surprised tribesmen, engaging in hand-to-hand combat with their makeshift axes and knives.

My eyes suddenly flung open when I recognized Teuila's father grappling with one of the tribesmen on the dusty ground. They rolled side-over-side a few times in the sand until Te's father gained the superior position. Then he raised his adze over his head and slammed it down, splitting the other man's skull in half.

Suddenly I heard the sound of another warrior's scream, and I looked up to see the crazed face of Manaia running toward me holding a flaming spear. Just as he reared back to fling the spike toward my helpless body, his face contorted in agony and he flopped to the ground with a large arrow sticking into his back. Standing a few feet behind him, Teuila stood wearing a lopsided grin. She nodded toward me, then she reached behind her back and grabbed a series of arrows from her quiver, felling the few remaining warriors still standing from the other tribe.

Within minutes, the battle was over as the warriors from the other clan lay sprawled on the ground around the fire with one or more stone objects embedded in their lifeless bodies. Te's father lifted himself off another dead tribesman, and after satisfying himself that the threat from the other side had been neutralized, he noticed Te' and approached her with an angry expression.

"*O lau o fae inerti?*" he shouted, acting surprised to see her.

"*Mea tau!*" she replied, holding her bow up and pointing toward the tribesmen she'd killed with her arrows.

The chief nodded in appreciation, then he recognized Manaia's figure lying on the ground and turned him over. Manaia groaned as he reached around toward the arrow still embedded in his back. Teuila's father said something to him, then turned him over on his stomach to inspect the wound. Then he grasped the shaft of the arrow and pulled it out of Manaia's shoulder and flung it onto the ground. He motioned to one of his men to bring him a tapa-cloth sling and Manaia sat up gingerly, placing his injured arm in the pouch. He glanced up at Teuila, pinching his eyebrows suspiciously, and she looked away from him disdainfully.

Te' strode up to my stake and began loosening the binds holding my hands behind the pole, but she paused when her father barked a command to her. She protested whatever he was saying, then he stormed toward me and pulled her hands away from the pole.

"What's going on?" I said, peering into Te's eyes. "What is he saying?"

"He wants to leave you tied up until he figures out what to do with you. He doesn't want to take any more chances that either one of us will run away."

"Oh Te'," I suddenly cried, overwhelmed to see her again. "I thought I'd lost you forever."

"Not as long as I live and breathe," Te' said, clasping the side of my face with her hands and kissing me firmly on my lips.

For now, at least, we were together again. But from the angry look on her father's face, I had no idea for how much longer it would last.

**28**

———

For the next fifteen minutes, the chief huddled with Teuila and Manaia as they gestured toward me in a heated discussion. Manaia seemed particularly agitated, pointing back and forth between me and Teuila like he was blaming us for the interclan rivalry. He walked over to where her father had discarded the arrow fired into his back and inspected it carefully, then he carried it back to the chief, shaking it angrily in Te's face. The chief muttered something to Teuila and she dropped to her knees in front of him, begging him to accept her version of the story.

Finally, he swept his hands in a dismissive motion and gestured to one of his guards to attend to me. The guard pulled a sharp adze from the side of his skirt and began walking toward me in a threatening manner. I could only assume from Te's anguished expression that her father had instructed him to kill me, and I closed my eyes, steeling myself for the worst.

*At least it will be quick this time,* I thought, tensing my body in anticipation of the final blow.

But instead, the guard circled around behind me and began sawing at my ties until my hands were free. I looked up at Teuila, breathing a sigh of relief, but she just peered back at me sadly, shaking her head. The chief said something to the guard and he pulled my hands behind my back and retied them, then he connected a longer cord, which he wrapped around his hand. Te's father pointed to three more guards and motioned toward the remaining villagers cowering in their huts, then he lifted his hand and waved it in a circle, indicating that it was time for the rest of us to return to the village.

The tribesmen got in formation behind the chief and the guard who was bound to me pushed me in the back with the butt of his adze, instructing me to join the line. Te's father said something to Teuila, then she led the way back into the jungle with the rest of the troop following dutifully behind. As Manaia took up the rear position, I looked back at the sad faces of the women and children peering on from the entrance of their huts and wondered what would become of them. The whole scene reminded me of something out of a Vietnam War movie, with me taking the place of the captured soldier having to do a forced march back to the prison camp.

———

By the time our band returned to Te's village, the morning light was beginning to stream over the lagoon and the women and children raced out of their cabins, overjoyed to see that their side had won the battle. The men were exhausted from the night-long march, but Te's father pointed to the middle of the square, motioning for them to begin work on something. The guard who was tied to me escorted me to the location where the chief had pointed and forced me to sit down in the sand. Then the rest of the group disappeared into the woods as they began hacking down trees and branches of different sizes.

When they returned, they dug four deep holes in the sand on either side of me, then they placed a long stake in each pit, being careful to shore each one up so that it stood firm and steady. I watched dumbfounded as they began erecting a webbed scaffold all around me from the smaller branches, tying the posts tightly together with cross-ties of threaded bark. As they scurried up and over the structure like spiders, Te' reached out her arm and held my hand while the wall slowly rose between us.

"What's happening, Te?" I said, horrified they was caging me up like an animal.

"My father doesn't trust us to be together," she said. "He plans to keep you in this enclosure under close guard until either your friends return or the next cargo ship passes by our island. He doesn't want to take any more chances that either one of us will escape before then."

I glanced up at the lattice of poles rising above me and noticed they weren't building any kind of door into the structure.

"Don't you think this is a bit extreme?" I said. "How am I supposed to go to the washroom?"

Te' frowned sheepishly as she pointed toward the back corner of my cage.

"There's a small opening at the base of your enclosure through which we can pass a bucket and plates of food. I'll make sure you're kept as clean and well fed as possible until the ship arrives."

I reflected back on the image of Nona carrying a bowl in and out of her hut while Te' was being held in detention. At least there she had the advantage of covered walls to protect her modesty.

"They want me to do my business in plain sight of all the other villagers?" I said, hardly believing my ears. "Jesus, Te'—this is worse than a Turkish prison. At least there, you have a modicum of privacy."

Teuila squeezed my hand as she looked at me painfully.

"I'll talk to my father about placing a drape over your enclosure. I know it seems harsh, but he could have decided on a far worse course of action. As long as you're still alive, there's a chance we can find a way to be together."

I glanced behind Teuila and noticed Manaia conferring quietly with the chief as they watched us suspiciously.

"What about Manaia? Doesn't your father believe our story about him being a traitor?"

"Unfortunately not. He thinks Manaia comported himself bravely in battle and that his injury was further evidence he was fighting for our side."

I allowed a slight curl to form in the side of my mouth.

"So he doesn't know that you shot the arrow that injured him?"

"He has his suspicions, but there were a lot of arrows flying in every direction during the battle. My father is convinced that it came from one of the other tribesmen."

"And I suppose he also doesn't believe that Manaia was trying to kill me just before he was injured?"

"There were too many people running around, and he was busy fending off his own attackers. It's my word against his."

"And he believes *Manaia* over his own daughter?!"

"Unfortunately, he's already seen where my allegiance lies, which is with you. He has no reason to believe Manaia had any motive to betray his own tribe."

"So what happens now? What will become of you once your father gets rid of me?"

Teuila glanced down toward my feet as a tear dripped down her face onto the sand.

"He intends to marry me to Manaia tonight after everyone is rested, in celebration of our victory over the other tribe."

"Even though you've made it clear that you want nothing to do with him?" I said, shaking my head in dismay.

"It's no use. My father doesn't understand how two women can be in love the way we are. He insists on following the custom our tribe has practiced for hundreds of years. He expects Manaia and me to produce lots of babies and live happily ever after. He's convinced that once you're out of the picture, I'll regain my senses and settle in to a normal family life here in Anuta."

My face tightened into a painful expression as I peered into Te's eyes, realizing how hopeless our situation had suddenly become.

"Maybe he's right," I sighed. "Maybe I'm just pulling you away from what is natural and right. Maybe I'm just another Western intruder chipping away at your culture, leading you down a path of destruction and heartache, like the explorers did with the people of Easter Island."

"No Jade," Te' said, clasping my arms with both hands. "It's just the opposite. You've opened my eyes to the joy of true freedom and helped me recognize the opportunities outside my tiny sheltered island. It's my *father* who's been oppressing me and my people. I'm just expressing my free will and following my heart to be with the person I love."

"Oh Te'," I said, reaching between the poles and pulling her close to me as the last of the tribesmen stepped away from my completed cage. "I love you more than you'll ever know. I just don't see how—"

Seeing that my enclosure was now fully secured, Te's father stormed up the path and grabbed her arm, pulling her away from me.

"*Alu mai te ai!*" he shouted, glaring angrily at me.

As he dragged Teuila kicking and screaming back to their hut, Manaia locked eyes with me and sniggered a lopsided grin. I collapsed my body against the webbing of my enclosure and began sobbing, knowing I'd never have another chance to run away with my island girl.

# 29

After Teuila left, one of the tribesmen planted himself in front of my cage and stared at me impassively, while the rest of the village resumed their usual activities. Every now and then, some small children ran past my enclosure, pointing at me and giggling. Most of the men had retired to their huts to get some rest, but the women were busy moving about the courtyard with handfuls of provisions, preparing for the big celebration later this evening. I glanced in the direction of Te's hut and noticed her grandmother shaving some taro root on the porch, trying not to look at me. Her hut was surrounded on each side by a guardsman holding a spear. Inside, the dwelling was quiet and still, and I wondered if Teuila had been tied up again to prevent her escape.

*So that's how it's going to be,* I thought. *The chief is going out of his way to keep the two of us separated and confined.*

I looked at my guard and shook my head. I felt more exposed than ever with my bare breasts on display for everyone to see, like some kind of hooker standing behind the glass in Amsterdam's Red-Light District. I crossed my arms over my chest and sat down in the sand, and before long fell asleep from sheer exhaustion.

A few hours later I woke to the sound of chatter and noticed some tribesmen erecting a long trellis-shaped structure in the middle of the square. A band of women followed closely behind, decorating the lattice with garlands of flowers. My skin felt hot from the overhead sun beating down through the open bars of my cage, and I pressed my fingers against my flesh realizing I was beginning to burn. I picked up some sand from the base of my pit and tried to coat my body with it, but it just fell off my skin like dry confetti. Peering up at the sun, I estimated it was around noon, and I wondered how these people expected a pale white woman to survive all day long, exposed in the tropical sun. It had also been almost thirty-six hours since I'd had anything to eat, and I clutched my stomach from the gnawing feeling in my gut.

Te's father disappeared into their hut, then a few minutes later he came out carrying a few bowls and some folded objects. He spoke with Nona and pointed in my direction. Nona placed some items in one of the bowls, then she took the materials from his hand and began walking toward me. Upon reaching my cage, she bent down and slid one of the bowls through the narrow hole at the bottom of the enclosure.

When I saw that it was filled with fresh fruit and vegetables, I picked it up and gobbled it down like I'd never seen food before. Nona nodded toward me and passed a hollowed-out coconut shell filled with water through the bars and I emptied it in three gulps. As my stomach began to settle, I looked at her and smiled, placing my palms together and bowing to thank her for her act of kindness. Even though I knew she couldn't speak English, I hoped she'd be able to share some news about Te'.

"How is Teuila?" I said, pointing toward her shack. I swiveled my wrists together in a shackled motion. "Is she tied up?"

"*Eh le lelei,*" she nodded, recognizing her granddaughter's name. Then she placed her hands over her heart and spread her palms in my direction. "*Na te misia oe.*"

I choked up understanding her meaning and swallowed hard, knowing that Te' was thinking of me. I looked at the other materials she'd placed on the ground outside my cage and recognized some woven mats similar to the ones Te' and I had made to line the floor of our treehouse.

"Are those for me?" I asked, motioning to the mats.

She nodded then said something to my guard, and he unfurled the mats and threw them over the top of my cage like two long table runners, one on each side. Nona straightened the leafy curtains until they extended all the way down to the base of my enclosure, then she slid one of the drapes aside so we could see each other.

"*Mai le Teuila*," she said, pointing to my newly created canopy.

I returned Nona's gesture, placing my hands over my chest and extending them toward her in gratitude.

"Thank you."

Then she picked up the last object on the ground, which looked like a small hollowed out stump. She placed it between her feet and half-squatted over it, nodding and pointing to me. I nodded back, understanding her meaning, then she pushed it through the little hole at the bottom of my cage and rearranged my curtains so that I was almost completely covered.

I placed my hand over my heart again and blew her a kiss, then she walked slowly back in the direction of Te's hut. As I watched her walk away, I reached out and rubbed a piece of the leafy matting between my fingers. The strands were still bright green and pliant, like they'd been recently harvested, and the weaving pattern was exactly the same as the one Teuila had shown me days earlier. I leaned my body forward and closed my eyes, breathing in the fresh scent of the pandanus leaves. For a moment, I imagined I could smell Te's scent on them too, and I wondered if she'd had a hand in making them. Either way, I was grateful she'd sent them to me as I sat down in the dark shade of my little hut and finished off the rest of the food Nona had brought me.

*At least they're not going to let me starve out here,* I thought, grimacing at the makeshift toilet bowl. *Looking after my other personal needs is going to be a whole other nightmare.* But the shade from my leafy umbrella was already starting to cool the inside of my cage, and

I soon fell asleep dreaming of making love to Teuila on the floor of our treehouse.

***

I awoke many hours later to the sound of singing and chanting coming from the courtyard. I pulled my curtain aside and saw the villagers seated in long rows on opposite sides of the floral-decorated trellis leading toward a giant bonfire burning in the middle of the square. The flames reflected off the face of Te's father sitting atop his chieftain's chair, flanked by his children sitting squat-legged on the ground beside him. As the tribesmen hopped and skipped around the fire, the women and children sang gleefully at the top of their lungs.

Standing stoically in front of the chief with his arms folded over his chest, Manaia peered expectantly down the path in the direction of the trellis. He wore a long grass skirt like the other tribesmen, but unlike the rest of the bare-breasted warriors, he wore a beaded vest festooned with brightly colored sea shells and an elaborate feathered headdress. Posing like a flamboyant peacock, he looked ridiculously overdressed for the occasion. But with his exaggerated sense of self-importance, it seemed to fit his personality perfectly. I fingered the unicorn-shaped shell that Teuila had reclaimed from the sand of the other village, wishing it were a dagger I could throw at him instead.

But Teuila and her grandmother were still nowhere to be seen. As the singing and dancing slowly increased in pitch and volume, I recognized some movement on the front porch of their cabin. Nona swept the front door mat aside, then Te' stepped out onto the portico looking like an angel from heaven. Wearing a white tapa dress dyed in a pretty floral motif, she wore a long wreath made of frangipani and jasmine around her neck and a crown of orchids atop her head. Her face shimmered in the moonlight, with a greenish-yellow dusting of turmeric powder and flower pollen coating her upper eyelids. I gasped at her beauty as her grandmother took her arm and escorted her down the front steps of their cabin.

As they strode toward the trellis marking the entrance to the reception, Te' glanced in my direction and I slunk back toward the rear of my cage. For some reason, I didn't want her to see me watching her as she prepared to get married. Whether it was from my own sense of dread at losing her once and for all or from some misguided feeling of not wanting to ruin her big day, I lurked in the shadows, closing my eyes listening to the chanting of the wedding participants. But after another minute or so, I couldn't resist the urge to see her one last time, and I pushed my screen aside to see the two of them walking under the trellis toward the fire in the direction of Manaia, who was grinning in front of her father like a Cheshire Cat.

*So this is the way they do it here in Anuta,* I thought, nodding at the similarities between the Polynesian wedding and those in the West. *The groom waits patiently by the altar, while his bride-to-be tantalizes him by slowly walking up the aisle as their loved ones eagerly look on. The only difference was that the mother of the bride, or in this case her grandmother, gives the girl away. Typical male-dominated culture, where the patriarch sits on his high horse as he watches his daughter given away.*

The two women walked together through the floral-covered trellis, then Nona disengaged and joined the rest of her family as Teuila approached the raging fire.

*How appropriate,* I thought, watching the shadows flickering over Manaia's smug face. *From the mother's arms into the fire.*

I half-expected Teuila to leap into the flames and self-immolate to escape the clutches of her treacherous groom. But then I realized that her father still had me to use as leverage to force her to go through with the ceremony. It was probably no accident that he'd placed me in the middle of the courtyard for everyone to see as a reminder of his absolute power over the rest of the village. He'd probably threatened to kill or torture me if Teuila didn't abide by his wishes and marry Manaia.

When Teuila got to within arm's reach of Manaia, he reached out and took her hand then they both turned around to face the chief as a hush fell over the crowd. Her father muttered a few words to them both, then he threw up his hands in exaltation, shouting to the rest of the crowd. Suddenly, the women and children poured off their benches, as they joined the tribesmen in excited dancing around the fire. At first, Te' seemed reluctant to join the festivities, but Manaia grabbed her hand and swung her boisterously around the fire with all the other celebrants. Whenever she came back around facing in my direction, I could see her glancing at my enclosure, but I squinted through the narrow breaks in the leaves, remaining hidden. I was too ashamed for her to see me trapped like a rat in my dark and dirty cage.

For the next two hours, the entire village sang and danced and feasted in celebration of Teuila and Manaia's union. After a while, I could no longer bear witness to the tragedy of the spectacle, and I curled up on the sandy floor of my cage, holding my hands over my ears trying to block out the sound of all the merrymaking. Eventually, the cacophony began to subside and I pulled my curtain aside, noticing the villagers slowly returning to their huts. Manaia and Teuila sat with her siblings finishing the plate of food laid out on the buffet, then her father said something to them, nodding toward one of the huts next to his own.

As the bride and groom stood up and began walking hand-in-hand across the sandy courtyard, I couldn't help noticing the bounce in Manaia's step as Te' dragged her feet through the sand. He seemed determined to consummate their marriage as quickly as possible, pulling her by the arm as she lagged two feet behind. They stopped at the base of the steps leading up to the cabin next to her own. Like the chief's, it was elevated much higher above the ground, signifying their newly elevated status.

*Unbelievable,* I thought, shaking my head in disgust. *All he has to do is marry the chief's daughter to elevate his status to second-in-command within the tribe. It's only a matter of time before he finds a way to take over command of the entire island.*

Manaia pulled Teuila reluctantly up the steps of their cabin, and just before they disappeared inside, she turned and glanced in my direction. My heart leaped out of my chest, and for a moment I considered flinging my drape aside and crying out to her to tell her how much I loved her. But Manaia yanked her inside and within minutes I heard the sound of pounding floorboards as he had his way with his new bride.

I closed my eyes and prayed forgiveness for ever having planted the seed of doubt in Te's mind. If it hadn't been for me, she'd never have known any other way than that of a man. I'd ruined it for her for the rest of her life. Teuila would forever pine for my tender touch as long as she remained on this far-flung island. I collapsed to the ground and sobbed, watching the tiny rivulets of tears roll away over the sand.

## 30

The next morning, I woke early with a sick feeling in my stomach. I'd dreamt Te' and I were swimming in our lagoon when a sea monster breached the surface and pulled her underwater. I reached out trying to grab her arm, but all I could do was watch the sad look on her face as she faded away into the depths. Realizing how accurately my dream mirrored the reality of our situation, I leaned over and retched into my wooden toilet basin.

Looking for a bit of light to pull me out of my depression, I pulled the blind across on the south side of my crate and noticed another guard sleeping in the sand a few feet away. I checked the other side and saw that my original guard was lying still on the sand with his eyes closed. The sun was starting to peer over the horizon at the far end of the lagoon, and with the village still quiet, I began to think about an escape plan. If I could just find a way to break out of my pen and sneak past the guards, I could return to our hiding spot and wait for Teuila to rejoin me. Once she knew I was free and safe, there would be nothing holding her back from escaping on her own.

I surveyed the construction of my cage and pushed it firmly on the side to see if it would give. But the heavy posts embedded deep in the sand at the four corners meant it wouldn't be as simple as toppling the tightly strung structure onto its side. I kneeled down and burrowed under the base of the enclosure with my hands, but the soft sand quickly backfilled into the hole. The guards were beginning to get restless, and I didn't want to take any chance at the digging sound pulling them out of their slumber. My only chance would be trying to untie the straps holding the poles together and slip out before they woke.

As I dug my nails into the cords and began loosening the ties, I kept a close eye on the guard on the south side of my crate. There were fewer huts between me and the forest on this side, plus I could use the shelter of the lagoon if necessary to hide underwater as Teuila and I had done at the swimming hole. But my finger slipped while untying one of the knots, and I squeaked in pain as it twisted against the wooden pole. The guard suddenly stirred and when he saw what I was trying to do, he leaped up and yelled at me, flinging a handful of sand in my direction. Some of the grains landed in my eyes, and I staggered back against the other side of my cage as they welled up in pain.

I batted my eyelids as tears streaming down my face, and within a minute or so I was able to recover my sight. The drapes had been pulled to the side of my enclosure, and the two guards barked at me as they thrust their spears in my direction. I slunk back onto the sand at the base of my pit while the guard on the lagoon side refastened the loosened ties, pulling them extra tight with double knots.

A few minutes later, Teuila emerged from the front of her hut and she began walking toward me carrying a few items. I smiled at her as I wiped the tears from my face, throwing a handful of sand into my bucket to cover up the smell of my vomit. As she approached my enclosure, she noticed the redness in my eyes and furrowed her brow with a worried expression.

"Good morning, Jade," she said, trying to cheer me up. "I brought you some fresh food and other provisions. How have you been holding up?"

"As well as can be expected under the circumstances," I smiled weakly.

Te' pulled the shades back across my enclosure, glaring at the guards for not giving me enough privacy. For a moment, I considered telling her about my failed escape attempt, but I figured it would just inflame their already raw emotions even further.

"Are you finding the drapes I made for you are keeping things a bit cooler in here?"

"Yes, thank you," I said, happy to hear that at least she wasn't being tied up in her hut.

"I thought you might like a bit more protection against the sun and the prying eyes of the villagers," she said, handing me a folded white cloth through the bars.

I unfolded the garment and smiled, seeing that it was a dress similar to the one she'd replaced from the previous night's wedding ceremony. I pulled it over my head then pressed against the bars, desperate to feel her touch. She reached out and squeezed my hands as we pressed our foreheads together.

"Te'," I moaned. "I've been thinking of you so much. I watched the ceremony last night, then I heard you with Manaia in the hut—"

"Don't pay any mind to that," she said, pulling back to peer into my eyes. "He may possess my body, but my heart will always belong to you. We just have to wait a few more days until things quiet down, then we can find a way to escape this god-forsaken place."

"What about the two guards?" I said, noticing the tribesmen still scowling at me. "How can we hope to escape with them watching me twenty-four hours a day?"

I glanced in the direction of her hut, fearful that Manaia or her father would see her with me.

"And what about Manaia? What if he finds us? I have a feeling that he and your father won't be as lenient if they were to catch us again."

"Let *me* worry about them," Te' said. "I know how to keep Manaia distracted. He's sleeping right now. We'll have plenty of opportunities soon enough. They'll never find us on the other side of the island."

I shook my head, remembering how easy it had been for the other tribesmen to catch me.

"Have you seen any sign of my sailing crew? The sooner we get off this island, the better. I think I've had quite enough of the tropics for a little while."

"There's been no sign of them. But my father says a cargo ship is due to pass by any day now. We won't have long before you're sent away."

She lifted a bowl full of figs and sliced pineapple, and I closed my eyes, breathing in the heavenly aroma.

"Are you hungry?"

I nodded, and she pushed the bowl through the hole in the bottom of my crate.

"This reminds me of our first day in the lagoon," I said, lifting the sweet fruit to my parched lips. "I remember waking up to the fresh scent of these hanging above our treehouse after we made love that night."

"It's all I can think about too," Te' said, squeezing my hands so tightly they began to turn red. "It's the only thing that keeps me going."

I looked at Teuila with sad eyes and frowned.

"I'm sorry, Te'. I should never have come to this island. If you had never met me, you'd never have known anything different—"

"I'd still know what it feels like to be abused by a man," she said. "If it weren't for you, I'd have never known what it feels like to be truly loved by someone."

"Oh Te'," I cried, thrusting my body against the front of my crate and throwing my arms around her. "I don't want to lose you. I can't imagine my life without—"

Suddenly, the flap covering Teuila's hut swung open and Manaia turned to face us, glaring angrily in our direction. He quickly descended the steps and began running in our direction, and Teuila turned around and began running toward the woods. But he already had a healthy head start, and he quickly closed the distance, tackling her in the sand. Then he picked her up and threw her kicking and screaming over his shoulder, snickering at me as he strutted back up the steps of his hut. Soon after, Te's father emerged from his cabin and nonchalantly sat down on his rocking chair.

*Teuila wasn't kidding about the men on this island*, I thought.

As the thumping sound resumed in Te's hut, the chief leaned back in his chair and began to rock it slowly, nodding to my guards to keep a close watch over me.

**31**

———————

For the rest of the day, I didn't hear from Teuila and wondered if Manaia had tied her up in their cabin to prevent her from communicating with me. Fortunately, Nona kept me well fed and hydrated, emptying my toilet bowl every few hours to keep my enclosure tolerable. I had plenty of time to ponder my situation, and the more I thought about it, the more hopeless I realized our predicament had become.

It would be nearly impossible to escape from my cage under twenty-four-hour guard. And with Manaia keeping a short leash on Teuila, she'd be hard-pressed to find a way to slip away before the cargo ship arrived. Almost as worrisome, I wondered why my sailing crew hadn't yet returned for me. It had been almost two weeks since they'd abandoned the island, and I couldn't understand why they'd left in such a hurry.

*Had they run into members of the other tribe who threatened to harm them if they didn't leave immediately? Had they aborted the search once they realized how large the island was and how much ground they'd have to cover to search all of it? Had Teuila's father convinced them that I was likely dead after they'd stopped by the village? Or were they going to get reinforcements to search for me more thoroughly?*

Either way, I didn't have much time before this was going to be out of my hands. There'd be very little I could do to salvage my relationship with Teuila once I left the island. It wasn't like I could come back with a team of mercenaries and forcibly abduct her. For all intents and purposes, Anuta was a sovereign nation and I'd be flaunting the rules of maritime law by interfering with their right to privacy.

And once I left, what chance would Teuila have escaping the island on her own? Even if she managed to evade Manaia's clutches, he and the rest of the tribe would hunt her down until they found her. With hundreds of miles of open ocean surrounding Anuta, there'd be no way for her to navigate to friendlier waters using one of the few remaining outrigger canoes.

The isolated beauty of the island was both a blessing and a curse. It was the tropical paradise where I'd found the love of my life, but it was also a refuge from which few could ever hope to escape. What right did I have invading their personal space, thinking I could steal away their most important daughter? Anutians had lived for centuries in peace and tranquility until I arrived. Teuila wouldn't even have known what it felt like to experience lesbian love if I hadn't contaminated their culture with my promiscuous Western values. I was acting like the typical arrogant American, thinking I could impose my superior Western mores on their backcountry civilization.

I slept fitfully that night, tossing and turning while trying to reconcile my selfish desire to hold on to Teuila with my knowledge that I had no right to intervene in the tribe's personal affairs. I awoke the next morning to the smell of fresh sea breeze wafting under the curtains of my hut. I pulled the blinds aside and watched the sun gleaming off the pristine waters of the lagoon as children ran playfully across the sand. Their mothers and grandmothers looked on from the porches of their huts as they prepared another healthy breakfast of fresh fish and locally harvested vegetables. On the beach, a team of young tribesman were busy chipping away at the trunk of a felled breadfruit tree, hollowing out a new canoe.

I smiled at the bucolic scene, realizing I had no right trying to interfere in their tranquil life. Suddenly, I noticed movement in the direction of Te's hut and I saw her grandmother walking toward me with a heightened sense of urgency. She had a strange look on her face, like she knew something foreboding was coming. When she approached my cage, she glanced at the guards nervously as she passed me a handful of fruit. A curl of bark fell to the sand and she gestured for me to pick it up. I leaned down and unfolded the husk, noticing some writing had been etched onto the inner skin.

"*Mai Teuila,*" she said, placing her hands over mine. Then she turned around and hurried back to her hut past the imposing figure of Manaia, standing on his veranda with his arms crossed.

I unfurled the parchment and read the message scrawled into the pulp.

*Cargo ship on the horizon. Will be here within two hours. Manaia is not letting me leave the hut. If I don't see you before you leave, find your way back to our treehouse. I'll meet you there as soon as I can. Thinking of you always, love Teuila.*

As I stood reading the message, my heart beat a hundred miles an hour. I wanted to scream out across the courtyard to tell Te' I loved her and would never forget what we'd shared. But that would betray the vow that I'd made not to meddle any further in their affairs. But I couldn't just leave without saying goodbye. I had to let her know what she meant to me. I ran my fingers through the sand at the base of my enclosure and found a small stone. Then I peeled off the top layer of the bark and placed Te's message in my pocket. I sat down in the sand and began to scratch a new message on the parchment.

*Dearest Teuila,*

*I'll never forget the delicate love and tenderness we shared during my short stay on your island. I'll carry the precious memories with me as long as I live. But I don't want you to pine for me after I leave. Your people share this wonderful culture of aropa, and in time I believe you will grow to appreciate the peaceful comforts of your community. I'll always be with you in mind and spirit.*

I signed the note with a heart symbol and the letter J scrawled inside. Then I pulled the curtain aside on the side facing the chief's cabin, noticing Nona weaving quietly on the front porch. I feigned a cough and she looked up in my direction. I looked around to make sure I wasn't being watched, then I motioned with my hands for her to come back toward me. I knew this would be my last chance to leave a message with Teuila before the ship arrived.

She placed some fruit in a bowl and carried it back to me, and when she slid it through the slot in my cage, I dropped the husk in the pot and looked up at her. She paused for a moment, and I nodded as she slid the scroll under her dress.

"For Teuila," I said, pointing to her hut. "Thank you for all your kindness."

I steepled my palms in front of my chest and smiled, bowing in gratitude.

*At least Teuila won't be entirely on her own once I leave,* I thought. *She'll still have the love of her siblings and grandmother to keep her spirits buoyed.*

As Nona walked back toward her hut, I closed my blinds and sat down on the sand of my crate and began to sob uncontrollably.

## 32

—————

For the next couple of hours, the village square was a bustle of activity as the children pointed excitedly toward the horizon and the men began bundling up piles of shark fins they'd caught on their recent fishing expeditions. A foghorn sounded from the direction of the lagoon, and my guards began dismantling my crate. Soon after, the bow of a large cargo ship glided into view beyond the cape. As a small skiff jetted toward the beach, Te's father and grandmother emerged from their cabin. Nona was carrying my handbag, and as they began walking toward me, I realized this was to be my final sendoff from the island.

I glanced in the direction of Te's hut and noticed that it was eerily still. It was obvious that Manaia was keeping her from me, and I suddenly began hyperventilating at the thought of not seeing her again. It seemed unimaginably cruel of him and Teuila's father to deny us the opportunity to say one last goodbye.

When the guards pulled the last of the ties away from my crate, they each grabbed one of my arms as Nona handed me my handbag. It was obvious that Te's father wasn't going to take any chances that I wouldn't be getting on the boat. I looked inside my handbag and noticed that everything was just as I had left it. It felt strange and surreal to see all the usual trappings of my old life lying in the bottom of the bag. There was my bikini, a bottle of sunscreen, my smartphone, and of all things—a business card, which must have fallen out of one of my travel guides as a bookmark. It was hard to imagine returning so abruptly to my privileged life on the mainland.

The guards escorted me down the courtyard toward the beach, and as I began stepping into the boat, I turned around one last time, hoping to catch sight of Teuila. Suddenly, she leaped out the front door of her hut with Manaia in hot pursuit and began running down the path toward me. This time she was the one with a head start, and it only took a few seconds before she traversed the full length of the courtyard and flung her arms around me. As Manaia pulled up behind her breathing heavily, the chief held up his hand and nodded, indicating he was going to permit us a few moments to say our goodbyes.

"Jade," Teuila cried with tears streaming down her face. "I got your message, but I don't understand. Don't you love me anymore?"

I pulled away and cupped Te's face gently in my hands.

"Of course I do, baby. I'll never stop loving you. I just wanted you to see the inevitability of our situation. You belong here on Anuta." I glanced at her grandmother and her siblings looking on from the porch of their hut. "You're surrounded by people that love you."

"But what about *you*?!" she said. "I thought you said you were starting to like it here? We could hide away on the other side of the island."

"If we stayed here, we'd eventually be hunted down. And your father will never let you leave this island."

I choked up, fighting to say the words.

"It's time to move on. I'm sure that once I'm gone, everything will quiet down and return to normal. You can still live a good life in this beautiful place."

"But I don't *want* to stay!" Te' cried. She turned to face Manaia and scowled. "I will *never* love that man. You're the only one that I want."

"Oh Te'—" I said, trying to hold back my tears.

Te's father suddenly motioned to the guards, and they grabbed her arms, pulling her away from me. I despaired at the thought of never speaking with her again and reached into my handbag, passing her my card.

"I don't know if you can send mail via the cargo ship, but this has my address if you want to keep in touch."

The boatmen started up the engine and pushed the skiff off the beach, and my face tightened in anguish as Teuila screamed and flailed, trying to escape the guards' grasp. I blew her a kiss and mouthed the words I love you, then the boat turned around and headed toward the cargo ship over the bumpy surf. When we reached the big ship, they threw a rope ladder over the side and I leaned over the gunwales, retching into the sea. I couldn't bear the thought of never seeing my island girl again.

After I got on deck, I peered over the railing toward the village lagoon, but Teuila was nowhere to be seen. For a brief moment, I considered asking the crew to drop me off on the other side of the island, then I realized I'd just be prolonging her agony. I asked the porter to escort me to my stateroom, where I cried myself to sleep.

**33**

---

It took me four full days to return home to Chicago. I had to have new credit cards delivered to a branch of my bank in Honiara, then take three flights to transport me from the Solomon Islands back to the continental USA via Sydney and Hawaii. But I was in no hurry to return to the comforts of my previous life. I didn't even buy new clothes en route to the States, happy to wear my tapa dress for a few more days as my fellow fliers looked on curiously.

It wasn't until I'd been home for a few weeks that I began to settle in to my normal routine. But I never stopped thinking of Teuila. Whenever I passed the pineapple stand in my local grocery store, I smiled recalling how she'd scaled the prickly tree to harvest some fruit for us to eat near our favorite waterhole. I cooked seafood on my barbeque and marinated it in lime juice, trying to remember how good the fresh-caught grouper tasted after we'd trapped it in the lagoon. But the only tangible memento I had of her was my little unicorn shell, which I placed on my office desk and gently caressed whenever I needed to let my mind wander back to the pristine waters of our private paradise.

One particularly lonely day, I opened the photo app on my iPhone, intending to browse through the few pictures I'd taken of

Anuta before getting lost in the jungle. I knew that I didn't have any photos of Teuila, but I wanted to see the pink sand and big leafy trees of the island again to remind me of the few blissful days we'd shared in our lagoon. I smiled at the pictures of Captain Ben and the rest of the crew of our sailing vessel, and my heart skipped a beat looking at the images of my fellow passengers enjoying our first catch in the lagoon.

But as I flipped through the pictures, my eyes suddenly widened when I came upon some photos of Manaia hunched over one of the village's dugout canoes as smoke poured from the inner hull. I paused for a moment, dumbfounded at how the villagers had figured out how to use the sophisticated electronic device. I knew that young children could quickly decipher the graphical user interface, and I assumed that one of Te's siblings had picked up my unlocked phone and begun playing with it before it ran out of battery power. The camera app was at the top of the screen, and they must have accidentally tapped the capture button while running around the courtyard.

I studied the photos for a moment and spread my fingers to zoom in on the images. The pictures provided unmistakable proof that Manaia had sabotaged the canoes shortly before the battle with the other tribe. But what could I do with them? I could try printing the images and sending them back to Teuila and her father. But how would that change anything? He'd just think it was another trick by the jealous American, who was manipulating her Western technology to accuse a rival of violating their custom of Aropa.

But I couldn't just stand by and do nothing. If there was the slightest chance to use the pictures to convict Manaia of his crimes, maybe the chief would excommunicate him from the tribe, or at least annul his marriage to his daughter. And if the wedding was overturned, this could open a window for me to return to the island and reclaim my girl. I rushed to the nearest photo shop and asked to have the pictures developed immediately then called the shipping company that had picked me up from Anuta to see when the next ship would be passing by the island. They said another ship was scheduled to return the following month and that they could deliver a package to the island for a fee.

I mailed them the photos together with a bank draft for two hundred dollars, with explicit instructions to deliver the package to the chief's daughter only. Concerned they might just take my money and run, I told them if they could return a note from Teuila, I'd send them another two hundred dollars as proof of delivery. Four hundred bucks was a pretty steep price to send a package overseas, but it would be worth it for my peace of mind knowing that her father at least had tangible proof of Manaia's treachery.

I waited over a month for some kind of word back from Teuila. Then another month passed. And another. Eventually, I resigned myself to the fact that there was nothing further I could do to convince the chief of Manaia's lack of fitness for his daughter. For weeks, I cried myself to sleep every night pining for my lost love, realizing that I'd never see her again. It seemed ironic that *I* was the one having difficulty letting go, not her.

Then one day, returning from running some errands, I noticed a shiny stone lying atop the welcome mat in front of my front door. I squinted at the object, then widened my eyes, recognizing the familiar shape. I picked up the gem and ran my fingers around the edges as my heart began to thump in my chest. It looked just like the stone Te' had picked up off the beach of our lagoon and said she'd keep it as a memento of our love.

I suddenly gasped and swung around to see Teuila's pretty face smiling at me.

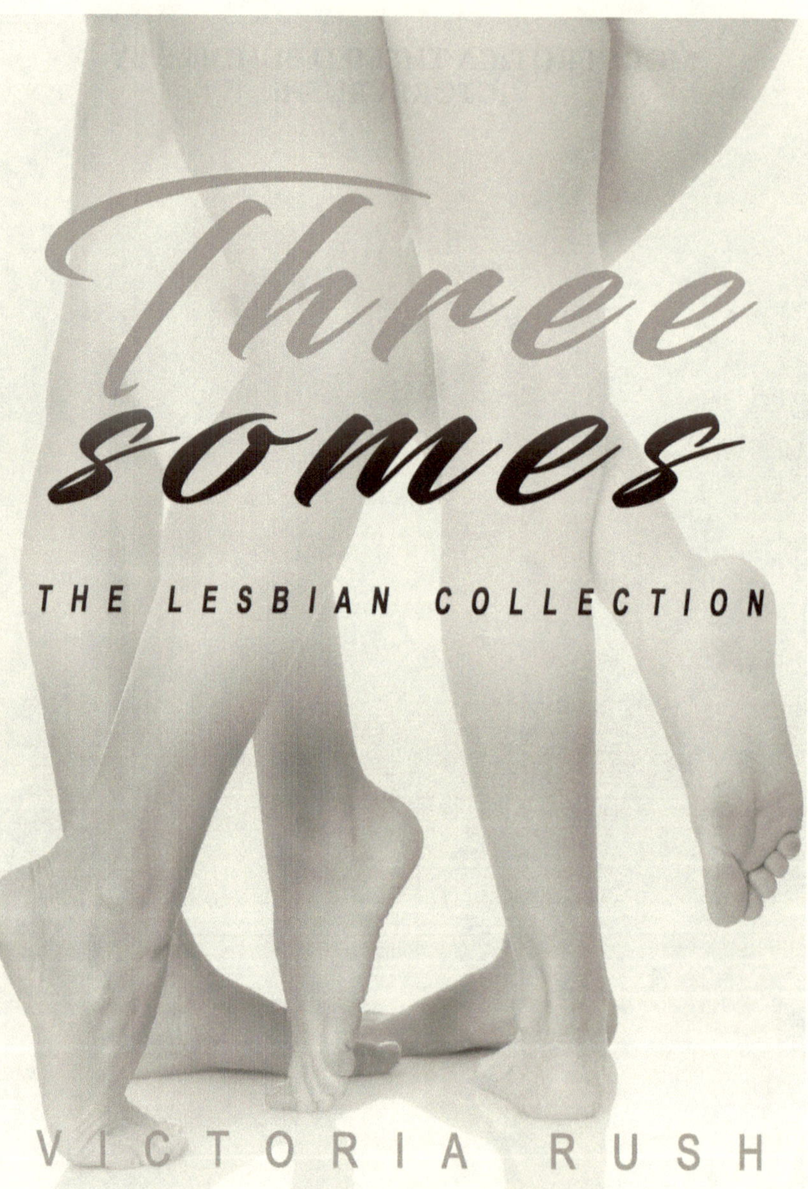

Three
somes
THE LESBIAN COLLECTION
VICTORIA RUSH
2 + 1 = a hundred ways to have fun...

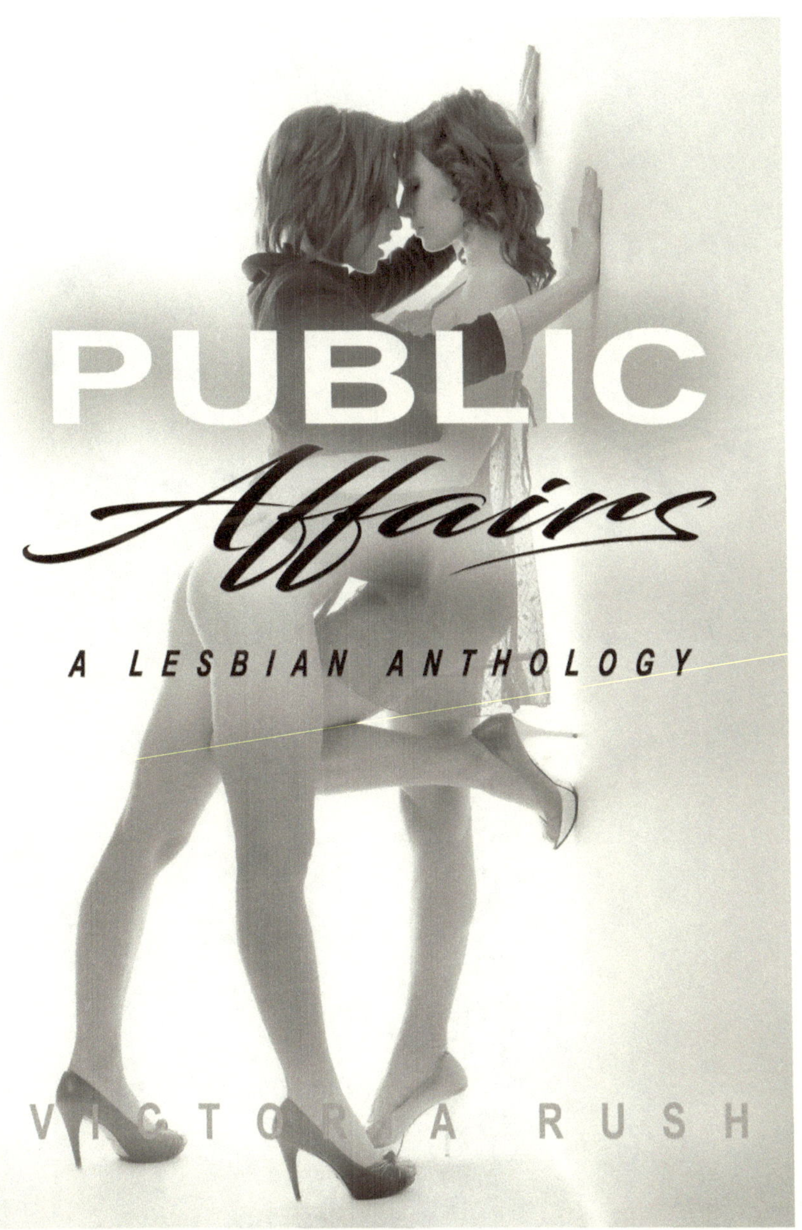


*Sometimes the biggest turn-on is knowing you might get caught...*

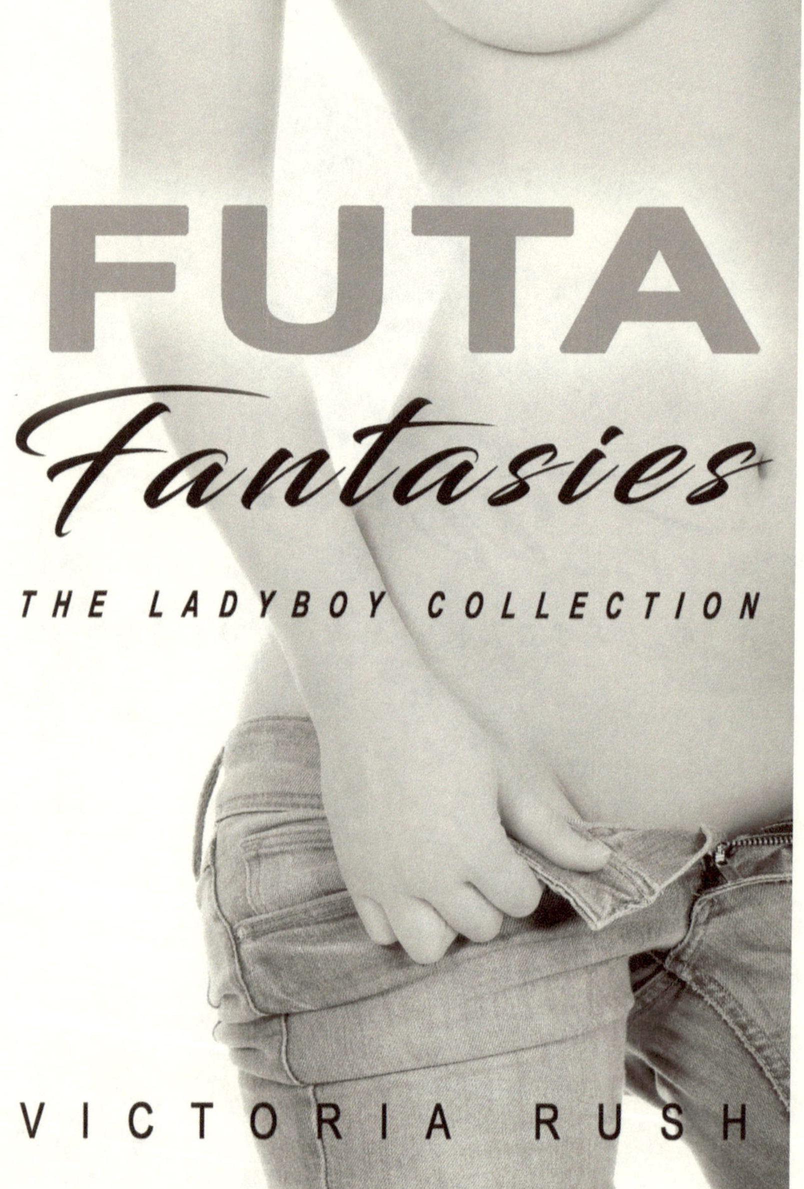


FUTA
Fantasies
THE LADYBOY COLLECTION
VICTORIA RUSH
Some girls have got a little more to work with than others...

First
Time
A LESBIAN ANTHOLOGY

VICTORIA RUSH

It's never as good as the first time...

*Sometimes it's more fun to watch...*